Amy Br... .... who .
worked for PBS and MTV. Her fiction and non-fiction have
been published in *Salon, Guernica, Time Out New York,* and
Redbook, among others, and anthologized in *Before and After:
Stories from New York* and *Lost and Found.* She has won fellowships
in fiction from the Edward Albee Foundation, Jentel, the
Millay Colony, Fundacion Valparaíso, the Constance Saltonstall Foundation, and the American Antiquarian Society in
Worcester, MA. She lives in Brooklyn with her husband and
two small daughters. *The Movement of Stars* is her first novel.

The Movement of Stars

AMY BRILL

PENGUIN BOOKS

PENGUIN BOOKS

Published by the Penguin Group
Penguin Books Ltd, 80 Strand, London WC2R ORL, England
Penguin Group (USA) Inc., 375 Hudson Street, New York, New York 10014, USA
Penguin Group (Canada), 90 Eglinton Avenue East, Suite 700, Toronto, Ontario, Canada M4P 2Y3
(a division of Pearson Penguin Canada Inc.)
Penguin Ireland, 25 St Stephen's Green, Dublin 2, Ireland (a division of Penguin Books Ltd)
Penguin Group (Australia), 707 Collins Street, Melbourne, Victoria 3008, Australia
(a division of Pearson Australia Group Pty Ltd)
Penguin Books India Pvt Ltd, 11 Community Centre, Panchsheel Park, New Delhi – 110 017, India
Penguin Group (NZ), 67 Apollo Drive, Rosedale, Auckland 0632, New Zealand
(a division of Pearson New Zealand Ltd)
Penguin Books (South Africa) (Pty) Ltd, Block D, Rosebank Office Park,
181 Jan Smuts Avenue, Parktown North, Gauteng 2193, South Africa

Penguin Books Ltd, Registered Offices: 80 Strand, London WC2R ORL, England

www.penguin.com

First published in the United States of America by Riverhead Books,
a member of Penguin Group (USA) Inc. 2013
First published in Great Britain in Penguin Books 2013

001

Set in 12.5/14.75pt Garamond MT Std
Typeset by Jouve (UK), Milton Keynes
Printed in Great Britain by Clays Ltd, St Ives plc

ISBN: 978-0-718-15992-4

www.greenpenguin.co.uk

Penguin Books is committed to a sustainable
future for our business, our readers and our planet.
This book is made from Forest Stewardship
Council™ certified paper.

MIX
Paper from
responsible sources
FSC
www.fsc.org FSC® C018179

ALWAYS LEARNING   **PEARSON**

For My Family

It is chiefly from the comets that spirit comes,
which is indeed the smallest but the most
subtle and useful part of our air, and so much
required to sustain the life of all things with us.

— Isaac Newton

A great soul will be strong to live,
as well as strong to think.

— Ralph Waldo Emerson

PART ONE
April 1845 Nantucket

1 . Crosshairs

Hannah bent over her notebook in the half dark of the tiny room at the top of the house, squeezing the remainder of her entry onto the very last lines of the page:

3:04 am, 12 mo. 4, 1845, she wrote. *Unable to resolve nebulosity around Antares. Object sighted at 22 degrees north has not reappeared. Further observations obscured by clouds.*

As if to underscore her failure, the candle at her elbow sputtered and died. For a moment, Hannah sat in the dark, fighting the urge to hurl it across the room, and closed her eyes. Mastering her emotions had been as much a part of her education as long division and multiplication. She hadn't thrown anything, or stomped her feet, or wept in public in over two decades. But now, at twenty-four years of age, unmarried, she sometimes wondered if she was even capable of feeling deeply about anything besides what she saw – or didn't see – in the night sky.

Only on the small porch affixed to her roof, after sunset, did Hannah allow herself to be thrilled by a glimpse of something new flickering among the celestial bodies, or overcome by wonder at their majestic order. Even the crushing sense of defeat she felt on nights like tonight, when the elements or her instruments obscured the beautiful mysteries overhead, moved her more than anything that went on in daylight. Or so it often seemed.

She had hoped to revisit the nebula she'd seen the night

before, near the Cat's Eyes in the tail of the Scorpion. A pale, luminous area like a suspended cloud with two distinct bands, one darker than the other, which threaded through the nebulosity from north to south like velvet ribbons. At the southeast edge of one, Hannah had observed a bright mist that seemed less distinct on one side. Sighting it, she'd felt like an explorer on the knife edge of the New World, the veil of possibility and promise suddenly thin enough to puncture with the slightest breath.

It was unlikely to be a comet, but unless she saw it again, she would never know. As soon as darkness had fallen she'd grabbed a new stub of candle and sprung up the steps to the roof-walk. But the sky had been thick with clouds, and Hannah blew out a long, disappointed breath and leaned on the railing, watching the clouds scud by overhead.

Since her father had taken a bank job that kept him away for long periods, Hannah alone conducted the nightly observations that her family used to calibrate the chronometers carried by whaling vessels to keep time at sea. She also made the necessary corrections to every such clock in the fleet when they were in port. In addition, she ran the house, kept the ledgers in order, and paid the boys who managed the small farm they kept a mile east of Town, even as it steadily lost money. Then there was her own job as junior librarian at the Nantucket Atheneum, from which she emerged at the end of each day, eyes aching, to return to an empty house and spend a few hours observing from their small rooftop porch.

Off-Islanders morbidly referred to the platform as a

'widow's walk,' for the women of Nantucket Island and similar environs who spent their days working themselves toward an early grave and their nights upon the roof, watching and waiting for husbands to return from distant whaling grounds. In truth, most of the women Hannah knew to have men on the whaling ships had little time or inclination to stand around on the roof waiting for anything. If her twin brother, Edward, were present, he'd have pointed out the irony of her having become exactly like those whaling widows she both pitied and scorned, without having married anyone.

But Hannah allowed her situation only an occasional crumb of pity. Waiting for the return of a brother was surely not the same as waiting for a husband, she imagined. Still, she'd thought of Edward every day in the two years and seven months since he'd shipped with the whaling bark *Regiment*, stealing away at dawn and leaving only a note behind:

Do not bear ill will to Mary Coffey, he'd written. *She is like a fair wind to your brother, tho not as forceful a gale as yourself.* But Hannah could no more alter her judgment than she could change the weather: he'd run off to prove himself marriageable to a girl who no more deserved his affections than the giant beasts he now pursued across the globe deserved their brutal fate. In his note he'd insisted that she pursue her observations and not be distracted by marriage or teaching or some other all-consuming female endeavor. But he'd offered no advice on how, exactly, she should go on living without her only sibling, friend and confidant.

After ten minutes, Hannah had given up on the weather

and gone back downstairs. She wished her father were there. She'd been hoping to show him the broken crosshair she'd repaired with a sticky strand of cocoon just the week before, knowing that he'd appreciate her ingenuity as well as her economy. Fixing the crucial, slender bit of wire herself meant saving the expense of crating the instrument in hay and shipping it all the way to Cambridge, where their family friends the Bonds oversaw the new observatory at Harvard. Plus, it meant she wouldn't miss a night of her own observations.

But the garret was empty. When she was a child, Nathaniel Price had been a constant presence beside her in this room and up on the walk, at all hours of the night, in all kinds of weather. Her first job as his 'assistant' had been to count seconds for him as a star made passage across his lens. At twelve years of age, she'd taken her position with utmost seriousness, and he'd handed over a tiny stopwatch he'd made for her out of old parts, with a polished brass case inscribed with her initials. She'd loved that little clock nearly to death, and when it stopped ticking for good and could not be restored, she'd laid it at the bottom of the trunk at the foot of her bed, wrapped in a muslin cloth, one of the few treasures she bothered to shield from the eyes and hands of her twin.

Since Edward's departure, though, their father had avoided the little room at the top of the house as if it was quarantined. Alone, Hannah had thrown herself into observing like a zealot at a revival, but her slavish regimen of sweeping the night skies had neither rekindled her father's interest nor revealed a single new thing in the Heavens.

If anything, her accomplishments seemed to shrink in

inverse proportion to the Universe itself, which was expanding at dizzying speed. In the last two years alone, there had been Faye's comet, De Vico's comet, and the resolution of more nebulae. The parallax of a half dozen fixed stars had been computed; new observatories had sprung up in Cleveland, Cambridge, Washington. It was all happening – but she had no part in it.

Hannah slid the telescope on its tripod closer to her desk, then pointed it at the wavering candlelight to examine her new crosshair again, hoping to buoy her spirits. But with only cobwebs and clamshells as her witnesses, the cunning morsel of her accomplishment was diminished.

Had she tilted the eyepiece a few degrees, she would have seen the world outside the small, diamond-shaped window focused in its lens. Nantucket Town, upside down: slate, mourning dove, granite, thistle. Grays hard as rocks and soft as shadows, cobblestones and shingles, sand and ash, as far as the dark slick of the wharves and the leaden, undulating sea beyond. Past the massive sandbar that protected the harbor, the bobbing masts of a dozen whaling vessels pierced the horizon line; west of them lay forty miles of open water to the New England coastline, and some three thousand in the other direction. In between, seven thousand souls resided upon her windswept Island, each entangled in a lifelong embrace with the sea itself. When blockade or blizzard made passage to the mainland impossible, life on the Island ground to a halt: no commerce and no industry, no wood and no currency, no news and no whale oil, which meant no light.

If she glanced at the window itself, she would have seen her own wavy reflection in its glass. Nearly six feet tall and angular in the extreme, from jawline to elbow to knee; thick coal-colored hair that reached the middle of her spine and resisted her attempts to contain it under the bonnet she wore anytime she was in public; fine lines etched around her large, dark eyes from squinting at the night sky for nearly a dozen years. In every part of her appearance Hannah was the opposite of most Islanders, whose freckled skin and pale blue eyes passed from generation to generation as surely as their views and customs. When she'd read Lamarck's theories about evolution, Hannah wondered if her own people were one of his dead ends, so perfectly calibrated to life on their Island that no further change was even possible.

Not one of them expected anything of her besides service to her father and, eventually – soon – to a husband. None of them thought her interest in the night skies would amount to any significant contribution, certainly not the discovery of a new comet – a wanderer – among the millions of fixed stars. Not when so many men, all over the world, were watching, waiting, sweeping with superior instruments, all scanning the same sky in hopes of spotting that singular celestial event.

But this was Hannah's intention: to find a comet that no one on Earth had yet seen. It was more than she could reasonably hope for, with no proper observatory, no hope of a higher education, and no instruments but the dear, battered, three-foot-long Dollond telescope and her own two eyes. But the part of her that soared each time she sighted a blazing wanderer crossing her lens hoped anyway, and she supported that irrational sentiment by observing as often as she could manage without abandoning sleep entirely.

If she could establish priority, her accomplishment would be stamped forever in the shape of her name. 'Comet Price' would earn her the King of Denmark's prize – a gold medal and generous sum to anyone, anywhere in the world, who found a new comet. Each time another such prize was announced, a part of her despaired, while another strengthened its resolve: *Next time,* it whispered. *Next time it will be you.* A platform from which to pursue her work would mean a chance to contribute to more than the tick-tock of the clocks that cluttered her workspace and guided the whalers on their global hunts.

But most important – and this she dared not consider too long or carefully – there would be a reason for her father to pay *attention* to their work the way he had before Edward had broken the beautiful geometry of their tiny family.

The first time she'd observed the stars from anywhere but the walk, she and Edward couldn't have been more than four or five. That was the year their father had taken them on their first overnight camping trip. Carrying battered canvas tent and poles, potatoes and bedrolls, they hiked two miles west along the Madaket road to Maxcy's Pond. Her father strapped the cookpot to Hannah's small pack, laughing as it clanked along with each step she took, first along their own narrow sand-and-dirt street, past all the neighbors on both sides. The weathered grey shingles clung to the squat saltbox houses like fish scales, and the lamps, just lit, cast a warm yellow glow into the late afternoon. As they headed out of Town, the houses grew farther apart, surrounded by farms with fields of high corn waving in the twilight, the Prices' own acre and a half tucked in among them, and then disappeared altogether, and the family had heard only the crickets and their own footfalls in the sea-damp air.

It was August. They set up their camp as twilight deepened, the evening punctured with the glow of fireflies. Their bellies were full of boiled potatoes and the blueberries they'd picked along the way, and as darkness descended, Nathaniel led the twins along a trail, slender as a willow tree, that opened into a small clearing. He laid out a scratchy old blanket and the three lay with their heads touching in the center, like the spokes of a wheel, as the stars glimmered into the sky. As the night deepened, Hannah tried to commit them to memory, each in turn, until they blurred together and she slept beneath them.

At dawn, Hannah went with Nathaniel to collect oysters at low tide, holding tightly to his hand as they waded among the shoals, and he named everything for her as it passed underfoot: mosses and crustaceans, water-weeds and tiny silver fish that darted among their toes – making her laugh and leap into his arms.

The memory of his bony shoulder pressed to her cheek now lightened her mood in the garret. Nathaniel had been her ballast, a fountain of curiosities in her child's world of hard benches at Meeting and lined copybooks at school. He had a brightness then that seemed never to diminish; Hannah often wondered if Edward's departure was but the final blow in a series of disappointments she had charted with her own eyes, ranging from physical to financial.

She inhaled deeply, as if she could still smell the humid, salt-soaked dawn of her childhood memory. It was enough to buoy her for the work ahead, even as the empty room reminded her that one upstanding daughter did not make up for one disobedient, seagoing son.

2. Timekeeping

By the time Hannah changed into her First Day dress and lit the fire, it was nearly six a.m. She was used to the echo-ey ring of fatigue, but there was no comfort in the thought of the morning ahead. The weekly ritual of silent worship at the Meeting House had once soothed her, the swish of skirts and conversation settling into quiet like sand to the bottom of Miacomet Pond. It was beautiful not for any divine revelation – not to her, anyway – but for the way the hours in the hard-backed pew seemed to stretch time like taffy. It had been the perfect place to think, to contemplate, to dream.

But as her schoolmates married or moved off-Island, meeting for worship had devolved into a chore, and she dragged her feet as she stirred together flour and salt for graham bread. If Hannah arrived early, someone was sure to try and engage her in gossip, or suggest that she attend this or that lecture or event. If she was late, a hundred pairs of eyes would observe her as she made her way to her seat, gauging her dress or her demeanor, wondering about her future.

She was just about to pour the batter into the pan when she heard a soft, rhythmic knocking, just audible over the hiss of the damp firewood. Someone was drumming gently on the front door.

Swinging it open, Hannah blinked twice. A dark-skinned

man stood in the dim, grey morning, a swaddled bundle tucked into the crook of his arm. A seaman of some lower rank, she decided immediately, examining him in one long glance. His boots were cracked white with salt, and though his pants and jumper were clean, they were inadequate for the weather. Studying his hands, she wondered if he was Ethiopian. He wasn't as dark as most Africans she'd seen – closer to the color of honey or new molasses. Perhaps he was Wampanoag or South American. He was as tall as Hannah, who towered over nearly everyone, which made averting her eyes awkward. She looked back at his hands. The contrast between the pink of his nails and the brown of his skin was strange, as was the white of his palms, cradling an object. She wished she'd put on her bonnet.

She cleared her throat and raised her eyebrows, hoping he spoke English.

'Is that a chronometer?' she asked, nodding at the parcel in his hands. It was nearly six and thirty; if she didn't get the bread done before she left for Meeting, she'd go hungry till noon.

'I am knocking upon the door,' he said finally, and nodded at the wide wooden entry as if it were faulty, which it was. It needed a whitewash, as did the rest of the house, and the useless door-knocker – an old brass hummingbird missing its beak – was still broken.

'And I heard thee,' Hannah said, choosing the formal mode of address reserved for elders, hoping that it would silence any further comment on the state of her door by a stranger of indeterminate race. She found the so-called plain speak of the Friends to be a useful tool for keeping one's distance, though hardly anyone under age fifty used it anymore outside of the Meeting House or conversation with their parents.

She held out both arms for the bundle he carried; he hesitated for a second, then passed it to her.

'Are you wedded to Mr Price?'

'Certainly not,' she snapped. Glancing at his face, she was struck by the unusual color of his eyes. Neither brown nor orange, they were a near-perfect match for a chunk of amber she remembered from the Bonds' mantel in Cambridge. She could envision it clearly, though it had been nearly two decades since she'd seen it up close, clutched tightly in George Bond's pale, sweaty palm. Transfixed, Hannah could practically hear his tinny voice: *You may look upon it but you may not touch it. It's not for girls.*

She let the cloth slip away from the clock, and its soft sweep on her hands pulled her back to the present. She examined the instrument. It had a burnished mahogany casing and a gleaming brass plate fixed to the top. Someone had polished it carefully: *Pearl*, it read. Hannah smiled and lifted the cover, making a swift examination of the face, its Roman numerals and hands stilled at half-three.

'Lovely,' she murmured. The chronometers were beautiful machines. She loved their magnificent springs, the special construction that allowed them to keep time at sea, in spite of the pitch and roll and humidity. This one was English, made by Arnold; it probably kept to within five seconds.

'I'm sorry?'

'How has it done for the *Pearl?*' Hannah asked, inspecting the casing to keep herself from staring at the man's features.

'I do not know,' he answered. 'I was not aboard her last voyage.'

'How did thee come to possess it, then?' She drew the clock closer to her body and took a second look at the man, wondering if she should take caution. Hundreds of captains, plus first and second mates, had brought their chronometers to the Price house to be rated over the years, but she couldn't remember a single one that wasn't white beneath his sun- and wind-browned skin.

'The first mate, Mr Leary, is giving it to me this morning, to deliver for Mr Price's attention.'

'John Leary? Are you a boatsteerer?' Hannah realized too late that she'd dropped the formal address.

'I was. I am now second mate.'

Hannah could practically see the man grow an inch taller as he said it. She decided he couldn't possibly be lying. It would be too easy to uncover such a deception: she knew Mr Leary, as she knew everyone who had grown up on the Island. And there was no reason to suspect him, aside from the color of his skin. A twang of shame for her suspicions vibrated in her body as she snapped the cover closed.

'It's a fine instrument,' she said, drawing the cloth back over its face. Normally she'd log all the required information right then, but she'd be late for Meeting if she did that. In fact, she was already late. And the house was empty.

'Can you return for it in a day's time? We can have it ready in the afternoon.'

She ducked inside, put the chronometer down on the little table beneath the hat rack, and made to close the door, but he looked so perplexed that she paused in mid-swing.

'I was told – Mr Price is not at home?'

Now Hannah was confused.

'Do you need to speak with my father? He's not here. If you must, you can walk with me: it's First Day, and he'll be at Meeting. But you'll have to wait. I need to douse the fire.'

He squinted at her.

'First Day. What you call Sunday. We order our days and months numerically.'

He didn't look convinced, but he nodded, and she stepped back inside. There was no need to explain that the plain calendar evolved because early Friends recoiled from using names for days and months derived from pagan deities. Perhaps he'd be offended by it – who knew what sort of God he worshipped? After hesitating for a moment, Hannah closed the door with a gentle click. The gesture felt odd – she was coming back a moment later – but she didn't want to leave him standing on the step in front of an open door. She didn't consider inviting him in.

Scraping the ashes, it occurred to Hannah that the sailor wasn't confused. He was worried about leaving the chronometer with her. Rocking back on her heels, she swiped her hands on her apron, then untied it and dumped it on the table before buttoning up her coat. Taking her bonnet from the rack, she knotted the strings swift and taut, then swung the door open again.

'You've no need to fear the fate of the *Pearl*'s chronometer,' she announced as she stepped onto the porch, yanking the door shut. 'My father will oversee its adjustment with due care.'

When he didn't respond, she marched down the flagstone path to the little gate, unlatched it, and then stood in the sandy street, waiting for him to follow. Hannah took a deep breath, hoping to quell the indignity of having to escort this sailor from who-knew-where to speak with her father because he thought a woman incapable of handling his ship's chronometer.

He was slow as a slug. Hannah took off walking, happy to let him trail behind. The notion of a woman handling such a delicate and important thing would likely unnerve all twelve thousand whaling men on Earth, save her twin — but Edward was the exception to nearly every rule. At the corner of Main, she forced herself to wait in case the sailor didn't know the way to the Meeting House.

By habit, she glanced up the street toward a three-foot-high stone obelisk in front of the Pacific National Bank, the markings on its face etched into her memory: *Northern extremity of the Town's meridian line.*

Five years earlier, she and Edward had navigated the heavy cart containing that stone toward its designated resting place, the wheels sending up a mighty clatter that rattled their teeth through their laughter. Nathaniel led the way, marching with the spades perched on his shoulder like a sentinel at arms. Hannah recalled the ping of pebbles flying as they dug, the not unpleasant burning in her arms and shoulders.

'You're listing, Hannah,' Edward had said, stumbling under the weight of the marker as the three of them guided it into place. 'I hope your membership in the weaker Sex won't mean broken toes for the men.'

Hannah rolled her eyes and adjusted her hands to counterbalance the weight.

'If the power of your reason exceeded your wit, we could discuss which Sex is truly the weaker.'

'As your elder brother, it's my duty to model my outstanding wit in hopes that you'll aspire to emulate it.'

'Elder by four minutes,' Hannah said, panting as they began to lower the stone.

'Best four minutes of my life.' Edward winked and nearly fell into the hole.

'Gently now, Prices,' Nathaniel murmured. A small crowd had gathered as they bent over the marker, and when the three of them straightened their backs, the patter of applause warmed Hannah's cheek and lit her body with pride for the declaration they had made: the precise location of their Island would now be known to all passersby. *We are here!* the stones announced, and would for eternity.

When the sailor caught up they turned onto Main, where the modest little houses clad in identical grey shingles, home to most everyone Hannah knew, gave way to a series of newly built mansions set back from the cobblestone street, away from the rattle of carts and pedestrians. The pomposity of these grand homes made Hannah wince. The Three Bricks, identical structures built for the three sons of whaling patriarch Joseph Starbuck, wore their porticoes like feathered ruffs; the white clapboard Barrett house boasted an enclosed cupola and enough chimneys to incinerate the rest of the houses on the Island. A few blocks farther on, the ostentatious residences gave way to the commercial stretch of mapmakers and milliners, bakers and fishmongers, along the main artery of Nantucket Town. Lutherans and Unitarians and Friends all moved in a steady flow en route to their various houses of worship. Among them were the residents of the black neighborhood called New Guinea, on their way to the African Baptist Society's Meeting House at the corner of Pleasant and York streets in Five Corners, just east of Town.

'Do you attend church?' Hannah glanced sideways at him, wondering if they had churches where he came from, or if it was an uncivilized, Godless place. It seemed unlikely, since his speech was elegant, if odd – somewhere between a clergyman and a deckhand. Yet there were many such places upon the Earth where people knew nothing of their Creator, or imagined there were many all at once.

'I am not religious,' he said. He walked with his hands at his sides and his eyes straight ahead. His stride was so steady he almost seemed to glide.

'Does your family worship?'

'They did at one time. When I was a young man. Now –' He paused. Hannah thought she heard him sigh. 'I do not know.'

The street became more crowded as they drew close to the Meeting House, and a breeze carried the smell of fish and rancid oil, tar and sawdust, up from the wharves a few blocks away. Margaret Granger, an unsmiling woman of some thirty years who ran her mother's shop, bustled down the opposite side of the street; her husband was aboard the *Regiment* with Edward. Margaret shot a quick, puzzled look at Hannah's companion, then hurried on her way. It happened twice more on the short journey to the corner of Fair Street, and Hannah's face was burning by the time they arrived.

She dropped back slightly as they crossed Main, stepping carefully on the uneven cobblestones. There wasn't anywhere to hide among the shuttered, two-story wooden storefronts, and it was too late to pretend she hadn't been walking alongside the man, even if she were inclined toward fakery. Nor should she: he'd come with a chronometer, and wished to speak with her father. There was no more or less to it. But she was equally annoyed with herself – for not having realized that strolling to Meeting alongside any stranger, much less this one, would stir scrutiny – and with her neighbors, who treated anyone they didn't recognize as an unwanted guest.

Scanning the near-identical wooden buildings nestled together like candlesticks, she aimed for the shadow of the awning over John Darling's Maps &c, at the corner of Fair Street. The wide, plain double doors of the Meeting House just down the street were obscured by a swarm of grey-bonneted women and black-hatted men, though three times as many could fit inside. The congregation seemed to diminish weekly; the vanished were evenly split between those no longer interested in adhering to the ever-tightening code of Discipline and those who'd been disowned after failing to do so.

Edward was among the former group, but had been well on his way to joining the latter when he left. He was spectacularly unconcerned about the possibility of disownment, which to Hannah seemed tantamount to being cast out of one's family. She was in the minority of her peers, though. With disownments being handed down daily for infractions as minor as wearing a colored ribbon or singing in public, the heads of her fellow congregants were as uniformly grey as the building itself. The handful of young people who did remain did so mostly out of allegiance to their parents or grandparents.

'If I want to bore myself to sleep,' Edward had told Hannah a fortnight before the *Regiment* sailed, 'I can do it in my own house well enough.'

'You're not supposed to sleep at Meeting,' Hannah had answered. 'You're supposed to wait for insight. Revelation.'

'I *am* waiting. No reason I can't wait here, where there's coffee. And the newspaper.' He'd reached out and squeezed Hannah's hand. 'Don't worry. I'm sure God can find me if He wants to have a word.'

While she waited for the tide of worshippers to diminish, Hannah tried to think of something to say to her companion, who'd circled back to stand beside her. Idle chatter was confounding. Should she ask him about the *Pearl*? About his origins? His proximity was unnerving, though his demeanor was calm as stone.

'What vessel were you with, before the *Pearl*?' she finally asked.

'I was boatsteerer upon the *Independence*, out of New Bedford.'

'The *Independence*? I heard about that ship. Over three thousand barrels and not a single injury or crew change the entire time. My brother read me an article about it.'

Edward had been trying to shore up his argument for joining a whaling crew, but Hannah had reminded him that far more whalers ended up dismembered, dead, or lost at sea than did qualify for interviews by the *Nantucket Inquirer*.

'We are having good luck upon the journey.' The sailor bowed his head a little. *He's modest,* Hannah thought. It was unusual for a whaler. Every one she knew enjoyed crowing about his superior skills with the reeling line or the harpoon.

'Did you by chance tie up with the *Regiment* on your journey home?' It was a long shot at best, but she couldn't resist asking.

'I do not believe so. But I am not consuming spirits, so I am not always in the festivities when our ship is meeting others.'

'I see,' she said, mentally correcting his grammar while peeking around the edge of her bonnet. If she stalled for another minute, the crowd outside the Meeting House would disperse even further. She sneaked another look at her companion's face. In profile he reminded her of an etching in a book at the Atheneum. But which plate? She risked another glance, and the image resolved. It was an etching that an enthusiastic pamphleteer had attached to a reprint of one of Mr Emerson's essays, from the series he'd published the year before. Hannah hadn't read the entire thing, but it had caused a fair amount of talk and argument among borrowers. 'Character,' it was called, and it began with a reference to Lord Chatham, who was depicted in the plate. The association between a great English statesman and a possibly illiterate black sailor was so bizarre that Hannah had to force herself to look away.

'That's our Meeting House there,' she said, pointing. People were streaming toward the doors. Now was the perfect time for her to approach. She'd drop into the flow and slip in without being noticed. But taking him along would call attention, not deflect it.

'Do you still wish to speak to Mr Price? If so, you'll have to come along.'

The sailor made his own survey of the crowd. A small muscle in his cheek flexed as he studied the scene. They stood side by side. Pedestrian traffic flowed past like current around a boulder.

He doesn't want to go over there any more than I do, Hannah realized. She could see it in his face. She was oddly comforted.

He made up his mind.

'I entrust you,' he said with a small bow. Hannah tried to acknowledge it with an awkward nod of her own, but before she'd raised her head, he'd disappeared into the crowd of worshippers making their way down Main Street.

3. Silence

Hannah moved toward the Meeting House with her head down, hoping her bonnet would shield her from the chatter that ran through the crowd. A grating chorus of titters and gasps made her look up, and when she did, she found Mary Coffey standing directly in front of her.

Mary frowned at her giggling companions as if to silence them, and they melted away like a queen's ladies. What was it about Mary that made everyone – including Edward – want to please her? Hannah studied her costume: a tailored dress of fine silk, though its color was plain brown, in keeping with Discipline. Its lace collar was an exquisite web of leaves and flowers, delicate as dragonfly wing. It was probably French. No doubt Mary had ordered it from a catalogue. It was the kind of thing Edward would have scorned, had he not been tricked by his emotions. A family like the Coffeys would never be sufficiently impressed by his accomplishments to ignore his lack of money and let him marry their remaining daughter. Hannah knew it as surely as she knew the names of the fixed stars. But Edward was blind to it.

'We have the farm,' he'd reasoned to Hannah. 'And if the Coast Survey contract comes through, there's that.'

Her brother's naïveté had made Hannah wince, though George Bond had been hinting for months that such a contract from Washington might come their way.

Dr Alexander Bache, the recently appointed superintendent of the survey, was parceling the newly expanded United States into nine regions, each of which would have its own baseline from which to triangulate every nook of coastline therein. Massachusetts was in Region I; according to George, the baseline was to fall somewhere around New Bedford, making Nantucket the perfect place for an official 'station.' If it was so designated, Hannah and her father could expect a crateload of new instruments, and a significant increase in their income as well.

The scope of the survey was controversial, but Hannah warmed to Dr Bache's vision: the disparate shorelines and peoples of the nation bound by geodetic certainty. A national coastline wide enough to encompass 20 degrees of latitude and 30 of longitude was hard to imagine, much less map, and she appreciated the orderly manner in which he approached the task, his appreciation for mathematical rigor. Plus, she'd heard he was willing to hire women as computers for *The Nautical Almanac*.

'Even if we received the Coast Survey contract, it would barely cover our own expenses,' Hannah said. 'And I don't think the farm has turned a profit in twenty years – I don't even know why Father keeps it. How do you expect to support someone who lives in a mansion and has servants?'

'The Coffey place isn't a mansion, Hannah. It's just a brick house. I've been inside. And look' – he did a mincing little dance around the kitchen – 'if I turn into some sort of dandy, you can call the constable!'

'Stop it.' Hannah swished at him with the flyswatter. 'You know what I mean.'

'I do,' he'd said, flopping onto the stool. 'But you're

mistaken. Mary's just like you. Well, no. She's not like you. No one is like you. But she's a lovely girl, and not spoilt like you think. I don't know why you think it, anyway. It's not like you to be so uncharitable.'

'I think she's false,' Hannah said flatly. 'I don't think you see everything there is to see.'

'And you do? You see only the saturated ends of the spectrum, my dear. Dark or light. True or false. Yet we live upon what might be the greyest place on Earth.'

Even under the cloudy First Day sky, Hannah found it painful to look at Mary directly. Her pale skin was nearly translucent, but her eyes were a bright, demanding shade of blue. In every weather, her gold hair shimmered as if reflecting summer sun. Gazing upon something so inarguably lovely was lulling. Whenever she looked at Mary, Hannah wanted to keep looking, and then she found herself tongue-tied and confused, awkward even in the simplest conversations.

Hannah had tried, as a child, to penetrate the mysterious web of Island girls her age. They seemed bound to one another as tightly as their stitches. The last time she'd joined a tatting circle had been when they were twelve or thirteen years of age. Hannah had sat rigid as a flagpole in the chair she'd been offered, and studied the hoop in her lap. The easy chatter of the girls around her was as unfamiliar and intimidating as a foreign tongue, and Hannah felt sorry that she'd come.

Tallulah Barnes had been there, Hannah recalled, and Lilian Archer, and Mary of course. Hannah had picked at her forlorn skein of slender thread until Tallie leaned over and gasped with a kind of shocked pity, and the other girls had ceased talking and gathered around.

'Hannah, you'll ruin it!'

Lilian had brightened for a rescue, laying her own work aside and turning to Hannah's.

'I'm certain we can put it to right,' she said.

'Hannah despises tatting, isn't that right?' Mary asked.

'Well, it takes practice,' Lilian offered, picking at the threads.

'My mother says that it's part and parcel of a lady's education. Tatting is, I mean.' Tallie rolled her eyes but didn't look as if she really thought the idea was silly. 'If we hope to marry eventually.'

All the girls had giggled, but Hannah hadn't understood the joke. Mary said something about a boy, and then there was silence, and Hannah realized that she'd been asked a question.

'Pardon?'

More giggling. Tallie and Lilian exchanged a look Hannah couldn't interpret. Her face had flushed. What did they want from her?

'Tallie was only asking what you thought about Peter Macy,' Mary said, not unkindly.

Hannah had kept her eyes on the mess of silken thread in Lilian's hands. What was she expected to say? She chose the truth.

'I haven't any thoughts of him,' she stammered.

'What about Nathaniel Starbuck?' Tallie asked.

'Or Zachary Phillips?'

'Zachary? Don't be absurd. Why would Hannah think on him?'

'Well he's quite bookish,' Mary said calmly. 'And Hannah likes books. Don't you, Hannah?'

'Maybe Hannah isn't interested in boys,' Lilian said, patting her on the knee. 'She's smarter than all three of them put together, anyway.'

'My mother says that women who read too much –' Tallie began, but Mary broke in.

'Hush, Tallie.' She took Hannah's hoop from Lilian and handed it back to her. 'It wasn't so bad after all. Go on with the stitch – you'll get it in time.'

But Hannah had shaken her head and risen from the chair so abruptly that the girls scattered like startled birds. They'd called after her, but she hadn't gone back, not that evening and not afterward.

It wasn't true that she never thought of boys; she just had no concept of what to say to one who didn't happen to be her brother. The other girls seemed steeped in such things; Hannah had often watched them as they giggled and ran after each other, and she even pretended she was speaking to Peter Macy once or twice, addressing her own wavering reflection in the glass windowpane of her bedroom. But she'd felt so foolish and vain that she never bothered to make the attempt in life. Over the years, her sense of ineptitude, along with her injured pride, had only hardened, and she'd shunned most of the attempts the women made to include her in their activities. Eventually, they had stopped trying, all except for Mary.

Whenever she looked at Mary now, though, Hannah saw Edward's empty chair in the garret, his empty trunk, his empty seat at the table.

Hannah scanned the crowd outside the Meeting House

for her father, but all the men looked alike in their wide-brimmed hats.

'Have you had any letters?' Mary asked, swaying slightly to try to meet Hannah's roving eye. Hannah looked back down at her. Mary's hand floated up to pat a stray lock of hair into place. Her fingers were white as worms.

'We haven't had a letter in at least a month,' Hannah answered. That was the excruciating truth. Each day, en route to her job at the Atheneum, she checked their little wooden box at Riddell's store – an ancient, dilapidated structure right in the center of Town, whose sun-bleached wooden shingles, sagging porch, and squeaky door belied its importance as the housing for all the Island's correspondence. The enormous canvas sacks stuffed with letters hung from the rafters like fat men on gallows, each labeled with a destination – *Pacific grounds*, *Cape of Good Hope*, *North Atlantic*. Women and girls flowed in and around them like a school of fish, hoping for news or trying to deliver their own. The bags were full of words describing deaths and births, grievances and reprieves. Above all, Hannah knew, they contained oaths of everlasting love. She averted her eyes from the bulging repositories of so many hopes and dreams; staring at them felt like inviting disappointment.

'I've had none for a fortnight,' Mary sighed. 'More. Let me think. The last one came the day we had Debating. You weren't there, were you?'

Hannah shook her head. She never went to the Debating Society, though Edward had insisted that she'd be a hundred times more convincing on any subject than most of its participants.

29

'The necessity of comprehensive education for both Sexes, for example,' he'd said one evening in their kitchen. 'Or the importance of proper alignment of one's furniture in the perpendicular.'

'As far as education goes, I doubt anything I might say at such a gathering would hasten an onslaught of colleges for women,' Hannah answered, sweeping as if the broom were responsible for the pathetic number of baccalaureate programs open to members of her Sex, all of which she could count on one hand.

'Of course, I attend only for amusement,' Edward added, a trail of crumbs from his toast with jam following him across the just-swept kitchen to his seat at the table.

'Is there any other reason you do anything?' she asked. 'Pick up your feet.'

He obliged, his knees knocking the underside of the table.

'You'd rather enjoy the spectacle of our local windbags pecking at each other's already porous arguments. With the exception of Mary Coffey, I didn't hear a single speaker that had a passion for their topic or an ability to express it in a manner not guaranteed to provoke immediate slumber. It's better than a tonic. Was that a snort?'

Hannah attacked the floorboards so that a little cloud of dust and ash rose around her broom.

'Mary Coffey? I expect your eyes overruled your ears if that's what you came away with.'

'I don't know,' he said, brushing crumbs carefully into his long palm. 'Maybe you'd be surprised.'

Hannah hadn't gone to Debating, and she declined repeated invitations from the Ladies' Temperance Auxiliary and the Book Club, which seemed anxious to have an Atheneum employee as a sort of trophy member. The thought of speaking in front of them was enough to cause her pulse to race and sweat to bead on her lip. All those eyes upon her. It was the last form of entertainment she'd choose.

As their neighbors drifted into Meeting, Mary prattled on about the Society's last meeting.

'The question that week was, "Has the world at the present time arrived at a degree of civilization to which it has never before attained?" I remember because Fritz – you know Fritz Gardiner – said something utterly surprising. Yet it made perfect sense. I love when that happens. Don't you?'

Hannah squinted at Mary.

'I suppose so,' she muttered, wondering when she could slip away without being completely rude, and Mary took it as a sign that she should go on talking, seizing Hannah's elbow as if they were now the best of friends, then tugging her in the direction of the wide double doors. Hannah was electrified by the contact, the strange sensation of being pulled close to another body. No one in the Price house was prone to embrace. Mary tipped her chin up toward Hannah's ear, and her warm breath tickled her neck.

'Anyway, Fritz said one must use caution when imposing one's own definition of civilization upon everyone else in the world, for each people have their own set of rules for living which we might find impossible to understand or support but which make perfect sense to them.' They paused outside the doors, and Hannah extracted her arm and fiddled with her bonnet strings, looking in vain for her father.

Worshippers crowded the entryway. Nearly everyone nodded at Mary first, then at Hannah. She felt pinned in place, queasy under the gaze of so many observers.

'Anyone who assumes that view could regard a murderer as perfectly justified in his own mind,' Hannah said, raising her chin and wondering if she was being baited. 'Certainly such a position isn't a Christian one.'

Instead of recoiling, Mary seemed to levitate with excitement.

'That's just what Dr Hall said! It promised to be an extremely interesting exchange. But unfortunately Mr Rubens brought up the un-Christian behavior of our own citizens at the antislavery rally in '42, and how throwing rocks and stones wasn't civilized in the least, and then all the men began shouting.'

Mary sighed, and flashed a bright smile at a young girl who'd offered a tiny, shy wave. The girl beamed and ran to catch up to her mother. Before Hannah could excuse herself, Mary went on.

'Hannah, you really should come to the next meeting. Edward always said you'd put us all to shame with your reason. And I'm certain he's right. Oh, there's my mother. Good talking to you! Very good.' She blinked rapidly and backed up a step, then turned and went toward Charlotte Coffey, who looked as if she'd eaten something unpleasant. Something she'd have to eat again.

Hannah felt a hand on her elbow, and then her father was beside her. Hannah exhaled, relief flooding her body.

She tilted her head to get a look at him. He hardly looked worn from his long journey from Philadelphia. If anything he looked refreshed. His brown eyes, so similar to Hannah's, lacked the dark circles that surrounded hers. He'd trimmed his beard and hair, eliminating the boulder-colored grey swoop that usually impaired his vision. Someone had mended the hole in the shoulder of his jacket with tidy stitches, and Hannah squinted at them, wondering who could have sewn them; the only needle she'd touched in months was the one she'd used to repair the crosshair.

'I was looking for thee,' he said. 'Dr Hall wished to say hello.'

'I'm sorry I missed him.' Hannah turned, expecting to see her old mentor and teacher.

'Thee shall have another chance – I've invited him to supper tomorrow evening.'

'Oh. Very well. I hope there's enough of the roast left over. I suppose I could do a chowder if someone has clams.' They began moving through the crowd, walking easily in step.

'Ever practical,' he said. 'We'll make it enough. He has simple taste. I'm sure a home-cooked meal from thee will warm him sufficiently, even if it be stone soup.'

'It may taste thus,' she said, only half joking. Among the many things Hannah wished her mother had lived to pass along was her renowned ability to cook. Ann Gardner Price had died when Hannah and Edward were only three years old, and Hannah had found it difficult in the years since to learn much about her beyond her cooking, though Miss Norris, the senior librarian and Ann's former classmate, had once said something startling: 'Thy mother was a force to be reckoned with,' she'd intoned, lowering her voice as if she were committing treason. 'She was never settled in matters of Discipline. Thy father indulged her, some said, though in my opinion there's aught a man can do about a wife with ideas.'

'What sort of ideas?' Hannah had asked, remaining perfectly still for fear that Miss Norris might stop speaking.

'Ah, well. She didn't much like keeping house, outside of the garden and the kitchen. She had a difficult time with all things plain, though she grew up in the Discipline, too. And she wasn't the quiet type. Questions, questions, questions – that was thy mother. Like a child in that way, she was. In any case, the past is past, and thee can be glad to take after thy father. Not a hint of impertinence in thee, I'm glad to see. One wishes the same could be said about thy brother. But boys, there's no sense in them but what a woman knocks in.'

Hannah and Nathaniel reached their row. The assembly began to settle as the Prices parted. Nathaniel dipped to the left while Hannah took her place on the right, with the women.

There was no need to look to know who was present. In the front, facing the room, Dr Hall took his place with the other elders. At their feet sat the Starbuck and Folger clans, along with the rest of the original families, descendents of the first Friends who'd made landfall upon Nantucket two hundred years earlier and never left.

Behind them, the Coffeys and their kin occupied two more benches, along with other families whose fortunes grew greater each evening as people up and down the eastern coast from Penobscot to Atlanta read and sang and prayed by lamps filled with right whale oil.

Farther back were the families whose fortunes depended upon those of the people in front: the mapmakers and milliners, importers and outfitters. Without the captains and shipowners and their families, they would be out of work, as would Hannah and her father. His job at the Bank was to ensure that the banknotes from New York and Rhode Island and Connecticut were exchanged for local notes the owners could deposit into their accounts on Federal Street. As their accounts grew, so would Nathaniel's – but he'd only been in the position for nine months, and Hannah had yet to see any increase in their finances.

She wondered if they ever would. For the first time in history, more whaling vessels were shipping from New Bedford than Nantucket. Her fishery still held its own – and proudly – but the economic winds were blowing west. There were the great manufacturing centers springing up across the eastern seaboard, promising jobs that took a man away from home for ten hours at a stretch instead of four years. There were mills and factories to be staffed clear to the Louisiana Territory, railroad track to be laid and land to be claimed.

Nathaniel Price frowned upon factory workers almost as much as he did upon whalers: he said they were too lazy to find an occupation of the mind. He believed in expansion, but not if one had to sacrifice intellectual pursuits or squander one's morals in the process.

Hannah peeked at her father. He sat silently, head bowed, as always, but he opened his eyes a crack just as she looked at him. He didn't wink before closing them as he had when she was a girl. Hannah sighed. Perhaps his job weighed upon him. The contract with the Bank took him to Providence and Boston, New Bedford and Philadelphia, every month. She wondered today, as she often did, surrounded by their neighbors' wives, if he still missed her mother.

As the silence deepened, Hannah remembered her long-overdue reply to the letter George Bond had sent over a week ago. She'd put it off because she felt herself unhealthy with envy, though she couldn't blame George for his circumstances. He hadn't chosen to be the son of the man who oversaw the greatest observatory in the United States. Nor had he chosen to be his father's assistant. If anything, the job had been thrust on him; George would rather be sketching a newt than observing a nebula. But he did his duty, as did she. It was one of the things that bound their friendship, along with the loss of their mothers at an early age. Their ongoing correspondence was full of playful jabs at each other's flaws and weaknesses. In his letter, George had told her that his father had been able to partially resolve the nebula in Orion:

I saw it too – it is truly spectacular. There are several clusters of stars, near the head, and then a mass about the trapezium. You should come to Cambridge soon and see for yourself. Though it pains me to say so, your presence would likely lighten the atmosphere of our ever-active, under-staffed hive – but knowing you, perhaps I'd be more likely to lure you with a promise of more work and less diversion.

Hannah envisioned the cloud of indistinct, milky light resolving into discrete bodies, as if in a dream: there, a pinkish star of the fifth magnitude; here, a cluster; there, another.

She would never see such things with the Dollond. The observatory at Cambridge was only a half-day away by steamer and carriage, but it might have been an ocean that separated Hannah and George. He diverted a stream of astronomical news and publications her way each month, and recounted a flurry of occupation and advancement in every letter, along with a regular exhortation to visit. Sometimes Hannah wondered where he found the time to write so often; he sent twice as many missives as she could respond to, and those notes she did dash off in return were nowhere near as long. His intentions were good, but the secondhand news only reminded her how small their garret observatory was by comparison. No matter how long and hard she looked, George could observe more in a night than Hannah could in a lifetime.

She tried to still her mind and focus on the object she'd seen in the night sky a few nights earlier. But as she recalled the milky nebula – if it was a nebula – and the dark ribbons threaded within it, the picture began to dissolve into inky darkness.

Dear Edward,

I hope you are well and under fair wind tonight, or this morning I suppose, where you are. We are ever in hopes of letters from you for none have come since 2nd month. Winter still grips us nights. I look forward to the milder days ahead, for this winter tried my fortitude. I wish you'd been here. But there is no use in that.

How go your advances in Navigation? Do you understand now how to work the preparations for taking a lunar? I hope so. If not I shall explain it in a different way, though by the time my 'lecture' as you will doubtless call it reaches you I am certain you'll already have worked it out.

Everything is the same, here. Phoebe Fuller came into the Atheneum a few days ago to interrogate me about poor widow Ramsay's reading habits; there have been a half-dozen more disownments. Lizzie was read out for singing songs while doing the washing, or some such. I half-expect Phoebe to disown herself by accident one of these days, if she should catch herself chatting with an off-Islander. I thought to tell her to let the poor widow be, but said nothing.

Father has been away much of the time on Bank business. I know you think he shall never forgive your decision but I'm certain if you wrote to him directly he'd be glad to hear from you. I wish you would — maybe it would encourage him to take more of an interest in our astronomical labors again. I imagine he is in hopes that when you return things will be as they once were, and we three can undertake the Coast Survey contract, should the

Bonds manage to arrange it. George is pestering me to visit but I can't see how we can take the time away.

I remembered recently that I once thought of leaving, too, when we were children and pretended at navigating our way across the dark Atlantic. I passed our playground the other day on one of my rambles — where that old log used to sit on the beach at Madaket. It all came back to me — I was the captain, and you were the cook and boatsteerer and 1st mate all at once — but now you are actually crossing the ocean and I am ashore, as always.

Please study and read when you can and also write to your loving Sister, HGP

4. Decimal Arithmetic

The next afternoon, Hannah heard the distant knock on the door downstairs and, annoyed by the intrusion, forced herself to put aside the equations she'd been wrestling with for weeks. George had sent dozens of articles and commentaries about the work of British mathematician John C. Adams, who was calculating the probable location of a never-seen planet that would account for the inexplicable aberration in the orbit of Uranus. Hannah had plugged in Adams' data and worked through the equations herself from top to bottom, but hadn't been able to replicate his conclusions. It was infuriating: Adams was but a year older than Hannah, and what had *she* discovered? If she couldn't even work down his equations with his own data, how could she expect to compute the orbit of a comet she had yet to even sight?

Her heavy lace-up boots echoed as she clumped downstairs and threw open the door as if it were responsible for all her failings. The *Pearl*'s second mate was waiting on the porch, his hands clasped behind his back. He wore the same jumper as the day before, but had a threadbare green scarf wrapped around his neck in addition, as if that could possibly protect him from the cold.

He lowered his head to acknowledge her, but made no move to enter. She hesitated, too. Normally, she'd have already entered all the required information about the timepiece and its vessel in the log, and could just return it and collect the payment. In this case, though, she'd put it off. And the *Pearl*'s chronometer was still up in the garret. A blast of cold wind gusted, and they wrapped their arms around their bodies at the same time.

'There's some information I need from you,' she said, shivering. 'Step inside.'

He made his strange bow again, then slipped past her into the hallway, pausing before removing his soft cap and placing it on the peg beside her bonnet. Hannah led him through the hallway, and she was halfway up the stairs when she realized he wasn't behind her.

The man had stopped at the entry to the sitting room and was staring at the half-filled globe of water hanging from the ceiling in the center of the room, a relic of her father's old experiments. As Hannah watched, a bar of late afternoon light passed through the room, and he started, staring at the colors it flung upon the opposite wall like wild birds.

'It's refraction,' Hannah said from the doorway. 'My father used to experiment with prisms. That's what it's called – a prism.'

'I am once seeing an illusionist make such a trick,' he said, still eyeing the display. 'In Fiji. From a stone he did conjure colors such as these.'

Hannah raised her eyebrows. 'This is no trick,' she said, vaguely insulted. But how would he know better? She shifted into her teacher's voice. 'Light rays separate into the spectrum when they pass through the water. Those are the colors you see upon the wall.'

As she spoke, the ray of sun ceased, and the colors

vanished. The sailor glanced around as if they might be hiding in a corner, and Hannah saw the room as he might: the set of hard straight-backed chairs, the table and mantel with no decorative flourish, the threadbare settee. Only the vines on the wallpaper and the woven rug had anything bright to offer. Hannah loved the spare alignment of the room, its angles and corners, but where she saw order, he likely saw a barren field. Her gaze lighted on his hair, and she wondered if it was as soft as it looked, or bristly as a wire brush. Then, embarrassed by her curiosity, she whirled around and went back up the steps.

'This way, please,' she said, ducking through the door off the landing that led up to the garret. 'Mind the rafters.'

Upstairs, Hannah busied herself locating the ledger for the fleet, flipping through the pages for the *Pearl*'s account. Not finding an entry for his ship, she turned to a fresh page in the ledger. PEARL, she wrote at the top as he edged into the room, hovering just inside the doorway.

'What is your captain's name?' she asked without looking up.

'It is Captain Coffey.'

Out of the corner of her eye, Hannah saw him take a very small step into the room, then another, appraising its jumble of items as if they were the treasures of a hundred ships' naturalists: conch and snail shells, specimens and minerals vied for space with the furniture and books. Sad bundles of sassafras and archangel hung from the ceiling. It was dim even on the brightest of days, but Hannah didn't want to waste a candle.

JAMES COFFEY, *Master,* Hannah wrote. He was

Mary's uncle. She frowned into the ledger, though it was no surprise. The Coffeys owned much of the fleet.

'First mate? Navigator? Vessel's first year in service? Current destination?'

He did not know some of the answers, and stumbled on those he did.

'Time in port?' she asked, trying for a less severe tone.

The last was met with silence. Hannah looked up. The man hefted a chunk of mineral in his palm. The stone was heavier than it looked, she knew, more dense, its true nature hiding beneath its humble coat. It was one of her favorites.

'That's blue labradorite,' Hannah said, surprised by his interest. Perhaps he was wondering if it was valuable. 'It's just a mineral,' she added, unnerved by the thought that he could be a thief. He could be anything.

'Blue?' he repeated. She nodded. Pushing back her chair, she reached over and he dropped the grey rock in her open palm. Plucking a metal file from a small hook on the wall, she drew it sharply against the stone, once, twice, then blew on it to clear the dust.

Rubbing her thumb against the deep blue she'd exposed, the color of a moonless midnight, she passed the stone back.

'Blue.'

He passed his own thick, callused thumb over the warm spot, then placed it carefully back on the shelf and swept his arm around the room, indicating by the gesture the whole of its contents.

'These are belonging to you?'

'To my father and myself, yes.'

43

'These?' He reached toward the telescope and sextant on the table beside it, his fingers hovering over them, long and graceful.

'These as well.' She paused. Were his questions a function of simple curiosity, or disbelief that a woman should have access to such instruments at all? None of the seagoing men who had passed through this room in the years she'd spent in it had ever shown such interest in its contents. They were only interested in getting their chronometers working, and paying a fair price for the service.

When he didn't elaborate, she went on with her questions, wanting the interview to be over.

'How long will the *Pearl* be in port?' she repeated.

He shrugged. 'We were to be leaving next week,' he said. 'But today I am learning there is a delay.'

'What sort of delay?'

'Money. Repairs. As always. I am not certain. I am speaking with Mr Leary this morning and he say perhaps a fortnight, or two. Or four.'

Hannah wondered where he passed his days and nights – if he'd let a room somewhere or if he had family here on Nantucket. She doubted it. Whalers from faraway lands drifted in and out of port like tides, with about as much emotion. This man, however, seemed worried, even sad, as he contemplated the uncertain stretch of time before him.

'What shall you do?' she asked, her voice softened by an unexpected rush of sympathy.

'I shall work at the smith. Mr Vera has been generous.'

Hannah nodded. Hot metal clanged and sizzled at

Vera's shed from morning to night, horseshoes and harpoons springing forth at astonishing speed.

'Are you Portugee, then?' she asked, writing down *1-2 mo.?* on the line next to *Time in Port*. Hannah doubted it. Joseph Vera and the other Portugee she knew were white.

'Nooooo, not Portugal,' he said, clicking his tongue. Stooping, he examined a stuffed pheasant under the mineral shelf, though he did not touch it. 'Azores.'

'Ah –?'

'Azores.'

She doubted that her tongue could replicate what he'd said, and she wasn't about to embarrass herself by trying.

'You call them Western Islands,' he added.

'Oh!' She tilted her head at him, not hiding her surprise. 'Is that where you come from?' She knew the place as a stopping point for provisions on the long road to the Pacific whaling grounds. Ships bound for home carried news from there, and letters, from those newly en route.

He nodded, but repeated in a low voice, 'Azores. That is the name.'

Hannah nodded to show that she had understood. Rolling the word in her mouth, she broke it into parts. Ah. Soar. Ays.

'And what is your name?' she asked, keeping her eyes on the page in front of her.

'Isaac Martin.'

She wrote his name in the ledger as if there were a place for it there.

'And your place?' she asked, pretending she did not remember from the day before.

'I am second mate.'

Hannah nodded, and waited to see if he had something else to say. When he remained quiet, she wrote his station below his name in her tight script, then reached for the chronometer and the soft cloth by its side.

'It was five and a half seconds off,' she said, bundling it up. 'You might want to tell Mr Leary that the escapement has a bit of wear on it: nothing to be very concerned about, at least not for this voyage. But when he returns to port, he might want to see about changing it. Or you might.'

She passed the bundle and Isaac accepted it, but didn't move from his spot. Instead, he slowly replaced the chronometer on the desk in front of her and pointed at it.

'You are fixing it?' he said.

'Yes. It's perfectly accurate now.'

'Can you show me?'

'Show you what?'

'How it works.'

'You wish to know how the chronometer works?' she repeated.

He clenched his jaw, crossing his arms over his chest and staring at it as if it was about to sprout wings.

'Well, I suppose I can.' Hannah looked around, flummoxed by such a strange request. It was the last thing she'd expected him to ask. 'Wait here.'

As she extracted another stool, grimy but solid, from the corner, a trill of excitement ran through her. Brushing it off with her hand, she dragged it toward the desk, then beckoned Isaac to it.

It had been years since she last taught schoolchildren;

the job as junior librarian at the Atheneum had offered far more than the $25 per annum she'd earned assisting Dr Hall, not to mention the chance to read anything she wanted. But she missed her students' hungry minds, powering their wonder with Truth. Her favorite lessons had explained how the Creator had puzzled their world together, the invisible, unbreakable connections among all living things.

She cleared her throat, then drew an old, dusty chronometer from the shelf and blew on it gently before wiping it off with her skirt. Then she put it down on the desk beside the *Pearl*'s instrument.

'The chronometer,' she said, tapping it with her quill, 'is a precision timekeeping instrument, built for seagoing vessels and used to determine longitude.' Turning the clock over, she unscrewed the small peg that kept it closed, then removed the entire back. Isaac winced, and she pretended not to notice. With sure hands, she removed the winding pin, the spindled gears, the escapement and balance wheel, pausing to admire the beauty of the spiral spring attached to it before laying it, light as a feather, in line beside the other parts.

'In order to keep time, a clock must measure out precise units with no aberration. It needs a source of power' – she paused and tapped the winding pin with her quill – 'and it needs to store that power and use it up in small increments, so that it keeps going over a long spell at sea. That's what these circular gears do.'

He was silent, but she went on, speaking slowly so that he might not miss anything.

'When these gears turn, they trigger this small lever – called the escapement – to move back and forth. This keeps the balance wheel moving, like a pendulum, and the motion of the balance wheel makes the gears rotate. The smaller one spins faster, to measure seconds, and the larger more slowly, to measure hours. The little hands on the clock that tell you the time are attached to these gears. Now, in a normal clock, the period of the balance wheel changes when the temperature changes, because metal expands and contracts with heat. In a chronometer, this little spiral spring at the heart of the balance wheel is forged from a mix of different metals that expand and contract at different rates, so the balance wheel keeps a constant period, and thus the exact time, at sea. Even when the ship pitches and rolls about, and in any type of weather.' In conclusion, she tapped her quill on the table-top like a conductor.

'The time,' he stated, pointing at the chronometer, his eyes narrowed as if he suspected it of trickery.

'Yes?'

'Why?'

'Why do you need the *time*?'

He nodded, staring at the instrument.

'Well, to determine longitude, of course.' She paused before continuing. 'Since the Earth rotates fifteen degrees each hour, one needs to know the time at the home port as well as one's local time, in order to calculate the ship's position.' When he didn't answer, she sank into her own chair. His question hadn't been about the function of the chronometer, after all; it had been about its purpose.

Hannah slowly replaced the panel on the chronometer

and put it back down on the desk. Had he been testing her? Her cheeks burned and she tried to will them cool.

'I wish to learn,' Isaac said. 'Can you? Is it possible?' He gestured to the sextant, the telescope, the books, then looked at her directly. 'I can pay.'

'You want lessons in navigation? From me?' She repeated each word clearly, so there would be no mistake, waiting for his response before she allowed herself to consider it.

When he nodded, she wondered first where he'd gotten the ambition. Navigation was an officer's duty, she supposed, and he was indeed now one of them. What came of it should be no matter. Yet she'd never known anyone of his color to advance farther than boatsteerer, save Absalom Boston – and that had been twenty years ago. When she was a little girl, black men had made up a much larger portion of the whaling crews that came in and out of port, but their numbers had dwindled as recent emigrants from England and Ireland and Germany began competing for the same jobs. And with the country increasingly divided over slavery, race relations were strained even on Nantucket, where free men of every color had lived and conducted business in close proximity to their white neighbors for decades.

Antislavery sentiment was as strong on the Island as anywhere in the Northeast, but Hannah had seen the bruises and welts on those who'd been pelted with rocks and cobblestones and who knew what else at the antislavery convention at the Atheneum just a few years earlier. William Lloyd Garrison, the leading abolitionist, had spoken out against churches' refusal to denounce slavery.

And though the majority of Nantucketers were staunchly opposed to human bondage – it was difficult to find a yard of cotton or a wad of tobacco on the Island – the man's sweeping indictment of the clergy overcame their civility.

And there was the matter of the Nantucket schools, from which the African children had recently been expelled, reassigned to their 'own' school as if they hadn't been perfectly fine right where they were. The African community had petitioned the Massachusetts state house for redress. Hannah wished the schools committee hadn't been swayed by the prejudice of what she was sure was a minority of Island residents, but the courts would surely correct their position.

Why should Isaac Martin not learn navigation if he wished to do so? Hannah was reminded of her own thwarted desire to study alongside the young men at Cambridge, the heat of her envy at their easy chatter, their overflowing libraries, the observatory to which they had access every night of their lives, regardless of their aptitude. Lessons lined up in her mind like workers reporting for duty. She sat up in her chair.

'But can you read and write?' she asked, bracing for disappointment.

'I can.'

'Oh. Well, good. And do you know the points of the compass?'

He nodded.

'What about maths? Do you know combinations? Can you reduce a fraction?'

Hannah reached for a volume that had been sitting on

her desk for nearly three years, untouched but for the feather duster, and slid it carefully across the desk in front of him, pushing the *Pearl*'s chronometer aside to make room.

Bowditch's *American Practical Navigator*, it read.

She turned back the green cover. Inside, two names were inscribed:

Hannah Gardner   Price Edward Gardner Price

Isaac pointed to Hannah's name with his long finger and tapped it gently.

'That's me. And my brother.' She turned the flyleaf over, feeling protective of their names, then paged through one delicate sheet at a time until she reached the first set of exercises. Bringing out a battered copybook with some blank sheets at the back, Hannah put it down in front of Isaac, pressing it open to a clean page and handing over a stub of pencil from a dented pewter cup on the desk.

'You can come once a week, or when you can manage, starting tomorrow. Evenings are probably best. But in the meantime, let's see what you can do with these.'

She watched him study the page. *Reduce* 1/5 *to a decimal.*

Pressing hard on the graphite, he slowly inscribed: 5.0 and then stared at it.

Hannah plucked the pencil from his fingers and put a line through what he had done, rewriting it in the reverse: $5\sqrt{1.0}$, then handed the pencil back.

'You were nearly right. Go on from there,' she said. He squinted at the page, taking what seemed like a very long time before putting the point of the pencil to the paper.

Isaac inscribed a curvaceous *2* beneath her angular scratches, then placed a careful dot in front of it.

Hannah realized she'd been holding her breath, and as he made his mark, she exhaled, letting go of the chair and clasping her hands on her lap.

'That is correct,' she said, keeping her voice steady. It wouldn't do to let him know she was excited. 'Go on and do the next one.'

If he was to be of any use to his ship's navigator, Hannah thought, watching him work, he'd need books. They could be borrowed; but she'd also need a quadrant, and an azimuth circle if she could get one. She sighed. It had been so long since she looked at the Bowditch. Edward had never shown much interest in navigation, though he liked observing, especially if she told him where to look.

I can teach this man, Hannah thought, watching Isaac work down the page of simple arithmetic. *Anyone who wants to improve should have the chance.*

She ignored the sentiment that flickered in its wake: no matter how accomplished a navigator he might become, she could not think of a single captain who would have him for an officer.

Dr Hall's spine seemed slightly more curved than Hannah remembered, his sheep-like, iron-grey curls tufting paler around his temples. It was probably guilt playing tricks on her mind that made him seem like he'd aged; she hadn't been to visit his house on Pineapple Street in months.

'Good evening,' Hannah said, once he'd made his way inside and hung his hat on the rack. 'It's good to see thee.'

'Hannah Price. Thee as well. I've missed the pleasure of thy company of late.' He straightened his glasses and cleared his throat. 'I hope it's those equations I provided that have been occupying thy time. Though I chose them as a challenge,' he added. 'I don't expect thee to have mastered them already.'

Hannah hesitated. Were his expectations that low? Certainly he didn't mean the comment to sting, but a flash of indignation threatened to voice itself anyway. *I finished them months ago,* she felt like saying. *It took me but a week. How long did it take* you?

'I've worked most of them down,' she said instead, choosing her words carefully.

He nodded but didn't say anything, and Hannah wondered if he'd heard.

'But what are thy thoughts about the orbit of Uranus?' she added, raising her voice. 'Is Mr Adams correct about another, undiscovered planet being the cause of its deviation? Or might the orbit be reconciled with the laws of gravitation?'

They made their way into the kitchen, where Hannah had set out half a roasted chicken and a pot of chowder. She'd ended up gathering the clams herself that morning, sacrificing two hours of work time to do it. Dr Hall took his time settling into his seat, then peered up at her.

'There are as yet too many unknown factors,' he said. 'I cannot draw a conclusion. Nor should Mr Adams or his contemporaries. Speculation is the cause of many erroneous hypotheses, which then lead our American observatories into the realm of frivolous and self-serving activities on their behalf. A game of proving oneself correct, at the expense of effort better spent upon the true portal to astronomical innovation.'

Hannah started as if she'd been slapped. The work of

American observatories – resolving nebulae, charting the entirety of the Heavens, even trying to photograph stars! – was revolutionary. She shared his reverence for pure mathematics, but to her mind the quest for astronomical knowledge unfolding across the nation was the opposite of frivolous. She'd give anything to be part of it.

Though her heart was pounding, Hannah held her tongue, remembering what it felt like to squirm under Dr Hall's fierce blue gaze, the clear color of September sky. As a teacher he demanded full effort on behalf of truth. The ability to defend one's work was a measure of moral fiber. He conflated the work with the student: poor work meant poor character. A wrong answer meant a lazy mind.

She had rarely flinched under his scrutiny, but that was because she never turned in poor work. She'd thrilled to his approval, and earned it, but she'd been lucky. Her father had taught her to count carefully, check her work, and be diligent. Thus she'd been rewarded with Dr Hall's attention. He'd provided her with work in the higher maths once her school days were done; without it, she'd have been unable to keep up with the progress of astronomy, no matter how many periodicals and updates George Bond posted.

During dinner her mind kept flicking back to the events of the afternoon, and the strange new student she now had on her hands, and soon enough Dr Hall was rising to take his leave and her father was offering to walk with him to discuss some matters. Hannah walked them to the door, and as Dr Hall approached the porch steps she leapt to kick some metal spars out of the way, then leaned down to take his elbow.

'I'm yet hale, Hannah Price,' he snapped, and she pulled back as if burnt.

'Of course,' she muttered. 'I didn't mean –'

Her father shook his head at her in warning, and she clamped her jaw shut.

Half an hour later he returned, and as she dried the last of the dishes she asked about the incident.

'Do you think Dr Hall might be fading? Physically, I mean,' Hannah asked while she stacked the plates back in the cupboard.

Nathaniel stared as if she'd suggested the moon was falling.

'Fading? He's a younger man than myself.'

'Barely! And regardless of his actual age, I think we should be mindful: he's all alone, and if he's in ill health –'

'He stated quite clearly that he's yet hale, Hannah. Perhaps if thee spent more time in his company thee would realize that he's as vital as any man hereabouts.'

Hannah sighed and slid the last cup and saucer into place.

'I'll have to make the time,' she said. 'Though I'm certain I haven't left any extra hours lurking about.'

She meant it as a joke, but her father looked serious as a sermon.

'Do that,' he said. It sounded less a suggestion than a command.

*

18 mo. 4, 1845
11:40 pm. Cloudy.

12:55 am. I have gone up to the walk to check again but the clouds obscure everything. I was in hopes of spotting the double star Zeta Ursi — I read that it is unusually bright this month, and may be resolved at a magnitude sufficient for the Dollond — and I fear that I may miss it. At this thought I am pulled down. In spite of all my industry Nature does seem to laugh in my face on nights such as this, as if to say, You cannot expect to See! And then I do feel weak-spirited. For when I cannot observe, it is as if the great beauty and order and Truth of the Heavens does dissolve and I sense only my own wretchedly small place.

5. The Plane Scale

Isaac was late for his first lesson, and Hannah guessed he had come straight from the blacksmith's. Grease stains shaped like continents mapped his hands and forearms, and he was sweaty and breathless, as if he'd run all the way. Instead of leading him upstairs, Hannah brought him into the kitchen, handed him a washrag, and pointed at the basin.

'I'll be upstairs,' she said. 'You remember the way.'

He nodded, but did not move toward the basin until she turned away. When he appeared in the doorway of the garret a few minutes later he seemed refreshed, though he hovered as if he was uncertain whether to enter the room.

'This will be your desk,' she said, beckoning him in and nodding at the stool, which now sat beside a small table. She'd placed it at a right angle to her desk, the stool on the opposite side, so that he'd face her; but, watching him angle himself into place, hunched over like a giant sunflower, Hannah wished she hadn't set it up that way.

'It's just for today,' she said, wincing at his discomfort.

'It's no matter,' Isaac said. 'I am used to minor spaces.' He gestured with one wing-like motion to the room itself. 'It is like a fo'c'sle.'

Lesson in hand, Hannah paused, considering the room's heavy wooden beams and cluttered shelves, then imagined it afloat upon the great oceans of the world: a waterborne observatory carrying her and her instruments around the Cape of Good Hope, Van Diemen's Land, the high cliffs of Madagascar. She'd observe stars never seen at northern latitudes; a solar eclipse; the Eta Aquarids and their rain of light. A buzzing tingle ran up her spine at the thought of them, as if lightning were striking nearby.

Settling herself on her chair, she tried to dismiss the fantastic image as she picked up her quill.

'Mathematics are the foundation of the navigator's work,' she began, tapping the quill on her desk once for emphasis. 'The proper use of the instruments and careful, diligent observations are also necessary. But without maths, you'll surely founder. Think of these lessons as the foundations of a house: we'll begin with the very base, and build upon it depending upon your aptitude and progress. Do you understand?' When he nodded, she slid a copybook and pencil across the desk. 'We'll begin with the plane scale.'

For the next few hours Isaac drew as directed, a series of careful lines splayed across the pages like fallen matchsticks. First there were parallels, then 'right' angles in triangles, and then more lines within and without those figures. When he offered his work, she felt a smile stretch her cheeks, and she had to work the corners of her mouth back to an appropriate line.

'Acceptable,' she said. His brow furrowed just a fraction, and she realized he might not understand. 'It's good,' she added.

Glancing up at the little window above the desk, she was shocked to see the nimbus of the rising moon, waxing three-quarters. If she wanted to sweep, it had to be now, before its light obscured everything else in the sky. Yet Isaac sat, as if more lessons were forthcoming.

She stood up, gathering her observing log, chronometer, and quill. Still he remained, watching her like a statue, until she stood at the bottom of the rickety, narrow wooden stairway that led up to the walk.

'Are you coming up, then?' she asked, not knowing what else to say. 'Mind the top step. It's loose.' Grabbing another pair of mittens from the peg near the door, she let an icy blast of air onto the steps behind her as she shouldered the door open. Isaac made to follow her, and their heads almost collided as she ducked back in.

'And take that coat,' she said, nodding toward Edward's old woolen parka. 'I have extra mittens.'

Isaac followed her out, carrying the coat in his arms, and paused as the door squawked shut.

'Have you ever been out on a walk?' she asked, her voice carrying easily in the still air.

'I have not,' he said. 'It feels like a night watch.'

He put his arms into the coat. It fit well. Hannah inhaled as if she could smell it from across the roof: salt and wool and dust; a hint of ferrous sulfate and gum arabic from an ancient accident with the inkpot; and still, always, Edward's scent, his particular mix of grime and woodsmoke and mud. Sometimes she wore the coat herself, just to feel close to him.

'But this air – so cold,' Isaac said, buttoning the togs and shaking his head. 'I have sixteen years of age the first time I am feeling a northern winter. I imagine I am dying.'

'And how do you find them now? Our winters, I mean.'

'I am like an old ship now,' he said. 'Cracking and creaking.' She smiled, following his gaze across the dark expanse of Nantucket Town, out toward the Harbor, where a few twinkles of light told of crews playing cards or singing or fighting. 'But it is not bothering me any longer. It empties the mind. Clears the body. There is pain, but it is good. It is necessary.'

He wrapped his arms around himself. She knew what he meant. When she rose in the morning, her own joints registered their protest against her age, the weather, her occupation. Her body felt heavier at its center, less lithe in its extremes. But she avoided thinking too long on it. It was immodest, for one. And vain. Worse, thinking about her body led to the desire to touch, and the few times that Hannah had ventured in that direction, in the dark under her quilt, she'd been too ashamed to even enjoy the sensation. An ailing elder cousin had once confided on her deathbed that she was grateful her husband had never seen her naked, and Hannah, at fourteen years of age, had felt that she understood her completely, and been thankful on her behalf.

In the east, Arcturus was already high. Hannah surveyed the sky as if she could see clear through the visible horizon in the distance and all the way to the planets Dr John Herschel, the great cataloguer of the skies, saw through the lens of his twenty-inch refractor, to Ceres and Pallas, and beyond. She set down her stool and began to speak, her voice sliding smoothly across the rooftop.

'Imagine that you are standing on the very surface of the Earth,' she said. 'Imagine there are neither trees, nor houses, nor mountains – aught but you, balanced on a marble that is floating in the Heavens. Of course, you're spinning with this marble, and also moving in a great arc about the sun, completing one circle each 365 days.

'Now imagine that you're holding an enormous parasol, the tip of which ends at Polaris – there.' Hannah pointed at the North Star. 'The circumpolar stars – those closest to Polaris – you may imagine as fixed upon the inside of the parasol. They rotate around the Pole Star but maintain their relative distance to each other. We can always see them. The rest of the celestial bodies rise and set as the Earth turns, seen only at certain times or in certain seasons.

'In addition, if you draw in your mind a series of lines parallel to the equator, circling the inside of your parasol at equal distances from the north celestial pole and each other, forming a series of concentric rings, you'll have a picture of the lines we use to measure the distances of stars from the celestial Equator.'

'They are the lines of latitude?' Isaac asked, his eyes trained on Polaris.

'Yes, as projected onto the celestial sphere. We call them the parallels of declination. Another set of such lines – the hour lines – corresponds to the lines of longitude. They encircle our Earth from the opposite direction, passing through the North and South Poles. We use these lines to measure the angle of a given star at a given time, relative to the horizon, so that we might deduce our location on the sphere by means of triangulation.'

Hannah glanced over at Isaac; his eyebrows veed together as if he was thoroughly perplexed.

'Think about it this way: the sun is our nearest star. It

appears to travel across the sky each day, taking 24 hours to make a full circle of 360 degrees, or 15 degrees of longitude each hour. If we measure the sun's exact position at noon, and we know the time at your home port, as well as the time at your location at sea, a comparison of the two will determine your longitude. Which is of course why you need the . . .'

She trailed off, hoping Isaac would finish the sentence, but he was silent. His eyes were closed.

She felt a flash of anger, chased by a pang of disappointment. Either he wasn't paying attention or she was boring him to sleep. Hannah tilted her head to get a better look at his face. The tender veil of light from the crescent moon silvered his cheek and brow and outlined his mouth. His lips were full as a woman's – not any women she knew, but those who frequented the taverns by the wharves. Slicked with paint and perfume. She wondered if his lips were soft, and then, shockingly, what they would taste of. Her skin tingled with gooseflesh and she shook her head, now glad his eyes were closed. She'd lost her place in the lesson. What had she been saying?

'The chronometer,' she snapped. 'Do you understand?'

Isaac sighed and shook his head slightly, then opened his eyes, keeping his gaze on the sky. He seemed to gather his words as he went, like acorns.

'Remembering all of this – I am thinking it is not possible.' He looked toward the door, raising his shoulders in a universal gesture of defeat. 'I should not be wasting of the time.'

'Wasting whose time?' she asked, trying to ignore the sense of panic that rose in her throat. 'It is complex, yes.

And you don't have the benefit of a higher education to support the work. But neither do I.' She folded her own arms across her chest. 'You're not expected to know it all right away. There's no reason you cannot become competent in a few months' time. If you choose to give up after so short a trial, though . . . I cannot help you.'

Hannah clamped her jaw shut, feeling as if she'd failed on her very first lesson. It was clear that he could learn; and, she was certain, she could do a decent job of teaching him. His humility was charming, but impractical. If there was any hope of advancing his position, he had to persist.

Isaac hesitated, and Hannah made up his mind for him.

'I have not yet dismissed you,' she said, beckoning him onto the stool beside the telescope. 'Please sit down.'

When he obeyed, Hannah was so relieved she slumped down herself, with her back to the railing and her knees pulled up under her skirts, then motioned to the eyepiece of the telescope.

'Look.'

Isaac hesitated for a moment, then leaned in, cautious, as if the telescope were an animal that might snap his eyeball out of its socket and swallow it. Once he had settled, though, he was silent for a full minute.

'Can you describe what you see?' Hannah asked.

'Another world,' he said, not removing his eye from the lens.

'Go on.'

'I see stars – many stars. Thousands. Like seashells. Or *flores*. Some are very bright, some are pale. Some are coming, going. There, but no there –'

He picked his head up. 'I'm sorry,' he said. 'It is difficult – the language.'

'I understand you,' Hannah said, envisioning the field. 'And your observations are correct. The very brightest stars we say are of the first magnitude. The faintest are eighth or ninth magnitude. And the places where you cannot distinguish quite what you're seeing – those are nebulas. They are the most interesting of all. No one is quite sure what they are. We study them.'

He nodded. '*Nebuloso*. I understand.'

'Good.' Hannah glanced up at the sky again. 'I'm going to observe now,' she said, and he rose, graceful as a cat. 'We can continue next week.'

'Thank you,' he said, bowing his head slightly.

The stool was still warm: she could feel it even through her coat and dress, petticoat and stockings. The sensation gave her a peculiar thrill. She put her eye to the telescope, refocused, and steadied herself, trying to ignore the heat that seemed to have reached her neck and cheek the instant she sat down. With precise motions, she moved the scope in a small arc, her actions so slow and steady that the change in position was barely discernible.

There were so many stars in the region between Pollux and Procyon that new objects were only visible on the clearest nights. The stars that formed the Twins, the Crab, and the Unicorn made passage across her lens. She swept from east to west and back, losing track of everything but each familiar star and the dark sky it swam upon.

When she finally looked up, nearly an hour had elapsed, and she blinked at Isaac, who was still sitting there watching her as if spellbound. She cleared her throat, but couldn't think of anything to say, and was grateful when he rose to his feet and nodded, then lifted one hand. Whether the gesture was meant to be a salutation or an exhortation to remain at her work, she could not tell. But she was grateful when he disappeared through the door without saying or asking anything more.

22 mo. 4, 1845.

3:52 am. Moon transit 7:26 pm. A clear night. All exercises completed. Sweeping SSE of Pollux again sighted the nebulae around what may be a double-star, though I could not find it in the catalogue. Yesterday I did not see it. It will require further observations to determine. No wanderers sighted. My student, Isaac Martin, did have his first taste of the Heavens this night, and was suitably dazzled. He is humble, but observant. Whether he will have the diligence necessary to succeed in his work is as yet unclear.

6. Nathaniel's Plan

If you could take a seat, for a moment,' Hannah said the following week, without looking up, when she heard the door to the walk shudder and squawk. The nebula she'd been observing would not resolve; it seemed to slip in and out of her field, a silken fog speckled with distant stars like a celestial egg. 'I'm still trying to get a clear look at this nebula. Until it's risen a bit higher, though, I doubt I'll be able to *see* what I'm looking at.'

When Isaac didn't answer, she raised her voice, but not her head.

'I left the beginning of the lesson on the desk downstairs; you may start on it if you wish.'

'May I?' her father answered.

'Oh!' Hannah bobbed up like a buoy at the sound of his voice and swiveled around. 'Hello. I didn't – I mean, I wasn't expecting thee.' Her stomach twisted with unexpected fear. She hadn't yet mentioned Isaac to her father, but he'd barely been home in weeks.

'So I guessed. Who's the beneficiary of thy lessons?'

'A new student. In navigation.' She instinctively omitted the details. She didn't think the color of Isaac's skin would bother him, but she still knew little about her student. He claimed to be temperate, but she couldn't prove it. She didn't know where he lived or what his history was.

Isaac could be dangerous, she supposed. But he'd

shown such reverence when he looked through the telescope. He might not be religious, but he'd been moved by the beauty of their Creator's design. That was surely a mark in favor of his character. And in any case, she'd convinced him that he could learn; now she had to keep teaching him.

Glancing back at the telescope, she rubbed her bare hands together to warm them.

'I'm glad it's you, though. Maybe you can resolve more of this nebula than I can. If indeed it *is* a nebula. I thought I detected some motion from a few nights ago.'

He stepped closer, the familiar high ridge of his forehead emerging out of the dark, and she scrambled off the stool so he could look.

'I came up to ask about the ledgers,' he said, but eased himself onto the small seat. 'Now, don't keep thy father in suspense. What am I looking at? Are you readying a challenge to Mr Adams' conclusions?'

'Do you see the body just a few degrees north of Antares, near that second-magnitude star? It's nearly in the crosshairs, and there's a fair bit of nebulosity. I'm unsure if it's the same body I saw a few nights ago.' She paused while he looked. 'Though, on the topic of Mr Adams, George just sent the latest summary of his findings.'

Hannah sat down on the cold walk and tucked her knees in close to her chest, wrapping her arms around them, and when her father didn't answer, she lay down on her back and watched the stars. Giving the weight of her calves and shoulder blades and head to the hard wood planks made her feel like a child again. Her eyes watered from the cold; her hands were stiff as old leather. But she felt happy. This was what she'd wanted. To work together, as they always had. To talk about what mattered.

The only thing missing was Edward. But the last frost was coming: Hannah had smelled Spring in the air the last few mornings, even as she tapped through the ice in the basin to wash her face. The *Regiment* would be home by shearing, in June, Edward had written; that was only two months away.

Her nose was running. Twin streams of salty tears ran from her eyes toward her ears.

'I believe what thee is looking at here *is* a portion of a nebula,' her father said.

'Really?' She sat up and squinted in the direction of the telescope. 'But I saw it three days ago and I'm fairly certain it's moved.'

'Perhaps it was another region of the same nebula, obscured in part by some atmospheric event.'

'It may be. But at this time of year?'

'I've seen it before, I'm fairly certain. Has thee seen any condensation of light toward the center? Or any suggestion of a train?'

'I thought I did, the other night, but the moon came up and I lost it. Then it was cloudy, and then it rained. This is my first view of it since then. You're probably right.' A pang of disappointment twisted through her.

'And in the Bedford catalogue?'

'Nothing. I should check again, though.'

'Well, I expect thee will pursue it until thee is certain,' he said, rising from the stool in one motion, his hands on his knees, then straightening his back.

'You know me well enough,' she said, unsure if he

meant that she should abandon the calculation. But why would she? If improbability was the deciding factor, she'd have given up sweeping entirely. The dark idea that her father believed her incapable of finding anything notable in the night sky crept up like a spider, and she brushed it away. It could not be that; if anyone knew her ability, it was he. She'd surpassed him in maths long ago. And her eye was far better.

'I'll keep watching it,' she said. 'But I'll check the catalogue again in case I missed something.'

Leaving the telescope on its mount, Hannah followed her father to the door and yanked it open for him.

'I've been corresponding with George about my meteorological survey,' she said, following him in but stopping on the top step and letting the door rest on her back. 'He insisted I send him the work; he called it my magnum opus of average cloudiness.'

Her father creaked down one step at a time.

'And what did George make of it?'

'He wrote that he thought Professor Henry might make use of it for some of the meteorological work he's doing . . . but I believe he might be overreaching. I can't see what my little observations could do for the National Institute, can you?'

He paused on the next to last stair, then turned and looked up at her.

'I think it's valuable work regardless of the Institute's current needs. Their mandate is to promote science, after all. But if George thinks it worth sending, I'm sure it is so. He surely wants only the best for thee. In fact, I'd say he's among thy greatest admirers.'

Hannah snorted, but let the door close behind her and came down two more steps, then sat on her hands to warm them. 'I was considering submitting it to *Silliman's*. Though I'm sure they've no use for it, either.' Hannah devoured each issue of the national science journal as it came into the Atheneum, though there was less about astronomy than she would have liked.

'Did George suggest that as well?'

'No. But they regularly publish such local findings: geographical bits and pieces, meteorological studies, and the like.' She rocked back and forth, waiting for feeling to return to her fingertips.

'Well, Hannah,' he said, then paused. 'I hope thee shan't be disappointed if they say no. I don't know that *Silliman's* publishes lady authors outside the botanical pages. Perhaps George or William would submit on thy behalf with a note. Ask them. It can't hurt.'

He turned and went halfway to the desk then turned again.

'I nearly forgot. Where is the ledger for the chronometers? I need to settle the Coffey accounts before the rush.'

The mention of Mary's name deflated Hannah's spirits anew.

'It's right there on the desk, under the Bowditch,' she muttered.

What would her father do if she *were* to actually discover a comet? Hannah wondered. Would he declaim it to all the land? Or insist that her findings be validated by a male eye – any male eye – in the vicinity? She imagined old man Shambaugh – the oldest whaling captain still living on the Island, who'd survived the War of Independence and the 1812 blockade and the freeze of '22 – bent over her telescope, double-checking her findings. She stifled a giggle at the thought.

'So it is,' her father said, sliding it out and tucking it under his arm. But he didn't leave. Instead, he sat down in the desk chair, clutching the leather-bound volume.

'There's another matter I wish to discuss with thee.'

'Oh?' Hannah was still sitting on the step, and he glanced up and beckoned her down. Gathering her skirts, she stepped around the trunk and sat down on the wooden chair she'd dragged upstairs from the parlor, to replace the ridiculous setup she'd inflicted on Isaac during his last lesson.

But sitting stiffly upright in a chair facing another person at such close range was awkward, she now realized. Even so, it was comforting to sit so close to her father. He'd lit the lamp before he'd come up to the walk, she noticed; he'd had no intention of observing to begin with.

He cleared his throat.

'As you know, I've visited Philadelphia a number of times on Bank business this year. Well, several months ago I was introduced to someone. A lady – a widow, actually, of some means. Though she's quite young. An accident it was – but some years ago. In any case.' He shifted and seized the ledger in both hands, as if he was about to open it and begin a spellbinding tale. Then he stared down at the cover as if stricken mute.

'Go on. A lady, you were saying.' Hannah's mind leapt ahead. He was going to get married. A woman, a stranger, would come to live with them. The idea was so odd and unexpected that she felt as if she were floating above it, examining it like a specimen. It could be good; it might be very bad. She envisioned a Philadelphia matron in their humble kitchen. Maybe she'd hire help. Or would she expect *Hannah* to be the help?

The lamp flickered. Hannah focused on the shadows the candle cast on the piles of papers and journals, the sum total of a dozen years of shared labor. She could smell the whale oil in the lamp, an acrid, sour tang that penetrated the very walls, but was discernible only at certain moments. Like the smell of a person upon a dress she leaves behind. Ann Gardner Price had left no such trace; Hannah had no sense of what her mother had smelled like, whether she'd hummed while washing up or preferred summer savory over sweet thyme.

What Hannah did know was limited to the traces that remained, like clues to a mystery that could never be solved. Through these few items – a framed catechism her mother had stitched in a rainbow of bright silken thread, now faded but still the liveliest corner of the room she'd slept in with Nathaniel; a silhouette that Hannah used to trace with one finger, as if she could summon some essence of the woman that way; and her wedding things, a trousseau tucked away in the upstairs trunk, crocheted linens bursting with intricate flowers and edged with colorful ribbons – Hannah had deduced that her mother had liked colorful things, and she'd nestled this bit of knowledge in her heart like a tiny nut, as if it could sustain her through girlhood.

She and Edward had been three years old when their mother died, of a fever so sudden and virulent that it took less than a week to burn her life away – as if she'd been no hardier than an ant targeted by a cruel boy with a lens on a sunny day. Hannah barely recalled the sweep of many unfamiliar skirts in and out of their kitchen, the garden, the parlor, though the echoey refrain of the mourners' comments had stayed with her all these years.

It is as the Lord wishes, the twins had been told again and again. *Thy mother is in Heaven now.* She remembered a long-ago conversation with Edward. They'd been six, or maybe seven. Sitting in a hollowed-out log at Madaket beach, playing ship.

'But *where* is Heaven?' Hannah had asked her twin. 'Do clams go there?' She went on muttering the names of the eight major winds. *Tramontana, Greco, Siroco, Ostro,* she whispered. *Maestro* was her favorite. The teaching wind. It filled the sails of their imaginary ship. Under the sand, invisible systems kept the clams alive until one dropped them in a boiling pot.

'I suppose so,' Edward answered. 'I suppose their Heaven is sandy.'

'So the sparrow's is full of thistledown?'

'And the fox's a warm lair.'

'But then, how would they know they were dead?' Hannah asked, alarmed.

'Maybe they wouldn't.' Edward drew a line in the sand with his toe, carving deep. 'Maybe that is Heaven.'

Hannah picked at a splinter on the wooden seat of her chair, enjoying the sharp sting when it pierced the skin beneath her nail. The whorl of the wood knot on the desk drawer blurred, obscured by a sudden sheen of tears and a powerful tug of nostalgia for the closeness she'd felt to

73

her father in the years that followed her mother's death. As a child of six, she'd huddled close to him under a moth-eaten blanket atop a hillside in the northern part of the state, her eyes grainy with fatigue but wide with wonder as they waited for the moon to darken with eclipse. His fingers tight around her shoulder, the thrill of discovery binding them against the outside world as the familiar belly of the full moon went fire-red above.

Hannah willed her tears back, and her defenses held; the hollow ache of loss in her belly diminished. Her father was going on about the lady's connections – something about the National Mint. Hannah had never considered the possibility of another wife for him, though such a move was logical, and certainly sounded advantageous.

'Hannah, thee looks as if I've told thee I'm deathly ill,' Nathaniel said.

She vaulted back to the present, and tried to reset her face. Of course he would find a show of emotion selfish, juvenile.

'I'm sorry. I'm only surprised. When shall she come, then?' Hannah asked. 'Will you wait until Edward returns to plan the wedding? Summer's the best time for it, I imagine. If you're planning a wedding, I mean. Is that what you're trying to say?' Words tumbled from her lips like grain down a chute.

'Hannah,' he said. 'Listen to me.'

She stopped herself from inflicting further damage to her fingers by sitting on her hands. Had he even written to Edward? She hoped he had. Hannah felt a nibble of possibility in her chest. Maybe this was the best possible way to repair the rift in their family: a woman in the house would soften her father's hard edges, help him accept Edward's decision and move forward.

'She is not coming here,' Nathaniel said. 'I – *we* – will remove to Philadelphia after the wedding.'

Hannah frowned. 'We? Thee and she, you mean? Does she not live there already?'

'I mean thyself, Hannah. Thee cannot remain here alone. I've thought long on this matter, and though I know thee would prefer to remain on the Island, I cannot in good conscience leave unless thee accompanies me. And there is much to recommend the city. Lucinda has many acquaintances there, and of course the Philadelphia Meeting is flourishing. There are any number of individuals that might be of interest to thee.'

Hannah closed her eyes, then opened them, as if to rewind the minute. But of course that was impossible. Time only moved in one direction. *Philadelphia. Accompany me. The city.* The tide of hopeful thoughts that had come in a moment earlier ran back into memory.

'Prospects, thee means,' she said, latching onto his last sentence. 'Thy wish for me is to find someone in Philadelphia to marry.'

'I wish for thy happiness, Hannah, as ever I have. Thee cannot accuse me of anything else.'

'Then thee must realize that I will be perfectly happy to remain here and continue my work. I have my job at the Atheneum. And our house, and the farm. Edward will be home in two months' time. I see no reason I should move off-Island.' She struggled to bring her voice down to level, beat back her rising panic. Her father would appreciate reason, not feeling.

His face hardened.

'Thy brother has proven that his comings and goings are based on aught but his own whim. If thee wishes to remain, I suggest thee begin to think on the prospect of doing so as half a household.'

'As a wife.' She folded her arms together over her chest, as if she could prevent herself from flying into pieces that way.

'Yes.'

'And imagining that there existed a man I wished to marry – and one who wished to marry me, which I can say with some certainty there is not – if my husband went to sea for years upon end as do half the "halves of households" on this Island, how would it be any different?' She knew she'd lost the battle to keep her feelings hidden, and a desperate confusion crept in, muddling her thoughts. How had she gone from discussing a celestial object with cometary properties to what felt like begging for her life?

'Hannah,' her father said, his voice stern. 'I've no interest in a theoretical debate about the differences between a whaling wife and an unmarried daughter. In fact, there are entirely practical options before thee which I see no good reason to deny.'

'What options are these?' She lifted her head, wondering if she'd missed something.

'Well' – Nathaniel glanced around, as if there were someone else there to overhear – 'Dr Hall, for one, has spoken to me of his great respect and affection for thee.'

'Dr Hall?' Hannah nearly shrieked, horrified.

'It is a reasonable idea.'

She lowered her voice, but her body was quivering, like an animal in danger.

'Reasonable? To join myself with a man for whom I have no feeling but scholarly respect, so that I may continue a life I've happily built for myself, and in the main by myself?'

His answer didn't matter: the truth was as clear as a harvest moon. Whatever life he desired for her was the life she was bound to. The idea that she'd determine her own future – find her comet, establish her place – had been a fantasy. It was her own fault, she realized. How foolish she had been to think she'd be permitted to triangulate merrily among the Atheneum and the Meeting House and her tiny garret observatory for as long as she wished. That the limitations and expectations that bound other women's lives would bypass her own.

'Nothing is settled,' he said. 'I await my Certificate of Removal from Meeting. It could be months, even a year. Other options may present themselves. Dr Hall is but one, though in his defense I will say that he is as like-minded an individual as thee could desire, in addition to being both well established and as keen a supporter of thy work as myself. He's told me on several occasions that he expects thee to surpass him, and that he welcomes that occurrence. There aren't many men who'll share that sentiment.'

Her father looked at her directly, and the sight of his deep-blue eyes, brows knitted with concern, overwhelmed her anger. Against her will, tears sprang up again. This time they spilled.

'Have faith, Hannah. Not one of us can intuit the future. The right path – or person – will appear, I'm certain. In the meantime . . . well, I'll let thee keep on with thy work.'

He rose and slipped from the room, leaving Hannah sitting beside the desk at which they'd worked in tandem for more than half her life. She had never considered leaving Nantucket. Her sand and shallows, salt and sawgrass, were as much a part of her as the tribal tattoos that marked the whalers from South Pacific islands far distant. Whenever she was off-Island, Hannah felt diminished, invisible as stars veiled by the bright clamor of the city. To leave forever would mean leaving Edward. It would mean leaving the Atheneum and all its treasures, leaving their familiar house and all its memories. It would be the end of everything she'd ever known. Worst of all, it would mean the end of her observations. It was unthinkable.

7. The Known Planets

Then her father left the garret, Hannah stayed in her chair like a prisoner, trying to clear the clouds from her mind and concoct a sensible plan. The only thing that looked like salvation was Edward. She'd be allowed to stay if he were home to act as chaperone and guardian – though he'd be first to point out that their roles ought to be reversed. Together, they could manage to oversee the farm and the chronometers, and even a contract with the Coast Survey, should one materialize.

The downstairs clock chimed her back into the present, and the fantasy of such a contract, along with the new instruments it would inevitably supply, vanished like a cloud of celestial dust. Sticky with unease, Hannah went to the garret door, opened it, and listened. The house hummed with silence. Her father had either gone to sleep or gone out.

She rummaged around the desk for the quill and ink-pot, then scribbled a hasty note on the back of a yellowed bill of sale: *Mr Martin: Come up to the walk.* When she'd posted it on the door downstairs, she climbed back up three steps at a time, as if she were being chased, and tried to pick up observing where she'd left off. But the cloud cover had thickened into fog. The nebula – if that's indeed what it was – had disappeared.

Hannah stayed next to the telescope for more than an hour, checking periodically like a mother with a feverish child, but the stars and everything else in the firmament ticked by invisibly. There was barely any wind, nothing to suggest an imminent change in the weather. A film of despair began to settle in her, lightly, like an illness just taking hold, as she contemplated her father's decision. There was nothing she could do to alter it, short of attaching herself permanently to a male – any male – who would contract to marry her.

The idea that she had always been powerless over her own future, but not realized it, was excruciating. She'd been propelled toward mastery – over her emotions, over her equations, of the biggest and most minute parts of the Universe – for her entire life. Dr Hall had demanded rigor, his teaching method requiring total expertise on one level before advancement to the next. Fractions came before geometry; simple maths before logarithms and algebraic equations. Until tonight, she thought she'd understood the rules that governed her life as well: work hard, sweep the skies, seek a contribution. Be rewarded. How could she have made so great a miscalculation?

Grinding her teeth, Hannah peered through the telescope again, desperate for something else to focus on. This time she didn't hear the door to the walk open or close. When she heard Isaac's deep voice at close range, she gasped, clapping her hand to her chest while trying to catch her breath.

'I'm sorry to be frightening you.'

'It's fine,' she muttered, embarrassed by her display. She

smoothed her skirts and squinted at the telescope. 'What did you say?'

'I have inquire what you look for? You seem to await.'

'I look for changes. New things in the night sky.' She steadied herself and glanced in his direction. He wore loose pants and a shirt under a woolen jumper and cap, and the same scarf wound about his neck. Hannah shook her head.

'You're underdressed,' she said. 'Take the coat from the peg just inside the door.'

He obeyed without comment, moving across the walk at his usual pace. A boatsteerer might move faster, she thought. The speed of the hunt, the small boats rocketing over the grey sea, the whiz of the reeling line: without a swift hand he should have failed or been maimed long ago, not advanced to his current place. Yet everything took him three times as long as it ought.

He returned, coat buttoned up to the chin. 'Why?'

'Why what?'

'Why do you look for this?'

'For knowledge,' Hannah answered. Was it not obvious? When he said nothing, she added, 'The pursuit of knowledge is the highest calling.'

'Knowledge?' he repeated, as dubious as if she'd said there were little men winging about on the moon. His doubt – on top of her father's, on top of everyone's – was infuriating.

'Yes. What about it, then?' she snapped. As he stood there like a giant puppet, she wondered if the entire enterprise was a waste of time. Maybe there was merit to the claims that his race was inherently lazy, incapable of industry or intellectual achievement. She hadn't ever thought it so, but then, she'd never really known any of them, had she?

He shrugged.

'It does not change . . .' He paused, fishing for the next word. '. . . certain things.'

'I don't understand what you mean.' She glared at the telescope, hoping he couldn't read her thoughts.

'How men are.'

She tried to parse his meaning from the thin sentence.

'Do you mean character?'

'Character.' The word rolled from his mouth with a smart flourish at the end. 'So much knowledge, yet men are . . . as animals.'

Hannah sat up, affronted.

'Men are certainly not animals, Mr Martin. We have dominion over the beasts. We have intellect. Logic and reason. Why would you believe such a thing?'

His face tightened, Hannah thought, a gesture so minute it barely registered.

'I have seen such behavior upon a ship – and elsewhere – that there is no other way of describing,' he said. 'In my experiencing, it is difficult to believe that knowledge alone can change this.'

'Do you mean violence?' she asked, wincing at the thought of men wounding each other.

'Some men are only understanding the language of force,' he said, then fell silent, leaving Hannah to wonder what he might have had to endure – or inflict – to arrive at his current position. It occurred to her that his advancement was no accident; for any man who wished to assist

Isaac Martin, there were likely a dozen who wished him ill, based on nothing but the color of his skin.

She sighed.

'That may be true, but it is my belief that knowledge does bring us closer to understanding the plan of the Creator, toward a higher plane, which is to say, the workings of the entire Universe.'

There was a long silence, during which she checked the night sky again and wondered if he'd understood her. A break appeared in the cloud cover, and she watched it for a moment. The nebula came into view, but was obscured a moment later. Disappointed, Hannah sat up, glancing at her student.

'You are seeing all of this?' His cheek twitched. *He's teasing me,* Hannah thought, allowing a small smile to crack the plane of her face. It relieved the tension, and when he smiled back, a full, warm grin, hers widened, too. He wasn't foolish. She felt something pass between them, like a current, and, unnerved, she looked away, breaking the connection by turning back to the telescope.

Gusting winds had cleared a wider swath of sky, exposing the area she hoped to study. She could just show him what she was looking for, instead of trying to convince him it was important.

'Sit here.' She waved him onto her stool. 'Quickly! I want you to see something.'

He slid into place without making a sound.

'Can you sight the very bright star nearly in the center of the field?'

While he looked, Hannah imagined the stars within the dense patch of sky under examination.

'Look carefully. Your eyes are an instrument, too. Observe the place just to the left of where the lines intersect in the middle of the lens, and then raise your sight just a few degrees north.'

'I see it,' he said a few moments later, his voice high, excited.

'That is Antares,' Hannah said. 'Antares is what we know as a fixed star. We think it is like our sun, which does not change its position. We have gone over the other fixed stars, and the planets.'

Isaac nodded but kept his eye at the lens.

'Now get up for a moment.' He leapt to his feet, hovering close while she leaned in and made a minute adjustment. 'Now look again, and describe what you see.'

They swapped places again, and this time he looked through the eyepiece for a full minute before turning his face to her.

'It is cloudy,' he said, sounding disappointed. 'I cannot see anything.'

'Ah,' she said. 'But it's a perfectly clear part of the sky, and the lens is in focus. Look again.'

He looked, but shook his head.

'I see only a cloud,' he said. 'A cloud full of light.'

'It's called a nebula.' She tilted her chin toward the distant smudge in the inky sky. 'They do look like clouds. But they aren't clouds. They're a mix of stars and nebulosity. Now, what is nebulosity?'

She paced the walk, continuing as if he'd been the one to ask. Her voice carried with no effort; the wind had died and the air was still and cold as marble.

'What is it made of? Is it reflected light? Is it dust, or

something else? What else is there besides stars, planets, asteroids? What are the bands of light and dark therein? Why do some stars move differently than others? All the planets and a number of stars change their position. Why don't the others? Why are they even there?'

She stopped behind him. Both their faces tilted toward the sky.

'We see so little of what there may be,' Hannah whispered, gripped by reverence. The urgency with which she wanted him to feel it, too – to yearn for revelation in every sweep of the night sky – was startling, and she cleared her throat before going on. 'Do you understand? It's immense beyond our imagining. The light from the very closest star takes nine years to reach us. Nine years! And yet, every day we see more and more. Some of us, anyway. With the right instruments.'

She could feel Isaac looking at her and see his profile in her peripheral vision, not twelve inches away. Her cheeks tingled, and then her neck.

'But what are you hoping to see?'

Hannah tipped her chin in his direction, though she didn't look at him directly. Instead, she stared at the telescope, the quiet gleam of the brass in the very dark. His question had reminded her of the conversation with her father, and a current of indignation mixed with rage sprang up. She didn't want to reveal her state of mind to Isaac, but her next question shot out like a challenge.

'What do you hope for, Mr Martin?'

'To advance my place,' he answered, careful with each word.

'As do I.'

Uttering the words emptied her of all desire to stand up, and she dropped down onto the floor beside him and tucked her knees up under her arms, sighing with relief to have the ground under her, familiar and solid. He half leapt off the stool, gesturing for her to take it, but Hannah waved him back without looking.

'Please. Sit. I prefer it here.' Scooting over a few inches, she leaned against the wooden rail. In one motion, Isaac swung the stool aside and seated himself opposite her, his back to the south rail, and crossed his legs. Then he tipped his head back and stared at the sky.

'How are you arriving upon this?' he asked.

Uppondis. Hannah understood his meaning, though his construction made her imagine the walk as a floating island in a vast sea upon which she'd been marooned. She smiled in the dark.

'My father taught me,' she said, resting her own head on the wooden post behind her. It was familiar as a cradle. 'When I was a child I'd count seconds for him during transits. And we used to go to Cambridge quite often. Family friends – a father and son – run the observatory there. They taught me about the instruments, how they work. We'd take them apart and put them back together for hours. The maths came later. In school.'

'It is a gift.'

She pulled her knees closer to her chest. Did he mean the knowledge itself, or its passage from others to herself? Either way, he was correct.

'I suppose so.'

Hannah bit back the urge to say more, surprised she'd said so much already. Revealing her state of mind to a stranger was as dangerous and unthinkable as revealing her body – at least, according to doctrine. She'd seen and walked among people from every part of the Earth her entire life – the sea carried them on- and off-Island as reliably as the sun rose and set – yet this was the very first time she'd ever had a private conversation about herself with one of them. Socializing with the world's people was grounds for disownment from Meeting these days. How had they strayed so far off course?

Releasing her knees, she stood up and gripped the railing.

'It's cleared somewhat,' she said stiffly. 'I should explain true altitude.'

Rising, Isaac came and stood on the other side of the telescope. If he was surprised by her shift in tone, he didn't show it, and she was glad to go back to the lesson.

'It's similar to refraction,' she said. 'Light from a celestial object is bent when it passes through our atmosphere, and the distortion alters our perception of its place. Only when it is directly overhead can we know its true altitude. Do you understand?'

'That the star is not always what it is appearing to be? Yes. I understand.'

'*Where* it appears to be.'

He nodded, studying the sky. A small smile darted across his cheek like a minnow, then disappeared.

'Where it appears to be,' he parroted.

As they watched, the cloud cover thickened, obscuring nearly every bit of light in the sky, and a sudden wind made her shiver.

'Rain's coming. We should descend.'

The garret seemed cozy in comparison to the roof. The glow of the little lamp was a welcome beacon, and Hannah moved toward the desk, wondering if she should dismiss him. But the thought of the empty house, the stack of dirty linens and aprons piled beside the washboard, repelled her. It occurred to her that she wanted him to stay.

The desire to remain in the company of anyone – much less Isaac Martin – was so strange that she wondered if she might be ill. Her head buzzed with questions. Had he indeed come from a Godless place? Who had taught him to speak as he did? Where would he go when the lesson was over? And, finally, did he wish to remain, too?

It seemed so, since he hadn't moved an inch. She scanned the shelf beside the desk, half hoping that her copy of Hutton's *Mathematics* would not be there. It was not.

'Do you want to see the Atheneum?' Hannah asked.

'The . . . ?'

'The Atheneum. Our library. It's very beautiful.' She kept looking at the desk.

'It is open at this time?'

'It is not,' she said. 'But I have the key.'

8. Reference Materials

They walked without speaking, honoring the deep quiet. It was almost one o'clock in the morning. Hannah felt unnaturally alert, tiny sounds unfurling around her. She imagined she could hear field mice scurrying across the Commons, rushes stirring in the wet breeze, dogs sighing in their sleep. Even the current slapping at the wharves a hundred yards away seemed audible. The air was damp and heavy with mist.

Hannah walked this route a thousand times a year, so she took long strides and kept her head down. As they drew closer to Town, though, she began to feel nervous. The Nantucket Atheneum was cherished by Islanders as a place of learning, dedicated to advancement and improvement. But it was a private institution, its volumes reserved for members who paid an annual fee for the privilege. Hannah had attended nearly every lecture at the Atheneum since she'd been old enough to understand the issues. She'd heard passionate appeals against capital punishment, in favor of a single currency, and on every aspect of the national expansion. Phrenologists and Millerites and Grahamites had been offered platforms; Mr Emerson had impressed everyone with his eloquence, if not his piety.

Then again, she reminded herself, knowledge was the very thing she sought for her student. There was no reason she ought not introduce him to the volumes therein, even if he wasn't a member. She was sure he'd treat the volumes with respect. And it was unlikely they'd be seen at this late hour.

A few lamps were lit along Main, and she and Isaac cast watery grey shadows across the paving stones. Along with their footfalls, she could hear the distant clamor from the taverns alongside the wharves. She'd never been inside, and could only imagine the women and men of ill repute, in poor humor from consuming spirits, and the liaisons between them.

Hannah slowed down and then stopped in front of Riddell's store. The door was never locked. Some women, she'd learned on her night walks, preferred to creep in and feel for a letter in their boxes under cover of darkness. She regarded them with a mixture of awe and pity; she would never allow herself to be so desperate. They seemed like prisoners of their own feelings, rather than their masters.

'I need to get the key,' she whispered to Isaac. There was only one spare key to the Atheneum, and it was housed in Hannah's letterbox, so it could be easily passed among the Trustees, chairs of the various Societies that met there, and the organizers of the lecture series.

He nodded, and stepped into the shadow of the portico, as if he, too, was uneasy.

At the door, her buoyancy flagged. What was she doing creeping around in the middle of the night with a stranger? Hannah's hand shook as she opened the door, and she froze when the little bell tinkled its familiar welcome. In the dim, the canvas mail sacks loomed over the small space. Shuffling toward her box, Hannah willed herself to focus on the task at hand: acquiring a copy of Hutton's *Mathematics* for use in her tutoring. Nothing more or less than that was occurring.

Sensible thoughts calmed her, and she thrust her hand into her box. Her fingers closed around a hard, sealed square of parchment. Holding it up to her nose, she squinted at it to be sure it was what she thought:

> *Hannah Gardner Price.*
> *Astronomer Extraordinaire.*
> *Librarian of Island-Wide Renown.*
> *Worst of All Seamstresses.*
> *Little India Street, Nantucket, Massachusetts.*

Hannah rolled her eyes, but felt a smile stretch her cheeks as she tucked the letter into the pocket of her coat. Edward never failed to try to amuse or embarrass her with his missives, but she didn't really care what he penciled on the outside. His voice, stretching across oceans, was precious.

She put her hand back into the box without hesitating again, and when her fingers found the ornate key to the Atheneum her fear dissolved. Her step was light again as she opened the door and rejoined Isaac.

'It's this way,' she said. 'Just down this street.'

As they approached the wide, unadorned building at the corner of Pearl, Hannah sped up, craving the familiar privacy of its interior. She felt nervous again, and was annoyed by her own lack of resolve. She had to wipe her slick palm on her dress so the key wouldn't slip as she fit it into the lock.

'It is a church?' Isaac said, leaning close so she'd hear. His voice at her neck sent a wicked shiver down her spine.

'It was, at one time,' she said, unlocking the heavy chain around the door handles, taking care not to send it crashing to the ground. 'Isn't it beautiful?'

Isaac stepped back so he was no longer standing under the portico, and took a long look at the building from the front. Hannah glanced to the left and right, but the street was empty.

'It is simple,' Isaac said. 'Plain. But strong.'

Hannah smiled in the dark. He might have been describing the people of Nantucket. There were those who used less charitable phrases – *peculiar*, for example. When her parents were children, and everyone had spoken plainly, the young ladies of Meeting had been referred to by others as 'thee and thou girls.' She herself had been stared at on occasion by visitors from off-Island who seemed to think they were watching a play upon a stage, instead of people going about their daily business in their own way, as they believed the Lord wished them to. Without adornment or preening, without false allegiances or pomp.

'Come in,' Hannah whispered, and he did.

In the entryway they stood still for a moment, letting their eyes adjust to the interior. In daylight, the long windows that came to a point at the top – the only decorative flourish on the building – provided ample light for reading and dreaming. Hannah didn't want to light a lamp, but she wasn't sure his vision was equal to her own. She took a deep breath, savoring the smell of the place: waxed wood and old parchment.

'Is there a candle?' he asked.

'No! Not here. Only the lamps. To prevent fire.'

She shuddered, remembering waking to the Portuguese bell tolling in the dead of night, the clamor of residents rushing to man the bucket lines. She'd been a child; the fire had begun on the edge of Town, near the wharves, and was contained before it reached the center. But she clearly recalled the gusts of smoke and ash, the wall of heat, the fear in her father's eye as he pushed Hannah and Edward from the scene, ordered them home when they'd followed him to the edge of the crowd, eyes wide and watering.

Nantucket's history was scarred by fire; the early settlers had built themselves a tinderbox of a town that on more than one occasion had burnt to the ground. Once, on a mapping expedition sometime around their sixteenth birthday, Edward had hurled himself down in the long grass atop the southern rise of Saul's Hills, where the town of Sherburne had once stood. It had been autumn, a bright day that blew them forward.

'Is it odd that once there was a town here?' Hannah had asked.

'Odd in what way?'

'Well, look at it.' Sky met raw earth in that place. Nothing but a strip of dry yellow grass ringing a large stone broke the surface. A cloud passing over the sun's face cast them in shadow. 'If our town burnt to the ground like Sherburne did –'

'It won't, if the Fire Brigade can help it,' Edward had said, and made a mock salute. '"Friend, have you emptied your ash-bucket this morning? Are you certain your broom is twenty paces from the hearth?"'

'I'm serious. What should be left of us?'

Edward had crossed his arms across his chest and lay back in the weak sunshine.

'Well, I suppose there would be plenty of baleen.'

'And?'

'I don't know. What else wouldn't burn?' Edward asked.

'Instruments,' Hannah offered. 'Metals. Quadrants. Sextants.'

'John's compasses.'

'The tips of Lilian's rolling-pins.'

'Are they not wood?'

'No, they're copper.'

'What else, Hannah?'

'Bone.'

They'd been silent, then, until Edward offered another: 'Gold.'

'Bone and gold. Is that how we shall be remembered?'

Edward sat up and reached over to sprinkle a bouquet of dry leaves over her head.

'I think you'll be remembered for more than that,' he'd told her as she rolled away from him. The sun had begun to dip below the horizon-line. 'Thy fine cooking, for instance. Thy delicacy. Thy sociability!'

Laughing, Hannah had risen and pulled her twin to his feet, leaves spinning in the fresh wind.

*

In the dark, echoey Atheneum, Hannah headed toward the reference volumes, letting her fingers trail over the neat edges of wooden tables and hard pews that had been repurposed from the original building. They weren't comfortable, but they helped the studious stay awake. Hannah approved of them, if not the frothy novels library-goers often hid beneath their guidebooks and catechisms.

She passed the cabinets of pamphlets, the monthly minutes of Associations ranging from American Anti-Slavery to Zoological, re-alphabetized by Hannah herself that morning, and then remembered her companion. She squinted into the room but couldn't see him.

'Mr Martin,' she whispered.

'Miss Price.' He was less than a yard away. The low hum of his voice barely broke the surface of the room; he didn't even have to whisper.

'Can you see well enough?' she asked, then winced. The man spent his life upon a whaleship. Of course his vision was adequate for a walk around a dim room.

'I am seeing,' he said.

Hannah wished he could come in daylight, then wondered if he might; she wasn't sure if he could become a member or not. A library should be open to all people, regardless of race, and New Guinea didn't have a library of its own, the way it now had its own school. Even if it did, she was sure the quality of the collection would be poor, just as the new 'African' school mixed all the ages of its students together instead of dividing them into appropriate groups the way the other schools did, for proper learning.

The crowds who'd come to listen to Frederick Douglass

speak at the Atheneum a few years ago had been mixed, Hannah remembered, black and white together. She turned to the rows of shiny spines that lined each wall, enveloping the room with possibility, and was comforted. Did it matter whether he could borrow books? He was here now; she could see to it that he had the materials he needed. With that thought, she dismissed the troubling idea that the people beside whom she worshipped each week in silence might deny this man his schoolbooks as they'd denied the colored children access to the school they'd happily attended for years.

'Hutton, Hutton . . .' She ran a finger across the familiar volumes on a low shelf not far from her desk, whose leather bindings she waxed, dusted, and otherwise prevented from being loved to death by borrowers. She knew the collection as well as she knew the contours of her own kitchen, from Homer's *Iliad* to Humboldt's *Cosmos*, *The Poetical Works of Sir Walter Scott*, Choffin's fables in French, and Plato in Greek. Books about the English seaside huddled in the southwest corner; Goethe and the philosophers nestled against the east wall. Hannah's finger halted its run on what she knew was a dark green spine with faded gold letters: *A Course of Mathematics*.

She slipped the volume from the shelf, and untucked the card from its pocket at the back as she made her way over to her desk. Edward always joked that her work-space at the Atheneum was the evil twin of her table in the garret. This one was free of clutter, always clear when she arrived and left. In the years she'd worked at the Atheneum, there was no task she hadn't completed in the amount of time allotted for it, no archive left unsorted or late-return gone unnoticed.

Hannah Price, she inscribed upon the card, and dated it.

'Mr Martin,' she whispered again.

This time Isaac didn't answer, and she peered into the room.

'Mr Martin?' Hannah couldn't see him anywhere, but he hadn't gone out, either: she would have heard the door.

'Here.' His voice was coming from one of the benches, but she still couldn't see him.

She walked over and peered down one row, then another, until she realized she was standing over him. He was lying down upon the bench, beneath the highest part of the roof, his arms tucked beneath his head.

'What are you doing?' she whispered. 'Are you unwell?'

'This space,' he said, making no move to get up. 'It has a greatness of air.'

His boots were on the bench. She meant to ask him to remove them, but her brain hit the wall of his sentence and stopped there. *A greatness of air.* She lowered herself onto the bench a few inches away from where his feet ended, and tipped her head back so she could see what he was looking at.

The ceiling soared above them to a neat peak. It was yet dark outside, but Hannah could make out the contours of the vast space. There was no ornamentation upon the ceiling, no worldly depictions of spiritual matters or colored glass windows to tint a worshipper's revelations. She felt at home here, as she once had at Meeting. She'd always thought it was because of the books. Now, doing nothing but absorbing the stillness, she felt something stir the way it did when she lay atop her roof or under a tree, gazing up at Creation.

'This was a Universalist Church, many years ago. They gave it over to the people of Nantucket to use as a library and a learning center.' She paused, then added, 'The Universalists are similar to Friends, in some ways – to our beliefs, I mean. They, too, favor abolition.'

'The abolition of slavery.'

'Yes, of course.'

'Your people wish to abolish it.'

'Yes. We've always been opposed to human bondage. It's a blight on humanity. And that slaveowners yet call themselves Christians.' She shook her head slightly, then rested it against the hard back of the pew again, considering the condition of those many thousands of enslaved souls. 'It's shameful.'

He said nothing, and she wondered if she had somehow offended him by bringing up the topic of slavery.

'We should go,' she said. 'I've found the book we need.' She held it up. The gold foil glinted.

Isaac sat up very slowly, swinging his legs down so he was sitting upright a few feet away from her on the bench. She couldn't see his face.

'I thank you for the entry to this place,' he said. 'It is rare for me to find such quiet. I am thinking it is not in the . . .' He paused, struggling for the right word. '. . . in the best of your intent.'

Hannah frowned, uncertain of his meaning.

'My best intent?'

'I am thinking it is a kind of danger. For you to bring me.'

'Oh. In my best interest, you mean.' He spoke the truth.

So why had she done it? She assumed that was what he wanted to know.

'You have the right to study, and to learn,' she said. 'As do I. As should everyone.' She stood up, feeling that she did not want to delve deeper into the matter. She'd answered his truth with her own. 'We should go now.'

When they went out, Hannah felt heavy and light at once. The melancholy came from conflating her situation with his own, and being reminded of it. The lightness, she wasn't sure. What did she have to feel giddy about? Suppressing a giggle that threatened to sneak out, she locked the door and slipped the key back into her pocket, trying to clear the rogue sentiment from her face.

They went down the steps side by side, and as they stepped out onto Pearl Street, footfalls approached, and voices: two men, striding alongside each other, deep in conversation. As they drew closer, she froze: one voice was unmistakably her father's. It was second week, second day, she realized: Meeting's monthly Business Committee must have run much later than usual.

There was nowhere for her to go; she stood still, though Isaac melted back a few paces, as if reading her mind.

'Hannah?' Her father and his companion paused, two black hats bobbing up at the same time, like apples in a barrel.

'Father.' She was still clutching the book to her chest. The other man moved on into the night.

'What is thee borrowing, then?' As he approached, Hannah lined up her sentences in her mind.

'It's a book. For a student. Remember I mentioned I'd

been engaged as a tutor in navigation? By a private student?' Hannah nodded almost imperceptibly to Isaac, who stepped forward and made a polite half-bow.

Her father looked at Isaac Martin one time – Hannah counted four very long-seeming seconds – then he turned his gaze back to Hannah and kept it upon her, though his question was obviously addressed to Isaac.

'Thee is engaged upon a whaleship, I imagine,' he said.

'Yes,' Hannah and Isaac said at the same time. Then she clamped her mouth shut.

'I am the *Pearl*'s second mate,' Isaac continued.

'Is she not in for repairs?'

'She is, sir, at this time. When she is fit we shall go.' Isaac scratched his neck and kept his eyes lowered.

'What volume is it?' Nathaniel leaned over to see the book in Hannah's hands. 'Well, that's rather advanced, Hannah.'

'No it isn't.' The book was a standard primer. Her father knew that.

'Well, thee may use whatever books you feel are appropriate, I suppose.'

'I shall try and do so.'

'And have thy lessons concluded for the evening?'

Hannah shifted the book from one arm to the other. 'I suppose they have,' she said. 'I was going to teach Mr Martin true altitude, but the clouds made it impossible to observe.'

'Well, then.' Her father grasped her elbow. 'I can accompany thee home.'

'Good,' Hannah forced herself to say. She turned to Isaac. 'We shall continue at the same time next week?'

He nodded. Hannah caught a glimpse of his face before he turned away, and read his concern. She could not tell if it was for himself or for her.

Hannah and her father walked without speaking until they had turned onto Federal Street.

'I'm surprised at thee, Hannah,' he said. He sounded more disappointed than angry. 'I'd think thee would know better than to wander about with a stranger in the middle of the night.'

'I only went from home to the Atheneum to get a book.' She patted her father on the arm, but she'd misread his tone. He stopped in the middle of the street and folded his arms. Hannah stumbled over her words in her haste to mount a defense.

'I'm certain no harm shall come to me in his presence.'

'And thee is sure of this on what grounds, Hannah? What does thee know of this person? From whence does he come?'

'He comes from the Western Islands,' she said, mentally apologizing for not trying to pronounce the true name of the place. 'But what difference does it make? He is a student. And a good student, at that. He's very diligent, and is learning very quickly. He came with the *Pearl*'s chronometer only a few weeks ago –'

'A few weeks?'

'– and he asked to be tutored in navigation so that he may advance his place,' Hannah went on. 'He's paying a good rate.'

She swallowed, shocked by how guilty she felt for something as simple as helping a man learn. The memory of the current-like connection that passed between them on the roof glinted, then disappeared.

'Advance his place.' Her father cocked his head as if he were suspicious.

'Yes.'

'Hannah.'

'What?'

'Where does thee think such a man might advance?'

'Such a man?'

'Yes. It's a noble idea, but –'

'It isn't my idea. 'Tis his own.' A spark of defiance burrowed into her chest.

'Regardless. I hope thee won't be disappointed if this boatsteerer –'

'Second mate.'

'– is disappointed in his quest. Advancement is a rare thing for his race, especially in these times. Thee knows this to be true. Or is thee naïve enough to think otherwise? Or, worse, encourage an unreasonable hope?'

Their whispers shot back and forth, faster and faster.

'I cannot believe thee would take such a position!' she hissed. 'Even the African school in Boston has a course in navigation. Why should he not learn it as a grown man?' Hannah wasn't a bit surprised that her father objected to her wandering around with Isaac at night. But he seemed to be condemning the lessons themselves. She'd always considered him tolerant, even progressive, on such matters. He'd objected to the segregation of the schoolchildren as strongly as she did. Now she wondered if it was because he no longer had any school-children.

'It's not my position, Hannah, and I do not say he should not learn, here or elsewhere. Whether thee ought provide the instruction is another matter.'

'What about Captain Boston?' He was the only example of a black whaling captain Hannah could think of.

'He assumed his duties over twenty years ago, Hannah. This man will find it difficult to advance in the current climate, is all I'm saying. And how does thee know that what he claims is true?'

'We've known John Leary since he was in short pants, and he's the *Pearl*'s first mate. If he hired this man, I imagine there's a good reason. But thee sounds as though he oughtn't even try to advance. Or is thee assuming that he cannot learn?'

He softened.

'That's not what I believe, Hannah.'

'Then I cannot understand thy point! What is thee trying to say?' With that, Hannah lost the battle to keep her voice level. His, though, remained smooth as a new sheet of copper.

'Mind thyself, is all,' he said, stepping back, snapping the cord of their conversation. 'He is a stranger. If thee wants to give the lessons, I won't forbid it. But I won't tolerate going about at night. It gives the appearance of impropriety where there be none. I expect thee will do nothing further that could jeopardize thy reputation – nor our standing at Meeting.'

He's worried about his Certificate of Removal, Hannah realized as he turned away and walked in the direction of home. *This has aught to do with my safety.*

She felt weak, and a little dizzy. He might as well have announced he was converting to the Catholic faith, or that he'd hatched a scheme to defraud an elderly widow of her life savings. That the person who'd taught her the very rules by which she ordered her days and nights – that things were either true or not true; that fact and reason were superior in every way to supposition and passion – would be concerned with appearances was sickening.

She wished to walk until she understood his position, the way she would work down an equation until she'd arrived at the proper conclusion. But her father paused, turning briefly in her direction. Hannah willed her feet forward, and when he was sure she followed, he turned and continued toward home.

9. Latitude

A week later, Hannah crossed the North Pasture in the glare of the late morning sun. Isaac was beside her. She'd been forming and discarding questions about his origins and experiences since she'd left a note at Mr Vera's smithery instructing him to come early in the day instead of after dark. Finally, she had settled on beginning with what was right in front of her.

'Does it look anything like this, where you come from?' she asked.

The sun seemed fixed at 45 degrees above the horizon, the sky a patchwork of deepening blues tinged with silver. The toes of her boots were damp-dark from the wet grass. A cluster of sheep bleated weakly, their thick, muddy winter coats the color of dirty snow. In a few weeks' time they'd be shorn to the pink. Hannah looked away. She hated the annual ritual of shearing, the chaotic terror of the animals. This year, though, the day couldn't come fast enough to suit her.

Look for my bony fingers clutching the mast by shearing time, Edward had written.

It's possible you won't recognize your brother after these few years but I shall know your face among a million till the end of my days — in spite of its gyrating into the most serious possible arrangement. From your last letter it sounds as if every Comet in

the Heavens should be shivering in terror if trying to escape The
Ever-Present Eye of Hannah Price. I am certain that by this
time you may have already claimed Priority and that your friend
and admirer George B. has built you a throne alongside the Great
Refractor in Cambridge. Tho I am equally certain you will refuse
to sit in such grandeur and instead claim a humble Footstool.

A gust of wind rustled the tall grass at Hannah's feet.

'I am not understanding.' Isaac cupped his hand to his ear. Hannah raised her voice.

'The island you come from.'

'Flores.'

'Yes. Does it resemble this at all?'

Isaac inspected the scenery. They'd come out on a footpath that would gradually give way from dirt to sand and sawgrass, and the track widened before them, leading them uphill at what could barely be called an angle. A gull circled, and he paused in his step, pointing to it.

'The name *Azores* – it is the name of a bird.'

'The Western Islands are named for a bird?' Hannah seized the tidbit of information like it was a revelation.

'Yes. But they name the wrong bird. The bird that has this name, Azore, this bird does not fly near my home. It is a mistake.' He began walking again, his stride matching hers, as if he, too, could walk for hours without tiring.

'You're joking,' she said, shocked. 'A mistake? Why did no one attempt to correct it?'

Isaac shook his head.

'I do not know. But the place is not like this. It does not belong to the finders.'

'The finders?'

'The people who are living upon it first.'

'The founders.'

'Yes.' Then he fell quiet again. As they walked, Hannah considered his statement. It was technically correct. Though Nantucket was part of the Commonwealth, and the Commons were shared among all the landholders, the nine original families who'd arrived in the seventeenth century and settled alongside the Wampanoag still owned most of the Island's property. Though Jeremiah Price – Hannah's great-great-great-grandfather – had not been among those settlers, he'd arrived shortly thereafter, ensuring that all the men who succeeded him would maintain their places at the front of the Meeting House and the back room of the Bank and on the various Committees that oversaw everything from schoolhouses to poorhouses to cemetery plots.

After another quarter hour, the trail began to ascend further. Hannah had set out lugging the satchel containing the sextant, observing logs, Bowditch, and the rolled parchment map she'd begun with Edward what seemed like a million years earlier. Two hard apples from the root cellar clunked in the pockets of her apron. When they crossed the Commons earlier, Isaac had plucked the leather bag from her shoulder as if it weighed no more than an ear of corn. She'd thought to protest, but was now glad she hadn't. Her dress was too hot for the day, and she envied his shirtsleeves and rolled-up trousers.

Fifty feet above sea level, with the sun fully risen above the horizon in front of them, they reached the top of a dune, and Hannah smiled as Isaac stepped up behind her and drank in a long breath. The Atlantic winked below them, deepest blue stretching impossibly distant, the little grey rooftops of 'Sconset's cottages puzzled together a half mile away, but the clock tower and high chiseled rooftops of Town were invisible. They might as well be marooned, like Defoe's famous character. Edward had spent dozens of hours in their youth trying to convince her to play Friday to his Robinson. The escapades he recounted, of mutineers and Spaniards and cannibals, ran together in her remembering.

'We are stopping here?' Isaac asked, and when she nodded, he released the bag, then lowered himself to the sand an arm's length away. Hannah watched him move, impressed by the ease with which he unfurled his long legs and arms. He propped himself up on one elbow and kicked off his boots, unencumbered by skirts or propriety. She could see now how it was on his boat, how his grace would be ballast amid the chaos of the hunt, the clamor of the chase. That his hands could tame a reeling line that might slice a man's arm clear to the bone as it whipped free; how the dead calm of his demeanor would clear the men's minds as they skimmed the surface of the sea as if in flight, clutching any part of the boat to avoid being tossed over and drowned while the whale surged forward through her dark world, not knowing she was bound to her attackers by the wound itself, the harpoon lodged in her. That her next ascent would be her last.

Hannah sank down beside him, tucking her knees up under her skirts and leaning forward to let the breeze cool her neck before beginning to draw the tools from her bag and set them out on a square cloth.

'To me, Nantucket looks like a woman asleep,' she said,

hoping he would say more about his origins. 'I feel relief each time I return. Though, in truth, I'm rarely away.'

Even as she said it, a tremor of excitement hummed in her throat. After months of what seemed like stalling, her father had finally arranged for them to visit the Bonds at Cambridge. The mammoth telescope they were installing there wasn't yet operative, but there were a myriad of other instruments she could use. The comet-seeker, for one. The thought of that special telescope, with a short focal length and wide aperture to admit unprecedented amounts of light, made Hannah want to spring to her feet and take the very next packet boat to the mainland and board a Boston-bound train.

'I am not seeing my home in . . . nine years,' Isaac said. 'I had only fourteen years of age when I depart.'

Hannah raised her eyebrows. At that age she'd been daydreaming about star passages during Meeting and tracking a family of snowy goslings near Maxcy's Pond. She'd certainly never been off-Island, save the occasional trip to Cambridge, where she and George had argued over the proper way to catalogue seashells and who sat where at dinner. She knew a few boys who'd lied about their ages so they could ship out without their parents' consent. When and if they returned, to a one they'd hardened into men. They were proud, to be sure. But stunted some-how, Hannah thought. Like a crop that had suffered an early frost. The hardship and violence of a whaleship was anathema to growth. Whenever she thought of Edward in such a setting, she had to push the thoughts away, guilty for wanting him to have chosen a less danger-ous path, one their father would have blessed. A position with a hydrographical party, for example, was something William Bond could easily have arranged. But Edward was loath to do it. The idea of being shuttled into an 'acceptable' position like some noble chess-piece made him itch.

'Was it – did you wish to leave?' Hannah asked.

Isaac gazed out across the open water.

'Yes. I remember when we row out, to the boat. The *Valiant*. In the dark. I am going at night, so the soldiers are not arresting me. I am leaving because I am not wishing to serve the army of Portugal.'

'I see,' Hannah said, rolling out the parchment map and anchoring each side with a stone, then smoothing it down with the palm of her hand. 'Were you alone?' She hoped not.

'My father is taking me. I can see my mother, and my sisters upon the shore. There is a moon – *lua cheia* –' He made a shape with his hands, like a ball of dough, and glanced at Hannah.

'A full moon?'

He nodded.

'And so I am having to hide, inside the boat.' He hunched down, to demonstrate. 'I am looking through a very small hole, in the wood of the boat. I see my family upon the beach growing small, smaller. Before me is a ship. More big than any ship I know. My island is growing smaller and then it is gone. I cannot see it any longer. Now there is only the ship.'

No one Hannah knew had ever related such an intimate story. His words felt like a spell, and she was transfixed. Isaac reached down and let a stream of sand run through his fingers, then lay back, face to the sky, one arm cradling his head.

'In answering the question,' he went on, in a tone reminiscent of Hannah's teacher voice, 'Flores is very different from here. First, it is green, from the top to the bottom. Not brown, grey, as here. And it is different in shape – Nantucket is – *como um gato* – as a – cat. A cat stretching, long.'

He glanced in her direction and Hannah nodded that she'd understood.

'But Flores is more looking as a bear, asleep.' He curled on his side, as if to demonstrate.

'Flores resembles a sleeping green bear?' Isaac was so curious. Childish in his way, yet with the confidence of a man. The contrast was bizarre but compelling.

'It is.' He rolled onto his back again. 'There are many hills, and clear water for swimming, and everywhere farms. The ships go to Horta, but men from San Miguel, Fayal, Corvo, and especially from Flores, from all places in Azores men join the crews.'

'Why especially Flores?'

'We are the most brave,' he answered, completely serious.

'Ah,' Hannah said, and began assembling the sextant. Index arm, indicator, arc, mirror. Anything she said would reveal how embarrassed she was for having presumed him incapable of more than a few cryptic phrases. Not only was Isaac articulate, he was far more poetic than she – or anyone else she knew. She feared that the wrong word would silence him. That he would reveal nothing further. Hannah kept her face neutral, hoping for more.

She needn't have worried. Once he'd begun to speak, it seemed, he could not stop.

'Also, everywhere on Flores is forest, and field, and flowers, flowers. That is what means *flores*. There are one thousand different kinds of flowers, and as many colors of green.'

Hannah imagined them, pale yellow-green ferns to sea-foam lichen, jade, emerald, moss.

'Flores is many places in one place. She is mountain and ocean. Rock and wind. All the year, wind.'

'Like Nantucket,' Hannah murmured.

'Everything is growing up – toward the sun. Climbing. And flowers, as I say. We grow many things, also. Sugar beet. Pineapple. Orange, on San Miguel. And . . . *uva?*'

She shook her head.

'*Uva.* For *vinho.*'

'Grapes.' Hannah had plenty of Latin to her credit. *Perhaps I could understand more of his language,* she thought, thrilling to the challenge. Even if she could not shape the words herself.

'And how far from the mainland is it?'

'Nine hundred miles.'

'Nine hundred?' She looked down at Isaac, eyes wide.

'Very far,' he said, and sighed.

'We have some flowers,' Hannah said, a little wistful, looking toward 'Sconset. 'By summer, all those cottages will be covered with roses. It's like a storybook come to life, except for the hordes of bathers from the mainland. There's heather, which of course you saw when we crossed the Moor. What else? We have sweetbriar and Russian olive, winterberry and larkspur. Hollyhocks as tall as you or I, though they don't always flourish. Hawthorn, tupelo tree, blue ageratum. Heart's ease . . . phlox . . . thyme . . .

'Corn and potatoes, which are the crops at our farm – you can almost see it from here. What else? . . . Rosemary. And the roses. I said roses. But they're wonderful. You'll see. If you stay long enough.'

They were quiet for a few minutes, listening to the boom of the surf below. She'd reminded herself of the hard grey chaos that awaited her in Philadelphia, and a hollow ache thudded like a funeral drum.

'And for how long are you remaining here?' Isaac asked, and Hannah wondered how he'd intuited her mental leap from his departure to her own.

'I don't know. I may not. I mean, I may have to leave.' Hannah hated the coldness in her voice. She was afraid of saying too much, dismayed that she longed to say more.

'And where will Miss Price go?'

'Philadelphia, perhaps.'

He frowned, as if he thought it was an awful idea. 'Why?'

'Because my father so chooses.'

'And why does he choose?'

'It's complicated.'

Isaac tilted his head slightly, and waited.

'I can't – it's difficult,' she stammered. The pocket of quiet was excruciating. She jumped to her feet, less gracefully than she would have liked, but without actually tripping. 'We should set up the sextant now. It's nearly nine.'

Relieved to be on her feet and doing something, Hannah dove into the satchel and drew out the remaining instruments, along with the old map.

'You can see that my brother and I were able to take a fairly accurate measure of our northern and western coastline – there.' She picked up a stick with which to point. 'We did so in a small boat, but it won't suit the open water on the southern side, unless we wish to be swept out to sea or dashed to pieces onshore. From here, though, we can use the sextant to establish our latitude.'

While she spoke, Isaac had wound himself into a squat so he could see the map, and as he knelt, looking over Hannah's shoulder, she became aware of how close he was.

She could smell him: woodsmoke, bootblack, sweat, and improbably a little bit of honey or marmalade, something sweet. Did he eat honey at breakfast? she wondered a bit wildly. What did Isaac Martin eat? She had never asked him to take a meal with her, had never even considered whether he might be hungry. She felt pulled toward him from her center, like a tide, and her stomach tightened.

She took aim at the southern edge of her map: *tap, tap*. Her hand was shaking a little, and she willed it to stop. It didn't. Nor could she slow her pulse. What was wrong with her?

She swayed a little, then stood, knocking one of the stones aside. The wind snapped up the free corner of the parchment, sending it aloft like a flag, and Hannah took the opportunity to scoot over to the other side while Isaac retrieved the weight and fixed the map back in place.

'Are you unwell?' Isaac asked. Hannah's cheeks were warm as fresh milk, but she shook her head strongly.

'I'm fine.'

Isaac stood up and turned so that he could survey the

area she'd just described. While his back was turned, she drew an apple from her pocket and knelt to leave it on the grass, in case he should want it, then changed her mind and put it back in her pocket.

Focus, she ordered herself. She put her hands on the sextant, and her mind was restored to what felt like its normal working order.

'Do you recall the lesson from the other day? About the parts of this instrument?'

Isaac nodded.

'Can you explain why the horizon and the celestial object remain steady regardless of whether you are on a moving ship or on land?' Hannah folded her arms across her chest. Isaac sighed and shook his head.

'Is it not possible – can you show the use of it?'

Hannah blinked and took a step back as if she'd been slapped. She had to rummage for her response, which she pieced together a word at a time like beads upon a ribbon.

'I'm planning to do so. But as I explained during our first lesson, you must understand why the instruments work, not just how to move their parts in this or that order. Just as you must understand the maths that underlie the equations. The precept, not only its execution.'

He set his lips and shook his head slightly as if she were speaking gibberish.

'It is a matter of the time,' he said. 'I do not have enough for . . . this.' He swept his arm across the sextant and the map, and Hannah winced.

'Your Sex is ever in haste,' she snapped. 'There is a right way and a wrong way to improve one's mind.'

'This may be so, but you are choosing the longest route for even the shortest journey.'

Hannah heard her own voice droning in her head like the incessant whizz of a mosquito: *To find the sailing distance of your ship in 2 hours if she goes 67 miles in 9 hours, you take 67 in your compass as a transverse distance, and set it off from 2 to 9 . . .*

She opened her mouth, then closed it again. In an instant, she was on her knees, rolling up the map, pushing pencils and parchments back into the bag.

Isaac knelt beside her. 'I was not meaning –'

One of the apples fell out of her pocket, and she ignored it as it rolled away in the sand, as if it were the offender.

'You are welcome to engage another tutor upon the Island or elsewhere if my instruction doesn't suit,' she said, hearing the words as if they were coming from somewhere else.

He leaned toward her as if to put a hand on her arm, but she yanked it out of his reach and he rocked back on his heels.

'I am doubting this is possible,' he said. Then, with unexpected tenderness, he reached for the fruit and cleaned it on his shirt before handing it back to her. She took it, intending to shove it into the bag with everything else and abandon him on the windy dune.

Let him try to find someone else!

But the sweet weight of the fruit and the look of sadness on his face combined to replace her anger with something more like sympathy. There might well be some other soul who could teach him navigation, though no one worth learning from sprung to mind. Isaac seemed to know that his ambitions had little chance of being realized, no matter how well he learned or how keenly he applied himself. She knew exactly how he felt. Her stomach knotted with hunger for advancement, for opportunity. Empathy dulled her anger. She sat back on her heels.

'I am sorry that I am offending you,' Isaac said, dissolving whatever remained of her sense of injury. She glanced at his face. It was solemn, clear of artifice. She saw only worry, and regret.

'I am seeing Mr Leary upon the wharves the day before today, and he is saying the *Pearl* is nearly fit. So . . . I am not having much time,' he went on.

'Yesterday,' Hannah muttered. She was still holding the apple, and she passed it to Isaac without saying anything, and drew the map back out of the satchel.

He bit into the fruit, taking half of it at once, then offered it back. The smell was tantalizing, and the gesture thrilled and repelled her at once. Hannah shook her head. She reset the sextant and pulled out her clock, then waited for him to finish the bite. It was difficult not to look at his mouth. She saw his throat quiver as he swallowed. After he'd wiped his mouth on his sleeve, he cleared his throat.

'In answering your question: it is because the instrument subtracts the motion from the reflection of the object through the mirrors.'

'Yes.' Hannah could not help smiling at the recitation, careful as a schoolboy's. She took her watch from her pocket.

'It's now almost noon. You shall take a sighting of the

sun, and then we'll calculate our latitude. First, find a good spot for yourself – oh, but don't kneel on the hot sand.' She pulled a swath of oilcloth from her bag and laid it in front of the sextant. 'When you're steady, pick it up the way I showed you.'

Isaac hefted the instrument's wooden handle in his palm. It was heavy. He tilted his head so he could see Hannah.

'Now, look through the eyepiece and adjust it until you've a clear picture of the sun. The filter will protect your eyes, but keep your finger on the index arm so that when you have the object in sight you can move the mirror without pawing around for the lever. Ready?'

Isaac nodded and put his eye to the sighting tube. Watching him turn the eyepiece skyward, Hannah thought of Captain Lewis at the forks of the Missouri and the great Yellowstone rivers. Hannah's father had read them excerpts from the journals of that man and his Great Expedition.

She remembered sprawling beside Edward on the hooked rug in front of the fire, age seven or eight, listening, rapt, to the section where Lewis has pushed to the very edge of the Continental Divide, negotiated with the natives there for horses, and on top of that celebrated his thirty-first birthday.

'"I had as yet done but little, very little indeed,"' her father read.

'But it isn't true! You've done so much!' Hannah cried out, and was answered with laughter from the adults in the room. How she understood Lewis now. He'd been entrusted with so much. Hannah envied him, though the idea of soldiering through uncharted forests and swamps was terrifying. It was the contribution she coveted: the opportunity to do something that mattered.

Isaac followed Hannah's instruction and sighted the horizon, then located the grey sea and uncharacteristically azure sky in one half of the lens, and the sun in the other. He swiveled the index mirror so that the bottom of the sun kissed the horizon-line.

'Why does your father wish to leave this place?' he asked, without budging from his position.

Hannah kept her back to him as she, too, looked out over the open water.

'He wishes to marry,' she answered.

'Ah. He is in love?'

Color rose to her cheeks again, but he could not see her face.

'I'm not sure. It's possible. Though I don't see how he could be.'

'Why?'

'Well, he doesn't ever speak of her. Not to me, at least.'

'Is he the kind of man to speak of these matters?'

Hannah shook her head, then remembered that Isaac was looking at the horizon, not at her.

'No,' she whispered. 'I suppose not.'

'And do you desire to leave? Are you not happy here?'

Hannah rolled the question over in her mind, finding it opaque on every side. Was she happy? It wasn't a question she ever asked herself. Her happiness – like her feelings – wasn't something she examined. She was happy when she had something to do. And everything she did was inextricably linked to the Island, whether in darkness or daylight.

'It's home to me,' she answered. 'I've no wish to leave. But if he insists I must go. I can't afford to maintain the house on my own.'

Hannah turned away from the distant horizon and folded her arms across her chest, watching him work.

'Do you have the arc of the angle, then?' she asked.

Isaac nodded.

'To one-sixtieth of a degree,' he recited, looking up and catching her eye. 'One minute of time.'

'That's correct.' *Look away,* she instructed herself. But she did not. The smell of smoke from a distant fire tickled her nostrils. The scent of her own body rose. A musk of damp wool and ink, milk from the butter she'd churned before dawn, ash from the fire and the book-dust that inhabited her very pores.

Isaac held her gaze.

'Your lesson – that time and distance are the same thing, at sea?'

'What about it?'

'I understand this,' he said. 'Not only in my mind. But in my self. The longer I am away from my home, the farther I feel from it.'

His loneliness was as clear as the noon sky. For the first time in her life, Hannah felt drawn toward the body of a man. She imagined herself kneeling beside him, an embrace that would relieve his suffering. Their bodies would be aligned perfectly – shoulders, elbows, ribs, hips. All their longing muted. She shuddered, then turned away, busying herself with the objects on the ground.

She could no more embrace Isaac Martin than she could announce her candidacy for President. Why would she envision such a thing?

'I need to be at the Atheneum soon,' she said, keeping her hands in motion. Observing log, pencil, compass. 'Can you see yourself back? Do you remember the way?' She risked one final glance in his direction.

He nodded, watching her the way one might observe a butterfly or bird in the wild. Hushed, but curious. As if he didn't wish to disturb her. At that thought – that he knew what was in her head, as he'd seemed to earlier; that his strange eyes cloaked some unnatural appreciation for the invisible – Hannah panicked. Her face burning, unable to utter a word, she took up her satchel and fled the hilltop, leaving the sextant and the apple core in her wake.

10. Cambridge

As Hannah bumped along the Boston Post Road beside her father three days later, the motion and the dust began to grind on her nerves. The blur of maple and elm, pine and fir – all the fine and stately forest she so rarely saw – made Nantucket seem bare by comparison. She imagined the settler who'd taken down the very last native tree on the Island some two hundred years earlier. How exposed he must have felt, how frightened of what would become of them. Her mind drifted back to Isaac. He must find his temporary home unbearable compared to the emerald world he'd left behind. His loneliness, and the shimmer of her vulnerability to it – like a sinister reflection – had stayed with her since she'd left him on the hillside. Even as she packed her valise and observing notebooks, her anticipation had been muted by the encounter, like a chill she couldn't shake.

It had been four years since she'd last visited the great observatory at Harvard. In the time since, her maths and her understanding of the Heavens had advanced greatly, and she hoped that William Bond would be pleased with her progress. William's praise meant as much as Dr Hall's; it was in his small clock-repair shop in downtown Boston that the friendship between William and her father had been forged over the troublesome timekeepers Nathaniel brought in for William's expert assistance. She'd always wondered if they'd also discussed the burden they had in common: raising children without the guidance of a wife.

As a girl, Hannah had learned to unlock the mysteries of the instruments piece by piece in the workroom of that tiny shop. The elder Bond had seemed a conjurer, able to coax a tick out of the most decrepit clock. His approach to fixing those mysterious instruments meant that Hannah and George spent hundreds of hours among the gears and wheels while Edward built towers and forts out of crates, and all three ran in and out of neighboring shops playing pirate. In this environment Hannah had never feared making a mistake: *If it doesn't tick, take it apart!* William had instructed as she and George disemboweled one cast-off clock after another. *Error is a doorway, children.*

When William got the commission to oversee the building and operation of Harvard's new observatory, Hannah was more excited than George. Her childhood nemesis and playmate had always been more interested in daylight than darkness. He was seven and twenty years of age now, but she still envisioned him with his leather-bound sketchbook and pencils, grubby fingers feather-light as he squinted over his subjects: milkweed pods and dragonfly wings, earthworms and bobolinks. Hannah smiled to herself, remembering his care with the treasures he pilfered from the banks of the Charles River and the Boston Common.

Then she sighed. George was as much a prisoner of circumstance as she was, though she never managed to work up the sympathy he'd demanded as a younger man. William needed George at the observatory, and George had done his duty as only son and followed him. In any case, had he pursued a career in Nature, his health would have suffered. He'd always been fragile, enduring bouts of catarrh that left him weak from coughing, and Hannah recalled him as red-eyed and wheezing throughout their childhoods. In the meantime, his sketches of nebulas and double stars, comet tails and moon craters, were the best she'd ever seen, and he still shared them with her at every opportunity, just as she shared her theories about advances in astronomy and her own progress or lack thereof. It was like having another brother, without the burden of having to mend his clothes and cook his food.

The carriage jolted over another set of ruts. Though she was excited to see the new building and instruments, their visit had another motive as well. *Lieutenant Phillips, the Super-intendent of the United States Naval Observatory, will be passing through the very week of your visit,* George had written.

> *We'll supper together, and my father is certain that you Prices will make sufficient case for your 'Nantucket station' that he'll have no choice but to assign you a contract. Hannah, I'm certain that the good Lieutenant will be as impressed by your mind and character as we Bonds continue to be.*

Hannah pushed the muslin drape aside and raised the window slightly, craving fresh air. Her father hadn't offered any advice or guidance on what they were to say to the esteemed Lieutenant to prove their usefulness to the Coast Survey. And George had mentioned that the man was insufferably arrogant. Perhaps she'd be fortunate enough to be seated far away at supper.

As the road gave way from track to paving stones, she

studied the tumble of shingled houses and hurried pedestrians. They weren't even in Boston proper, only the outskirts of Roxbury, but already her senses felt assaulted by the buzz and whistle of the city.

'It gets bigger every day. Where do all these people come from?' she asked her father.

'From everywhere, apparently,' he answered. 'The area's grown by some forty thousands in the last decade alone. They're building fast as they can. The boardinghouses are booming, though timber's at a premium.'

The cluttered, haphazard streets and crowds of people choked together like weeds made Hannah dizzy and she sat back; but as they turned onto the span of the Canal Bridge, suspended over the water, the breeze along the Charles touched her face and she sat up again. She could make out Harvard Hill and the green knolls surrounding the buildings, and a thrill spiraled up to the tips of her ears.

Along Cambridge Avenue, every corner was occupied by groups of young men engaged in conversation. The students spilled into the street, clutching their books, and she imagined each of them crouched before the comet-seeker at the great observatory on any given evening, while she squinted through the Dollond, alone atop her roof. The coach jammed to a halt again and again, jolting her each time, and Hannah's awe began to curdle into envy.

Why wasn't she rushing about with an armful of books? Hannah was certain that the majority of these boys had not the least interest in or aptitude for observing. Yet they had the right to be here, while she did not. She stuck her head out the window of the coach and frowned at a boy in a velvet jacket who was lingering in the street, shouting at a group of his companions. At first he didn't notice her glare; when he did, he winked and made a little bow. She ducked back into the coach and yanked the curtain closed.

Perhaps she was being ungenerous. Surely some of them must have a passion for astronomy. Then, watching the flow of students around the Commons, she thought of Isaac Martin, leaning over his copybook. The heat of his cheek beside her neck as she peered into the lens. She shivered. *We are not so different,* Hannah thought as they turned on Summer House Hill. *Neither of us is welcome here.*

The observatory was located on a hilltop, with a clear view in every direction, and it loomed above the carriage as they approached: a squat, square structure topped by a majestic copper dome. Hannah drank in the sight, imagining what it would be like from the inside. And there was William Bond himself, at the top of the fresh-laid steps, ushering out what looked like a group of students. He was no more than five and a half feet tall, if that, with a shock of white hair tufted like a meringue. He wore a battered, faded black overcoat that flapped when he flung both arms wide to welcome them.

'Prices!' he called, turning to address the air. 'The Prices have arrived. Nathaniel, my friend.'

As her father stepped down, the men clapped each other on the shoulders, and Hannah waited by the side of the coach.

'And dear Hannah. How are you, clever girl? Come,

come along, George will be thrilled to see his old friend. Goodness, you are tall. Here's the way. Your father tells us you've advanced remarkably of late.'

Warmed by his delight, Hannah let him take her elbow and steer her toward the great wooden door, feeling guilty for coveting his students' access to the powerful instruments. William Bond was living proof that the eye was the mightiest of all the tools at an astronomer's disposal. If anyone had ever accomplished more with less, she did not know of it; the man had observed the 1811 comet for months before anyone in the other sixteen States had even registered its existence. And he did it with a home-made telescope.

'He exaggerates. I've seen nothing not known to you and even to George,' she said, 'in spite of my very best efforts.'

'Well, come inside, come in.' Directing the driver to take their belongings to the house and install them in the guest rooms, William ushered them into the shadowy portico beneath the marble carapace, ignoring the to-and-fro of workers and students.

They stepped inside the great room. Hannah stood still, gazing up at the underside of the dome. She could make out the seams that marked the apertures, and imagined that when the dome was opened later – and she was certain that it would be – the mysteries of the Universe would slip through easily as an egg yolk cracked upon the side of a pewter bowl. She was enveloped by a sense of calm as she gazed around the space. It was thirty feet in the round, broken only by the massive telescope in the center.

'It's marvelous,' she breathed.

''Tis.' George materialized beside her, a head shorter and thin as a reed. His hair was just like his father's, save the color. George's was a sandy brown and matched his eyes, which were the color of maple sap. The freckles splashed across his nose like a spray of stars lent him a childish air. She gripped her old friend's shoulder in greeting.

'And what's this?' she asked. The great refractor was mounted on a granite plinth nearly twice Hannah's height, and an odd contraption – like a staircase on wheels – ran along a track, encircling the instrument.

'Father designed it as his observing chair. It raises and lowers as well as going round the base. But it's not operating as yet. Not until the refractor's ready.'

'Fantastic.' Hannah looked over at William, who was speaking to Nathaniel and gesturing at the dome as if he were conducting an orchestra. The elder Bond smiled at Hannah, then clasped his hands together.

'They're setting out supper at the house; Lieutenant Phillips is already there, and we have some other guests as well, so we should get along,' William called. 'The comet-seeker is still down there, too.' He bobbed his halo of white hair at Hannah. 'Eventually they'll manage to move it up here. But in the meantime it bides its time, waiting for a diligent eye.'

Hannah thought his comment was for her, but then, seeing George draw up, realized it was a barb aimed at him. She stepped closer to her friend in solidarity, and he squared his shoulders and slipped his arm through hers.

'Shall we?' he said.

Hannah nodded but didn't budge.

'Wait a moment,' she muttered, holding George back as their fathers moved toward the door. When they were gone, she let go of his arm and circled the mount twice, peering up at the twenty-some-odd feet the telescope extended, widening toward the objective.

Hitching up her skirts, she climbed the six little wooden steps attached to the ingenious chair so that she could get a better look at the refractor. It was a foot wide at its narrowest point, where it tapered toward the eyepiece. She could only imagine how much light the lens, fifteen inches around, would collect when it was finally, firmly in place.

'I promise we'll come back as soon as the sun has set,' George called, and Hannah climbed down, holding her long skirt out of the way.

'Esteemed guests and colleagues – a toast!' Lieutenant Phillips intoned, halting conversation around the large oval table all at once. George rolled his eyes at Hannah, who'd been seated to his right, as if to say *I warned you;* she pinched his elbow in response, hoping Phillips hadn't seen the expression. The last thing they needed was to offend the officer from Washington who'd been charged with oversight of the Coast Survey. Though William Bond was ever in good standing with the Depot of Charts and Instruments, it was this man who presided over the station assignments. If there was any hope of delaying the proposed move to Philadelphia, earning a year long contract to assist him was it.

He gestured with one beefy hand to the people assembled around the table. Mr Hapwell, a writer of some esteem, sat beside his wife, Lucia, who wore a bright blue silk dress with draping sleeves and a shirred collar that veed prettily into a dainty silk rose. Hannah fidgeted in her seat, feeling self-conscious in her high-necked brown dress and plain wool shawl the color of yesterday's ashes. She hadn't even combed or rebraided her hair after the long journey; as Phillips droned on, lauding the attributes of American astronomers in general, Hannah took in the details of the unfamiliar room. Usually, when she was in Cambridge, they spent so much time with the instruments that meals were an afterthought.

The walls were papered in yellow, just a shade lighter than the exterior of the colonial-style house, which squatted among a row of similar structures a short walk from the observatory. Garlands of pale flowers cascaded across the walls in gentle waves.

'For these two generations of Bonds we are inestimably glad, for without their perseverance and industry we would not be here to toast the latest expansion of this great nation's sight!'

'To the expansion of the Universe!' George, a bit flushed, attempted to raise his glass, but Lieutenant Phillips ignored the flutter of hands toward stems, cleared his throat, and nodded.

'That is right! We applaud the work of these great men, who nightly peer into the Soul of Heaven itself!'

Hannah looked sideways at George's face, frozen somewhere between embarrassment and disbelief, and pressed her lips together so that she wouldn't laugh. The man's résumé was practically gilded: he'd published extensively on oceanography, contributed a great deal to the understanding of naval meteorology and navigation and was not yet forty when he was appointed head of the U. S. Naval Observatory. In the fifteen minutes she'd been seated beside him, Hannah had also learned that he had no love for the Temperance movement, suffragettes, snake oil salesmen, Millerites, Grahamites, Catholics, or Jews.

For her part, Hannah had succeeded in speaking exactly three words – 'The salt, please' – and was certain she'd made no more impression upon the Lieutenant than the crochet-work upon the tablecloth edging.

'Without the labors of these fine men, our astronomical endeavors would falter in comparison with our European counterparts. Thus I do raise *my* glass,' he said, picking up his glass of port and lifting it up in the air, holding it there until all the guests followed suit, 'to William Cranch Bond and George Bond, who expand our manifest destiny ever upward! To the Bonds!'

'To the Bonds!' everyone at the table repeated.

As soon as the toast ended, Hannah found herself the unfortunate focus of a lecture on the merits of expanding the Texas border, along with its laws, southward.

'Do you not agree?' Lieutenant Phillips barely glanced at Hannah, though he was clearly speaking to her. He looked around for a servant to refill his glass. The cuffs of his dress coat were adorned with medals and ribbons that tinkled whenever he moved. Hannah knew she was expected to say that she did. Should she? Phillips was about to launch his next series of thoughts when she delivered her answer.

'The constitution of Mexico does prohibit slavery in

no uncertain terms, I believe,' she said, addressing the peas on her plate. 'And the law of the land should apply equally to all of its inhabitants.' To her dismay, her comment fell into a lull in the volley of conversations around the table, ringing out clear as the dinner bell.

'You're correct, Hannah: Mexico did abolish all slavery from its territories,' said George from her other side.

'Dear girl, why should Americans be subject to the laws of another sovereign? We did cast off that restriction some sixty years ago. Next you'll suggest the payment of taxes to the Mexican government.' The Lieutenant laughed loudly, gazing up and down the table.

'Well, because it is the law,' Hannah answered, wishing she could sink into the silk upholstery of the chair. The piece of roast meat upon her plate sat in a puddle of rapidly congealing gravy. Her throat and chest tightened and she pressed her napkin to her mouth before choking out her final thought. 'And because the inclusion of another slave state into the Union is unconscionable.'

'I agree completely,' Lucia Hapwell chimed in softly, after a long moment had ticked by in silence. Her husband examined his dinner roll.

'The sentiment of the Friends, as you know, Lieutenant, has always been toward manumission,' William Bond called from the far end of the table.

'Of course, of course.' Lieutenant Phillips swirled the dregs of his drink in the air as if to summon a spirit that would refill the cup. 'As are those of many good and pious men. Yet . . .'

Straightening up, he cleared his throat and then paused as if framing his words carefully.

'Those with no personal stake have yet to offer a viable economic alternative, to say nothing of the social ills that might be borne from releasing from centuries of bondage a people whose nature inclines them toward that very condition.'

A tiny bead of red clung to his moustache. He waved his free hand in the air as if to clear the fumes of her comment. Hannah thought of Isaac. Servitude was the last thing he was suited for; if anything, he seemed more independent of thought and action than anyone she could think of. The urge to fling the remainder of the Lieutenant's drink in his face rose in her, and she busied herself with the napkin on her lap, hoping her disgust wasn't evident.

'In any event,' he continued. 'The one has aught to do with the other. We're speaking here of expansion, and none can argue that the people of this continent have not the capacity – or the appetite – for it.'

Looking around the table, the Lieutenant nodded regally to William Bond and then to George, as if only they truly understood his meaning.

'Well, in *this* room, all eyes are fixed upon the Heavens,' George offered, and everyone laughed.

Slumped in her chair, Hannah was relieved until Lieutenant Phillips leaned toward her again.

'I'm told you are an ardent observer of the Heavens yourself. Have you seen anything of late I should report to Washington?' He chuckled and cut off a chunk of meat, putting it in his mouth and gnawing on it.

A delicate lace curtain floated on the window behind him. It was nearly dark.

Hannah steeled herself and made ready an answer, though she was loath to speak to him: *I've been studying a nebula.* By the time she'd taken a sip of water, though, and cleared her throat, he'd already turned back toward William.

'And what do we think about Franklin's proposed route?' he asked. 'I'm told they're outfitted quite handsomely. Have you read about it?'

Hannah exhaled. The men went on. She pushed her peas around on her plate, willing the sun to sink faster.

Two hours later, Hannah could barely sit still, so anxious was she to return to the observatory. The men sat around a small mahogany card table; Hannah had chosen the worn settee closest to the window, but could not focus on the conversation at hand for more than a minute before her gaze was drawn back to the deepening violet sky. Lieutenant Phillips had taken his leave with the Hapwells after dessert, and Hannah pitied the kind couple, who'd be trapped in their coach with the man for the better part of an hour.

'If they expand the Depot of Charts and Instruments, they'll certainly need more computers to calculate the tables for all the planets. Of course, you'd need better instruments,' William said, swirling his brandy and paying no attention to his hand of whist. 'At the very least a comet-seeker and a zenith, probably an equatorial.'

'We'd also need a housing for them,' Hannah added from her position halfway across the room, roused by the mention of better instruments. 'We'd have to build out. What about a subscription?' She looked at her father, then

William. 'The people of Boston paid nearly the entire cost of your building. If Washington provided the instruments, don't you suppose we could raise the funds –'

'I agree,' George interrupted, excited. 'I'm certain people on Nantucket would support it. I – we – would be happy to assist in whatever manner. Though if you're to remove, Nathaniel, to whom would you entrust the daily operations? You surely can't manage it from Philadelphia, and I don't know that Lieutenant Phillips would consent to leave it in Hannah's hands – though, of course, we know they're more than capable.'

'Nothing has been settled on that front,' Nathaniel said, looking to William for support.

'When Edward returns, he can oversee the project – in name, at least,' Hannah offered, wishing she didn't sound like she was pleading. She'd managed to put the issue of her own future out of her mind since coming to Cambridge. But the reality of her position was as clearly outlined as the framed silhouettes on the west wall of the room.

'Is that settled, then?' William asked, looking from father to daughter. 'Well, that's wonderful news.'

'There is no such settlement,' Nathaniel answered. 'Hannah has attached herself to the idea that Edward shall return and remain, but I have no such faith. He's proven himself to be immune to the interests and wishes of his family. I expect from him no commitment to anything besides his own fancy – should he even return to Nantucket at all.'

'Of course he'll return,' Hannah said firmly, though a cold blade of fear sliced through her chest. 'He said he'd be home by shearing.'

'I thought he was interested in joining a research expedition,' George offered.

'And isn't he engaged to marry the Coffey girl?' William added.

Hannah and Nathaniel shook their heads at the same time.

'I shan't speculate on my son's future,' Nathaniel said. 'Nor on that of the Nantucket station. Should such a contract be offered, I shall determine how best to execute it at that time, and no sooner.'

The Bonds exchanged a concerned look. Hannah swallowed her protest, but keeping quiet only made her feel more imprisoned. Nathaniel would decide her future, because it was his right; she might as well be a servant. The room felt claustrophobic, her chest tight, so Hannah did the only sensible thing.

'I'm going for some air,' she muttered. Her skirts swished as she left the room.

George found her sitting on the steps of the observatory, in the dark.

'Hello,' he said carefully. She moved over an inch to show that he was welcome, though she didn't feel like talking. George lowered himself onto the step next to her and tried to catch his breath.

'Are you all right?' she asked, though her own voice was unsteady.

'Quite. Just need a moment.'

The only sound was the distant tinkle of a cow's bell, and somewhere a carriage's wheels kicking up gravel.

George picked up a pebble from the ground beside him and tossed it into the night.

'Do you want to come inside?'

'No.'

'Why not?'

'Oh, George,' Hannah sighed. 'I don't have the will to observe at the moment.' In truth, she felt like she might never regain it. What was the point? In the light of current circumstances, all her labor seemed a folly anyway. Her career – if she could even call it that – in astronomy was and always would be governed by the whims of men. Her father, Edward, even George, whose volley of journals and articles kept her up-to-date.

'I understand you're in a difficult position. But when has Hannah Price not mustered the will to continue her work?' He tossed pebbles one after the next. 'If it were me in your situation, I'm certain you would insist that I return to my observing at once, personal matters being no excuse for lack of diligence.' With his chin up and his eyebrows creased, he was an excellent mimic. But his attempt at levity only made her feel worse.

'But you *wouldn't* be in my situation,' she stated, not bothering to keep the misery out of her voice. 'You couldn't be.'

George blinked rapidly. 'Well.'

'You wouldn't be in my situation because you are a man, and by that simple accident of birth into one Sex versus the other, you are granted reprieve from the condition of . . .' She paused, trying to come up with the right word, and when she did she spat it out like a bit of unripe fruit. 'Servitude.'

She'd never uttered such a thing out loud, never given name to the swirling sense of dissatisfaction and longing that was muted by residing on an island where women and men were educated as equals, and women ran more than half the businesses and all of the households, in practice if not in theory. Here, though, among the instruments and students, she saw herself clearly.

'Hannah. You are no servant.'

'I didn't think so either until recently.' Even in the dim light of the lamp beside the steps, she could see her friend's concern. It was no use. There was nothing he could do. She reached over and patted him awkwardly on the hand, feeling guilty first for her candor and then for pitying herself at all. The indulgence of it left her feeling sticky.

'You cannot leave Nantucket. What would become of all your work? We must think of a way that you might stay, regardless of Nathaniel's plans. Or Edward's.'

The crescent moon, which had risen early, moved slowly toward the horizon.

She picked up a handful of pebbles and flung each in turn toward the invisible fence, hoping for the satisfying ping of contact. Two minutes later George said, 'We must make sure that Lieutenant Phillips reassigns Nantucket a place in the Coast Survey. At the very least, that will get you another year. Your father wouldn't abandon such an important contract just to get married.'

'Well, I did nothing tonight to advance our cause. If anything, I harmed it.'

'I doubt that. But you still need a secondary plan.'

'Such as?'

George shifted and glanced in her direction, then looked away and hopped to his feet as if he'd been bitten by a mosquito, though he didn't move from the step. The moon dropped another degree of arc.

'Well,' he stammered, looking into the distance and then down at Hannah. 'You could get married,' he said into the quiet.

Hannah shot him what she hoped was a withering look. 'And to whom would you have me contract myself?'

'Well. I suppose that's the issue.' He cleared his throat. 'But if it meant the difference between your being forced to live in Philadelphia or your staying on Nantucket, we could – I mean, I could ... You could marry me.' He thunked back down onto the step beside her, staring at his hands as if they'd grown extra digits. 'I've no plans to marry anyone else. And then you'd technically be married, so you could just go on. As you were. So to speak.' He raised his head and looked her in the eye, and a long second ticked by in which Hannah was rendered mute by a combination of tenderness for his effort and awe that he would make such a selfless offer – if indeed it was selfless.

She felt her face flush with a sudden reinterpretation of his many invitations to visit, his ongoing interest in her calculations, her ideas, and her weather reports. As they stared at each other, his face – earnest, embarrassed, and vulnerable – answered her question.

For a moment, she thought she might laugh, and she cleared her throat to keep from actually doing it. The sound broke the spell. George looked back down at his hands, then drew a breath as if to say something more, but didn't. Hannah knew she ought to speak, but she felt frozen in place, though she managed to avert her eyes so as not to embarrass him. The idea of a courtship with George was ridiculous not in spite of but because she was enormously fond of him. But what if his help, his interest, his assistance over the years, had all been tainted by an ulterior motive? And how could it have been, when she hadn't a scrap of romantic feeling for him?

'George. That's the kindest and most generous offer I've ever heard,' she finally said. She would treat his proposal as exactly what it must be: an offer of assistance to a friend, no more or less. 'But if I wanted a marriage of convenience, my father would be more than happy to arrange one much closer to home. The truth is I've no desire to marry anyone. But I certainly wouldn't want you to give up a chance for a true match.'

She almost reached over and put a hand on his shoulder, but such a gesture would seem pitying at best, misleading at worst; he saved her by reaching over and pressing another little stone into her palm. His was moist. He let it linger there for a moment, and when he spoke again Hannah thought she heard a waver in his voice that hadn't been there before.

'Well, I'll think on other options, but you should give it a bit of thought,' he said. 'Maybe you'll find that it's not the very worst idea. I mean, perhaps it wouldn't be so bad as you imagine.' There was an awkward pause, and he cleared his throat before going on. 'In the meantime, you'll have to try for the King of Denmark's medal. At least that one comes with some currency.'

Hannah laughed, her voice ringing out like a shot. A

dog began barking nearby. She was more aware than ever of how unlikely she was to earn such a distinction.

'I'd put my odds at one in a million,' she said softly, rubbing her thumb against the smooth pebble he'd handed her.

'Well, it can't hurt to dream,' he said. 'And you're more likely to find a comet than anyone I know, myself included.'

She smiled, grateful for the praise, then felt vain and a little foolish. Hannah was glad when he hopped to his feet.

'As you're not one for dreaming, I'll rephrase in language you're sure to understand: Shall we work?' He offered her one skinny arm, and she allowed him to pull her to her feet, though he let go as soon as she was steady.

She followed him up the step toward the door, amazed and annoyed by how little he knew of her true thoughts after so many years of friendship.

Hannah certainly did dream. And when she did, she imagined herself among a group of women she could number on one hand: Mary Somerville, the brilliant Scottish mathematician, writer, and translator of Laplace's *Mécanique céleste*; Margaret Fuller, the first full-time female book-reviewer in the United States, who was now reporting for the *New York Tribune* from Europe. Though Hannah hadn't read Fuller's strident tome, *Women in the Nineteenth Century* – the book had caused a row in every house on Nantucket it had appeared in, she'd heard – she fully appreciated the obstacles those women had to hurdle to attain such positions.

What Hannah admired most, though, was that their success had resulted not from some aberration from 'normal' female pursuits, but from following the dictates of their own intellects and aptitudes, and – without a doubt – working very hard. They'd earned the freedom to pursue their work, and had an income to go along with it.

The clatter of the chain around the door to the observatory made her jump.

'Do you feel as if you hold the key to the Universe entire?' she joked.

'Nay,' George answered, pushing open the great carved door to the dim interior. 'I'm a mere gatekeeper for the likes of you.'

'Rubbish.'

Hannah followed him in, pausing in the new dark of the interior. George lit the lamps with his slender hands until a series of watery reflections encircled the dome like an ancient cave of mysteries.

'Are you ready?' George ran his hands through his shock of hair, making it stand up even further, and nodded to the odd-looking cast-iron handle by his side.

'Ready for what?'

'To open the dome, of course. Go on and give it a turn.'

'You can't be serious. It's fourteen tons.'

George patted the little handle as if it were a lapdog.

'Always in doubt. Trust your friend and come here.'

Hannah crossed the room but examined George's face before she touched the crank, to see whether he was teasing her. She saw only a crinkle of excitement at the corners of his blue-grey eyes, and the hint of a dimple where he was trying to hold back a grin.

She grasped the black handle and began to turn, expecting to need every ounce of her strength to make it budge in the slightest. But she put it in motion with barely any effort. High above her, the copper-sheathed dome grated, then squawked. As she turned the crank, the thinnest of dark lines appeared between the copper plates, the crack of night sky widening with each passing second, like a curtain opening on a dark stage.

'How is it possible?' she called to George. He leaned in close to her ear to answer, though both their necks were craned at awkward angles so as not to miss a second of the show above. His hot breath on her ear made her cringe.

'There are dozens of iron balls fitted along the track,' he explained. Fifteen seconds passed, then twenty. She kept turning the crank, wondering at the clever design of the device. Each turn revealed more of the velvet sky ticked with stars. Ten seconds more and the crank reached the end of its revolution. The dome was open, the night exposed. She released the handle. Cool air flowed into the tower.

'Well done. Shall we go up?' George led her to a slender staircase on the south side of the tower. Hannah was shocked when he paused at the top and then pushed open a little door she hadn't even seen from below.

'Balcony,' he explained, and disappeared through the opening.

Hannah followed him, and found herself on a tiny platform fixed to the side of the dome like a barnacle. George stood beaming beside the very comet-seeker she'd dreamed of earlier in the day.

'But your father said it wasn't yet here.'

'I had it brought up during dinner,' George said. 'I knew you'd want to have a go at it.' Hannah could do nothing but stare at the instrument until he reached over and poked her in the shoulder. 'Go on.'

'I don't have my notebook,' Hannah muttered, eyeing the five-and-a-half-foot telescope squatting on its little mount. George lowered his head to his hands in mock despair and pushed the little stool toward her with his toe. She sat down but continued to admire the instrument without touching it, bending to examine its clockwork and base from a safe distance.

'The eyepiece is a Huygens,' George said. 'The lens is nearly seven and a half inches. Can't believe we bought it by subscription. Good people of Boston, we salute you.' He issued a crisp salute in the direction of the city. 'And you, Miss Price.'

Hannah finally leaned in and put her eye to it. She knew the numbers, how much light the aperture would admit; still, she wasn't prepared for the breadth of the field. She was swept into the pockets of dark and pops of light she'd never observed in this section of the sky, though it was this exact section she'd been sweeping for weeks, from home.

My sight has been parched, she thought. She had not known. And now here was the quenching light. It was as if she'd been quilting in ten different rooms, each containing a solitary square, and now, here, was the entire glorious blanket.

Hannah said nothing for a good ten minutes; when George touched her shoulder she nearly flew out of her seat.

'George,' she said, bobbing back toward the lens, unable to stop looking. 'I need a notebook. Can you please get me a notebook?'

Pearl-grey morning light filled the round room when Hannah crept down the stairway. George was snoring in the strange observing chair, his head tilted back and his mouth open. She tapped him on the knee, but he didn't budge. For a few moments she stood gazing at his familiar face, wondering again about his proposal.

She squinted, as if blurring the picture would help her see him in a new way, as a partner in life, in work. The image wasn't so difficult to conjure, but when it edged toward the other side of marriage – the physically intimate side – the curtain fell. Though she had no direct knowledge of such couplings, the idea made her shudder.

Throwing her shawl over him, Hannah crept out into the dawn, clutching her notebook, trying to shake her discomfort by focusing on the bright sparks in the night sky she'd been observing. They felt like the embodiment of possibility, the antidote to the uncertainty she felt about the future.

George was right: she was more likely to find a comet than most people, in spite of the limitations of her lens back home. Hannah could practically feel it: a wanderer, cloaked by reflected starlight, lurking among the millions of stars she'd just swept. If she looked long enough, she knew she would find it. It was only a matter of time.

11. *Uma Cometa*

Hannah didn't see or hear from Isaac Martin for nearly three weeks after she returned from Cambridge. She'd left a note for him at the shop the day she returned, instructing him to come in the evening to continue the lessons, but it had gone unanswered. As days with no word stretched into weeks, the number of reasonable explanations for his absence thinned. Hannah moved among her roof-walk and the Atheneum and the Meeting House, the promise she'd felt in Cambridge dwindling along with her hopes.

He might have given up his position on the *Pearl* and left Nantucket on another vessel; he could have left the Island for some reason he didn't wish to share; he may have been injured or disabled by some accident. It was the last that her imagination seized upon, and she suffered the idea that a hot iron spar had impaled or dismembered him; that a stray spark had flown into his eye and blinded him; that he'd been run over by a wagon or knocked unconscious in a brawl he had nothing to do with.

These scenarios – and the emotions they brought with them – had made her nauseous with anxiety, especially when compared with her cold reaction to George's proposal. She'd cycled through dozens of memories, but recounting the many ways in which George had gone out of his way to assist and enlighten her, or otherwise counter her isolation over the years of their friendship, did nothing to inflame any kind of passion in her. All it did was deflate her indignation about his motives. George hadn't been false; she simply hadn't noticed his interest, if it existed, because it wasn't reciprocal.

Her thoughts about Isaac, on the other hand, tormented her, rising at odd intervals, furtive as dreams. After two weeks of swatting them away like flies and muttering to herself in public, she paid a boy to go to the boardinghouses in New Guinea and to Prison Lane, to make inquiries, but he reported no residents of either by the name of Isaac Martin. She walked by Mr Vera's shop a half dozen times but didn't see her student, and each time she'd rushed off, embarrassed, whenever someone came out or passed her on the street.

Then she began to wonder if he'd simply given up, overwhelmed by the drone of her voice and the march of equations. The warm rush of relief she felt when she saw him sitting on her step at six o'clock in the evening, in the second week of May, combined with the sudden pounding in her chest, unnerved her so that she was almost rude.

'Did we schedule a lesson for this evening?' She clutched the tub of butter she'd just borrowed as if it were a priceless curio.

He clutched a worn copybook in one hand; the other was tucked into the pocket of his loose white shirt. His hair was shorter, the tiny curls wired close to his skull. Hannah followed the angular line of his jaw to his chin, then his mouth.

'I am sorry for not being in contact,' he said. *Nobeyn contaque.* His voice was gentle as a lullaby.

'I see.' Hannah stepped around him and opened the door. Her father's hat was not upon the peg.

Why did you not send word? she wanted to ask, but stopped herself, not wishing to pry. Nor did he need to know she'd been thinking of him. Now that it was obvious he was unharmed, her worry felt humiliating. She hoped he hadn't heard that she'd been asking after him. Perhaps she should send him away.

He followed her inside and stood like a humbled schoolboy, head bowed, as if he expected to be dismissed. But she was the one who'd insisted he continue the lessons, after all. Sending him away wouldn't serve any purpose.

'I hope you remember where we left off,' she said when they were upstairs, trying to keep her voice neutral. She'd prepared lessons weeks ago, but where were they? When she glanced at Isaac, he reached into his pocket, drawing out a stone the size of a quail egg, and placed it on the edge of the desk by her arm.

The stone was a deep, iridescent green. Luminous white waves marbled through it in parallel. Hannah picked it up and cradled it in her palm.

'Malachite. How lovely. Where did you get it? It isn't native.'

'From a friend.'

Hannah raised one eyebrow.

'He say it is jade, but I am knowing no. Still, I am wishing to . . . possess it.'

Isaac seemed to be struggling with his words more than usual, watching her turn it in her fingers and place it back on the desk.

'It's very nice. You can begin your collection with it.'

'Nooo,' he said, drawing the vowel out. 'It is for you.'

'For me?' Hannah looked at it again, then at Isaac. He nodded.

'It is a gift.'

'I cannot.' It wouldn't be appropriate for her to accept. As it was, he had yet to pay her anything for the lessons, and she hadn't asked. Maybe he meant it in lieu of the sum he owed. The stone had no such value; still, a tickle of pleasure ran up her spine at the idea that he'd thought of her in his absence. She shook her head.

'You can. It is yours.' The sudden urgency in his voice was unexpected, and Hannah glanced at him, surprised. This was his apology, then. She picked it up again and weighed it in her palm, then sighed.

'Well. I thank you.' Hannah carried the malachite to the specimen shelf and nudged aside a chunk of pyrite and a faded peacock feather to make room for it in the center. She blew a veil of dust from the logbook hanging nearby, and added: *Malachite. Unknown origin. A gift of Isaac Martin,* 1845.

She made her way back to her desk and rummaged around until she found the lesson she wanted. Looking over her notes in the margins, she found one to herself: *Wanderers,* she'd written.

'Have you seen anything since last time?' he asked, peering up at the small window.

His interest was gratifying. Since she'd returned from Cambridge she'd not had a single conversation about her observations. It was like devouring a feast and then starving for weeks. The words tumbled out.

'No. Although at Cambridge they have an instrument made specifically for comet-seeking. An enormous telescope, with a huge field. I did think I saw a comet from here a few weeks back – it behaved like a comet – but then it turned out to be nothing. Well, not nothing – a portion of a nebula, probably – but not a comet.'

'*Uma cometa,*' Isaac muttered, and shook his head. 'You are looking for this?'

'Yes. Are you unfamiliar with comets?'

'Only that we are wishing not to see. It is – for the men – a bad thing. A dark sign.'

Hannah sighed, amazed that such notions persisted in modern times.

'Superstition and myth. There's no such thing as a bad omen. Though it's not uncommon to believe in them,' she added, in case he felt slighted. 'I'll explain.' She looked around for her pointer, which had gone missing, and had to settle on a pencil stub. *Tap, tap.* The rhythm was soothing.

'A comet is a celestial body of eccentric orbit,' she began. 'It appears and sometimes reappears at regular intervals, but always has a bright nucleus, brightest toward the center, and often a long train which trails behind it like fire as it crosses the Heavens. They're sometimes referred to as wanderers. You can see it without a telescope if its orbit comes close enough to our own. In fact, I'm certain you've seen one. A spot of light traveling across the sky at a steady pace, much slower than that of other igneous meteors – shooting stars, for instance.'

Hannah peeked at Isaac to see if he understood, but was met with an inscrutable gaze – somewhere between bemused and bewildered.

'A comet nearly always has a tail,' she added, and, thinking he might not know the word, looked around for something with which to demonstrate; finding nothing, she tugged at one of her long, coiled knots of hair until it released from its mate and unwound in her hand. She held it out to one side.

'A tail of light, like this,' she said.

Isaac nodded, and his gaze went from her hair to her neck, exposed to the collarbone where she'd unbuttoned it earlier. Hannah felt like her corset strings were being yanked tight, but she wasn't wearing any such contraption. As she rewound the tresses and hid them away again, she hoped that he couldn't see her hands shaking with fear. Not of him, but of the blood that rushed to her belly, and lower, when he looked at her.

He turned his gaze back to the little window above the desk.

'Why do you look for this?'

Hannah paused. How could she explain the desperate beauty of that blazing arrow careening across the Universe on its own unique course, inexplicable yet predictable? If she could locate it, chart it – understand its geometry and the play of gravity and the composition of elements working upon it – there were any number of doors it might unlock, ideas it could unleash.

'We've been trying since the beginning of Time to understand them,' Hannah said. 'The early Christians thought they were fireballs flung at Earth by an angry God. Thomas Aquinas thought they were portents of revolution, or war, or bad weather. The Chaldeans thought they were a sort of planet.'

She shook her head, trying to order her thoughts. Isaac had an odd look on his face: surprised, amused, she couldn't tell. He probably thought she was a fool. Perhaps she was.

'Yet we still know so little about them. Do they never cease to carve the elliptic? Where do they begin? How do they end?'

The desperation she heard in her own voice made her want to cry. Whether it was for the comet or for his understanding wasn't clear. But the swell of emotion was bracing, clarifying. It occurred to her that she hadn't answered his question. She took a deep breath.

'The truth is that anyone may see a comet, Mr Martin. Anyone who is diligent, who watches carefully, night after night, might see something that no one has ever beheld.'

She raised her eyes to his.

'Even a woman with no formal education. Even here, on this Island. With a simple telescope, and no assistants, and no support. Do you understand now?'

Isaac nodded. When he spoke, his voice was gentle, but serious.

'Close your eyes,' he said. 'We will look.'

'I don't know what you mean,' she said.

'We will imagine it. The *cometa*.'

'Oh.' The idea was so puzzling, she paused to be sure she'd understood him. Then she shook her head. 'Why?'

'Why not?'

'Because it doesn't make any sense. What's the point?'

'It is a kind of preparation. Like imagining the whale, just below the surface. Her life, her habits, her dark, her light. Until you can feel her movement. She is rising to the surface. She is coming to the air. It is a kind of . . . calling.'

I don't believe in this, Hannah thought. It felt worse than nonsense. Closer to heresy. She felt as nervous as if he'd suggested that they dance.

'My grandmother is saying that the present is a shadow on our soul,' he offered, sensing her hesitation. 'The future, shining, is calling our attention. So we must be welcoming what we desire. In the mind.'

He reached out his hand, and she opened hers to it before she had time to think. The shock of contact vibrated through her entire body. His hand was warm and dry. When he curled his fingers through hers, she stared at the pattern of their fingers, dark and light. *Piano,* she thought. *Zebra.* These common words grounded her, lifting the net of fear. She felt as if she might float away.

'All right,' Hannah whispered. It would be no different from silent worship. Opening herself to unseen revelation. Perhaps his way would yield what hers never had. 'Show me.'

'Close your eyes.'

Hannah did, but reopened one a crack to be sure he was doing the same. He was. At rest, as if in sleep, his face was peaceful and beautiful. She shivered a little, her pulse thrumming where he touched her.

'Are we in a boat?' Hannah asked.

'Yes. We are in the Pacific. So it is warm. And very dark. No moon. Many stars.'

At first there was nothing but the odd sensation of midday stillness. Then, as she settled, warm air seemed to flood her body. A wind whose name she did not know lapped at her cheek, tickling her nose with the jasmine and citrus of green islands impossibly distant.

'We are looking to the stars,' Isaac said.

Hannah looked. The boat rocked. She felt the creaking in her ribs. She knew, from books, what the sky over the South Pacific would reveal, and she saw it entire, as if she'd been beneath it a thousand times. There was the Southern Cross; there was Eridanus and Hydra.

Isaac uttered something sharp in his language. She could feel the scurry of boots across the deck, the squeal of the rigging as the limber boys climbed and called.

Some men cried out in fear; others laughed. Hannah could see the comet so clearly it burned the insides of her eyelids. Seized by a sudden fear, she opened her eyes. As if on cue, he did the same, then reached for her other hand, gathering it softly in his own.

'Before Pope Urban IV died, in 1264, a comet appeared,' Hannah whispered.

Heat radiated from her fingers up through her wrist, twisted into her forearm, elbow, shoulder, throat. She swallowed, sending the warmth into her core.

'It disappeared when he died. The people thought the two events were connected. Scribes recorded the event. The tail was over one hundred degrees of arc. Half the elliptic.'

Her hands were hot under his touch. Was he burning, too? Was she imagining it?

'*Tu acharás,*' he said. 'You will find.'

Hannah shook her head. Her mouth was dry, but her brow was damp. She wanted to lick her lips. She wanted him to lick her lips. She felt her face contort, flinching from the lewd image.

They broke apart. Isaac put his hands on his thigh, then into the pockets of his shirt, and looked up toward the little window.

'*Nebuloso,*' he muttered.

Hannah left hers where they were, paralyzed by fear. *This should not have happened,* she thought. *I should not have allowed this.*

'We should look at logarithms,' she muttered.

He nodded, but neither of them moved.

She stared at her desk and cleared her throat.

'Or perhaps that's enough for today.'

The heat of her desire and her shame did not lift, though she tried to focus on work. What had she meant to do before he came? Was there something she'd been reading? *Right ascension,* she thought. *Meridian altitude. Eclipse.*

He nodded, then rose, the chair squawking on the wood floor. He took a few steps toward the door, then paused.

'About the payment.'

Hannah put her hands on the desk and studied the candlelight playing upon them. Dark, light. *Piano. Zebra. Cometa.*

'Yes?'

'I am having . . . It is difficult. I am working on the mainland. This is why I am not coming. Before.'

Hannah pressed her lips together, relief coursing through her. So he hadn't abandoned her. He'd been away. She peeled off her words one by one, like wet clothes. The effort of revealing herself was mighty.

'You might have told me,' she said to her hands.

She wiggled her fingers. The light played on and off the surface of the desk like sun upon waves.

'I know.'

Before he could say anything else, something that could not be forgotten or changed or ignored, she spoke again. This time she made certain her statement left no room for an answer.

'Pay what you can manage.'

She didn't look up again, and when the garret door clicked shut behind him she sank into her seat, all her strength gone.

PART TWO

June 1845 Nantucket

12. Reunion

Shearing Day dawned bright and hot as coal. It fell on the fifteenth day of the sixth month, cleaving the year in two. The date made perfect sense to Hannah, who charted its approach as keenly as another woman might have welcomed her wedding day. As the sheep fog that enveloped the moor and Commons in a thick, wet haze gave way to the warm, bright days of June, she swatted away any whisper of doubt caught muttering and scampering around her periphery, grasping the echo of Edward's five-month-old letter as if it were a buoy.

I'll be home by shearing, he'd written. And though she'd heard nothing since, she'd kept the specter of Philadelphia at bay by refusing to consider the possibility that the *Regiment* wouldn't make it to port in time for the festival. He had to come.

A wavy, indistinct blur rose from the little city of tents in the meadow north of Miacomet Pond, where the animals had been washed the day before. The encampment buzzed with women in muslin summer skirts and eyelet bonnets, their sleeves rolled up to their elbows. The men were overseeing the division and shearing of the animals, or doing the work themselves, while their mothers and wives and daughters filled the tent-tables with the fruits of their labors.

Hannah hated the huddled and helpless pens of animals,

the spectacle of their exposed skin. She would have preferred to avoid the whole event. She was sweating profusely in her navy linen summer dress, even with its sleeves rolled up and collar unbuttoned. She drew off her bonnet and shielded her eyes against the glare, scanning the crowds for the boy she'd dispatched to the wharves to wait for a flag on the horizon. The air was tangy with grease from the doughnuts Lydia Black was frying in bacon fat, and tart with apples from the cider Fayth Shambaugh – the old whaling captain's young wife, who sold the best pickled vegetables on the Island – was pressing in her tent. The scents mingled with the sizzle of lamb on an open-fire spit, the sticky sweetness of molasses buns, the lulling aroma of fresh-baked bread.

Hannah lifted her coiled braids from her neck in hope of a breeze, and fanned herself with an ostrich feather.

Miss Norris hustled up, leaning on her cane.

'Miss Price! Wonderful to see thee.'

'Miss Norris. I'm glad thee is hale.'

'It was just a sprain, dear. I'm surprised to see thee here, though.'

Hannah grimaced and sipped her lemonade. At least a dozen people had said the same over the course of the last three hours as they trailed by her tent. Compared to other families' tents, Hannah's spread was simple: roasted meat and two pies. But it had taken what felt like a stupendous effort for her to lay it, from trading a half bushel of summer squash and two laying hens for a leg of lamb, to surreptitiously studying the Atheneum's battered copy of *The American Frugal Housewife* for a week straight.

A bead of sweat rolled down her neck and continued

to her shoulder blades, making her squirm. She didn't want to make small talk, but there was nowhere else to go. Conversation swirled around her, and her eyelids grew heavy.

She'd spent the previous night roaming the rooms of the house, restless, and by dawn, when she'd heard the low hum of town selectmen and elders leading the sheep from the Commons up to the pens, she was shaky and distracted. Hannah scanned the crowd again as the men began pouring into the encampment from the shearing pens. A fiddler struck up, and Hannah dragged her stool into a small triangle of shade in front of her tent and slumped onto it.

It was so hot. And she was so tired. Hannah struggled to keep her eyes open. It wouldn't do to fall asleep. But the heat blurred the very air, and her eyes fluttered. She was on a boat, or a mountaintop. Before her, a vast plain of deepest blue. The ocean reflected all the familiar points of light in the Heavens. In her dream, she was meant to create a map of the firmament from the undulating waves.

'I cannot be certain which are fixed,' she cried to someone she could not see. 'They are all in motion!'

Her distress mounted as the vessel pitched. Each streak of light that crossed her field of vision was immediately obscured by a wave.

'But I saw it!' she cried. And then Isaac Martin was beside her on the roof-walk. Yet it was not her house. The platform was wide-planked but unstable.

'Take care,' Isaac whispered. The tiny, invisible hairs on her neck rose, magnetized. 'Do not look down.'

But she did, and the world was upside down; she was

floating through the sky itself, flying toward the stars but looking back at Earth. She reached for Isaac but he wasn't with her. She struggled against whatever force carried her, but only moved farther away.

Hannah woke and bolted upright, wiping her brow.

'So boring to wait for one's brother to arrive,' Edward said. 'Anyone in their right mind would do the obvious thing and sleep through it.'

The next minute disappeared in the twins' embrace, which was silent and fierce. Hannah was overwhelmed by relief. As her brother's bony arms wrapped around her, she understood at once that the women of her Island survived the years of worry and longing by releasing them from memory, easy as kites, when their beloveds returned. The curious sensation made Hannah suspect that mothers who labored and tore and bled their babies into the world forgot that pain in the same way, and for the same reason.

Hannah and Edward drew back at the same time and surveyed each other.

'Where's the rest of you?' Hannah asked, looking him up and down, a lump in her throat. She'd felt all his ribs through his clothes. His hair still stood up in random tufts, and glinted gold over new patches of grey. His brown eyes, so like her own, were now set in a weathered face that looked ten years older and five shades darker. But they still sparked with humor.

'Did I not report on the cuisine in my letters? I thought I would have described the king's feast we enjoyed nightly.'

'If you had, I'd certainly remember, since they were so few and far between I easily committed each word to memory,' Hannah said, reaching for Edward's hand and pressing it to her cheek, overwhelmed.

'A tear? Can it be? Heartless Hannah, don't ruin your reputation!' Edward whispered, grinning and tipping his forehead so it touched hers. 'I'm home and all's well. And anyway, you haven't even said hello to your new sister!'

'My what?' She looked around as if a small girl-child was going to appear in a puff of smoke.

Edward turned and nodded, and Hannah realized that Mary Coffey had been standing beside him the entire time. She stepped up and smiled at Edward, and he took her hand in his own. It looked like a lily in a tiger's paw.

'Look,' Edward said, pushing the little hand at Hannah. 'See what this brave girl has let herself in for.'

Mary wore a plain gold band upon her fourth finger. It glinted in the sun, and Hannah stared at it, calculations whirring like gears set in motion: the number of hours that Edward could possibly have been on-Island; the failure of the boy she sent to the wharves to spot the *Regiment*'s flag. The impossible span of years ahead in which this could not be undone. Mary and Edward stared at her, expectant. She should say something.

'How?' she whispered, turning her face to Edward. 'When?'

'Early this morning,' he answered softly, lowering Mary's hand but not letting it go. 'I rowed myself in from the Bar. A Reverend Jenkins – a friend of mine from New Bedford – performed the ceremony for us at dawn. He came in on the packet last night.'

Edward smiled down at Mary. Hannah was numb. She felt the way she had the time she swam too long in early season and was pulled out by a riptide she couldn't fight. Swimming parallel to shore until she was too tired to continue, what she'd fixated on was her own foolishness, her poor assessment of the tides and the conditions. In crisis, treading water, she'd processed facts: the likelihood of her freezing to death before regaining her strength; the nearest location of a crosscurrent.

When Hannah turned to Mary, her voice was as cold as the icy water that had nearly claimed her.

'And your family? They have approved?'

'They knew I'd never give Edward up no matter what they said,' Mary said, beaming at Edward. 'And I'm of legal age to marry, so . . .' She shrugged as if her disregard for their wishes were of no more consequence than a pest in the storehouses. 'Of course, they'd rather we had a proper exchange of promises at the Meeting House,' she went on. 'And I'm sure we'll oblige at some point. In any case, they won't deny us our happiness.'

'Nor would anyone who cares for us,' Edward added, his eyes warning Hannah to be kind.

She turned away, toward the tent, unable to look at either of them.

'You must be hungry,' she managed. 'I'll make you a plate.'

The next few hours passed in a haze of heat and well-wishers. Hannah sat upright on her stool beside the tent, feeling like a distant, elderly cousin instead of a sister-in-law. She hadn't had a single moment alone with Edward, though every so often he reached over and squeezed her hand or handed her a cup of lemonade. It felt more like a funeral than the celebration she'd envisioned.

'I'm going for a walk,' she announced at four o'clock. No one seemed to hear. Edward and Mary were sprawled on the grass a few yards away. She had her head in his lap, and he was stroking her hair as he spoke to John and Libby Abbott and the Johnsons, two young couples Hannah and Edward had grown up with.

She stepped closer to the shadow of the tent so no one would see her watching. As children, they'd collected frogs and pinched each other across the benches at Meeting. But as adults those boys and girls had found each other again, and now they were joined by a mysterious bond Hannah did not understand.

Envy fired a hot streak through her chest. What was the defect in her that she had never felt such affection? Was it of the body? The spirit? Surely she was plain, but look at Libby. Her cheeks were round as a squirrel's, and she had two chins and no sense. She talked all the time without making a point.

Hannah turned her back on the offensive scene and went round the back of the tent, then strode up to the top of the hill without stopping until she came over on the other side, which was empty. Once there, she halted and then knelt, squatting as a series of sobs ripped through her, one painful heave after another. She covered her face in case anyone should see her, then shielded her brow so that she appeared to be searching for something on the ground. Her thoughts felt muddled, and she had no sense of what to do next. Return to the tent? Go home?

Hannah's head snapped up like a rabbit. Had Edward even told their father? She wiped her cheeks with her sleeve. Rising, she brushed off her dress and composed her face to a semblance of normal – though she felt anything but – and walked the rest of the way down the hill, the clamor of the tent city fading behind her.

With everyone at shearing, the streets were hushed, and the squeak of the door when she opened it and her steps on the floorboards seemed to reverberate through the empty town.

Her father was sitting in the kitchen with a half-empty cup of tea and a stack of correspondence fanning across the table. He didn't look up when she came in.

'Has thee been to the tents?' she asked, checking the kettle. It was cold.

'Mary's father came to see me this morning,' he stated, glancing up at Hannah as if to admonish her for being coy. 'I apprised him that I'd no prior information concerning the event, and that if I had I'd certainly have alerted him in time to prevent it.'

'Would thee have?' She was surprised in spite of her own fantasies about how the union might have been stopped.

'Of course,' he snapped. 'Thy brother is in no position to marry. Though I'm certain he has some ridiculous, impractical scheme in mind.'

Hannah bowed her head and sighed, hoping to mollify him.

'I had a letter from William Bond today, ahead of one that he advises us to expect later this week,' he went on. 'Apparently we've earned a small contract from the Depot of Charts and Instruments to operate a Nantucket station for the Coast Survey.'

He snapped the page he was reading so it crisped to attention.

'Really?' Hannah picked her head up. 'The Coast Survey?'

'Indeed.' He passed William's letter to Hannah. As she scanned the brief lines, a rush of hope bloomed in her chest like a field of flowers all opening at once. But her father looked grim.

'Is this not wonderful news?' she asked carefully.

'It should be,' he said, gazing at her over the top of the page. 'But it pains me to say that I do not know if we can accept it.'

'But why would we not accept it? It's an excellent opportunity! And think of the instruments.' She pressed her palms down on the table, taking comfort from its solidity, hoping that whatever the reason for his hesitation, she could settle it. She willed herself to stay calm, clear the sticky cloud of fear from her voice.

'I'm not certain that Lucinda will consent to wait another year for my presence in Philadelphia,' he said. 'And as previously discussed, it is unlikely that the contract will hold if I am not in residence to oversee it.'

Hannah's heart hammered against her ribs, but she managed to subdue her fear enough to keep her voice level.

'Could Edward and I not maintain the station together? With thy supervision, of course.'

Birds were fighting in the mulberry tree outside the window; the pair burst out at intervals, leaves flying in their wake. In the absence of other human sounds, their chatter seemed unnaturally loud.

Her father's voice turned unexpectedly tender.

'Daughter,' he said, 'I must advise thee to clear thy head of the notion that Edward will remain here.' Was that pity in his face? She had steeled herself to defend her brother, not herself, and now was unsure how to go forward with her argument.

'But why?' she asked, hating the quiver in her voice, vulnerability making her feel more like a child than a grown woman capable of running a station of the national Coast Survey. 'Has he said as much?'

'I expect he shall announce his plans tonight. The Coffeys are holding a dinner. At their home.' He moved his newspaper the rest of the way down to the table and peered over his glasses at Hannah. 'It's not for a few hours yet.'

'But thee will attend?' She smoothed her skirt, which was patched with flour, stained dark with cider and butter. A button-size spot was still damp from her tears. She left her other questions unasked. There was no use in querying her father any further about Edward or pushing for a reconciliation. He felt as betrayed by Edward as Hannah did, she realized. But she'd diverted her pain into a kind of moat, buffering her from despair. Nathaniel had allowed his to harden into a wall. Maybe his way was better. At least he hadn't had all his expectations dashed.

'Yes, I shall attend,' her father said, going back to his work. 'If we're lucky, the situation won't tarnish our business relations with the Coffeys. The last thing the Bank – and this household – needs is the wholesale withdrawal of the accounts and chronometers of the entire fleet.'

'Does it really matter at this point?' Hannah muttered, losing her will to put on a professional show for her father. 'If we're to remove anyway, what difference can it make?' If her father decided to remove to Philadelphia without mending his bond with Edward, she'd have no chance of staying to run the station.

'Those of us whose support remains dependent upon the finances of this household are in no position to comment upon its needs, I should say,' he answered calmly, then went back to reading.

Shame weighing on her like a boulder, Hannah rose, careful with her feet, and left the room without saying anything else. She felt branded, like one of the penned sheep up by the pond, with a giant *F* for *Failure*.

She was nothing but a burden to the household, in spite of her meager income from the Atheneum. That's what her father was saying. She'd failed to find a comet or anything of note in the Heavens; she'd failed to find a husband or even look for one. And apparently she'd failed in predicting the outcome of Edward's journey and her own future.

The Coffey dining table stretched from one end of the room to the other, half the length of a schooner. On the walls of the room, portraits of previous generations of Coffeys glared down upon the diners as if in horror that one of their own had secretly married a Price of little means. Hannah felt stiff as an overstarched tea towel in a brown, high-necked First Day dress she'd been wearing since high school. It was meant for cooler days, but she couldn't get the blue one clean in time. Once, she and Edward would have scoffed at the idea of supping at the Coffey table in their best clothes. Now he sat across from her, barely visible through the twisted metalwork of a brass candelabra that dominated the centerpiece.

Even surrounded by Mary's imposing family – her parents, John and Charlotte; her sister, Eleanor; and her two brothers, Elias and Elijah, and their wives – not to mention two Nantucket selectmen, Dr Hall, and his own disapproving father, Edward looked serene. Hannah wondered if her father had even informed Edward about his own plans to marry and remove.

She'd yet to have a moment alone with her brother, and his proximity was excruciating. All she wanted to do was steal him away, to walk and talk. The simplest things. But they were trapped in this grand room, where everything from the windows to the table to the gilded edges of the china was burnished to a mirror-like sheen. Everywhere she looked, Hannah saw herself, wavy, distorted. Her place setting seemed crowded with cutlery. There were three spoons, two forks, and what looked like a silver toothpick with two prongs at the end.

It was a ridiculous assortment for one person, but she was glad to have something to do with her hands while the conversation flowed around her. As the soup was served and removed, and plates of carved roast meat and potatoes were passed, Hannah felt the chatter more than heard it, until Elias caught her attention.

'I don't see the allure of Philadelphia, myself,' he said to the table at large. 'Outside of the Mint, of course.' Hannah glanced at her father, seated beside her to the left, but he didn't seem to notice.

'What about Constitution Hall?' Mary offered from her place next to Edward. 'That was a grand building in its time.'

''Twas, until a mob burned it down,' Elijah said.

'There's the Independence Bell,' Elias conceded. 'I suppose that's something.'

'A seventy-year-old bell?' his brother sniffed. 'I'll take Boston any day.'

'If the mob had read the Bell carefully they'd have thought twice about routing Mr Garrison's antislavery forces. Does thee know why, Edward?' Dr Hall asked from Hannah's right elbow. She'd been surprised to see him, then grateful that she'd at least have someone to speak to; but he'd been unusually reserved, and spoken more to her father and the other selectmen than to Hannah.

'Hannah?' Edward asked. She shook her head.

'Leviticus 25:10.' Dr Hall put one finger to his chin, waiting to see if anyone knew the passage.

'"Proclaim Liberty throughout the land unto all the inhabitants thereof,"' Nathaniel intoned.

'Those who support slavery aren't civilized enough to care,' said Elias' wife, Sally. 'They'd happily melt the Bell down for reuse as shackles.' She lifted her chin but her eyes sparkled. Her pretty defiance was a kind of flirtatious parlor game, Hannah thought. Sally, along with every other woman in the room, seemed crisp in her muted silk dress, a silvery grey color reminiscent of a cloud. While all the women were technically in keeping with Discipline as far as their attire – no one wore bright colors or plunging neck-lines, and there wasn't a ribbon or ruche in sight – Hannah still felt thick and common as a dandelion in a field of pop-pies. Her hand fluttered to her hair, which she'd haphazardly pinned into a knot that threatened to undo itself with every move she made, and she wondered how these women kept their hair so neatly ordered and plaited into intricate coils.

Someone helped them, she realized. An instant later, a memory blazed through her: her mother's hands, hover-ing at her neck. The gentle, lulling tug of braids woven in, a splash of bright blue ribbon wound round the ends and tucked away, like a hidden gem only revealed at bedtime.

The soup was cleared by black women in matching long skirts and snowy white aprons. The sensation of her mother's hands receded. Hannah found her gaze drawn to their hair beneath their snug caps, wondering if it was similar to Isaac's. A pang of what felt like hunger ran through her at the thought of him; she hadn't seen him since their strange shared vision in the garret nearly a month earlier. Embarrassed by her ignorance, she resumed playing with her silverware, though she supposed she ought to eat something.

'I heard the bell ring once, when old Tippecanoe passed on,' Elias said.

'Did you?' Edward asked. 'What did it sound like?'

'Quite loud,' Elias answered. 'Rather like the sound of thousands of free Africans overrunning the country. Lib-erty Bell indeed.'

'Elias! Really.' Sally clicked her tongue. Hannah winced at the crude comment.

'What? I'm no friend of the slaveowner, but sudden,

wholesale manumission? They must be mad. It'll be a disaster.'

'More of a disaster than the continued subjugation of an entire race of men, women, and children? I cannot see how,' Mary snapped, and Hannah looked up, surprised at her fervor.

'That's because you've never looked farther than your own Island shores, where all the bunnies run free and happily together,' Elias answered. Mary and Edward exchanged glances, and Hannah saw her brother shake his head and whisper something to his new wife. Mary smiled.

Hannah felt overheated, nauseated by the bloody platter and the overcooked green beans. Hoping for distraction, she turned toward Dr Hall.

'Have you had a look at the latest volume of *Silliman's Journal*?' she asked.

He nodded.

'It lacks the depth of a scholarly endeavor. I'd rather hoped for more substance from our national science journal.'

'I thought much the same,' Hannah said. 'There's nothing on astronomy at all except a short description of the observatory at Cambridge. And nothing on Charles Babbage's latest analytical engine design. Though I suppose that's technically an English innovation.'

Mary had bent her head low and was laughing at something Edward was saying. Hannah wondered what he was making fun of. He'd made no effort to include her in their conversation – though with a piece of brass the size of a small tree between them, it would have been difficult. Still, she felt snubbed, and the sting of rejection made her even more unhappy to be there. She tried to focus on what Dr Hall was saying; something about Horace Mann. She'd read that article, hadn't she? Hannah rummaged in her brain for its thesis, and was relieved when she retrieved it.

'I found the article about Mr Mann's school heartening,' she said. 'Not the part about the training methods for women teachers; thee did a fine job of instructing me on that front without any formal "method." But as far as it advanced the idea of equal education for all people.'

Dr Hall bowed his head slightly, absorbing the compliment, then put a forkful of peas in his mouth, chewed, and swallowed. Hannah pushed her food around on her plate.

'I'm told thee has a student of late.'

Hannah controlled her features, though she could feel the blood rush to her cheeks.

'It is true. In navigation,' she said mildly, wondering who had told him about Isaac. What they had told him. 'Only the rudiments, of course: he'll be halfway around the Cape before we could even scratch the deeper surface. Yet he advances.'

She paused, hoping the conversation would end there. When he didn't answer, she glanced at him, and was reminded again how much he'd aged since he'd been her teacher. Perhaps she'd misread his question.

'Does thee miss thy students?' she asked.

'Some more than others,' he answered, turning his head to look at her. His eyes seemed paler today, the icy blue of a glacier. At such close range, the effect was bracing: instead of the old mix of excitement and fear she'd felt as a schoolgirl when he paid attention to her, she now felt acutely conscious of his physical proximity. She could see the iron-grey stubble on his cheek, the whorl of thinning hair on the back of his head. Her cheeks warmed as his gaze lingered, and her father's words in the garret back in April returned with burning clarity: *Dr Hall has spoken of his great affection for you.*

Hannah looked back down at her plate, mortified by the idea that her teacher could be attracted to her; it was perverse in the extreme. When John Coffey cleared his throat, Dr Hall turned toward him, and the clink and buzz around the table ceased. Hannah exhaled.

'We wish to acknowledge the presence of the Price family at our table,' he said. There was a tiny crumb marring the sheen of his deep-blue jacket, and Hannah kept her eye on it. His voice betrayed no emotion. He might have been speaking to an assembly of workers at one of his storehouses, or to the men's Business Meeting about a bylaw.

'And our esteemed friends as well. We are grateful for thy company, though as you know this event was rather unexpected.'

A ripple of laughter went round the table, though not everyone was smiling. Hannah caught Edward's eye for a moment, and she felt more than saw his discomfort, though she was sure no one else did. She was seized by the urge to protect him from this theater. But how? Should she rise from her chair and inform everyone that Mary was not deserving of a hair upon her brother's head, much less his heart? That her devious capture of his body and spirit was not the Coffeys' to despair but the Prices'?

Edward looked back at Mary, and curled his hand over

hers. Hannah felt her heart shrinking like a sponge being wrung out.

'Edward and Mary have joined themselves in the contract of marriage, and we gather together to acknowledge the promises they spake to one another, and in hopes that their union may prosper,' John finished.

The assembled bowed their heads briefly to acknowledge his words. Hannah thought she saw Elias roll his eyes, but she averted her own before he saw her looking.

'What are your plans, then?' Sally called from the other end of the table. 'Shall you set up housekeeping at the Prices'?' Someone at the table tittered; Hannah couldn't tell who.

Edward and Mary exchanged a look, and Edward nodded. Hannah studied his face through the branches of the candelabra. She closed one eye, then another; in the wavy candlelight she saw something new in his face. His light was still there, but there was gravity as well. He was no longer a boy, she realized.

'Some time ago, Edward wrote a letter to Captain Zachary Thomson, who is leading a cartographic expedition to Jerusalem, to express his wish – our wishes – to join their party,' Mary said.

Hannah wasn't sure she'd heard correctly. A collective gasp went around the table.

'Really?' Elias said. '*The* Captain Thomson?'

Edward nodded.

'Jerusalem?' Charlotte Coffey repeated, her shock visible to all.

'And,' Mary continued, 'he's had his answer. We've been accepted.'

She beamed at her husband. Edward looked across the table at Hannah.

'We wished to speak to everyone separately earlier today,' he said. 'But with all the hubbub by the tents, our nearest and dearest did vanish like runaway sheep.'

Hannah would not look at him. Jerusalem was a half a world away. To her right, Dr Hall said something about the Dead Sea, the science of salt. How it buoyed everything, yet could sustain no life. The Jordan River was mentioned; someone's father had been to Nazareth, seen the lake upon which Jesus allegedly walked.

Dr Hall opined that the story had its basis in the aforementioned sea; Charlotte Coffey said she believed her Savior had walked upon freshwater.

Hannah felt frozen in place. But her gaze was drawn to Mary, who seemed as happy and hopeful as any new bride. Hannah imagined the journey before her, the places she would see. The moon above Jerusalem lighting the white stones. Stars like runes, ancient and meaningful, spreading overhead.

'I'm feeling unwell,' Hannah whispered to Dr Hall, and pushed her chair back from the table. She focused on the pale pink roses on the carpet beneath her feet. Its thick pile caught the legs of the chair, making it difficult to stand.

She heard Edward say her name. But Hannah continued through the grand foyer with its polished floors, and out the door with its ostentatious brass knocker in the shape of a right whale, and then she was in the street, striding toward the home she was about to lose, under the only night sky she would ever observe. It was difficult to think clearly, now that her only hope for a future of her own choosing had announced his plans to depart for the other side of the world. It was her worst nightmare, what everyone had warned her of. Edward was leaving, and there was nothing Hannah could do to stop it.

And then Mary was running to catch up, calling her name with her sweet, trilling voice, but Hannah didn't break her stride until Mary seized her elbow and yanked her to a halt.

'Please! Let me speak.'

They faced each other like adversaries about to duel.

'You must know that Edward wanted to share our plans with you personally, but you disappeared amid the festival,' Mary said, trying to catch her breath. She let go of Hannah's elbow and brushed it with her hand to smooth the sleeve. Hannah pulled her arm away.

'Your plans,' she echoed.

'Yes.'

Mary straightened her shoulders and stared back. The sight of her calm brow and clear eyes was infuriating.

'Unbelievable.'

'Why is that, Hannah?' A hint of something hard crept into Mary's voice.

'Where do I even begin? First, there is the matter of this being Edward's home, and where his family is. This is where he belongs. And second, there is the matter of your own – fitness.' Hannah spat the word out as if it tasted bad.

'Fitness for what?'

Mary's voice carried genuine confusion, but Hannah paused for only a fraction of a second. Then she ceased to think at all.

'For anything, as far as I can tell. For industry, to begin

with. Do you plan to twitter with the birds and the fish all day long? Will you don your finest silks, your French lace, on the crossing? Will you assist with navigation? Collect specimens? Take a lunar? Read a chart? What *are* you fit for, indeed?'

Mary recoiled as if Hannah had slapped her.

'How dare you?' she whispered. 'You know nothing of me. And apparently nothing of your own brother. I've shown you only interest and kindness, and in return you judge me. Not only me: you judge everyone! From the safety of your rooftop, or the blockade of your desk. Deeming us worthy, or unworthy, in the main, without knowing a thing about our nature. It's remarkable, really. For all your industry, you see so very little. I pity you,' she finished, a sob catching in her throat. 'Once Edward is gone, you'll have no one at all.'

Mary turned her back and fled in the direction of her house, leaving Hannah standing in the middle of the dark street, adrift as a ship with no mast. Her rage receded, but she still felt like the victim of a cruel scheme to strip from her everything that mattered.

The house on India Street would only remind her of all she had lost. She couldn't go back to dinner. Rooted in place, Hannah thought she could feel the Earth spinning on its axis, while she remained stuck in place, pinned to its surface by the invisible, unseen force of gravity itself.

13. Gravity

Three hours later, at nearly ten o'clock, Hannah was walking east, away from Town, her feet finding their rhythm only after a quarter hour of what felt like a slog through a swamp. The ground was softer than it had been earlier in the day. With twilight a gentle fog had returned, and she could only see a few feet in front of her as she passed through Newtown Gate, heading toward the south pasture. She was slowed by the bulk of the Dollond and its stand, which she'd swaddled in a woolen blanket with great care and stuffed into a canvas carry-bag now slung across her back like a large child.

It will lift, she told herself, the grey mist swirling before her like a series of veils.

It did not. Ten minutes later, having lost the track twice, she turned back, defeated.

If she was inclined toward magical thinking, or believed in spirits, it would have been easy to convince herself that every element in the Universe was conspiring against her.

Instead, she resolved to go home and work on the Adams equations again. Thinking about the dizzying spread of signs and symbols was like an antidote to the poisonous memory of Mary's face backing away, wounded. But Hannah's eyes still burned with a gritty mixture of dust and resentment.

She shifted the heavy satchel from one shoulder to another and squinted at a blurry figure about her height that was walking toward her along the Polpis road. She couldn't make out his features. As he approached, though, his head bowed but his stride long and easy, familiar with the ground in a way that she recognized, she knew that it was Isaac Martin.

A dozen bats began flapping wildly in the dark of her belly. Hannah held her ground until he was near enough to hear her speak without shouting.

'Mr Martin,' she said, and he raised his head.

'Miss Price,' he answered, a smile seeping across his cheek and widening into a toothy grin. 'Why am I finding you here?'

'I felt like walking,' she said. 'I thought to observe –' She shrugged a shoulder to indicate the bag, and he immediately reached for it. She rubbed her shoulder where the strap had cut in, grateful. 'Thank you. Unfortunately, the elements are not cooperating.'

He shouldered the bag, then turned in the direction she'd been going and offered her his elbow. She hesitated for a second, then linked hers through.

'So we are walking,' he said.

Hannah swallowed and willed her feet to move in time with his. The warmth of their coiled limbs was distracting at first. But as they moved along the road, the fog wisping around them and the ground damp underfoot, she forgot to think about the place where they were joined. They were well matched, as if they'd been walking together for years, and they went without speaking for some minutes, their feet falling two by two on the loamy soil.

'What is the word from Mr Leary, then?' Hannah said after a quarter hour, surprising herself with her directness.

Isaac shook his head.

'He has disappeared again. Like an illusionist, this man.' He kicked a pebble with the toe of his boot. 'I had to go to the office of an agent to inquire.'

Isaac's face was tight. She'd heard about ship's agents. They'd sign a dog on as a deckhand if they could get a double fee for the four legs. Yet the owners depended on them more and more to pull crews, since local boys no longer fought for spots on a journey likely to take them away from home for four years in pursuit of the giant creatures they'd fished out of waters closer to home. When Hannah was a child a typical whaling trip had been two years at most; by the time she was assisting Dr Hall it had been three. Now it was closer to four.

'What did the agent say?' Hannah asked Isaac.

'He say – said – that the *Pearl* is going nowhere.'

'What?'

'He said they are deciding to resheath her copper. That it will be another month.'

Hannah shook her head and clicked her tongue in sympathy, but a current of relief ran through her at the idea that he wasn't leaving yet.

'Why would Mr Leary not tell you such a thing?'

He shrugged.

'I am not important?' he said.

'But you are second mate!' Hannah answered, indignant, stopping in her tracks and pulling him to a stop, too. Only then did it occur to her that the right or wrong of it wasn't the part that troubled him. It was work that he needed. She wondered if he had any money at all.

'What shall you do?' she whispered.

He shrugged as if he wasn't concerned, but she wondered if he was only trying to spare her from worrying.

They started walking again, and the mist thickened, then thinned. Hannah realized they were near Five Corners, in New Guinea. She'd passed through this part of the Island, where colored families – some Nantucketers for three generations at least, others newly arrived clutching their papers – built their houses and ran taverns and boardinghouses and businesses of their own. There was an excellent seamstress in New Guinea; Hannah recalled hearing someone mention that she was unusually reliable for someone of her race.

'Have you observed anything of late?' Isaac was asking.

They passed Newtown Cemetery and turned south onto Miacomet Road. Their boots scraped against the grit. Hannah could barely see Isaac, only puffs of steam ahead of him. Several times she heard footfalls approach and fade. But she didn't see anyone, and no one gave any indication of noticing her. Isaac's warmth felt like a salve, and she clung to him.

'I've barely had time to observe. It has been difficult. At home.'

The words snagged, as if she had splinters in her throat. Isaac didn't respond, and Hannah considered how she might go on without saying too much. Once, a young girl, a neighbor about her age who belonged to the Catholic Church, had explained to Hannah about confession. The idea of sitting in a dark box, whispering her vanities and lusts to a male priest considered God's living incarnation on Earth, made Hannah cringe. Yet she felt something like what she imagined the pious would feel upon entering that enclosed space, unburdening themselves upon a compassionate – though quite human – listener.

'The *Regiment* is in port,' Isaac said, his voice soft as the mist. 'Your brother is returning?'

Hannah cleared her throat.

'Yes. But he is not staying on the Island. Which means – in all likelihood – that I cannot stay, either.'

They'd walked half the length of Miacomet Pond when Hannah stopped short, taking her arm from Isaac's, then walked to the edge of the road, which came to an abrupt end, and squinted at the brush.

'Follow me. There's a path here that leads south.'

He obeyed, trailing her into what looked like a thicket. She popped out onto a footpath that snaked around the edge of the water, running south for another quarter mile before turning parallel to the horizon and the edges of the dunes that led down to the shore.

Hannah took a deep, cleansing breath. A handful of stars emerged overhead, where the fog had thinned. The tiny breakers salted the air. They picked their way along the path to its end, where it widened into a small circle of sand, sheltered from wind by the brush and the dunes.

As soon as Hannah paused, Isaac settled onto the ground without squirming and surveyed the sky, and she dropped down next to him. She should set up the telescope right away: the bank of clouds to the northwest would be overhead within a half hour. But she hadn't the will to move. The moment she'd stopped, the full weight of disappointment had landed on her, sapping her energy.

'You are upset,' Isaac said a minute later. 'About your brother.'

'Yes.'

'And you do not wish to leave.'

'I do not,' she whispered. 'But I cannot stay, unless I find someone to marry within the next few months. Or make some stupendous discovery that awards me a large sum of currency and a better-paying position.'

There was no point in dwelling on the absurdity of either scenario. Hannah climbed to her feet and looked over the bluff, feeling like a surveyor at the boundary of the New World. She gazed out over the tumbling surf below, wondering how Isaac saw her. Fierce and strong? Stiff and serious? Did he grasp the gravity of her situation, how powerless she was over the forces that controlled her? There was no way to know. Nor should she care. She was his tutor, she reminded herself. *Tutor, then.*

'Did you do your reading on the subject of gravity?' she asked, wrapping her arms around herself and turning toward him.

'I am not having the time,' he said. 'I am sorry. I am working off-Island all week, and then the sheep.'

'You worked the shearing today?'

He nodded. No wonder he sounded tired, Hannah thought. He must have risen well before dawn. She wondered where he'd been going when she ran into him. She eyed the bulging leather satchel of his own he'd set down alongside hers.

'Don't apologize. In fact . . .' She reached into her bag and drew out a slender volume of Sir Isaac Newton's *Principia*, then realized it was too dark to read. 'We can have a lesson about it now and you won't have to do anything but listen.'

Isaac put an arm over his face, pretending to hide.

'Newton is speaking of the planetary system,' she began, ignoring the gesture and settling herself more comfortably on the ground beside him, leaving enough space between them for a loaf of bread, or a bucket of ash. She lay the book gently on the ground beside her and closed her eyes, paraphrasing from memory.

'"The primary planets are revolved about the sun in circles concentric with the sun, and with motions directed towards the same parts, and almost in the same plane,"' she began, propping herself on one elbow, then opening her eyes to check if he was asleep.

'I am listening,' he said, without moving.

'All right. Well, Newton goes on to posit that mechanical causes cannot account for the regular motions of the planets or the irregular motions of comets. Rather, he says that "This most beautiful system of the sun, planets, and comets, could only proceed from the counsel and dominion of an intelligent and powerful Being."'

Hannah paused and switched elbows, glad for the excuse to move a few inches closer to Isaac. His body radiated warmth. Even as Hannah spoke, she was aware of being drawn toward him, as if by an undertow.

'And that if the fixed stars are the centers of other like

systems, they must all be subject to the same dominion of One; especially since their light, and the light of the sun, and the light from all systems are of the same nature. To prevent them from falling upon each other due to gravity, our Creator placed those systems at immense distances one from another.'

Isaac sighed and stretched out his arm so that it grazed her elbow.

Move away, she commanded herself. But her body would not obey. Hannah felt her elbow bend, her shoulders and chest and neck lowering to Earth, her head coming to rest upon Isaac's arm. Even after she'd stopped moving, the sinking feeling continued, as if she lay upon a featherbed of infinite depth. The clouds had obscured nearly every star. The dark was heavy as a blanket.

'We are like these systems,' Isaac said a few seconds later. Hannah could feel the vibration of his voice echo through his body and into the arm on which she rested. It felt like low thunder. She wanted to press her hand to his throat, feel his voice hum there.

'How so?'

'We are put upon the Earth by the same Creator, if there is such a one.'

'Yes,' Hannah said, feeling no urge to insist upon His existence.

'We were placed at immense distances from each other.'

'We were,' she said.

'And yet the same forces work upon us.'

Hannah closed her eyes. Loneliness and longing pooled in her bones, weighing her down. She moved incrementally closer to him, until his fingers curled around her shoulder and she could feel his breath on her forehead. The cold current of warning that cut through in harsh bursts was not strong enough to move her. She willed it away, basking in the warmth, the weight of her bones beside his.

'They do,' she whispered, feeling like Time itself had stilled for this instant only, granting her a reprieve from worry that she had not earned.

14. Borrowers and Lenders

When Hannah opened her eyes, the first thing she saw was a grey sky shot through with pale blue and silver. Her dress and hair were heavy with dew. Beside her, Isaac's chest rose and fell, steady as a tide. His face was peaceful.

Breathe, she told herself, tamping down the panic rising in her throat by focusing on that action alone. When she'd calmed herself enough to feel that she could move, she sat up, careful not to make a sound. How had she let herself fall asleep here? The idea of facing Isaac was overwhelming. She had no idea what men and women said to each other in such a situation. Though they'd shared nothing but slumber, Hannah felt as exposed as if they'd been intimate. She had to go, and quickly, before it got any later. Her only hope of avoiding a scandal was to get home without being seen.

Her arms and legs were stiff, but she managed to rise without waking Isaac, or looking too long at his face, lest she be pulled again into wrong thinking.

In daylight, the truth was easy to see. The tentacles of desire were sticky and invisible, treacherous. They'd reached into her most sensitive parts, exploited her weakness and her need. Hannah crept away from Isaac, nauseous with remorse. Even the pungent scent of her own body seemed different. But all her senses were suspect. She had to be vigilant. His scent, his voice – his face – she must avoid them.

With her carry-bag over her half-numb shoulder, Hannah tiptoed away. When her feet found the sandy trail that led back around the pond and onto Miacomet Road, it took all her strength to resist the urge to run.

Instead, she walked fast. The road was empty until she came to the outskirts of New Guinea, and from there on more people appeared each minute. Hannah fell in with the steady stream of bakers and shop assistants and servant girls flowing toward Town.

Feeling anonymous among the many was a strange solace. By the time she reached Federal Street, Hannah had composed herself. She tiptoed into her house, which was silent, and willed the stairs not to squeak. Before slipping into her own room, she paused in front of Edward's, imagining him and Mary asleep together. Were their limbs entwined, the flesh of one inseparable from the other? Was her head upon his arm, as Hannah's had lain on Isaac's? Was Mary peaceful in her happiness or had Hannah's words been harsh enough to disturb her rest?

Regret rose, bitter as bile. But she could not strike what had been done. And if she didn't put the telescope back in the garret, wash her face, change her dress, and go straight to the Atheneum, she'd probably lose her position on top of everything else.

The cool, quiet interior of the library soothed Hannah's ragged nerves. For the next eight hours, her actions were simple and straight as nails. She logged half of an archive, filed a stack of periodicals, and gave a brief tour to a handful of tourists from Virginia whose loud voices rattled her nerves.

At two o'clock, desperate for occupation, she turned to the cabinet of curios with her duster and polishing cloth. Hannah had personally begged, borrowed, or otherwise acquired each item in the collection over her years at the Atheneum, including the cabinet itself. It was as nearly as long as a coffin, and fashioned of English rosewood, with a series of double glass doors that each had its own tiny brass lock.

Inside, carved ivory chessmen from Cameroon nestled near Scottish scrimshaw. There was a feathered, embroidered headdress from Feejee and an elaborate gold filigree bracelet from Egypt. And on the very top shelf, a tiny carved wooden girl sat upon an equally tiny chair, her chin resting in her hands. The captain who'd donated it to the Atheneum said it was Japanese, and it had the classic, simple lines of art from that nation. The girl sat like a comma, a gesture in wood. Hannah had never been fond of dolls, but the little figure had tugged at her from the moment it had arrived. She put the girl in a different spot in the cabinet each time she opened it, as if it would benefit from viewing the other artifacts at a new angle.

She'd just dusted the wooden girl and put her in the center of the headdress when Isaac Martin walked into the Atheneum. He entered the room and removed his cap when he noticed a pair of young ladies who'd been browsing through pattern books looking at him. They stared at him for a moment, then one nudged the other and she nodded to acknowledge the gesture. Then they ducked their heads back down into the pages like plovers diving for dinner.

Hannah kept command of her features, though a lurch of fear roiled her belly. What was he doing here? She hoped no one would notice that her hands were shaking. In case they should, she crossed her arms as if she felt a chill.

He crossed the room, a book tucked under his arm. Hannah's eyes darted to his face, then away, but in that brief moment she could see that he was struggling to keep his face from showing anything but a student's polite distance.

Hannah put her hands in her pockets and fumbled for the miniature key-ring, then the key for the door in front of her, relieved to busy herself locking it.

'Mr Martin,' she said. 'You've brought a book.'

'I have,' he answered, sliding it across the top of the cabinet. It was her book, from the night before.

'I thank thee,' she said. 'I hope you found it illuminating.' She stared at him directly, willing him to be cautious. He didn't look nervous in the least.

'I have many questions,' he said. 'I am finding it difficult to understand.'

'It's not so complicated,' Hannah said, glancing around to see who was near. There was the pair of women, who seemed engrossed in a catalogue; Miss Norris, who was copying out a passage for an elderly trustee. Hannah turned back to Isaac.

'The rules that govern the Universe are quite clear,' she

said. 'I should think our lessons would have helped thee grasp that concept.'

He nodded, but kept his hand on the book.

'And yet, you have instructed that these rules cannot explain all things in the Heavens,' he said. He seemed amused, but Hannah felt the opposite. 'Are there not elements that are not obeying these rules?'

'What is thy question, exactly?' Hannah snapped. Miss Norris looked up, as did her visitor.

Isaac leaned forward over the cabinet slightly, so that only she could hear him. The scent of his skin reached her, and with it the memory of his body beside her. Hannah swayed a little.

'Can I come this night?' he asked. 'For a lesson? Time is short.'

Say no. But the tentacles reached into her throat, down into her chest, deeper, into her very core, sucking the words away. She nodded.

'Come at dusk,' she whispered.

He straightened his back, took his hand off the book, and left the building, not looking at anyone, though everyone in the room turned to watch him go. Hannah put her hand where his had been. It was warm.

At four o'clock, she watched the last of the day's visitors – a boy of about twelve, with hair the same orange color as his father's and every one of his three brothers: a lesson in hereditary properties if ever there was one – bound down the steps and race toward home. She was about to close the door behind him and finish the day's tasks when a familiar figure appeared on the steps and hailed her.

'Dr Hall.' Hannah opened the door again and stepped forward to take his elbow, feeling a flush creep up her neck when she remembered how she'd run away from the Coffey dinner table the evening before. 'Come in, please.'

He glanced at the key in the lock but didn't pause.

'Good,' he said, and stepped through the portico. Hannah pulled the door closed behind him, flipped the card to *Closed*, and followed the clack of his cane into the shadowy space.

He paused before her desk, then settled into the chair in front of it and laid the cane across his knees. Hannah settled in her own chair, hands folded on her desk like the pupil she had been, attentive and diligent. When he did not immediately speak, she cleared her throat.

'I regret taking my leave so abruptly last night,' she said. 'I was not myself.'

He shook his head.

'Regret is a wasted emotion, Hannah,' Dr Hall said. 'It offers no comfort to the soul, for what's done cannot be undone. This, on the other hand . . .' He picked up the cane and swung it in an arc, indicating the bookshelves surrounding them. 'Shakespeare. Milton. Plato. Euclid. Here is where comfort lies. In knowledge. Especially when shared.'

She flushed, remembering his pointed comment at the table the night before, then glanced at him, hoping she could gauge his intentions. Maybe she'd been mistaken in thinking his attention was anything besides the sincere interest of an aging mentor, lonely for company.

Dr Hall's thinning tuft of grey-black hair was swept up off his high forehead, silver spectacles dangling from a chain around his neck, giving him the look of a ruffled snowy owl.

'We've rather traded positions, it seems,' he said.

'I'd be loath to even try and approximate thy command of the classroom.'

He brightened, then fiddled with a magazine on her desk before peering up at her with a curious expression.

'On the subject of students, I'm interested in hearing more about thine. We didn't get to finish our conversation on the matter the other evening.'

Hannah hoped her face didn't reveal anything.

'Did we not?'

'Thy private student. A Negro crewman of the *Pearl*, I believe?'

'Second mate. He's from the – the Western Islands, I believe,' she answered. Hannah wondered first where he'd gotten such detailed information, and then if he was about to subject her to a lecture about the man's prospects for advancement. Or worse.

She paused and slipped the lesson she'd been preparing for Isaac under a pile of papers on her desk.

'I didn't realize thee had a passion for the improvement of the lower classes,' he added. 'I never saw it in thee before.'

'I harbor no such passions,' Hannah said, unspooling each word with caution. 'It is a matter of a fee for services. Nothing more or less.'

'I hope it doesn't interfere with thy own work.'

'I don't see how it would.'

'Well, I thought thee fully occupied by thy position here, and I'm told the Coast Survey contract has materialized.'

'It has,' Hannah said, seeing an opportunity to change the subject. 'We're hoping for new instruments from Washington.'

She stopped short of saying more: any discussion of the Coast Survey was sure to lead to one about Hannah's future.

Dr Hall was nodding as if there was more he wished to say, and then he held up a hand as if to stop her from going on.

'Yes,' he said. 'I'm aware. But there is something about which I've been remiss in not speaking to thee directly. I shall speak it now, if thee will hear me.'

Hannah flinched. Her efforts to hide her lapse in Discipline – not to mention reason – had not gone unnoticed, after all.

'I believe thy father has spoken with thee of my . . . I don't wish to say offer. Nor can I say feeling, for though I hold thee in the highest regard, I certainly cannot profess a romantic sentiment of the kind exalted by thy peers – or, of late, thy brother – in these times.'

He waved his hand in front of his face as if to dismiss all sentiment from the ether.

Hannah moved her hands from her lap to the edge of her chair and held on, trying not to be overtaken by the urge to laugh wildly from the combination of relief and disbelief. Had any woman, anywhere, ever entertained a proposal that began thus?

'In any case,' he went on, pinning her in place with his stare, 'what I wish to say is that thy position is untenable.

When thy father removes, thee will be in need of a new situation, whether it be now or a year from now. As I say, I do not pretend to veil this situation with any kind of romantic puffery. Rather, we are two like-minded adults, and should we commence to join as husband and wife, I believe the result will be mutually beneficial. Thee might remain here and continue thy astronomical work and studies – indeed, I would insist upon it.'

'And what can thee expect to gain from this . . . arrangement?' Hannah asked. She no longer felt like laughing. Instead, she was confused. His interest wasn't a matter of romance, as he'd clearly stated.

'I'm not a young man, Hannah. I don't travel as I once did, and without the school . . . well, thy intellect as a daily companion would alone be enough to suggest the idea's prudence. And thee will find me agreeable to whatever work thee wishes to pursue.'

A pleading note crept into his voice, though his eyes held a hard certainty.

'You want to marry my mind?' she said.

The vulnerability he'd allowed a moment before vanished.

'I didn't mean to offend thee,' she said, hoping to soothe him. 'It's only that I'm surprised. Thee has the best mind I've ever known. And there is good sense in what thee suggests.'

Her words vibrated with their own truth. There *was* good sense in his reasoning. He offered ballast, a means for her to stay on the Island and continue her work. At least there was no emotion attached to the offer, which removed the awkwardness she'd felt about George's proposal. What Dr Hall's lacked in warmth it made up for in practicality. And what other options did she have?

She felt the sensation of Isaac's hand upon her shoulder, curling her body toward his in sleep. Hannah flushed.

'I will consider it,' she said. 'I cannot give an answer at present.'

Dr Hall nodded once and rose, hooking the cane over his arm, suddenly nimble. Hannah kept her head low as she followed him to the door, where she stepped in front to hold it as he passed through. But he paused and seized her arm.

'Take thy time. But, in the meantime, resume thy visits,' he said. 'I have missed thy company.'

He held on a moment longer, though she didn't utter another word, then went down the steps in the last of the late afternoon sun, leaving her with an uneasy mind and the faint impression of his hand upon her arm.

15. An Admonition

Hannah was still unsettled when she went out into the humid late afternoon, and once she was at home waiting for Isaac to come for his lesson, everything she touched went wrong. In the space of an hour, she burned the leftover mince pie she was heating for her dinner, pinched her thumb in the kitchen cupboard, and knocked over the small ceramic bird that had sat upon the windowsill for as long as she could remember. It landed on the floor and broke in two, its tiny bird head flying across the room like a bullet.

Everywhere in the kitchen there were signs of a woman: two fresh aprons upon a peg, the chowder pot scrubbed to gleaming, the wood floor swept, and the two long benches arranged neatly at either side of the table, like good students. Apparently Mary's first order of business as a Price had been to tackle the mess Hannah had made preparing for Shearing Day.

Hannah wanted to think that Mary had hired a girl to come in and do the work, but she felt a wife's hands in the order of the room. There was a warmth that had not been there before. Then she remembered how cruelly she'd spoken to Mary, and winced. She'd been too harsh. Sinking onto one of the benches and looking around at the sparkling cookware, Hannah waited for tenderness to descend like a butterfly and land softly in her heart. But she still saw Mary as a gilded bird, not a worker bee. So what if Mary had swept a floor and scrubbed a pot? That didn't make her a good match for Edward.

Her thoughts flickered to Dr Hall. She'd always considered him a clear thinker, with morals as straight as a slide rule. Hannah smiled again when she thought of his proposal. What was the phrase he'd used to disclaim any sentiment associated with the institution of marriage? *Romantic puffery.* He'd gotten that much right: Mary and Edward were perfect specimens. It was clear that he assumed Hannah was like-minded on the subject and bore not a shred of sentiment. That she would view his offer as the only practical choice for a woman in her position, a reasonable outcome for two people bound by an intellectual passion and a shared community. All of which was true.

The longer she turned his proposal over in her mind, though, the more it troubled her. Dr Hall's age wasn't the problem. The intensity of his gaze at the engagement dinner and his grip on her arm at the Atheneum had demonstrated his vitality; he might as well have stood up and beaten on his chest. But as her thoughts drifted from the practicality of a union with him to sharing his bed, his small body in his nightclothes, his hands reaching for her under the covers, she shuddered, then shook her head to clear the grotesque vision.

Hannah brought her hands to her face and massaged her temples. She felt bruised all over from her night on the ground beside Isaac, and fatigue weighed on her as if her bones had turned to iron. How had she fallen to such a state? And why had she invited him to her house?

She should have told him to stay away. But it was already done.

Time is short, Isaac had said. Hannah needed to decide what lessons to retain, which to cast aside along with whatever feelings she harbored for the man. They were useless, possibly dangerous, and above all distracting. Rising from the bench, she made her way through the parlor and up the steps, feeling better the moment she entered the garret. This was where she belonged; the pure relief she felt among her books and instruments was like the cool of a pond on a scorching day.

But she'd barely gotten situated at the desk when she heard footfalls. Hannah jumped up, chin raised, clutching a sheaf of papers.

'Sorry to disturb,' Edward said, stepping into the room. He paused and looked around, his gaze hovering on the little window, then the rocking horse, and finally on Hannah herself.

'I thought so much of this room in my absence,' he said, walking to the shelf of minerals and checking its contents. He picked up half a geode the size of a sea urchin and studied its gleaming core, then put it back in a different place. 'I imagined you at work, bent over your equations, ever industrious. I was certain by the time I returned you'd have established priority on a bevy of new objects in the night sky.'

Hannah swallowed.

'I'm sorry to disappoint,' she said, scratching her neck. 'I can assure you it's not for lack of trying.'

'Hannah,' her twin said, stepping closer, then stopping. 'I feel that I need to say something to you. A few things, actually. But I don't quite know what to say. I think I ought to be angry with you for how you spoke to Mary. She wouldn't tell me what you said, but I don't think you were flattering her needlework.'

'No,' Hannah whispered.

'Well, I don't feel angry. If anything, I feel responsible for your horrible behavior.' Edward cracked his knuckles. The crunch of bone on bone made Hannah wince. 'Which is to say, I know you better than anyone in the world. I should have confided my plans. But I knew you would try and dissuade me. I might have been swayed.'

He began to pace the room in tight circles, past the desk and the collection shelf, the trunk and the staircase, the broken furniture, and back past the door again.

Hannah shook her head.

'I doubt I've any power to sway you. If I had, I'd have used it four years ago and stopped you from leaving –' She paused, cutting herself off. *Leaving me,* she'd almost said. The wound felt as fresh as if she'd found his empty trunk and hasty note only that morning, not four years earlier. He was the only person she'd ever felt herself with, shown her true feelings to. The sting of his abandonment still smarted. And he was doing it again. She'd never told him how she felt. Her gut twisted with the effort of containing her grief. Would it not be best to say nothing? Was that not what they had been taught?

Edward seated himself on the old stool. He was waiting for her to speak, as he always had. She owed him truth. Her chance was now or never.

'Why did you do it?' she whispered. A tear sprung into each eye, and she allowed them to fall.

'Oh, Hannah.' Edward's voice cracked. 'I had to. If I hadn't, my life would never have been my own. My path and yours are so different: I've no head for numbers, no aptitude for astronomy or maths. When I look at the Heavens, I fall asleep.'

Hannah smiled through the tears. She'd found him dreaming on the walk dozens of times.

'Father had my options laid out like a suit. It was accounting at the Bank or going to University, and you remember my marks. William Bond would have had to beg for my admittance anywhere, and I've no interest in sitting in a classroom anyway. I would have failed. But worse, I'd have been miserable. And an embarrassment to the Price name.' Edward's imitation of Nathaniel fell short; Hannah could see how much their father's disapproval pained him.

He leaned toward Hannah, reaching out with both his hands until she raised hers to clasp them. Even if he hadn't spoken another word, she would have forgiven him. How could she not? He was her twin. Denying him happiness would only compound her misery.

'Here's the thing,' Edward went on, keeping hold of her hands and looking her in the eye. 'I know that you are the most loyal and noble of sisters that ever did walk this Island or any other. I know that you think you know what course is best for me, and that you decided in your mind that Mary is not that thing. But you don't even know her. You've based all of your actions on assumptions rather than fact. If you did your work that way, every ship in the fleet would be wrecked in no time. Mary has always admired you. She told me a dozen times that she wishes she had an occupation that she could devote her mind to, something to which she could commit herself the way that you've committed yourself to the Heavens.'

He released Hannah's hands and stood up, running his hands through his hair and looking around for another place to settle. He sat down on the desk. Hannah frowned, but he swung his legs like a child.

'Of course, now she can commit herself to yours truly. But, more to the point, not only were you mean to Mary, which she will of course forgive, but I've heard talk of behavior that makes me question whether you really are my sister or an impostor with a remarkable resemblance.'

He reached out and rapped gently upon her head with his knuckles.

'Where are you, Hannah? What are you doing roaming about the Island with your student at all hours of the night, toting your telescope like a rifle? Do you think that thus armed you could ward off idle talk?'

He folded his arms across his chest and tilted his head at her.

Hannah felt her jaw drop and snapped it shut as she fished for a response. But even if she'd known what to say, she probably couldn't have choked out the words. The idea that her neighbors were observing her with two sets of eyes – friends and foes at once – and then whispering about her, slandering her, made her feel sick.

'Oh, don't look so stricken!' He reached out and mussed her hair as if they were talking about a schoolyard slight. 'It's me: Edward! I don't care a whit about your friends – and I'm assuming that you've taken this wayward sailor under your wing to nurture his latent navigational talents to the best of your ability.' He paused, as if considering which direction he wished to go.

'In any case, as I say, I trust that if you've befriended this person, whatever his hue, that you've good reason. But there are many hereabouts who do care. Enough that I've heard word of it two – no, three – times in the forty-eight hours I've been here.'

He shook his head and sighed.

'I'm supposed to do my brotherly duty here and warn you of this or that consequence: disownment, diminished prospects.' He pantomimed a gasp but then settled, serious again.

'All I really care about, though, is your happiness. And what makes you happy, Hannah, is work. I'm sorrier than you know that I cannot stay here and provide a base for you to keep on with your observations. I've thought on it for months, ever since I learned of Father's engagement. And if you must know, Mary thought we should stay. It was my decision to apply for the expedition.'

Hannah sank into her chair, grateful for the wood at her back. She looked at her brother, with whom she'd shared every moment of her life prior to his departure. There was no more familiar set of features, no frame more comforting than his own. That he would separate from her – that they would cleave like a tree with one trunk and two divergent branches – had never seemed possible. Yet he would go. She could not follow. Nor could she stay. She could not look him in the eye.

'You must do what your happiness dictates,' she said, her voice hoarse. She cleared her throat.

'I don't expect you to forgive me, but I hope you'll

understand. If not now, later. Staying here would be like clinging to the past instead of reaching for the future – for you as much as for myself. Even if you do move to Philadelphia, it won't be the end of your work, though I know you think it will be. If anything, there are more opportunities there; at least it's a city, not a tiny island mired in its own history.'

He moved toward the door.

'I'm going to meet Mary at John and Libby's, if you want to join us,' Edward went on, pausing on the top step. She knew he wanted her to look up, to give him a sign that she had understood.

She shook her head and turned her face toward the desk.

'I'm going to work,' she lied. 'But thank you.'

His feet pounded down the steps, the cadence loud and familiar. In all likelihood she'd not hear that rhythm again: he'd be gone before summer's end. As the footfalls faded, she wondered if she'd ever think of him again without feeling a hot iron pressing on her heart. But the lonely ache that accompanied that thought was almost more than she could bear.

16. Lunar Distance

Hannah waited for Isaac on the top step of the porch, her foot tap-tapping in time to an invisible chorus. When she saw him approach, she jumped up and slung her bag over her shoulder, then hurried down the path.

'We're walking.' Hannah ignored the dent of concern in his brow, and when he reached for her bag she held on to it. He was lugging a satchel of his own again, and it appeared full to bursting.

'Leave it,' she said. 'You've enough to carry.'

He shrugged and fell into step beside her, the early evening light muting the edges of everything in their path. She was careful to maintain a reasonable distance between them, and kept her head down and her gait quick. They walked an arm's length apart until they were well out of Town, and both were quiet until they emerged onto the tiny bay beach north of the harbor. The crescent of sand was empty. Lamps had just flickered on in the taverns by the wharves; Hannah could hear the laughter of men and the tinkle and clank of mugs filled with spirits.

Hannah released the pack and sighed, then unknotted the string and drew out the bundled parts of the Dollond, piecing it together with hands swift as gears. Tripod, tube, eyepiece: in a matter of two minutes, the telescope was assembled on a flat boulder that might have been dropped there by a giant for their use.

Then she turned to Isaac.

'All right, then, Mr Martin,' Hannah said, clearing all sentiment from her voice. 'As of this moment, we are no longer on land.'

He raised his eyebrows and crossed his arms over his chest.

'Where are we?'

'We are at sea, of course. Since time is short, we need to accelerate your training. In this exercise, I will act as first mate.'

'You?'

'That is correct. And you are the second mate. Which is your position. You shall assist in taking a lunar observation.'

Hannah kept her eyes on his shoulder and the landscape carved behind it: the roofs and steeples of Town, the flat edge of the harbor. The stars above.

'Yes, sir,' he said, then turned toward the sea. The orb of the moon had just risen above the horizon, silvering the foam of the breakers and the damp sand under their feet, painting everything pearly grey.

Hannah nodded toward the telescope.

'Do the necessary preparations and let me know when you're done. I'll use the sextant to take the angular distance of the moon and – What star might we use, this time of year, Mr Martin?'

He tilted his chin toward the sky.

'Capella. Are you –'

Hannah interrupted before he could ask anything she did not wish to answer. *Only the work,* she thought.

'Correct,' she said. 'I'll take the angle while you take the

altitude with the telescope once you've done the preparations.'

He stared at her for an agonizing series of seconds. She
could practically hear the tick of the metronome she'd
used as a child to help guide her as she counted seconds
for her father during transits.

She picked up Bowditch's *Navigator* and handed it
to him.

'Page 166,' she said.

He took it from her, then hunched over it, his back
toward her.

'Are we in west or east longitude?' he asked, cordial as a
shopkeeper. But he did not look at her again, and the current that had carried their conversation at the Atheneum
was gone. He'd made himself a stranger again, and Hannah wasn't sure why she felt sad when that was exactly
what she'd intended.

She paused.

'I don't know,' she said. 'Where do you want to be?'

'Home,' he said immediately.

Hannah imagined him rowing into his own island. Its
layered miracle of green upon green. His family greeting
him. Perhaps a girl. She imagined a woman with skin the
same hue as his, dark hair blown about by a warm wind,
free from the constraints of a bonnet the size of a pump-
kin. Light eyes that lit up when they saw him. A wad of
envy lodged in Hannah's throat. She saw them embrace,
felt his arms encircle the other woman. His chin tilting
toward her, his body leaning into hers.

'Fine,' Hannah snapped. 'West, then. Pretend you are a
day's sail from your own harbor, in fair wind.' The residue

of her jealousy was as grainy and unpleasant as a mouthful of sand.

Isaac nodded once, to acknowledge the instruction, then bent over the text and his copybook. Hannah couldn't see his face, but she imagined deep lines etched into his forehead where he squinted at the page. She drew out a pocket watch and waited for him to signal that he was ready.

She meant her voice to ring out, but it emerged as a whisper.

'Time,' she said. Her stomach tightened like a fist.

He recorded his time, and, a half moment later, the altitude of the moon according to the telescope. At the same moment, Hannah took the measurement of the moon's angle with her sextant and wrote it in her log.

She brought the log to him and handed it over, then returned to her seat and drew her book back into her lap. Isaac gave no indication of his state of mind.

Ten minutes later, after he'd pored over tables and minuscule numbers in the half-light, he brought his computations over to her. The instant she took the copybook, he sat down, unlaced his boots, rolled up his trouser legs, and stepped into the shallow water. For the next ten minutes, while she scrutinized his work, going back to the Bowditch and the telescope, repeating each of his steps, he stood in the water as if at anchor, gazing at the horizon.

'Well,' Hannah said when she'd finished going over the work, closed both books, and laid them one atop the other beside the Dollond, 'you've performed your duties admirably.'

Isaac stayed where he was, his back to her. Hannah took a few steps closer but stopped short of the water.

'Are you not happy? It's an advanced calculation you made.'

He folded his arms across his chest, something she noticed him do whenever he wasn't at ease. Everything – the shape of his shoulders and back, the surface of the water, the bubbling little waves rolling onto the shore – was silvered by the nearly full moon, which was rising quickly above the horizon. To the east, though, thunderheads had already gathered. A long minute passed before he turned toward her.

'What is happening?' he asked.

'What do you mean?' Hannah studied the ripples on the surface, each a tiny mirror of the sky above.

His voice softened.

'What is upsetting you?'

She shook her head and clamped her lips together, feeling like a stubborn child. But he could not possibly understand her feelings. She wasn't sure she understood them herself. Turning herself inside out would do nothing to advance her comfort. Already her life felt destabilized, like a boat tilting atop a wave. She felt unbalanced even thinking about what Edward had said. There was no point in discussing it with Isaac.

But he held his ground.

'Something is happening. I feel it.' He sucked in his breath through his teeth. When he spoke again there was a hard edge to his words. 'I am having eyes and understanding. Do you think that I am blind? Do you think I am a child?'

Hannah raised her head and crossed her own arms. 'I can't speak to you like this.' When he didn't come any closer, she reached down, unlaced and removed her boots, then drew off her stockings and hitched up her skirts, feeling as exposed by her bare knees and ankles as if she were naked. Then she waded out to where he stood.

'What is it you want me to say?' she asked, hating how blunt her words sounded.

'What is true. What is happening on this day. Why you are angry.'

'I'm not angry. Not with you.'

Isaac waited. His eyes narrowed as if he could see through her.

'Please. Don't look at me that way.' What if he could see into her? What would he see? Hannah bit her lip, wishing herself invisible, and a moment later just the opposite. She wanted him to see everything, and nothing. It made no sense at all. In any case, he had no right to ask for her thoughts. They were not his to claim, like a lost valise.

'This is a small Island, Mr Martin. People here speak of things they see, they speak to each other and then others know, too. People make assumptions. They draw false conclusions about what they have heard or seen, but know nothing of.'

She glanced around as if a group of people would materialize on the empty beach and assume that they were witnessing . . . what? A lover's quarrel?

'You are worried that people are seeing us this night? Together?'

'More than this night.' She let go of her skirts, not caring that they soaked through instantly, and unknotted the strings of her bonnet, which were cutting into her neck.

They stood a foot apart, facing each other. He was still in the water. The moon went behind a cloud, and she could not see his features clearly.

When he spoke again, his voice was stiff, as if belonging to someone else.

'I understand,' he said. 'You wish our lessons to cease.'

The wind changed. The ripples on the water reversed direction. More clouds appeared, scudding across the sky. Still they stood. Every second that ticked by felt like a door swinging shut.

'No,' she said, amazed that he didn't know that she felt exactly the opposite: that she wished to be near him all the time; that he distracted and perplexed her mind, taunting her with feelings she could not indulge. 'That is not what I wish for.'

How could he see her? She was hidden. Reaching up, she drew off her bonnet, holding it by the strings. It filled with air like a balloon. Without thinking about it, Hannah let go. It gusted away, then floated toward the beach like a poppy, airborne. The wind loosened her hair and blew it across her face. She raised her head, baring it to the elements as if she could purge her shame that way.

'What are you wishing?' Isaac asked. 'What do you want?'

'I want to be near you,' Hannah said. 'But I wish I didn't.'

She half hoped he hadn't heard. But his face told her that he had.

I've wounded him, she thought. She hadn't meant to. Her words had gone wrong. She should not have tried to reveal herself. Instead of stepping toward him, though, she turned away, sloshing back toward shore. The first raindrops fell, pelting her head and neck.

Isaac stayed where he was, even as she laced up her boots, rolled the telescope into its cloths, and shoved the books and the sextant and everything else into her satchel.

'Are you not coming back to Town?' she called, hunching her shoulders against the rain. Water streamed down her forehead and neck; her hair was soaked.

Thunder clapped and her heart jittered. Still he remained.

'Isaac!'

A flare of lightning lit the cove and the marsh and his face. He shook his head.

'You should be going,' he said.

'Are you staying here? It's unsafe. At least come out of the water.'

He crossed the distance between them in six long strides. Then his hands were on her shoulders. The rain spattered like the flutter of bat wings. He held on tightly, grasping her, his eyes angry and tender at the same time. Was he going to hit her? Kiss her? Hannah held her breath.

But he released her and stepped back as if snapping out of a dream. She exhaled, shivering.

'It is impossible,' he said.

'What do you mean? Just come off the beach –'

'No. Not this. You. You are – I cannot understand you. What you – why you are choosing –' He put his hands over his face, pressing his palms together as though he were praying. When he lowered them, the intensity was gone, as if he, too, had decided to abandon whatever it was he'd been trying to say. He took another step away from her. Instead of being relieved, Hannah felt a crushing disappointment.

'I am having nowhere else to go,' Isaac stated, as if announcing the catch of the day or the price of milk. He nodded at his bag. 'This is everything. I am sleeping where I find myself.'

He took another step away from her, as if they were doing a parlor dance.

'You've been sleeping outside?' Hannah asked. The idea of him without shelter against the rain and wind made her shiver more violently.

'It's not important,' he said.

'It isn't right.'

Isaac shrugged. The rain came harder, beginning to soak.

'My room at the boardinghouse is becoming unavailable,' he said. 'She does not say why.'

Hannah stared at him, blinking away the water.

'Come with me,' she said, swinging the bag around so she could hug it to her body, protecting the telescope.

He shook his head.

'Already you are suffering,' he said. 'I will not create more trouble.'

'It's not important,' she echoed. They stared at each other. She'd failed to reveal herself in words, in deed. He could not see her, after all. She should be relieved. *Walk away,* she thought. Leave it here.

Instead, she reached for Isaac's hand. When she made

contact, clarity flooded through her. He looked as surprised as she felt, but he gave his hand to her. She weighed it in hers, imagining the delicate systems within. Blood, nerve, bone. She curled her fingers around his.

They walked this way until they reached the edge of Town. When he let go, it felt like losing a limb. The streets were empty, the paving stones slick and rippling. She couldn't hear the bell ring on Riddell's store when she entered, and she paid no attention to the mailbags as she reached into her letterbox for the key to the Atheneum and handed it to Isaac.

'It works on the side door as well,' she said. 'Be out by dawn and replace it here in the morning.'

'If I'm caught? I'll be arrested.' He shook his head.

'I'll vouch for you.'

In the doorway they paused. She had to go right and he left.

'I'll meet you at the Atheneum tomorrow, after midnight,' she said. 'We can finish our lessons there.'

He nodded, saying nothing. The last thing she saw before she turned toward home was the black glint of the wet key in his hand.

17. Conflict

For the next two weeks, Hannah and Isaac fell into a routine that neither of them acknowledged would ever change or alter. Hannah's daytime orbit maintained its usual course. Isaac slipped into the library well after dark each day, when borrowers and lecturers had all gone home. Each night, Hannah imagined him stretched out on one of the benches, contemplating his home, the Heavens, the journey before him.

They didn't speak about the hours that stretched between their meetings. On the nights she came to the side door and slipped inside the cottony silence of the Atheneum to sit beside him on the floor between the stacks like islands upon a planked wooden sea, they pored over equations for everything from latitude by double altitudes to methods for finding the apparent time at sea. He did not touch her during those weeks. Nor did he revisit their words to each other the night of the storm. They did not speak of what would become of them during his absence. She did not talk about Philadelphia. He did not mention the *Pearl*.

Instead, they floated upon the cushioned nights among the books. When her lectures exhausted them, she read out loud from an array of texts: more of Humboldt's *Cosmos*. Mr Emerson's 'Character' – though she hesitated before showing him the image of the man he'd reminded her of the first day they had walked together through Town. But he did not laugh at the comparison to an English nobleman. Nor was he offended. He took the book from her and bent over the image, examining it as if it were being presented as evidence at a trial.

'Fascinating,' Isaac said after a full two minutes of scrutiny. 'He is a white man, no?'

'Clearly, yes,' Hannah said, uncertain of his meaning. 'He is English.'

'My great-grandfather was English,' Isaac said. 'Maybe we are relating.'

'I doubt you're related to Lord Chatham,' Hannah said. 'But I wasn't suggesting you resembled him directly. You've some aspect in common that's not specific to your features. The way you carry yourself.'

'Why would we not be re-lay-ted?'

'Well, for starters, he is white and you are . . . not,' Hannah said, feeling a little foolish but sticking to the facts.

Isaac leaned back on his elbows and tilted his head at her like a barn owl, then shook it as if he were very sorry for her.

'What?'

'Black or white. This or that. How are you believing that all things proceed in this way?' he asked. He looked as if he were about to laugh, but his chin pointed at her like a challenge.

'I'm only stating the truth,' Hannah said. She frowned at the book in her lap, but its sentences and paragraphs ran together.

'I am not white. He is not black.' He held out a palm for each word, as though they were pieces of fruit she was to choose. 'Everywhere in this world, even on this Island – especially here – people are not one or the other. Are you never seeing people the color of wood? The color of honey? The color of . . . *amêndoa*.'

She shook her head.

Isaac hesitated, tasting for the word.

'Al-mond,' he pronounced, and wagged his finger at her. 'Only people your color are thinking everyone else is one thing and they are another.'

'And in your few months here you've become an expert in what all white people think?' Insulted to be lumped together with every pale denizen of the Island, regardless of their education – not to mention the world at large – Hannah rose and took the book back to the philosophy section, reshelving it with a satisfying hiss of leather on leather.

'My opinions are forming before I am coming here, Miss Price,' Isaac said, assuming a serious posture. 'But since I am losing my place to work, and also my room, I am beginning to understand better.'

'You think it's because you're not white,' Hannah said, crossing her arms. 'But there are dozens of black families that have lived here, and been employed here, for decades. As long as my own family, in some cases. The Friends were first among those who freed their slaves voluntarily –'

'So you are saying before.'

'We are categorically against human bondage.'

'I was not speaking of this. Why do you?'

'You're speaking uncharitably about my people.' Hannah felt her spine stiffen.

'You say you speak only in truth. Yet you know that your people are sending the black children to different schools than the white children. Your people are throwing rocks at those who speak here against slavery.' Isaac's choice of words sounded like an accusation, and Hannah felt a storm brewing in her throat.

'That only happened one time,' she stated. 'And it happened because Mr Garrison spoke ill of religion, not because he encouraged manumission.'

'Your people are hoping that I will be disappearing. They are helping me to disappear,' he went on, as if it were obvious. The bitterness in his voice was unmistakable. 'And you are thinking this is for another reason than my color? And our . . . arrangement?' He held out his hands.

Her mouth snapped shut. She wanted to tell him that the schools committee did not represent the majority view of Islanders. That a white Friend and barrister had helped the African community petition the Commonwealth on the matter of school segregation. That she had not noticed the whispers that seemed to float in her wake like veils in recent days.

'That cannot be,' she said instead. 'People of every color are welcome on this Island.'

'If it is being profitable,' he answered, clicking his tongue as if she were a schoolgirl. 'And if it is not crossing the Newtown Gate. Especially at night. With one of its daughters.'

The sharpness of his words surprised her, and though he hadn't raised his voice, Hannah felt as if she was under attack. Isaac Martin had spent only a few months on Nantucket; she'd been here her whole life. How dare he question its people, their principles? Had her people not employed him, even advanced him? Had they not offered him opportunity when they might have passed him over? Had she not done the same?

'I think, Mr Martin, that you do not understand this place. We try to live according to Discipline, which prohibits interaction with the world's people so as not to distract us from our spiritual duties. Many people here don't accept those who take too much action on behalf of social causes for that reason, though their underlying beliefs be the same. Of course, there are some who hold that the races are different in nature. That the children of savages cannot learn as well as the children of civilized people. But most of us – like most reasonable people – do not believe that. It's been proven that they can, given the opportunity.

'And furthermore,' she tacked on, feeling as if her lecture was falling flat even as her temper rose like mercury, 'doors on this Island opened to those fleeing oppression even when it was not prudent, when it might have endangered the families therein. Even this door right here is open to you,' Hannah said nodding in its direction. 'In daylight, you may attend lectures here. You may improve yourself along with any other resident. Should you so choose.'

Isaac shrugged. She could read no emotion on his face, though his eyebrows raised slightly.

'The children of savages?' He looked around, as if a pack of wild animal children were about to spring out from behind the gardening section. 'If I am having children, will they be savages?'

'Of course not!' Was he purposefully misinterpreting her words? 'That's absurd. Why would I believe such a thing?'

'I think you are not knowing what you believe,' he said, and shook his head again. 'What you are saying is only what you have been teach. Taught. That what does not look like you or sound like you or pray like you is bringing danger.'

He wiggled his fingers in her direction as if summoning a bogeyman.

'At least I can say that I believe something. That I'm guided by clear principles. What guides you, Mr Martin? You wander about the globe hunting whales, earning a living, but what is the larger purpose? What might you contribute to the betterment of society? What knowledge?' Hannah hated how her voice had risen to shrill, but his casual posture – leaning back on his elbows, one ankle crossed comfortably over the other – was infuriating. He was utterly lacking in respect.

Isaac sighed as if he found her position amusing but tiresome.

'I am not thinking that knowledge is my contribution to this world. I have traveled the world, I have earned my place, I have advance to this position. Now . . . I am here.'

He tapped the floor of the Atheneum with his knuckle. The hollow knock echoed.

'Can that be all you aspire to? All you wish for?'

He tilted his head at her like a portraitist seeking a new angle.

'You did not ask what I wish for.'

'No. I did not.' She paused, the question drifting between them like a feather.

'I am not wishing for anything,' Isaac finally said. 'I am not a child, imagining a life that cannot be. Dreaming without purpose. I have hopes: that my family is well, that their harvest is strong. That the *Pearl* will have a good crew, fair winds. That I will earn what I deserve, so that I can go home. That I can walk the way that we are walking, with earth beneath my feet. I have hopes. I have desire. But wishes – no.'

He patted the floor beside him, then held out his hand to her, like an elder beckoning to an errant child at Meeting. One who had strayed, by accident or intention. The smugness of the gesture wounded her more than his words. Did he think he could dismiss her very principles with a pat of his hand? That she, too, should live without goals, abandoning her values, in favor of . . . what?

She stared at him, her eyes burning. He'd abused her community, accused her of parroting their teachings. Called them hypocrites. He was an empty shell; he was godless and errant; she desired him and detested him. He was wrong about everything. He was right, and it was awful.

Each time she was with Isaac, she lost hold of herself. The feeling that her foundation was unsound was terrifying. Hannah did the only thing she knew how to do in the face of such confusion. She turned away and went through the door into the dark night without saying another word. But as she strode away from the Atheneum, she felt anything but satisfied.

18. Changing Weather

Hannah kept her head down as she walked toward the Atheneum the next morning. The air was humid, thick with fog. Her neighbors were indistinct blurs across Main Street, dark smudges that hummed and moved. She'd been up most of the night after leaving Isaac, turning like a leaf in the wind for hours, unable to sleep. In her half-conscious state, his words took on different meanings each time she reheard them. Accusation, admonition, lullaby: *This is what you have been taught,* he said, again and again, until dawn broke, grey and heavy as her dress, as her heart.

She barely looked up until she reached Riddell's store. As she approached the familiar porch, its steps bowed by the weight of hope, a blurry crowd resolved, then parted as she stepped on to the stoop. Margaret Granger, Karen Pope, Aliza Starbuck, and two or three others fell silent as Hannah passed.

'Good morning,' Hannah mumbled. No one responded, though Margaret nodded a curt acknowledgment, then ducked her head, quick as a plover. Hannah pushed on into the store, wondering what had put everyone in such a foul humor. The bell broke the hush with its harsh jangle.

She hadn't checked the letterbox in days, but was still surprised to find not one but two folded pieces of parchment inside. One bore George Bond's familiar scrawl; the other had nothing but her name inscribed on it in carefully blocked print. It bore no return address or any other indication of its origin. Clutching both, she went back out onto the porch and settled on the top step to unfold George's missive, ignoring the small flock of women still gathered by the railing.

10 June 1845. Cambridge.

Dear Hannah, Forgive the short, and late, nature of this Letter. We have been back and forth to Ohio two times this month, to assist Mr Loomis, and I have also been sent to Washington, so time for letter-writing has been scant. But good news! Which I'm sure thy father has already carried home to you – Nantucket shall have a place in the Survey this coming year, and the Survey itself shall be overseen not by your Favorite shepherd of Good Works, Lieutenant Phillips, but by Admiral Davis himself, who has a well-deserved reputation as a man of Science and also is a very decent fellow.

She scowled. This wasn't necessarily good news; her father still hadn't decided whether or not they'd accept the contract. She'd inquired about it once since the day of Edward's return, and been informed that she would be told when he'd settled his mind on the matter. As if it were of no more consequence than whether he preferred chowder to broth for supper. Hannah gasped when she read the postscript:

PS: *Monsieur Rainault in Paris has established priority on a new comet he sighted in May, sometime around the 19th – just announced in Astronomiche Nasrichten. R. A. 16h 29m 24s Did you not mention that you observed a body near Antares around then, just before you came to Cambridge? I wonder if it was the same.*

Her hand flew to her mouth. The object she'd been observing in May *had* been close to Antares. The idea that she might have seen – but not reported – an actual comet was horrifying. She'd have to go back into her logs. There wasn't enough time before work, but she couldn't last an entire day without knowing. The eyes of the women on the porch bore into her as she leapt to her feet.

She ran all the way home, skirts flying, ignoring the stares of passersby and her wildly beating heart, flung open the front door, and raced up to the garret without even pausing to remove her bonnet. She shoved aside the flotsam that littered her desk, not caring about the papers and quills that flew to the ground. Where was the log? She paged through the volume with frantic haste.

Here: she scanned the entry quickly, then unfolded the page from George again, staring at it until the letters and numbers blurred. A ragged sob caught in her throat, but she choked it back. The object she'd seen was undoubtedly the same body that would bear the name of the French astronomer who had first reported it. It was too late for her to claim priority. The idea that she had found a comet after all – and found it first! – wasn't comforting in the least. What were the chances of it happening twice? She'd likely lost her only chance for recognition.

Hannah sank into her chair, drained. The other note, which she'd forgotten about, poked her in the thigh. She unfolded it.

A single line unspooled across the page.

WHERE IS YOUR KEY? – *A Friend.*

A blanket of needles rose from Hannah's toes to her throat in a matter of seconds. She looked up and around as though someone were playing a prank. But she was alone in the garret.

It was heavy stock, not a student's copy page. And the handwriting was neat and firm, blocked out in square, purposeful capital letters. An adult's work, not a child's. As she stared at it, the letters began to squirm, and she folded it up quickly, fighting the urge to shred it to pieces. Anger overtook her fear like a shark snapping up a minnow. Who would dare send such an outrageous, cowardly thing?

Hannah leapt to her feet and stormed down the stairs, forgetting about her lost comet in her haste to return to Riddell's store. The women on the porch were still absorbed in their chatter, and none looked up, though Aliza Starbuck glanced in her direction, then whispered something to the others.

She pushed open the door so hard that the bell nearly flew off its little hook. Mrs Riddell and the other two patrons stopped what they were doing to turn and stare. Forcing her feet forward, Hannah shuffled to the desk. Mrs Riddell's skin was dust yellow, like a paper ghost. Her hands were gnarled with age, but she sorted the stacks of parchment with the professional speed of a faro banker. She didn't smile. Had she ever? Hannah couldn't recall. She leaned closer, hoping to keep the conversation private, and cleared her throat.

'Does thee recall seeing anyone put a note in my box of late?' she asked.

'I don't track comings and goings,' the woman answered, barely pausing as she sorted the pile of mail. Her hands flew. 'Especially after hours.'

The woman raised her watery blue eyes to glance at Hannah. In the instant they made contact, Hannah saw an unmistakable glint of contempt. Then she turned away and tilted her chin at the person behind Hannah.

'Can I help you?' she asked.

Hannah stepped aside, grateful to be hidden again behind the wall of letterboxes, and, with her back to the door, reached inside her box again, feeling around with her fingertips. The key was not there. Hannah's mouth and throat went dry, though she wasn't sure if her fear was for herself or for Isaac. She'd told him to return the key, and she assumed he would do so. Either he'd ignored her instruction, or someone else had taken it from her box. Pulling her hand back and tucking it into her pocket, she curled it around the offensive note and went back into the street.

Not one person she encountered between Main and Fair had a greeting or comment, for which Hannah would normally be grateful. But now the silence seemed ominous, as if every passerby knew or imagined something about her, or about Isaac, that would cause trouble for them both. But when her thoughts tumbled too far ahead, she reined them in, forcing herself to focus on the cobblestones at her feet, the filing that lay ahead. The idea that one person on Nantucket knew about her and Isaac and saw fit to communicate it via anonymous note was bad enough. The thought that everyone knew was too much to contemplate.

In daylight, the Atheneum seemed too bright, like fresh paint on old wood. As she sorted through the pile of paper on her desk, the crawl of script across the pages swam. Even Miss Norris, who was usually in good spirits no matter what the day held, seemed agitated.

'Thee is late again, Miss Price,' she clucked as Hannah slid into her seat.

Hannah glanced at the clock. It was seven minutes past the hour.

'I'm sorry,' she said, drawing off her bonnet and smoothing her hair.

The senior librarian pursed her lips and fondled her key-ring, which was as spindly as a sea urchin.

'Also,' Miss Norris said, 'I've found a number of volumes out of place in the last week or two.'

The woman shoved a frayed copy of Margaret Fuller's *Woman in the Nineteenth Century* at Hannah like an accusation.

'I found this in the natural history section.'

'I see. I'll reshelve it.'

'And there were three pattern books among the gardening volumes.'

Hannah rubbed her forehead.

'Is thee all right, Miss Price? Is anything troubling thee? It's unlike thee to be inattentive to thy duties.'

'I'm quite fine, Miss Norris. I slept poorly, is all.'

She squinted at Hannah over the bridge of her eyeglasses.

'Thee ought to try a tonic, dear. And leave off some of thy other activities. One cannot be distracted in this job. Detail, detail.' Miss Norris' neck pecked forward to emphasize each syllable.

'It's everything, yes, I know. I apologize.'

Only when Miss Norris had clinked away with her keys and her pamphlets did Hannah wonder what 'activities' she was referring to. Could she have written the note? It seemed unlikely. Miss Norris might be provincial, even narrow-minded, but she wasn't the sort of person who would creep about penning anonymous threats. The more she thought on it, the more opaque the identity of the note writer became. Nantucket people – Friends especially – were known to be forthright. No one she knew would deliver his or her thoughts in such a stealthy way. It stood to reason that the culprit was an off-Islander with some grudge against Isaac or herself, or a youngster up to a prank. Her arrival at this conclusion didn't offer any comfort, though, and she had to force herself to focus on the tasks at hand.

All the rest of the day, Hannah felt surrounded by an invisible, impenetrable fog. Patrons who normally swarmed around her desk for assistance drifted by or wandered around the shelves on their own. Even the widows, who came for company and to hear their voices bounce off another human being instead of their cats and bedposts, seemed to be avoiding her. Only the children were themselves – buoyant, noisy, ever in need of a handkerchief and a watchful eye on their reading material.

By four o'clock, when she closed the door behind her and walked toward home, Hannah was certain that fatigue was playing tricks on her mind. Ann Folger, who usually twittered on until Hannah made any excuse to get away, glanced up as she approached, then dashed across the street. John and Lilian Archer, who were strolling arm in arm down Vestal, nodded as Hannah approached, and she smiled, relieved – but then Lilian whispered something to her husband, who shook his head and seemed to pull her past. Lilian must have shaken free, for a moment later she was back.

'Hannah Price,' she breathed, bright-eyed, as if Hannah were a theater star just emerged from the stage door, and seized her hand.

'Lilian,' Hannah nodded, and squeezed back, hoping the woman would release her. 'How are you?'

'Well, very well. Excellent, really. You know, the Anti-Slavery Society is planning a major event here, on the Island. The regional meeting! A major event, as I said.'

'I thought the Society had a difficult time finding a big enough meeting space,' Hannah answered, tugging to get her arm back. 'Since the trouble a few years ago, I mean.'

'Well, that's why I wanted to speak with you,' Lilian gushed, moving her hand to Hannah's elbow. She was at least a foot shorter than Hannah, and clung to her arm like a child. 'We thought perhaps you could help with the Atheneum's trustees. To persuade them that the rightness of our cause should prevail over fear of what a few uncivilized individuals may attempt.'

Hannah was confused. She'd never attended any meetings and had avoided even those speakers who might have engaged her in another context. Their stridency offended her sense of propriety; Hannah was certain that if the minds of men were to be moved, no amount of haranguing would do the job. They had to change because their consciences moved them to it. And that was only accomplished by devotion – to whatever spiritual law one adhered to. To family. To work. Industry brought clarity.

Hannah yanked her arm free. Why on earth would Lilian mistake her for an agitator?

'I've no influence with the Atheneum's trustees, I'm afraid,' she said. 'And I'm certain they'd not risk the collections by hosting such an assembly. What if there were a repeat of what happened in Philadelphia?' Everyone knew about the burning of Constitution Hall during an antislavery rally inside – how close Lucretia Mott and her family had come to being burned alive.

'Oh.' Lilian dropped her hand and glanced back at John, whose arms were folded across his chest. His head was cocked and his eyebrows raised; a caption under a caricature of his stance could only read, *What did you expect?*

She looked back at Hannah and smoothed her crumpled sleeve.

'Well, I hope we see you at a Society meeting soon,' she said. 'The more supporters of our cause that take action, as you have, the better for all of us!' Lilian leaned in and raised herself to her tiptoes, aiming her next whisper at Hannah's ear.

'Don't be swayed by the chatter of idle tongues! Keep up your work!'

And then she rushed off to join John, though he didn't offer his arm again. Hannah watched them go down the street in the diminishing light, fear ticking erratically in her stomach.

By the time she reached home, Hannah was desperate to speak with Edward. But the house was quiet. The newlyweds' trunk loomed in the hallway like an unwanted guest, waiting for the things they'd purchased at the outfitters' in New Bedford. She contemplated going somewhere else, to check her creeping assumptions against an objective mind. But she could think of no one except Isaac Martin. And she wasn't ready to see him yet. She had no interest in further debating her nature and beliefs with him – especially not today – and doubting herself further could not possibly lead in the direction she wished to go. It was work that would brighten her mood and lift her spirit.

Hannah went into the kitchen, grabbed the last of the morning's graham bread from the kitchen counter, and, in her rush to get upstairs, knocked over the cup of cold tea she'd left sitting on the table the previous afternoon. It clattered to the floor, its contents soaking her skirts and her left foot. Groaning, she dumped her food on the table, mopped up what she could, and then, holding her soggy hem in her hands and muttering to herself, ran upstairs to change her stockings.

She didn't see Mary round the landing, her arms piled high with a tower of stacked and folded linens, until they collided on the second step.

'Oh!' Half the pile tumbled from Mary's arms, the cloths unfurling like sails. She swayed, one arm flailing like a rudder, and Hannah reached out and grabbed it, holding on until Mary steadied. When Hannah's pulse slowed, she released her grip, and Mary burst out laughing.

'So you don't wish me dead after all,' she said, and sighed with mock relief.

'Oh, I'm kidding! I'm only kidding,' she added, seeing Hannah's face, which must have reflected her horror. She patted Hannah on the arm like a grandmother, then began gathering up the cloths as if nothing had happened.

Hannah wasn't sure what to say. She hadn't seen Mary since the engagement dinner two weeks earlier, though Mary had left her looping, high-bridged cursive signature – *Mary Coffey Price, Mary Coffey Price, Mary Coffey Price* – lying around on so many receipts, letters, and bills of sale that Hannah could probably forge it perfectly. Every time Hannah had seen the signature, it felt like an accusation, but there hadn't been a private moment in which she could try and express her regret for the outburst the night of the dinner. She'd never been fond of apologies: they seemed insincere, a vain attempt to earn a reprieve for one's lack of control or poor behavior. Now that she was in the strange position of owing one, she had no idea how to begin. Feeling paralyzed, she watched Mary gather up the napkins and towels for a moment, then forced herself to stoop down and help.

'I'm sorry,' Hannah muttered. 'I wasn't looking.'

'No, I'm sorry. I was blinded by washing. It's my fault.' Mary rose and carefully shifted the pile from one arm to the other.

Her own arms full of sweet-smelling, slightly damp cloth, Hannah stood awkwardly on the step.

'Have you . . . did you find everything you needed? In New Bedford?' she asked, grasping for some neutral topic.

Mary nodded, gathering the pieces one by one in her free arm and laying them atop her pile.

'We did, thank you. Though of course we're limited by

budget and space. We've got to fit a year's worth of – well, everything – into that trunk down there.'

Both women stared down at the old sea trunk, which loomed between door and landing. Hannah wondered when Edward had taken it down from the garret, and what he'd done with the things therein. She'd only gone into the trunk one time, when she was sixteen, and some embarrassment – real or imagined – had sent her fleeing to the privacy of the garret and into her mother's trunk.

The sweet decaying smell and the sting of vinegar had risen from it when she creaked it open, a veil of dust wafting through the glow cast by the candle. There had been letters, bundled neatly in a stack, but Hannah had allowed her hands to fall into the soft cloths beneath them, swimming down into the depths. Napkins and runners, the slippery silk of a gown, the soft wool of a shawl in a rich earth-brown hue – not knowing what she was feeling for, Hannah had worked her way down, toward the bottom, until her fingers closed around the hard edges of a book. Hannah had caught her breath and leaned back on the trunk, paging through the slender volume as if it contained revelation itself.

But the journal had been a mere chronicle of a young wife's everyday life, in agonizing domestic detail. There were lists of items to be bartered, sold or bought; recipes for chowder and pie; tatting patterns and herbal remedies. There were almost no insights into the writer's mind, nothing about her hopes and desires and dreams. No wisdom for a lonely daughter. Hannah had returned the book to the trunk along with the yellowing papers and swaths of linen and silk, her longing for the guidance of a ghost muted by disappointment.

What had Edward done with their mother's things? Given them to Mary? Piled them in a corner? It shouldn't matter. Hannah had no use for wedding things. But the idea hurt like a paper-cut, sharp and invisible.

'I've wanted to speak with you,' Hannah said stiffly. She folded the remaining napkin into an imperfect square, then shook it out and began again. 'But I haven't had the chance.'

'You're like a spirit, wisping round. We've wondered when we'd catch you,' Mary answered, patting the pile like it was a baby.

'I regret what I said to you the night of your announcement.' The words sounded more formal than Hannah meant them to. 'I was not myself.'

'I understand,' Mary said at once, placing the entire stack down on the top step and seizing Hannah's arm. 'I've wanted to speak with you, too. It was thoughtless of us to have sprung it all upon you that way. We shouldn't have. We got carried away.'

Hannah felt like a marionette, her wooden limbs and pins stiff with age. She managed to nod but could not summon the warmth in her voice that was called for.

'Edward must do what is right for him. For you both.'

Mary unleashed a dramatic sigh and shook her head. Her golden curls bounced back and forth.

'Hannah, you don't need to make a brave effort. I know it must pain you greatly.'

She dropped down onto a step and patted the space next to her. Hannah forced herself to gather her skirts and sit down, though she longed to flee to the garret, where quiet waited.

'I, too, am sorry, for what I said to you. But it's still true: you do judge everyone. Or you seem to. Especially me. I've always admired your intellect, and your work. My entire life I wished for an occupation like yours, something I could practice and improve upon, commit myself to. But my family offered me little in the way of intellectual opportunity. Of course, I did all right in school – but they disapproved of me speaking at Meeting, even when I wanted to. I was invited to Debate in other cities, at other Societies.' She glanced sideways at Hannah, as if she was afraid to seem boastful. 'But my parents felt my prospects were best served by perfecting my manners and my tatting.' Mary's disdain was clear.

A gust of surprise swept through Hannah. She'd never imagined Mary as a woman who felt hemmed in by circumstance, nor one who resented her situation.

'Edward is the first person I ever met who treated me like I was smart, who saw me clearly,' Mary continued, her voice now edged with a challenge. 'This journey – it's not only for him. It isn't ill considered. And I don't expect or need servants.'

'I understand,' Hannah said, and meant it. She'd seen the work of Mary's hands. And her eloquence reminded Hannah of Edward's comments about her Debating skill, and how Hannah had dismissed it. The notion that she'd been entirely wrong was humbling and humiliating in equal parts. Hannah sighed, giving in to the idea. It made her feel oddly free.

'At least you did perfect those things,' she said. 'I never

did. If I hadn't had astronomy, I'd have – well, I don't know what I would have done. It's always been there.'

'It's a calling,' Mary said, so sincerely that Hannah felt a rush of actual affection, though her enthusiasm was a bit cloying. 'I'm glad for you. And I'm sorry I was unkind. I've no wish to wound you. We're sisters now. I know you've no experience with that strange state, but I do. I'll have to teach you.'

This sudden intimacy was so unlikely it seemed comical. Hannah snorted, trying to stifle a laugh, but that only made the compulsion to giggle even stronger.

'Is this going to require a show of sentiment or some sort of feminine ritual?' she sputtered. 'I'm afraid I'll be a total failure at either.'

'Neither nor.' Mary straightened her back and stretched her neck. 'In fact, it requires nothing other than what's already occurred.'

'What's occurred?'

Mary began to gather up her linens again.

'Well, we've said cruel and unhappy things to each other, and been forced to live together without speaking, and we've both suffered from the idea of the other, and that we'll have to share Edward forever because we both love him.'

'And?' Now Hannah felt threatened by tears, and she swallowed fiercely to drive them back. What was the matter with her lately? Her emotions seemed to be staging a revolt she couldn't put down. She wished she could hide her face, but there was nowhere to go. Mary moved up a step so that they were eye to eye, not six inches from each other.

'And,' Mary said, her gaze locked on Hannah's, 'we'll continue to do so, but eventually we'll love each other, because we must, and because it's the only outcome that's reasonable, and you, Hannah Price, are the most reasonable person I've ever known, in spite of your horribly critical nature and your utter lack of personal style.'

It was like listening to Edward. Suddenly Hannah saw why her twin loved Mary and why she loved him back.

'And you, Mary Coffey, have turned out to be a good deal deeper than your shallow exterior promised. You're right about one thing especially.'

'What's that?'

'I've no idea how to be a woman's sister.'

Mary sighed, and bowed her head a tiny bit so that her forehead touched Hannah's for a split second. Before Hannah could absorb or react to the tender gesture, though, Mary had moved down a step, breaking the bond.

'It's a shame you'll only have a few weeks to practice,' she trilled as she passed, but her eyes were sorry, and Hannah felt a tug of sadness, too.

When she finally pushed out onto the roof, the sky was a cloudless expanse of deepest blue, moonless and pulsating with distant stars. A clear night sky onto which she could pour all of her attention and pin all of her hopes – this was her reward and her respite. Turning her attention to the telescope, she trained her eyes on the Heavens.

19. The World's People

Ah, Meeting,' Edward said on First Day the following week, yawning. 'How I've missed the opportunity to study my neighbors for hours, waiting for one to share a revelation that occurred to them as they stirred their tea or forked hay.' He assumed a theatrical pose, hand to ear, and cocked his chin at the ceiling. '"Neighbors, this day I did envision that my heart has been too hard in the matter of my son Barney's affection for fiddle music."'

'Edward.' Mary shook her head and swatted him with a napkin. Then she went back to brushing the crumbs from the table. 'You should take a lesson from Hannah. She goes to Meeting faithfully, as do I. It wouldn't hurt you to sit still for a few hours and settle your mind. It darts like a hummingbird from one thought to the next.'

'I cannot agree,' he answered, sweeping her into his lap. 'It would be immensely painful and cause untold suffering. Plus, has anyone been outside? We should take the advice of this intrepid entrepreneur.' He tapped a finger on the copy of the *Nantucket Inquirer* that was open on the table. 'In his advertisement here he claims that Sea Bathing is not only "a delightful indulgence" but also "necessary" and "invigorating."'

'Ugh.' Mary wiggled free. 'The thought of joining the hordes of invaders stampeding our lovely beaches all season makes me ill. I wish they could all be contained to one corner of the Island, and leave the rest of it for us.'

Hannah smiled, but studied the grain on the table until Edward released his wife. Mary straightened her apron and flipped the johnnycakes. Their intimacy made her ache: when their ship left port in just a few days' time, they'd go over the horizon together, while she remained behind. Nantucket had always been the only home she ever wanted or knew. Now it loomed in her imagination like a desert island.

'All right, ladies, I shall attend,' Edward said, looking alarmed by Hannah's expression. 'But don't be surprised if there's a general outcry when I appear in the Meeting House. The rafters may fall with the weight of the assembly's dismay. Prodigal son and all that.'

Hannah thought she ought to say something comforting, but there wasn't much to add. In the three weeks since the engagement dinner, their father had spent only two nights at the house, and one of those she'd been at the Atheneum with Isaac and hadn't seen him at all. She'd seized the other as a chance to mend the rift between the two Price men before it was too late.

The only reason her father and Edward had even come together at the dinner table was because Hannah didn't tell either that the other would be present. She'd hatched the plan the instant her father had come through the door with his valise and ledger, obviously exhausted from his travels.

'I planned to take the evening packet back,' he said as

she dried her hands and helped him off with his jacket, though he sighed with relief when he had hung his hat on the rack and unlaced his boots.

'I haven't had a chance to speak with thee of late,' Hannah had said carefully. 'Stay for supper. I've questions for thee. About . . .' She rifled through her mental files for something to dangle before him. '. . . a chronometer. It's been giving me trouble. I thought thee might have a look.'

He ran a hand through his hair, which needed trimming again.

'In this season? What ship is it attached to?'

Hannah fumbled for an answer, annoyed by her own lack of imagination as much as her anxiety. It wasn't an alibi for some grave offense, after all. But she couldn't think of any ship's name but the *Regiment* — the last ship on earth she wished to name in his presence.

'I'll bring it down when thee has washed up,' she answered. 'I've got something on the stove.'

Rushing to the kitchen, she flung the big black pot on the fire, frantically blew the embers to life under it, and managed to get some water and potatoes inside before he came through the door. He didn't seem to notice the smoke, or the fact that nothing smelled like supper. But he hovered instead of settling, wary as an animal, shifting in his seat every time the wind knocked the shutter. His discomfort was shattering: he clearly didn't want to see Edward, though Hannah held on to the idea that if they all sat down together, everything would be set right.

In an effort to prevent him from leaving, Hannah produced a chronometer with a loose spring from the garret, which he easily set to right; then she brought down the new copy of *Silliman's*, then the latest *Proceedings of the American Philosophical Society*. In between, she threw things into the pot – a carrot, an onion, two mealy tomatoes, and the half bucket of clams Edward and Mary had collected at Madaket that morning. Too much salt, not enough butter – she barely knew what she was doing. It was ridiculous, she thought, tasting the stew and then throwing in two more potatoes, hoping they'd absorb the salt. They were a *family*. But they no longer felt like one.

Edward and Mary blew in at sunset, their laughter pealing through the house. When the door slammed, Hannah winced, blood thrumming in her cheeks. Her father looked as though he'd eaten something bad, though she was relieved that he had the courtesy to arrange his features less offensively as the couple entered the kitchen.

'Nathaniel! How wonderful to see thee!' Mary hardly paused for an instant before she crossed the kitchen to offer her hand to Nathaniel, who returned her affectionate squeeze with an awkward pat.

'Father.' Edward stayed in the doorway, stooping slightly to avoid hitting his head on the frame. 'Has the Bank given thee time off for good behavior?'

Nathaniel glanced at Hannah, who was saved by Mary.

'It's wonderful that we can dine together as a family,' she chimed. 'I'll set the table. Hannah, can I assist? Is there bread?'

In the bustle and clatter of seating and serving, Hannah was grateful for her sister-in-law's ability to talk for all of them with no apparent effort. When they were all finally facing each other across the table, there was a lull as everyone spooned their stew at once. Hannah blew on hers and looked up to find Edward looking back at her. He raised his eyebrows, and she willed him to exhibit a crumb of deference.

'The commander of Edward's expedition to Jerusalem was with Franklin in Alaska,' Hannah said in her father's direction when she'd managed to swallow.

He looked up briefly.

'So I'm told,' he said. 'Was he not passed over for the Northwest Passage journey later in the year?'

Edward folded his arms across his chest and looked at Hannah as if she were to blame for the barb.

'I failed to interrogate the captain about the blight on his résumé when I applied for the position,' he said.

Nathaniel didn't flinch, though Hannah saw a muscle in his cheek working. She was already sorry she'd orchestrated the meeting: it was too soon, she saw now. Like stripping a bandage from a weeping wound.

'I'm certain he promised his wife he was done with the Arctic,' Mary said. Edward smiled at her, and Hannah exhaled, relieved.

'I for one am very glad you're headed to a temperate clime,' Hannah said. 'The thought of you in the Arctic is awful.'

'In answer to thy earlier query, my work at the Bank does not afford me the leisure to indulge my fancies, be they domestic or global,' Nathaniel said, looking at Edward directly. Hannah watched her brother flush as he stared into his soup.

'Perhaps the Coast Survey will give thee a chance to enjoy thy pursuits as thee once did,' he said, his voice soft.

She was grateful he chose to speak plainly to their father. She hadn't heard Edward use a *thee* or a *thou* in a long time.

Hannah held her breath. Their spoons scraped the pewter bowls.

'It is unfortunate that we shan't have the opportunity to find out,' Nathaniel said, sitting straight as a fencepost, and setting his spoon down beside his bowl. The gesture had an undeniable finality. Hannah sank into her seat. 'Since thee has decided to depart, there's no one to whom I may entrust such a contract.'

Edward laughed, a harsh, hoarse sound. He put his spoon down, too.

'I don't know why you'd even consider entrusting it to me in the first place, since the only person in this house qualified for it is your daughter.'

The sound of Nathaniel's fist landing on the table made all of them jump. Soup sloshed everywhere; Mary's hand flew to her mouth. Hannah gasped.

'Because you are my son,' he said through clenched teeth, rising from the table.

Time seemed to pause. Hannah, Mary, and Edward all stilled in their various postures, like the doomed of Pompeii. Hannah had never seen her father lose his temper, never seen him make a violent gesture or utter an oath. It was over, then. Hannah felt as if she were waiting for the table itself to tip over and sink into the floorboards as the last of her hope drained from her body.

It was the kind of day when grown men and women abandoned their shops and crops to go swimming. Were it not

First Day, Hannah was sure, a good percentage of Meeting-goers would already have their ankles in the waves.

As they drew close to the Meeting House, Mary pulled forward, and Edward was drawn aside by an old school friend. Hannah let the crowd swirl around her, feeling dozens of pairs of eyes light on her and flit away like butterflies. Muffled whispers surrounded her. What was it Lilian had said? *Don't be swayed by idle chatter.* But swayed from what?

Her next thought flashed with the clarity of lightning, the terror of exposure: *We were seen.* Hannah could feel the blood drain from her face at the idea of an observer, cloaked by the thicket; her body and Isaac's, curled together. Since she'd stormed out of the Atheneum, she hadn't seen or heard from him, but she'd thought of him nearly every day since. Each time she tried to clip him from her thoughts as if he were an invasive vine. But the memory of his words – and his face – wasn't easily blunted.

When Edward popped up beside her like a buoy, Hannah jumped, but he didn't seem to notice. She trailed behind him into the Meeting House with the flow of worshippers, and once she was inside the cavernous space, Hannah felt her spine relax a little, her shoulders return to level. Mary appeared and slipped onto the bench beside Hannah. Why did she always behave as if the best day of her life had just gotten under way?

As the assembly settled into quiet, Hannah's dark humor melted into something tolerable. Her imagination had gotten away from her; it would be nearly impossible for anyone to have seen her and Isaac that night. And as for Mary, she shouldn't harbor ill will, especially here. This was Hannah's home as much as the house on Little India or the Atheneum. The smell of the wood and the white-wash and the collected bodies of her neighbors was as familiar as the 'Sconset roses in June or the pungent, earthy peat of the Commons in September.

Hannah allowed herself to be soothed. As the minutes ticked by, the feeling deepened, and she forgot about the strange looks and odd behavior of her neighbors over the past weeks. She failed to think about Philadelphia, or about Edward's imminent departure, or the break between him and their father. She didn't consider the chance she may have missed by failing to give notice of the comet – if it *was* a comet – that she'd seen before Monsieur Rainault, before anyone. She didn't even think of Isaac.

Ten minutes later, someone rustled nearby. Hannah looked up. Hester Starbuck, Aliza's mother, had risen to her feet. When someone was moved to speak in Meeting, they did so. There was no formal procedure. One needed only to rise and say what he or she was moved to say. On some days no one spoke at all. On others, several people wished to share some revelation or other with the community.

'My mind has been restless,' Hester began, 'my con-science troubled by some things I've witnessed among my neighbors. I turned within and sought guidance from the spirit there, and was moved to speak. It is without malice that I implore each member of this Meeting to be thus guided, especially in their associations.'

She thudded back into her seat and folded her arms as

if satisfied. A number of people around her nodded; some glanced in Hannah's direction. She looked around to see at whom they might be directing their gaze. A moment later, the silence was disturbed again as Ann Folger rose to her feet. She, too, gazed toward Hannah as she spoke.

'I was drawn in recent days to the journal of our fore-bear George Fox. I knew why when I came to the passage "As the people of the world have mouths full of deceit and changeable words I was to keep to yes and no in all things; that my words should be few and savory, seasoned with grace." I was moved to share this passage today for the benefit of those among us whose associations with such people may distract them from the true path.'

She lowered herself into her seat like a plump hen settling on her roost. Now Hannah knew that the gazes of her neighbors were directed at her, even as she stared straight ahead at the back of the bench in front of her. Mary inched closer, as if in support, so that their skirts ran together in a curtain over the edge of the bench. One after another, people rose and spoke their pieces, until Hannah no longer heard the words being said, only caught snips of phrases.

No one has the slightest prejudice . . . Even the most studious mind may be turned away from the Light . . . Persons who have not had the benefit of a religious education cannot be held responsible for the danger they pose to any individual spirit, but the danger exists nonetheless.

Then Mary was on her feet beside Hannah. The separation of their bodies was almost painful. Hannah felt exposed. Panicked, she looked across the aisle at Edward. He shrugged, his face a mixture of confusion and concern.

Mary's face was flushed, and a rare frown creased her forehead. When she spoke, her voice was mild only on the surface, like silk draped over stone.

'So much revelation upon the same topic in one week is truly surprising,' Mary said. 'I myself have been contemplating a different passage from the Book. "My friends, as believers in our Lord Jesus Christ, the Lord of glory, you must never treat people in different ways according to their outward appearance." James, I believe.'

She aimed a sweet smile at the elders upon the altar at the front of the room and sat down again. Her hand crawled over to Hannah's and grasped it. In spite of her gratitude for the show of support, Hannah pulled away. She did not want to be comforted or consoled; she wanted to escape. Her muscles braced to rise; her knees and ankles thrummed with desire for flight.

But she stayed in place. A series of images like a deck of playing cards fanned out in her imagination. She saw herself as a child, stealing away with a book while her schoolmates played their games, laughing at jokes she did not understand. Pounding up the stairs to the garret, away from company, from lectures, from anything that would require the mincing dance of chitchat. Fleeing the shearing festival, and then the engagement dinner, rather than revealing her feelings to Edward and Mary. Running from Isaac Martin, again and again.

All around her, the hiss and rustle of silk and wool, the

smell of lemon oil and sawdust. Hannah basked in the deep familiar for seconds that ticked by like hours, like years, a lifetime of at-homeness. Then she rose to her feet.

A new silence layered itself upon the old as the staccato tickles of motion in the cavernous room ceased. No one coughed, or yawned, or scratched. They turned in unison to watch Hannah as she spoke, as if she herself were a celestial object streaming across the night sky.

'I have something to say,' Hannah said. She focused on Dr Hall's knees, which were at her eye level where he sat upon the altar. His cane lay horizontally on the floor at his feet. A beam of morning sunlight nearly bisected it, but the angle was off. An X, then, instead of a cross.

'I have always been guided toward Truth by indisputable fact,' she said. The room was so still the drone of flies sounded like train engines. 'I am an expert observer. I do not say this to be boastful. I speak only what is known to me. My eyes are trained to see objects in a dark sky that would be invisible to most people in this room.'

An orchard of pale faces tilted toward her, waiting.

'I have spent most of my life pursuing that Knowledge that would lead to a great contribution from our small community. Some discovery that would illuminate a dark corner of the Heavens. And all that time I have sat here, in this seat, and believed that the Light that guided others was also guiding me. It is only now, today, that I understand I have been mistaken.'

A collective hiss as the assembly inhaled in unison like a reef swaying under a wave.

'I believed that turning inward was the path to right

behavior. I believed that the "world's people" would distract and distance me from the Light within.'

Hannah directed her gaze at Ann Folger.

'And yet, it is only through my association with such a person that I have been able to unbind myself from this stricture.'

The squeal of wood upon wood as Dr Hall rose to his feet. The cane slid out of the perpendicular when he kicked it with his toe. Now it was lit in the parallel, glowing like Pharaoh's enchanted staff.

Hannah looked up.

'We thank thee, Friends, for these words. Enough has now been shared on the topic of the world's people, and our association with them,' he said.

Ann Folger rose again.

'She is making an acknowledgment, brother. We must hear it.'

'I am doing no such thing,' Hannah stated. Her voice reverberated in the air overhead. 'I have nothing to acknowledge but the pursuit of Truth as my own conscience guides me.'

'Does thee contend that such an association falls within the acceptable bounds of Discipline?'

It was Phoebe Fuller who spoke, from her place beside Dr Hall. She spoke from her seat, her powerful voice ringing out, silencing the frantic buzz that had broken out among the congregation.

Hannah felt frozen in place, a field mouse under the eye of a hawk.

'I do not,' she said.

'Then is it thy position that Discipline is dispensable?

Or have thy observations revealed a spiritual path that thee cares to share in the event that we should all follow in thy footsteps?'

Hannah shook her head, all language having run out of her like milk from a cracked bucket.

'I don't believe that she –' Dr Hall said, but Phoebe silenced him with one hand raised.

'Let Hannah Price speak for herself,' she said.

Hannah swallowed. *You are only saying what you have been taught.*

'It is my position that the determination of truth from deceit does not rely on one's island of origin, nor upon one's occupation, nor upon the hue of one's skin. It is my position that the world's people pose no greater or lesser harm than any individual within our own esteemed ranks.' Dr Hall sank into his seat as if being pulled down by an anchor. Ann Folger stared, slack-jawed.

'It is my position that determining the state of one's spiritual health is best left to each individual. I do not believe that this Meeting nor any other association of persons possesses the ability or the right to make such an assessment.'

Once she had said the words, Hannah felt dizzy with understanding that they were truer than any she had uttered in the past months. Possibly years.

She bowed her head beneath the weight of it, the gravity of what she'd done bearing down on her. But as she turned and walked up the center aisle of the Meeting House for the last time, the heaviness lifted, and as she got closer to the door, relief flooded her body, lightening her bones, bearing her the final few yards until she was outside, in the daylight, invisible.

20. An Appeal

When the double doors closed behind her, Hannah hesitated. She blinked in the brightness of day, then turned away from Town and began to walk west. Air and sky, dirt and leaves, these were what she needed. Things devoid of malice. Without realizing it, she chose the path she'd taken with Isaac the day of the storm. It was the first time in months she'd walked without toting a bag filled with instruments and books and maps. *My armor,* she thought. Stripped of it, her body felt buoyant.

Poofs of dry dust shot out from beneath her boots with each step, dispersing and settling again upon the surface. Her footsteps would disappear with a gust of wind, all evidence of her passage erased as sure as the wake of a whaleship would disappear before its mate could scramble up the rigging. Evidence so easily dispersed seemed a perfect metaphor for the day; everything she thought she knew about herself and her neighbors had proven to be upside down. True was false; friends were foes. Sincerity, hypocrisy, humility, vanity – she doubted she could even tell one from the other anymore.

She turned onto the sandy track leading out to the beach. As she emerged onto the dune, expecting nothing but the twinkle of the waves below and a stretch of fine empty sand ahead, she stopped short. A lone figure sat upon the bluff, his back to her, leaning upon his elbows in a familiar posture.

Hannah took a step back, ready to flee by force of habit. But no – there would be no more of that. What she'd put in motion could not be recalled. As she stood, feeling frozen in place, she realized that she'd chosen this spot, among all the others on the Island, in hopes that she would find Isaac here. He was the person she wanted to see; she had nothing to gain by leaving. If anything, she owed him an apology. He'd called her attention to Truth, and she'd refused to see it. *You are only saying what you have been taught.*

She forced her feet forward. They felt like they were boiling in her high boots. As she drew near, he turned his head and smiled. He didn't seem angry. Hannah unclenched her fists, which she'd shoved into her pockets, and dropped down beside him as if she'd done so every day of her life.

'I am surprise to see you here,' he said. 'Are you not meeting this day?'

She shook her head. And then everything before her blurred as tears sprang to her eyes, spilling hot and shocking upon her cheeks and dripping onto her dress.

'What is happening?' Isaac asked, his voice gentle but fringed with worry.

'I'm sorry,' Hannah said. But a big heaving sob ripped through her. She bowed her head.

Isaac did not ask again, but he leaned toward her and drew her in. She let the ballast of his body support her as she wept, his solidity a small miracle amid the ruin. She cried for the loss of Meeting, for disappointment at how her individual neighbors, all people of conscience and faith, had hardened over the years into a unit so rigid it could not bend. Or would not.

She cried for the loss of her brother, and for the pain she'd caused Mary. She cried for Isaac, who had suffered because she had allowed herself to get too close to him. And she cried for the Island, the place she loved more than any other, her home that no longer felt like home. Yet she knew no other.

Finally, spent and aching, Hannah raised her head. Isaac looked down at her, his concern mixed with affection and confusion. As always, a hint of amusement. His own complicated face. How she adored looking at it.

A bright bit of color waving in the slight breeze caught her eye, and she looked to the east. A quilted bedroll was laid out upon the sawgrass. Isaac's satchel lay beside it, his familiar green jumper peeking out from the top.

Puzzled, she turned to him.

'It was raining last night,' he said. 'Everything is drying now.'

Hannah shook her head a little.

'Have you not been sleeping in the Atheneum, then?'

He shook his head.

'Not since our last meeting.'

Hannah pressed her lips together, but before she could answer, he squeezed her shoulder as if to show her that he wasn't angry.

'I decide to sleep here, under the stars. But don't worry: I replace the key in the box that very night.'

Hannah bit her lip. She'd checked her letterbox ten times in the last week, but the key had not reappeared. Her father's words, months ago in front of the Atheneum in the dead of night, returned as if he were whispering in her ear: *What does thee know of this person?* She swept her mind for signs of doubt, and found none. And though she didn't mean to consult her feelings, they made themselves known, like the insistent hymn of a pious neighbor. Isaac cared for her; he would not lie to her.

As if in answer, he sat up a little and released her, wrapping both his arms around his knees and looking out over the surf below. A half mile away, a couple was wading in the water. The woman held her skirts in one arm and the man's elbow with the other. Hannah sighed and dried her cheeks with her sleeve. She didn't want to think about the key now, or about what would happen when she went home that day, or woke up the next.

Isaac tilted his head in her direction, his eyes gentle.

'Do you wish to say what happened?'

'I'm adrift.' She didn't want to be vague, but if she told him what had transpired, she knew he'd feel responsible. 'Do you remember when you told me that I was only saying what I had been taught?'

He nodded, his eyes questioning.

'Well, it's become clear that what I have been taught, and what I believe, have diverged. And what I thought would happen when Edward returned – I was wrong about that, too. I'm –' Hannah struggled to keep from crying again. 'I feel as if I've been cut in two. Have you ever felt anything like that?'

It was hard to imagine that he had. Isaac seemed as even-keeled as a canoe cleaving through still water. She envied his composure, which came not from a rigid code of Discipline, as hers had, but from something else.

He gazed out at the water again.

'I'm sorry to hear about your brother. The feeling you describe – this makes me think of my own brother.'

'Is he on a whaleship?'

'He is dead.'

'I'm so sorry. I didn't know.'

'It was a long time ago,' he said, glancing at her as if to comfort her. Her distress must have read on her face. 'An accident. In the water.'

'What happened?'

'We were in the boat, my father, grandfather, Paulo, and myself. He was like a fish. Nine years of age. He slip into the water and my grandfather did not see. He was rowing. The oar, it hit him.'

Hannah imagined the crack of the blow, cries of the men from the water, rowing fiercely toward shore, his brother's limp body a delicate arc over his father's out-stretched arms. The sound of his mother's wail rising, his grandfather's silence afterward. Edward at that age had been all arms and throat, mischievous and gentle and clumsy and coarse all at once.

'You must miss him terribly,' she whispered.

A smile flickered like a candle across his face. He stretched his legs out in front of him and leaned back on his elbows in the sand.

'I remember him laughing. The time to cry is past. We

are passing through this pain: we cry for him, pray for him, remember him. We tell our stories. Now I am only happy to think of him.'

Hannah thought of the silence around her own mother's death, the smothering of any outward expressions of grief. 'I wish we were able to speak of such things. When I lost my mother, I was so young, and when I got older we never spoke of her.'

Isaac looked horrified.

'If you do not speak of it, where does it go?'

'Where does what go?'

'The suffering.'

Hannah paused, then reached for his hand and curled his fingers into a fist before lifting it to her heart, holding it there, covered with her own.

'It stays,' she said. Bowing her head, she allowed her lips to rest on the small stretch of his hand that was exposed, the soft underbelly of his palm. They sat this way for some minutes, no sound but the breakers whispering against the sand.

'I must tell you something,' Isaac said, not looking at her. Hannah felt like lobsters were pinching her gut. She raised her chin and released his hand.

'The *Pearl* is ready to sail. I have word from Mr Leary last night.'

'When do you go?' Hannah asked.

'The day after tomorrow.'

She inhaled. Heat and salt. Only a tiny hint of Isaac, as if he'd become the place. Sand and sky and skin comingled. There was no imagining her Island without him now. If she could even call it hers.

Hannah dug both her palms into the sand, burying them to the wrists.

'So there is time for one final lesson,' she said.

He smiled.

'If you are willing.'

'Come tonight,' she said, rising as if she'd gotten marching orders.

'To the Atheneum?'

'No. Come to my home.'

'Is it wise?'

'It's what I want.' She paused, wondering how much to say. Their relationship was no longer about the lessons, or his advancement. When she was near him, Hannah felt both exhilarated and free at the same time, the way she felt when she was observing. The idea of parting from him was excruciating.

Hannah hovered above Isaac for a moment, shielding him from the sun. Backlit, she imagined herself silhouetted by light, her features blurred, indistinct. The sensation of his embrace returned to her, warming her body like sunlight. Her hand came to rest upon the tight curls that covered his skull, light as a dragonfly. They were soft, moss-like. She'd expected them to be more resilient, like springs.

'I'll see you then,' she whispered, and turned toward home, to face whatever awaited her there.

Hannah found her father at the kitchen table. When he looked up, he looked more sad than angry.

'Thee has disappointed me,' he said after ten seconds passed in cold silence.

'I was not meaning to,' Hannah said. She sounded like Isaac, and the accidental mimicry struck her as funny, though there was nothing humorous about her present situation. She coughed to cover her smile. 'It has naught to do with thee,' she added, hoping to soothe him.

Her words had the opposite effect. Nathaniel sat even straighter and raised one finger, though he did not point it at her. Instead, he tapped the table in a rhythm as steady as a metronome's, each syllable an ominous drumbeat.

'I defended thee,' he said. 'To those who questioned thy devotion, I said, "An undevout astronomer is mad." To those who said thee flouted Discipline, I stated that thy discipline was unparalleled as a matter of temperament. To those who said worse – well, they did not make their claims aloud. Not to me, anyway. Thy standing was already imperiled. But now –'

He shook his head. 'Now, daughter, I'm afraid thee will have no choice but to remove with me. I see no prospects for thee here. In fact, thee might consider doing so immediately. I'm sure there will be plenty for thee to occupy thyself with in setting up our new house-hold.'

Hannah sank down on the bench and picked a hangnail. 'The Atheneum provides plenty of labor,' she muttered.

'Hannah.'

She looked up, startled by his sharp tone.

'Thee clearly does not realize the gravity of the situation. I guarantee that thy position at the Atheneum is being reassigned as we speak.'

His statement stood between them like a glacier. She couldn't see through or around it. She shook her head.

'What does one have to do with another? I don't understand.'

'Does thee know of a single trustee who does not cleave to Discipline like a barnacle to a boulder?' he said. 'Is thee so naïve as to think they will disregard thy actions at Meeting – and elsewhere – and continue to entrust thee with guidance over the most vulnerable minds on the Island?'

'I cannot see why my guidance should be questioned when so many of the devoted hold views that are vastly less Christian than those I expressed today. They claim to be pious but their actions speak otherwise. They say they hold no prejudice against the Negro race but recoil when one comes too close. They abhor violence but hurl cobblestones at those who voice unpopular opinions. Not to mention the conditions aboard their whaleships. They –'

'Enough.' Nathaniel stopped tapping and looked at Hannah directly. His voice was gruff, as if the effort of expressing emotions snagged his words like thorns. 'There is no "they." No collection of conspirators. Thee does a disservice to thy own character by speaking so. It pains me. If thy mother were with us –' He paused, and Hannah wondered what aspect of Ann Gardner Price he was remembering. A walk in the garden? Their wedding day? Her body heavy with two lives growing within her? A flash of envy raced through her. She had nothing to counter with but her own self, forged from the flesh of that very woman.

'I believe that thee meant to do good,' he added, as if reading her mind. 'But thee has done harm, Hannah. To thy name. And to mine own, regrettably.' He shook his head a little, then raised his chin. 'Thee will cease these lessons immediately.'

Hannah raised her own chin, aware of how similar their profiles were. Like two views of the same coastline. But she felt like a stranger. If his invocation of her mother was meant to shame her, it had the opposite effect. She felt a surge of power.

'I believe my mother would be inclined to stand on the side of Truth, as I believed thee would,' she said. 'I believe she would be proud. I certainly don't see why she would be ashamed. Was she not a clear advocate for Truth as she saw it? Did she not challenge a notion if she found it unreasonable?' For the first time she could remember, Hannah felt the spirit of Ann Gardner spark to life in her. Perhaps she was not solely her father's daughter after all.

But the look of pain on her father's face – as if her words had struck a physical blow – doused her newfound zeal. Hannah swallowed and lowered her voice.

'In any case, the *Pearl* is leaving port on third day,' she went on. 'My student will be aboard as second mate, hopefully with the ability to assist the captain and crew with their navigational duties. There's no need to cease the few remaining lessons we have time for.'

All traces of hurt and sadness vanished as he rose to stand over her, as if he needed the higher position to cement his authority.

'I will not discuss it further,' he stated. 'All communication with this person will cease at once. I will hear no more idle talk on the topic of my daughter's associations. And I wish to hear no more from thee about the behavior of thy elders or anyone else. Thee has irrevocably tainted thy opportunity for a match hereabouts, and I'm told by William Bond that thee did not even consider George's offer seriously, though I cannot imagine why. I wonder if thee gives any thought to the repercussions of thy actions at all. I don't know anymore.'

He opened his mouth as if he were going to say more, but did not. Instead, he rose stiffly and left the room.

Hannah remained seated, her heart still pounding from the exchange. She'd never invoked her mother before. It was as if her conversation with Isaac had cracked a dam she hadn't known existed, and now all sorts of ideas and feelings about that woman threatened to pour through. It was disturbing and exciting in equal measure, the first new idea of herself she had ever entertained.

Then she remembered what her father had said about her job. If it was true, and she was to be removed from her post at the Atheneum, she'd have no chance of staying on Nantucket. He was in no mind to support her. What she needed to do was go to Dr Hall and make her case for keeping her job. If anyone on the Island would advocate on her behalf, he would be the one.

She found him on the porch of his neat house, a fixture as steady and recognizable as the weather vane on the roof. Hannah knew every well-swept corner of his home, from his chronologically ordered library to the procession of teacups in every room, all half-full of lukewarm brew. As she approached in the grey twilight, calm descended, as if this were any other summer evening and she was on a mission of intellect, not mercy. She'd walked the path from her house on Little India to his on Pineapple for nearly twenty years; she could practically hear the blows of hammers from the summer they built New Wharf, the clang and thud from the old shipyard, and above all Dr Hall's own voice, urging rigor, helping her weave equations into Time, into distance, the way other women turned skeins of yarn into blankets, sweaters, socks.

He was as passionate as anyone she'd ever known about the value of knowledge, the importance of improvement. Surely he would support the rightness of her actions, even if he hadn't stood up in Meeting and said so. He had much to lose, she reasoned, by making a public statement on her behalf; but surely a quiet word with the Atheneum trustees was well within his realm of influence.

Dr Hall stood as she approached.

'Thee needn't – please sit.'

He lowered himself into his seat without bending his back. It had a regal effect. When he'd settled, he gestured to the chair beside him. She sank down, relieved to be tucked away in this familiar corner. From Dr Hall's porch, it was easy to pretend that nothing had changed. Behind the long, low candle warehouses across the street, dim streaks of light crisscrossed the horizon, the last remains of sunset. A few sparks glinted on the Bay. Hannah could hear the slap of water on the piles, seafoam sucking back from shore, and the distant cawing of the gulls circling the inner harbor. A hundred tiny boats bobbed in unison as if they were no more than paper shells. She inhaled deeply, a sigh of pleasure that sent a shiver down her back.

Dr Hall spoke first. He seemed in no hurry to get his

words out, and his tone was such that Hannah had to lean in to hear.

'What occurred at Meeting was unfortunate,' he said. 'I imagine thee is suffering some regret.'

Hannah rocked a little in the chair, enjoying the slight breeze created by the motion.

'I regret that slander and hearsay made their way into a place I have always regarded as the realm of Truth,' she said, picking her way carefully. 'I knew that people questioned my actions with regard to my student.'

'Yes.' Dr Hall wasn't offering a twig of encouragement. A film of unease floated down from nowhere, and she planted both feet to stop the chair from moving.

'I answered a request for improvement, and provided an opportunity for betterment to one who deserves such a chance. No more or less,' she said, wishing she didn't sound defensive.

'At the expense of thy own opportunities, it now appears.' Hannah couldn't read his tone. Was he accusing her, or empathizing? He gazed out over the water, impassive, his cane resting across his lap.

'That's why I'm here, actually.' She cleared her throat. 'My father believes I'm likely to lose my position at the Atheneum. If that happens, I'll be forced to leave the Island immediately. I hoped that thee could intervene. If it comes to that.' Hannah dipped her head. She wasn't trying to appear humble, but felt humiliated in a way she hadn't anticipated. She'd arrived full of righteous energy, sure that Dr Hall would clear the way for her to remain in her post. Now she felt like a supplicant.

The seconds ticked by. His silence was excruciating.

'It's a delicate situation, my dear,' he said, still not looking at her. 'Many of our neighbors feel that thee has not only skirted but flaunted Discipline in this matter.'

'And thee is in agreement?' For a moment she felt a tenderness that bordered on pity. He'd been alone as long as she'd known him; his awkward proposal of marriage, even his rigid classroom posture and harsh manner, were all a function of loneliness. If he was long-winded, prone to issuing judgments and soliloquies, it was because he hadn't anyone to practice any other kind of conversation with. It was easy to sympathize with his lack of social graces. Undoubtedly some people thought the same of her. Hannah wondered if he'd ever courted a woman besides herself – if you could call it a courtship. Who might he be if he had someone to help him see himself?

'My own feelings on the matter are irrelevant,' he stated. 'As thy instructor and a friend to thy father, I regret the current state of affairs. As thy prospective husband I might be able to sway the opinions of the Trustees in the matter of thy position, but in our current situation I see very little I may do to lighten the stain upon the Atheneum caused by thy activities.'

Hannah's warm feelings dissolved. Perhaps she'd misheard.

'You won't help me because I haven't consented to marry you?'

Dr Hall sighed as if he found it tiresome to explain himself. When he spoke, his voice was emotionless and taut. He might as well have been delivering a lecture on natural philosophy.

'I am of the opinion that thee ought to have given me thy decision long ago. As thy teacher, I've guided thee in every aspect of thy education. I gave thee all the tools thee needed to accomplish thy goals, even the pursuit of a comet. It was I who taught thee to push for the precepts behind the equations, the underlying order of the Heavens. I ensured thee an income at the Atheneum. What more must I do for thee, Hannah Price, in return for thy simple companionship as my wife?'

She was struck as if the words were physical blows, and Hannah fired back, too appalled to tamp down the volcanic energy of her anger or maintain the pretense of a respectful form of address.

'Yes, you did a fine job of nurturing my mind and supporting my aspirations, as did my father and Edward both. But above all you taught me to pursue truth. Truth! *The highest calling*. Did you not drill it into me? And now you're suggesting that I consent to be your wife in order to secure my position at the Atheneum? Do I strike you as a woman that would make such a vile contract?'

She'd never felt such fury, or allowed it into words. She'd stood up while speaking, and her fists were balled so tightly her fingernails dug into her palms. It felt good, so she squeezed harder.

'It's regrettable that thee abandons thy manners and thy plain speech at the first rush of emotion,' he said mildly. 'Though it is encouraging to see a feminine fire burning in one who excels at hiding her passions.'

Hannah backed away, hovering on the edge of the porch step.

'You don't see me as a peer at all. For all your talk of

equal education, you see my shape, not my mind. At the end of the day I'm but a woman.' The words were bitter in her mouth. Her body was a prison. How unfair that she would be trapped in it until the end of her days.

'Does a zebra gaze upon its mate and see plaid, my dear? Thee should be grateful for thy blessings, the role thy Creator has reserved for thy Sex.'

Hannah stared at him, barely hearing the words. Her Sex, indeed. It was the cause of all her suffering.

'I urge thee to reconsider my offer,' he went on. 'If not for thine own sake, then for the sake of those who may be affected by thy decision. Thy father, for instance. He still awaits his certificate of removal, and it will be a challenge for him to continue in his position if he's in poor standing with the Philadelphia Meeting. Or thy . . . student. Who appears to have a surprising familiarity with the collections of an institution not even open to one of his race. And excellent night vision.'

'You left the note in my box,' Hannah whispered, the truth seeping in like poison. 'Where is my key?' she hissed.

'I was trying to help thee, Hannah. As I am now. Thee has no further need of the key to our Island's most cherished institution.' Dr Hall blinked once, twice, owlish. Was he mocking her with this façade of concern? In the twilight, on his rocking chair, his frailty made a bizarre contrast to the power he wielded.

'It is not too late to make an acknowledgment,' he added. 'That, in combination with an announcement of our engagement, would surely mend any rift between thee and thy neighbors. Think on it.' He folded his arms and began to rock, as if she were a student and he had dismissed her.

Had she been a sailor, she'd have spit at his feet.

Instead, she shook her head and measured her words.

'On the contrary,' Hannah said, each word heavy as a cannonball as it fell. 'I shall do my best never to think on it again.'

She turned her back on him and went back the way she'd come, grateful for the shelter of the encroaching dark.

21. Double Stars

A note on the hall table informed her that Edward and Mary were out looking for her.

If you get this before we return, Edward had written in an uncharacteristically serious postscript, underscoring the last line, *Please Stay Here.*

Hannah sighed and dropped the note in the tinderbox, wondering what Edward would say about the day's events. She couldn't imagine he'd find much to laugh about.

As she unlaced her boots and went upstairs, she kept seeing Dr Hall standing at the head of the classroom. His zest for knowledge; his passion for unraveling the mysteries of the Heavens; his devotion to Truth – all of it had been real, as far as she could ascertain, and equal to her own. How could he have succumbed to such base behavior?

The answer was obvious but ugly. It was because he desired her, and believed he had the right to acquire and display her like a stuffed pheasant. Hannah splashed cold water on her face, glad for the bracing shock, and pressed a clean cloth to her nose, inhaling the lingering smell of summer air.

Dazed, she wandered back down into the kitchen and found a plate of sausage and potatoes Mary had left for her. Grateful, she slumped into a chair, suddenly more tired than she'd ever been in her life. It was unbelievable that the first stars had only just winked into visibility.

She heard the front door open and close as she picked at the cold remains of her dinner, and though she heard Edward calling, she had no strength to answer.

He burst into the kitchen and stopped short.

'You're here! Why didn't you answer?'

Hannah shrugged, and he slid onto the bench beside her, propping one elbow on the table and resting his head on his hand, studying her.

'You need not stare,' she snapped. 'I've had enough scrutiny for one day.'

The words stung even as they left her mouth, but Edward didn't seem offended. Instead, he sighed.

'I feel partly responsible for what happened today. I ought to have – I mean, had I been here, maybe I could have. I don't know.' His face was mournful. 'I'm not the watchdog type, but I might have saved you the indignity of being clawed at like that by a bunch of righteous prigs.'

'What could you have done? Ordered me to stop giving lessons to Isaac? And in any case, it doesn't matter. You weren't here then and you won't be here next time, will you? Not that there will be a next time. Since I'm leaving.'

She dropped her fork on the plate so that it gave a satisfying clatter, then swept up the dish and took it to the sink so she could turn her back to him. Her simmering anger threatened to boil over, but another confrontation would only bring her more pain.

Edward rose, too, and came over to the sink. His voice had none of its usual swagger. Rather, he seemed like he might cry. He put a hand on her shoulder.

'I've thought on it all evening,' he stammered. 'And I've

decided – well, Mary and I – that if you want us to stay, we will.' He swallowed. 'I won't draw this out, but I ask you – as my sister, my twin, my much better half – to consider, before you give your answer, whether staying here is what you truly wish for. Ask what this Island holds for you – for any of us – and whether you might be happy here after all that's happened.' He paused, sighing deeply. The sound seemed to come from a place in him Hannah didn't recognize.

She couldn't look at him. Instead, she kept her hands in the basin of soapy water, as if hiding them would some-how shield her from the confusion already swirling through her.

'Don't answer now,' he said, stepping away. 'Think on it. If we are to stay, I'll have to alert Captain Johnson as soon as possible. But that's not your concern,' he added. 'You decide as your heart dictates.'

Hannah finished washing and drying her plate and fork, then dragged herself up to the garret and out onto the walk. She didn't want to observe. Not tonight. What she wanted was to sit under the familiar blanket of stars and be comforted by their steadfast light, orderly and unchanging.

Edward's offer was what she'd hoped and wished for all this time. A way to stay on Nantucket that required noth-ing of her. She could go on with her observations, maybe go back to teaching. Surely the African School would have her. Why didn't she feel relieved?

His question hovered in the warm night air like the drone of an insect. Could she be happy here now? Knowing that her neighbors had betrayed her, that their judgment would be as eternal as the stars themselves? The life she had wanted to continue here would be no more. What a new life would be like was an unworkable equation. *Not one of us can intuit the future,* her father had said months ago, when she had wept over the idea that she would have to leave. How right he had been.

Especially now, when the Island itself and her life on it were bound inextricably to Isaac. No matter what she chose to do, he would not be here. There would be no more lessons, no more excursions, no more conversations. She would not feel his body beside her again, hear the deep thrum of his voice. Even if she stayed, it wasn't likely he'd return, for what did this Island hold for him? She leaned heavily on the wooden rail. Perhaps sometimes Isaac would think of her as he took a distance or calculated his ship's position. At that dismal thought, her heart lurched in her chest. The thought of separating from him was painful enough to contemplate on its own; the idea that he might not feel the same sense of loss made it unbearable.

Squinting at the sky, she watched the cloud cover, wondering if it would thicken or diminish. She could look for Albireo, in the Swan, if it cleared. She ought to at least set up the telescope. But she remained fixed in place, heavy with uncertainty, and, after a few minutes, stretched out in her usual spot and closed her eyes.

Isaac climbed the tree soundlessly as a cat. When he whispered her name, Hannah bolted upright and choked back a shriek.

'Shhhhhh.'

He put a finger to his lips, clinging to the stout branch just below the walk.

'What are you doing?' Her heart was pounding so hard, she clapped a hand to her chest to try and calm it.

'Watching you sleep.'

'There's a door.' Her legs felt like they were in irons. Standing up was an enormous effort.

Isaac didn't answer but shimmied closer to the walk and sprang easily over the railing, dropping lightly to his feet.

'I did not wish to be seen.'

He looked around the walk.

'You're not observing.'

Hannah shook her head.

'I had no heart for it.'

She sat down at the edge of the walk, and he did the same. They watched black clouds scudding across the dark canvas of the sky. Here and there a star blinked through, and then was gone. It wasn't worth trying to identify them. They came and went at will, like the men in her life. Dr Hall and her father, Edward and Isaac, beloved, despised, betrayer, supporter – it mattered not: they had freedom of movement while she had none. They could bask in their desires, where she was shamed by hers.

'I am not knowing what to say,' Isaac said, glancing at Hannah. She kept her eyes on the sky, resentment twisting her gut.

'There is nothing to say. You will go, and be a good navigator.'

'Tell me what you have been observing,' Isaac said. 'I wish to remember the sound of your voice.'

'I've been trying to study double stars.'

Hannah's voice shook, then steadied. Being so close to him was making it hard to speak.

'Double stars?'

'Stars that share a common gravitational force. They move about the Universe together.'

A gust of hot wind blew loose more of Hannah's hair, and she slapped at it when it brushed her face, enjoying the sting of her palm. Isaac reached over and moved a lock gently aside. Her forehead burned where he touched it, and she resisted the urge to seize his hand and press it to her cheek, to her neck. Her breath was shallow and quick.

'But why are they together?' He seemed genuinely puzzled.

'They are bound by gravity.' *Like me.* Though she was constrained not by some Heavenly force but by her Sex. Hannah swallowed, tried to regain her thoughts so she could explain.

'We don't know,' she whispered. 'One star is nearly always brighter than the other. But they change positions relative to the other; sometimes they eclipse each other as they make their orbits. Sometimes we can only see one or the other.'

In the dark, Isaac leaned close to her ear.

'But they are always together, moving through the Heavens.'

'Yes,' she said, or thought she did. Gooseflesh on her arms made the fine hairs stand up like sentinels.

Isaac bowed his head so that his mouth was beside her ear.

'I wish I can speak to you in my language,' he said. He

turned his head so that his forehead brushed the soft dent of flesh at her temple.

'Speak,' she whispered.

The music of his voice, then. What was he saying? She could not imagine, did not care. His lips at her ear made her shiver, though her body in its wool dress felt like it was boiling.

When he kissed her, she disappeared. There was only sensation: his breath, warm, pungent; his lips sweet and wet. The sensation was like falling in a dream. She fell, but there was no landing.

Instead, she was suspended in the fall itself, the warmth of his hands on her cheeks steadying her. She allowed the seconds to unfurl. But she counted, as she had when she was a child, upon this very roof. Ten, nine, eight ... Tendrils of heat snaked through her body like fuses. She put her hands on his arms, shocked by the softness of his skin and the strength beneath. Six, five, four ... His mouth moved to her cheek, her jaw, her neck. She gasped, a shiver buzzing down her spine and landing in her belly.

Three, two, one. Isaac's fingers moved to the buttons at her collar, and the pulse of desire hardened into a thud of fear. His mouth found the hollow at her throat, and she gasped with pleasure. But when he unhooked one button, then the next, panic seized her chest. Her legs felt like jelly, and her hands fluttered like wings too weak to beat him away. She did not try to stop him; the pleasure of his mouth on her skin was so great, she could not form words. He unhooked another, then another, exposing her to the top of her slip, and only then did she find her voice, and her strength.

'Stop.'

She broke away, inhaled as if she'd been drowning. Air rushed in. She welcomed it. Air was pure; air was the matter of the Universe.

Her desire was as terrifying as a huge wave, propelling her toward and away from something she only understood in shadowy, unexamined glimpses. A vision of something bestial, a naked coupling, violent and dark, descended on Hannah like a swarm of locusts, and though her body commanded her to go back to him, she could not make herself do it. The combination of lust and sorrow and fear made her feel sick.

She shook her head and grasped the railing, blood pounding like an ocean in her ears.

'I cannot,' she said. The words gave her power. She backed away another step. Now there was space between them. Enough room for a wagon wheel, or a cradle. Control of her limbs returned and Hannah took another step, her throat constricted with shame.

Isaac stared at her, confusion woven across his face. He, too, gripped the railing and slowly straightened his body, then wrapped his arms around himself. When he spoke, his voice was low and hard, cracking at the edges.

'I am a savage? This is how you are seeing me?'

Sav-ahj, she heard. Even an ugly word sounded like a song in his throat. Hannah shook her head. Isaac's eyes darted around the walk as though he were seeking an escape, then they returned to her face. Her cheeks burned, and her throat felt dry as bone. She wasn't sure if she was more ashamed of her desire or her fear of it.

Overwhelmed, she did the only thing she knew how to

do: clamp her jaw shut and reset her features, cutting off all traces of emotion. It was like drawing the shutters in a house that was on fire. But it worked. He recoiled as if slapped.

Isaac reached into the pocket of his shirt and drew out a small square parcel wrapped in crumpled brown paper and tied with a bit of string.

He held it out to her like an accusation.

'What is this?' she whispered. She wanted to look at him, fly to him, but could not move. Her palms were damp, as if she'd just woken from an awful dream.

'It's your money,' he said. A hissing ugliness in his voice. As if she'd betrayed him. It wasn't what she wanted. Could he not see her wounds?

'That's not necessary,' she said. Why had she not said his name?

He dropped the package on the ground like a hot coal. The *thwat* of paper on wood made her jump. *Help him understand,* she told herself. *Stop hiding.* But by the time Hannah opened her mouth to try to make the words, he was already gone.

22. Conflagration

Hannah woke up in the garret, in her chair, in her dress. Something had jolted her from her dream, in which she was walking barefoot along an unfamiliar trail, in a green and tropical place; she had been lost in the dream, and wandering. It came again: a bell, clanging. Then voices.

'Fire! Fire! All hands!'

She bolted upright and almost cracked her head on the doorjamb rushing down the stair. In the hallway she collided with Mary, who was tying on a dressing gown.

'Where's Edward?'

'He ran out at the first bell. We should go.'

'Yes! Get dressed. Wait! No.' Hannah shook her head, clearing the last of sleep from her brain. 'You should stay here and wet down the outside walls. Put whatever things you can in the wheelbarrow – in case.'

Mary nodded.

'All right. Be careful!'

'You, too.' Hannah rushed down the steps, grabbing the fire bucket from the peg by the door.

'Take these!'

Mary thrust a handful of wadded linen into Hannah's hand and nodded toward the kitchen. Her voice shook.

'Wet them so you can cover your face if the smoke is bad.'

Hannah obeyed, grateful, and then stuffed the damp cloths into her apron and went out into the street.

In the moonlight, it was easy to see that everyone had heard the call. Doors were open up and down her street, neighbors rushing in the direction of Main. The tang of smoke permeated the air, and there was an orange glow flickering under the silvery cloud cover, but Hannah couldn't tell where it was coming from. As she joined the flow of people rushing toward Town, she caught a man's arm.

'Where?'

Whoever it was didn't turn or stop.

'By the wharves, I think.'

Hannah let go of the stranger's arm and turned onto Main. It was thronged like a parade, loud and thick with bodies. The bells of the Methodist church were ringing, and the clatter of carts and shrieks of the alarms collided with the calls of the fire wardens in distant streets so that nothing was clear. The air was smoky, and amid the press of bodies and the clank of buckets and boots, Hannah couldn't make out anything but the bright sparks hissing into the air from rooftops not far ahead.

The crowd surged toward the water, the smoke intensifying as they passed Gardner, Winter, Pine. Now Hannah could feel the heat, and as she bumped up against a group of women, the crowd seemed to break apart. She stepped to one side and peered down a side street. Men and women of every hue and persuasion, from every part of the Island, were calling to each other, rushing about with wheelbarrows and carts, buckets and carpets. Over the heads of the crowd, she caught a glimpse of orange flames shooting from the roof of Geary's hat shop and Washington Hall next to it.

'It's going to jump,' someone cried. 'Everyone back! Back!'

As a wave, the crowd retreated. Then people were moving and dividing, parting like the Red Sea to allow a volunteer company through. In their heavy coats the men were grim-faced and determined, shoving their pumper and coils of hoses as fast as the wheels would allow over the uneven sidewalk.

Clutching her bucket, Hannah looked around in the chaos for something to do, and spotted Miss Norris, her hands wrapped around her own bucket, rushing toward the corner of Centre Street.

'Miss Norris!'

'Oh, Hannah!' The older woman looked terrified; Hannah could see the orange of the flames licking at the buildings on either side of the Hall reflected in the woman's wide eyes. 'Good, you're here. Come on.'

She turned to follow but both women froze as a great cry went up. The crowd turned like a flock of birds as a spark found a home atop a building across Main. In less than a moment, flames shot from its landing place, devouring the dry wood.

'Miss Norris!' Hannah thought she was whispering, but really she was yelling. It was so loud, she couldn't hear the difference. 'Can it – could it reach the Atheneum?'

'It will reach everything if it's not stopped!'

Miss Norris seized her arm and yanked her along, and Hannah allowed herself to be pulled into Petticoat Lane. A crowd was gathering in front of Mrs Johnson's dry goods shop, and seeing how many of the women were wrapping damp cloths around their noses and mouths,

Hannah fumbled for hers, and did the same. Every woman on the Row had been drawn to this spot, it seemed, to try and protect their shops. She could make out Ruth Edwards and Mrs Rotch and Margaret Granger; in the crowd she spotted Constance Early, the tavern owner, and Eunice and Sarah, the milliners; Peg Ramsey; and even Phoebe Fuller.

'Every carpet you can find, then, and we'll work in teams!' Mrs Johnson yelled from the porch over the heads of the women. 'This half –'

She split the crowd by pointing one thick arm at it.

'Collect carpets. Take every cart you can find. Five or six gather and load, while the others bring 'em back.'

With the ease of an officer, she commanded the women.

'You all stay here and form a bucket line from the nearest pump. We'll need to wet down every wall between here and the fire. Tie up your hair well and mind your skirts!' She squinted, then coughed.

'Go, go!'

The women rushed off in two directions, and Hannah fell in line with those forming a squadron between the nearest pump and the surrounding buildings, shoving her hair down into her collar. The women moved from house to house, passing and hurling the water as it came, dropping back as the company moved out of the way of the flames. They came quicker than Hannah could have imagined.

They passed buckets, from hand to hand, as the smoke thickened. From the corner of Federal they fell back to Cambridge, to India, to Oak. Hannah could see nothing but the hands in front of her, the hands behind her. Her shoulders burned and her knuckles ached, but she held her place. She could hear, as if through a haze, the calls of the fire brigades, the thunder of footfalls around them as people ran to and fro, the clatter of carts as the women dumped piles of carpets in front of Mrs Johnson's store, and then, as that building erupted, in front of Mrs Chase's, and then the cobbler's; and then, instead of a street of familiar buildings, there was only a bonfire of enormous proportions, mountains of roaring fire that hissed and shrieked like attractions at a nightmare carnival. Hannah was mesmerized as the flames shifted shape, roofs and walls collapsing, the structures of the buildings themselves disappearing. Sparks flew in every direction as a flaming wall fell toward their fire line, and the women retreated, backing toward Broad as the fire company swooped in with the pumper.

Dazed, Hannah was rooted in place by the fantastic sight of the next building collapsing in on itself like a toy house made of matchsticks and paper; when someone took her by the elbow and drew her out of line, she went, stumbling without seeing who led her, for the woman was covered in soot, her head wrapped in wet cloth.

'The Atheneum.'

She didn't think, but clasped the woman's outstretched hand. They ran, heads down, holding on until they reached the steps of the great white building, which glowed with reflected firelight like a garish sunrise, illuminating everything bright as day. Hannah clutched the cloth to her face and fumbled for the key, then realized that she no longer had one. She shook her head, mute with despair.

'Watch out.' The other woman pushed Hannah aside,

raised a boot, and kicked out the glass window beside the door. It shattered easily, the sound tinkling like raindrops amid the thunderous roar of the fire.

Kicking out the remaining glass, Hannah led her companion into the dim space, her wet boots slipping on the slick floor, rushing for the side door, only to find it already propped open: a few souls were hauling books and collectibles out the door with no clear order, only trying desperately to keep them from the flames.

'Wait! Wait!' Hannah yelled, waving frantically. 'Start with these. Here! Here!' She grabbed a volunteer by the shoulders, wheeled him around, and pointed to the shelves behind Miss Norris's beautiful desk, the rare books and special volumes. He nodded and redirected himself.

Hannah dragged her chair closer to the bookcases, throwing precious volumes down from the shelves as fast as she could gather them, barely seeing whether anyone was there to save them. Minutes went by, or seconds: she wasn't sure. She squinted at the reading room, which was strangely bright. Was it dawn, then? Then she felt the heat. She climbed down from her perch, fumbling over the books at her feet, and skidded across the floor to the door.

She could see the fire line working like a beast with a hundred hands, the silhouettes of men on neighboring rooftops, women watering down the walls. The blaze was not a hundred yards away.

'Hannah!'

She squinted into the smoke.

'Edward!' They reached for each other's arms as if they were drowning.

'You shouldn't be here! The whole block may go at any

moment.' Edward's eyes were wide, frightened O's in his soot-covered face.

Hannah shook her head, yelling over the din.

'We must try to save the building! Or at least what's in it. Can you get help?'

'Half the company's down at the docks, trying to move the oil!' he yelled back. 'The other half's split between the bank vaults and the line.'

He bent over, coughing, and she held his shoulders. When he rose, tears were streaming down his cheeks.

'I'll bring who I can,' he said. 'But you cannot remain.'

Whirling around, Hannah ran back into the building and nearly collided with the other woman who had an armful of books.

Both woman flinched as a series of explosions rocked nearby buildings.

'You should go!' Hannah yelled into her ear. 'It's not safe.'

The woman pushed past her and dumped the books in her arms into a wheelbarrow, then pulled the wrap from her head and ran her hands over her pale forehead and golden hair, leaving twin trails of black soot across them.

'Be safe, Hannah,' Mary said, covering her hands with her apron before picking up the handles of the wheelbarrow and shoving it toward Broad Street, away from the fire.

'You as well,' Hannah whispered. Then, in the chaos of men and books and objects she had acquired and catalogued, cleaned, and stored, wrapped and unwrapped, as if the future of civilization depended upon it, Hannah forgot everything but salvaging what she could, until she stepped outside and a spark landed on her apron, and another on her arm. The air was so hot, it seared her nose and throat, and the flames, now on both sides of the building, threatened to engulf her if she lingered another moment.

Another explosion, then another, almost knocked her off her feet. It felt as if the Island itself was under bombardment by the fleets of all Europe. Hannah hesitated, unsure which way was safe.

Edward shoved her in the right direction.

'It's the warehouses. The oil, the candle-houses. Go! Now!'

Then she was running through a narrow channel amid the burning buildings, swerving around fire wardens and citizens. Every building on Broad Street was either on fire or blown away entirely. She ran, unsure of which direction to go. South Water, North Beach, Broad, Chestnut, Oak – fire in every direction, people running, some with buckets, some with children.

At Centre Street she was turned back by a member of the fire brigade, his face and hands coated in soot, his eyes narrowed against the smoke.

'You'll have to go round. Go round!' he bellowed to the swell of people.

Hannah ran. Gay Street, Westminster, Huffey, Liberty: here, the houses were untouched but the occupants were carting goods away from their homes or into them like barn animals set loose, trying to predict whether the wind would blow in the direction of fortune or calamity. Hannah pushed her way through the street until she arrived, breathless, at the Bank building, which stood like a brick sentinel at its corner. A lone figure emerging in a rush nearly knocked her over.

It was Josiah Smyth, the Bank director.

'Mr Smyth!'

Relieved to see someone she knew well, Hannah clutched the man's shoulder with her soot-blackened hand, and he put a comforting hand over her own, misinterpreting her gesture as worry about the money inside.

'The vaults have been cleared, Miss Price. All cleared.'

The man had a wildish look; he scanned the air in front of him as if a swarm of bees were coming for him.

He patted her on the arm and scuttled down the street. Hannah leaned against the brick building, grateful for something solid to steady her.

The corner was eerily silent, though she could still hear the distant cries of the firemen and the crowds, the occasional reverberation from an explosion shivering the earth underfoot. As if in a dream, she watched something float by, carried on an invisible wind, then another, then another, a peaceful drift of airborne parchments.

Hannah rubbed her eyes, struggled to her feet, and saw that the whole street was littered with such pages, drifting on gusts and swirling into piles like autumn leaves, unmoored. She snatched one from the air.

Dearest Martha, Hannah read, and scanned quickly down the page:

The men say that salt water and long absence will wash away love – but the water must be saltier than brine and absence longer than life to wash away the love I feel for you . . .

Dropping it as if it was on fire, she grabbed more yellowed scraps:

> *... People wonder at many things in the sea, but I wonder at the sea itself – that vast Leviathan rolled round the earth, smiling in its sleep, waked into fury, fathomless, boundless, a huge world of water drops ...*
>
> *My darling Horatio. Would that thee were with us and we were al together onse mor lik the family we once was ...*

Horrified, Hannah gathered the pages in her arms. These were private words, now exposed like skin. Where had they come from? The mailbags at Riddell's? There were old pages and new, some crumbling, some on child's copybook paper, others on backs of invoices.

Here was a grocery list in a woman's beautiful hand; here was a bill of sale for a horse with one brown eye and one black; here was a love letter, words that belonged to no one but the two souls between whom they passed.

She pushed pages into her pockets until they bulged. Turning to snatch another from the air, she noticed that the door of the Bank was wide open. *Up,* she thought – and then her feet propelled her forward, the desire to see, from above, what devastation the fire had wrought overcoming her fatigue and her fear. She darted into the wide lobby, its vaults gaping open like toothless beasts, and raced across to the stairs, then up and out onto the roof. She paused, blinking. What she saw in the distance could not be possible. She crossed the roof like a sleepwalker until she was at the parapet.

Nantucket Harbor was on fire. The wharves and the

ropewalks, the harbormaster's shed and the sail lofts, supply boats and every other vessel moored nearby, all of them ablaze like flaming pieces scattered on a chessboard.

Not only that: the Bay itself was in flames. The waters of the harbor were alight, slick with oil spilled and dumped from the storehouses – oil meant to illuminate the homes and stores and libraries of all the United States, all of it on fire upon the surface of the very water that had carried it home. The whole of the Island was illuminated in a ghastly orange glow.

Isaac. Hannah turned, fleeing the rooftop and rushing back through the desolate lobby of the Bank, until she was outside again.

With the last of her strength, Hannah stumbled in the direction of the wharves, looking for Isaac in every face, haunted by the image of the ships on fire in the harbor, the massive explosions at the wharves, imagining the worst. Among the dazed and wandering residents of Nantucket Island she saw no one who resembled him. Finally, when she could walk no more, she turned toward home, only to collide with the harbormaster himself, who blinked back tears as he righted himself.

'Miss Price,' he said. His fringe of white hair stuck out like a strange halo and he was covered in ash from head to toe. He'd lost his jacket, and in shirtsleeves and suspenders he had the look of a clown on the front lines of a war. 'An epic calamity.'

'The *Pearl*, Mr Starbuck. Has it – was it consumed?' Hannah studied the man's soot-covered face, twin tracks of his tears streaking down his cheeks.

He shook his head.

'The *Pearl* set sail earlier this evening,' he said, scratching his head and staring toward the horizon. 'She was the last ship out. Set to go tomorrow. But they changed orders. Lucky boys.'

A fresh tear tracked down and landed on his belly.

'The worst is over,' he said. 'It's all but ashes now.' He swept his hand in a wide arc, encompassing the still-burning skeletons of the fleet, the harbor, all of Nantucket Town. 'You should go on home.'

'Thank you,' Hannah whispered.

She wandered through the desolation, dawn cracking the horizon. The heat and smell were awful, smoke curling up from the ruins. Halfway there, she stopped and picked at a hole in the elbow of her dress until it gave. Ripping it off, she pressed the fabric to her face, but its reek was hardly better than the air itself.

There were dozens of acres of ash, shopkeepers and homeowners scavenging in the thin light, dazed as wounded soldiers. Hannah passed people she could not recognize; she couldn't tell if it was because they were strangers, or friends disguised by soot, or whether her own mind, contorted by grief and fatigue, was no longer working properly. One woman paced to and fro in the ruins of what might have been a house, a ball of bright pink yarn in her fist. A man walked by gripping the back of an armchair. Another wielded a single shoe with a polished silver buckle, holding it out in front of him like a divining rod.

By the time Hannah trudged up the final stretch of Main before turning onto her street, knots of tourists from 'Sconset and Madaket had gathered on the perimeter of the ruins like mourners. By some grace, Vestal and India and the streets surrounding them had been spared, and Hannah felt a mix of gratitude and guilt that they'd been so lucky.

When she got to her house, the door was wide open. Hannah pounded past the parlor, then up into the garret, and finally out onto the walk, where she found Mary clutching the railing and staring dazed at the smoldering remains of their town, and then the two women were bound in each other's arms, weeping; but Mary was soothing Hannah, stroking her forehead as she wept black and bitter tears: for the town, and for the fleet, and for Isaac, who was gone, probably forever. Isaac, whom she had hurt because she could not overcome what she had been taught, because she was weak and foolish and fearful. Isaac, whom Hannah loved as surely as she loved the dunes and tides of the Island itself, as surely as Mary loved Edward.

Mary rocked Hannah back and forth as she would one day rock her children, Edward's children, *shhhhhhhhhh*ing Hannah, who did not even know whether she was speaking out loud, though the words repeated themselves like a dirge, like a prayer:

All is lost. All is lost. All is lost.

PART THREE
March 1846 Nantucket

23. Regeneration

Her last day on Nantucket was freezing cold. Hannah made her way to Main Street, her cheeks numb. Her woolen stockings itched. The cobblestones hid under a thin layer of black ice. At least it made it easier to say good-bye, she reasoned; leaving the Island in Spring might have broken her spirit entirely.

The sound of music and conversation wafted in her direction from the stage on Main, where the lighting of the new lamps was under way. From the sound of it, most of Town had turned out. Hannah hadn't planned to go, but there was no point in spending her last hours sulking in the garret, which smelled like the clean pine of a new coffin. In the watery, late-afternoon winter light, emptied of its mysteries, it was nothing but a room at the top of a smallish old house, filled with wooden crates and burlap sacks. The only evidence that it had housed Hannah's dreams and industry for twenty-six years was the Dollond telescope, which she'd left perched on its tripod like a gull on a weather vane. From a block away, Hannah could pick out Mr Geary standing in front of his new hat shop. He looked hale, at least from a distance. In the months that followed the fire, his gaunt presence hovered over the hammering and framing like a ghost, his remorse as thick as fog. Hannah was sure he'd never again leave a candle burning in his shop at night.

She skirted the crowd, looking for a familiar face. Mr Cobb, Mr Worth, Rebecca Swain, and a dozen others were lined up in front of their shops like proud veterans about to be decorated. Fishmonger, mapmaker, Citizen's Bank: every business now had gleaming glass windows and new lamps to go with them.

The crowd itself, though, seemed thin. The fire had accelerated the slow and steady exodus that had begun years earlier. Nearly all of her schoolmates had moved off-Island, pulled by the mills of Worcester, the ports of other American cities, and the lure of land cheap as dirt in Missouri and Wyoming and Oregon.

At least a half dozen ships had sailed for western shores the autumn after the fire, carrying away hundreds of families. More Islanders had fled over the winter, tired of doubling up like kittens with their neighbors while the Town rebuilt its candle-houses and wharves and library. With so few residents to begin with, and most of those homeless and deprived of their livelihoods, it had only seemed right for Hannah and her father to remain through the long winter to help their neighbors rebuild, solicit donations, and organize and distribute the clothing and provisions that arrived daily from the mainland along with a handful of intrepid entrepreneurs and hoteliers looking to capitalize on the sudden availability of seaside property. It would be different by summer, when the sunseekers from the mainland filled the streets with their chatter and festivities, undeterred by the previous summer's calamity, oblivious to everything but their own holidays. The realization that she wouldn't be here to be annoyed by them this year was bittersweet.

As Alderman Lacy took the stage, the musicians on the bandstand struck up a new tune. He praised everyone in attendance for their tireless devotion to reconstructing the Town. Hannah shivered and stuck her hands deeper in her pockets. Even through the cold, she could smell new wood and tar. The lamps looked like bare saplings. At the alderman's signal, the first one – in front of Mr Geary's shop – was lit.

When its light shone out over the crowd, a great cry went up, and Hannah found her own voice swelling alongside the rest, as if the hat shop were Bethlehem itself. Hannah wouldn't be here to see the rest of the Town grow up again, as it had two hundred years before, and again after the War for Independence. But knowing that the place would persist – a rock in a river of calamity – filled her with pride.

As the voices of the assembly died away, the small light glowing against the blue hush of early twilight reminded Hannah of Isaac's first look at the Heavens through her telescope. Her chest tightened under its layers of muscle and bone, silk and wool. Why had she separated from him at all? Why had she privately allowed the very forces she'd publicly rejected to guide her actions?

The answer, circling like a hawk, descended again, fierce and cruel: because she could not help it. Discipline, prejudice, modesty, shame – she wasn't even sure how to pick apart the threads woven into her actions on the roof. The only thing she knew for sure was that she had wasted the only chance she would ever have to show Isaac how she felt about him. If she had another opportunity – if Time could eddy like a tidal pool, swirling her back to that moment – she would behave differently. She would allow Isaac to touch her, allow herself to feel instead of think. To desire without denial. The notion made her inhale sharply, then puff out a sigh of steam in the chill air. There would be no such chance.

All in a row, the lamps were lit along Main Street, and after them came smaller ones set carefully in the window of each new storefront, so that the crowd was bathed in a warm yellow glow. As everyone turned to the tables full of doughnuts and hot cider, Hannah felt a soft hand on her shoulder.

'Hannah!' It was Lilian Archer. How did she always manage to find Hannah in a crowd? Her cheeks were rosy and her hands rested on her enormous belly. 'Is it true that you're leaving?'

Hannah nodded, grateful for a scrap of company.

'It is the truth. Tomorrow morning, in fact.'

'And Edward? How does he fare in the Holy Land?'

'Well, Mary is a far better correspondent, but as I understand it, they are by turns filled with awe and utterly exhausted. It's quite a lot of labor they signed on for. But they're happy.' It seemed impossible that eight months had passed since Edward had offered to stay on the Island, so that Hannah could stay, too. His offer had echoed in her memory dozens of times since that day, but she never regretted her answer. Accepting would have meant sacrificing his future for her own. Such a profound act of selfishness was difficult to envision, much less enact.

And even if she'd been inclined to convince him to stay, it wasn't at all clear that she wanted to. Amid the ashes of Nantucket Town and its Atheneum, her reputation, and especially her relationship with Isaac, she'd been unable to find a shard of life on the Island that promised to sustain her. Everywhere she went, from her own rooftop to the bluffs over Madaket to the shoreline at 'Sconset, she was haunted by the memory of Isaac's company, and the sting that accompanied it. She had missed Edward when he was away, but she'd known he would return, provided he survived the journey. It helped that he had written, erratic as his letters may have been. With Isaac's absence, she had none of these consolations.

Hannah had seen Edward and Mary off, and by the time the packet carried them away – possibly for good – on a hot August morning a month after the fire, Hannah had convinced herself that redemption would not come from an act of mercy by any man but from her own diligence and effort.

Lilian shook her head and crossed her arms.

'I cannot imagine Nantucket without you. You're like the lighthouse. Or the Portuguese bell.'

'A relic, you mean?'

Lilian's eyes widened, and Hannah laughed.

'Oh, no! I meant . . . you are the best of us, Hannah. What we were, anyway.'

Lilian glanced around and Hannah followed her gaze. Only half the faces around them were familiar, and of those only a few wore bonnets or wide hats. Most wore modern fashions.

'I don't know what we were, Lilian,' Hannah said, bending so that Lilian would hear her. 'Nor what we are. But I'll miss thee.'

The plain address was tender on Hannah's tongue,

though she was surprised that it had slipped out. Hannah hadn't addressed anyone but her father that way since her disownment from Meeting; the idea of tailoring her speech for those who'd censured her felt like hypocrisy. Their Discipline had proved flawed beyond reason; her intellect, or perhaps her ego, had balked at offering its architects even a morsel of honor. Hannah had been surprised that she didn't miss the silence more: her nostalgia was reserved for a kind of inner peace she no longer associated with her neighbors and elders.

Outwardly, she was the same woman she had been before; the idea of suddenly donning a wardrobe of colorful prints was laughable. But she no longer walked with her head down, focused on the tasks she needed to accomplish. Instead, she found herself wandering about the Island the way she had as a child, examining the flora and fauna and collecting seashells solely for the sake of their shapes or the way their iridescent bellies caught the light. And she had adopted her mother's old habit of winding a bit of colored ribbon into her hair before tucking it under her bonnet – when she even bothered to wear it.

Lilian looked genuinely sorry.

'Did you find renters, then?'

Hannah nodded. Only a week earlier, Nathaniel had finally contracted with a young couple from New Bedford who planned to purchase seaside property for an inn but hadn't yet found the 'perfect haven.' Mrs Hatter, a petite woman with perfect diction and an endless array of dresses with matching slippers, said it was hard to believe anyone had lived in the house at all, so immaculate was its condition.

Hannah would rather have seen the house occupied by people who weren't strangers, but the Hatters were the only candidates they had. Residents who'd chosen to remain were pouring their savings into rebuilding their own homes while lodging with family or friends, and wintering in the ruined town had little allure for mainlanders. So Nathaniel had signed the contract, and Hannah had crated the few items she hadn't already shipped to Philadelphia: two pewter bowls, a few books, their bedding. There was nothing left to do now but say good-bye.

'And what about your observations?' Lilian was asking. Hannah puffed out a sigh, steam swirling in the dim light.

She'd spent the months since Edward's departure in methodical pursuit of a wanderer, with no results besides eyestrain and fatigue. She ignored the journals George sent, wasted no time savoring his awed praise for her lost prize:

M. Rainault's comet should indeed have been Comet Price, he'd written. *If thee had only sent notice all the world would know it too. But I shall always refer to it thusly.*

She'd read his letter on a frigid January morning, after a night of fruitless sweeping, and attacked the garret like it was the cause of her suffering. She dismantled the old models of the Universe that cluttered the desk, and their thunderous landing in the woodpile was so satisfying that she'd swept the contents of the specimen shelf into a box, too, ignoring the smash and tumble of the fragile treasures.

Her fingers shook when she unpinned her father's favorite quotation from where it had loomed over her desk for more than a decade: *An undevout astronomer is mad.*

But she'd stormed downstairs with it pinched between two fingers like a stinking dishrag, blown the embers into flame like her life depended upon it, and cast it into the fire.

Even that heresy hadn't made her feel redeemed, or free. As she watched the flames lick the edges of the old parchment, testing and then devouring it whole, Hannah was reminded of the fire, of the drifting scraps of love and remorse she'd stuffed into her pockets, which led to thinking about Isaac. She'd dragged herself back up the stairs, heavy with sorrow, and stood over the box of specimens until she found the chunk of malachite he'd given her, and she plucked it out and polished it on her skirt, then sat down at her desk with it in her hand, soothed by its solid weight.

Isaac had faith in her; that much she knew. Whatever he might think of her character after the way she had treated him, there was no doubt in her mind that he believed in her ability to find a comet. She put the stone on the desk and stared at it, then took a sheet of paper from the back of her observing log, which was the only book left uncrated in the garret. *Dear Isaac,* she wrote, then paused. What could she say that would undo the damage she had done? And what good could come of it? He was gone; she was leaving; and even if she stayed, and he miraculously returned, then what? There was no future she could imagine in which a union between them could flourish, short of one that unfolded on a distant, desolate island where no one cared what color anyone else was. Was there such a place?

An image of a verdant island rose, a jewel cushioned by

the blue Atlantic: Flores. Hannah imagined setting up a small observatory there, teaching schoolchildren. Isaac working his family's land, catching fish for their dinner. Teaching her the words in his language that she would need to know: *star*, *map*, *love*. She would learn to garden; perhaps there would be children.

The image was so fantastic, Hannah had to smile in spite of the tears that sprang to her eyes as the vision dissolved. She knew nothing of Flores or its people, but they were unlikely to smile upon the foreign white bride of one of its sons. And what happiness would she find on distant shores, with no friends or family, no intellectual life and few correspondents? The mail took long enough to get from Cambridge to Nantucket; she could only imagine receiving news about astronomical innovations, new discoveries, and responses to her own sightings and findings months after they occurred, instead of just weeks. And, most important, she had no evidence to suggest that Isaac wanted anything to do with her.

It was a dream she did not allow herself again. Instead, she'd kept the malachite on her desk as a reminder of Isaac's words to her on a night that felt as if it had taken place a lifetime earlier: *Tu acharás. You will find.*

Every night, after dinner, she'd gone directly to the walk with her telescope, willing a comet to appear as if its luminous tail and bright nucleus would somehow by its distant light repair the condition of her spirit. But it had not obliged.

'Unfortunately, a comet has yet to reveal itself,' Hannah said to Lilian. 'To me, anyway.'

'Well, we'll miss you, Hannah. Take good care.' Lilian

squeezed her shoulder and Hannah reached up and grasped her hand, squeezing back. She didn't trust her voice to answer without shaking.

As the cheers of the crowd died down, Hannah fended off the depressing thought that the reeds and rocks of Nantucket would no more miss her than they'd miss a tern that alighted and then withdrew. When she spotted her father a few yards away, she was glad for the distraction, and she waded through the crowds until she was beside him.

'Did thee see the lighting?' she asked.

'Indeed.' He paused, as if unsure of what to say, then glanced at her as though guilty of something she hadn't yet caught him at. 'We've a long day tomorrow. Is everything ready?'

Hannah nodded, mute, wondering how he felt about leaving the place where he'd been born and raised, then married and had children of his own. His face revealed nothing, and it didn't matter, anyway. There was nothing left to say on the topic of their departure. There was no work for her here. Edward and Mary were gone. The house was packed. The farm had been sold. The Prices of Nantucket would remove in the morning.

'I'm going home for a final sweep of our skies,' she said.

Without warning, her father stepped closer and wrapped an arm around her. His rough coat scraped Hannah's cheek and she turned toward him, inhaling his particular, woolly smell. Her eyes filled with unexpected tears.

'My best memories will remain on this Island, my

daughter,' he said, leaning close to her ear, his voice raspy. 'With thee especially. I have no doubt that thy mind will find its occupation and more in Philadelphia. I think – no, I'm certain – that thy mother would agree.'

It was the closest he would come to forgiving her transgressions. His attempt at tenderness made her chest ache. But she didn't feel soothed. If anything, her melancholy deepened. What her mother would have thought, or felt, was a mystery Hannah would never solve; whatever power she'd drawn from a vision of that woman as an invisible advocate or guiding force had burnt out. Her father was the sole guardian of his memories of Ann; the fact that Hannah did not have her own could not be blamed on him. She was glad that he, at least, drew comfort from thinking he was doing the right thing.

Nathaniel Price cleared his throat and gave her a bracing squeeze, as if readying a soldier for the battle ahead. Then he squared his shoulders and turned back toward the bandstand.

Hannah stepped out of the nimbus of light surrounding the revelers, but she didn't feel ready to go home. Instead, she wandered down Main in the deepening twilight until she reached the wharves. Not a trace remained of the bobbing skeletons that had haunted the waters for weeks after the fire, dispersing in bits and washing up as far as Amagansett and Penobscot. A few of the destroyed whaleships had been rebuilt: the *Peregrine*, the *Centennial*, and the *Wauwinet* were moored off the bar, their shiny copper sheathing and fresh-hewn masts waiting for orders. Hannah wondered if they'd get their crews in New

Bedford, which had more shipyards and a deeper mooring, not to mention employable men.

Hannah circled back through the narrow streets, feeling like a hungry animal in search of prey. Each familiar quadrant had been reconfigured: corners in perpetual shadow had become bright as day; the frameworks for new wooden buildings popped bright as wildflowers from the grey paving stones. Without her even realizing where she was going, her feet carried her to the corner of Pearl and Federal.

The new Atheneum squatted in the footprint of the old like a gleaming white monolith. It was two stories high, a neoclassical structure with two enormous Ionic columns soaring like guardians to the peaked portico. She wondered what it looked like inside. Was the philosophy section still tucked into the north corner? Did the light at the day's end still slant across the floorboards like an ancient sundial?

Hannah's exclusion from the rebuilding had been complete. She hadn't been invited to be part of the planning process or the soliciting of new books; the Trustees had answered her written offer of assistance with a note befitting an illiterate stranger:

We are grateful for thy offer but thy assistance is not needed at this time.

All at once, Hannah fiercely missed the life she'd led before. Before the fire, before her disownment – before Isaac came, before Edward left. Her days had once ebbed and flowed with readers and questions, anchored by her sturdy desk, her tiny wooden girl amid her cabinet of wonders. All of it had gone up in flames.

The conversation she'd had with Edward so many years earlier, on the hill where they'd gazed down on their Town, returned to her again:

Bone and gold. Is that how we shall be remembered?

Hannah turned back toward India Street, her shoulders hunched, heavy with loss. A last sweep of these familiar stars; then she would say good-bye.

24. A New Object

By the time she got home from the lighting ceremony and up to the roof, night had fallen. The air was searing cold, but the sky spread above Hannah like a giant velvet wing speckled with stars. She pulled on her mittens and bent over her log. As she flipped through, she caught glimpses of her own entries from the past months:

4 mo 9 – a Pleiades occultation . . . waning moon already within the constellation as it rose . . . spotted Alcyone and Taygeta along her dark limb. Just before dawn swept from the far western side of the constellation clear across. No wanderers sighted.

22 mo 11 – Swept all around Aquarius, which is yet dim but contained between Pisces and Fomalhaut, just above the horizon to the South. No wanderers sighted.

16 mo 1 – Cygnus reveals nothing new, though a bit of cloudiness did catch my eye a few degrees southeast of Deneb, stretching toward Albireo. No wanderers sighted.

27 mo 2 – . . . nebulosity has resolved, nothing unusual. No wanderers sighted.

She'd worked her way around to Polaris, the Pole Star. *Back to the beginning,* she thought. An echo of her first rooftop lecture to Isaac drifted into her head: *Imagine that you're holding an enormous parasol, the tip of which ends at Polaris.*

She fastened the telescope into place and readied her chronometer. Before she looked, Hannah filled her lungs with cool air, hoping to clear her mind. Then she leaned in to the eyepiece.

The spread of stars above her was as soothing as a lullaby. Instead of scrutinizing the quadrant of stars in front of her lens, Hannah allowed herself a moment to appreciate the array. What an architect of great imagination was their Creator. She was overwhelmed by gratitude for the beauty of the Heavens. Even if she couldn't observe much in Philadelphia, at least she'd been given the gift of these years to explore the realm of fixed stars and wanderers, elusive as they might be, the nebulae in their veiled mystery. Sighing with pleasure, she readied her mind for sweeping, and focused on Polaris.

It was the first thing she saw: directly in front of her lens, a few degrees northeast of the Pole Star, a small, nebulous body occupied a space that had been empty the night before, and every night as far as she could recall. No star resided in that spot: she knew it as well as she knew the number of fingers on her own hand.

Hannah stared at the body for three full minutes, withdrawing her gaze only long enough to scribble an entry in the open logbook in her lap:

Circular body, 5d. above Polaris. Slight nebulosity, faint. Night uncommonly clear – nebula?? But which??

A cloud drifted over the body in question. Hannah

bolted across the walk and down the steps, then stopped short, confronted by an army of crates. Where had she packed *Celestial Objects*?

She pried the lid off one crate, than another, rifling through hay and crumpled newspaper, feeling with her fingers for the peculiar heft of the volume, the telltale crack in its spine. In the third box, her fingers curled around it, and she drew it out and paged through, her mind hopping from one possibility to another.

A new nebula, a portion of an old nebula, some other object well-known to the astronomical community but not to her? Hannah checked the maps and charts, confirming her first thought: there was no star logged in that position. Standing upright in the garret, the book cradled in her arms, her skin seemed to vibrate. She felt as awake as she'd ever been in her life.

Hannah raced back up the stairs and looked for the object again, finding it easily: a faint smudge on the dark palette of the sky. The longer she stared at it, the more she doubted. How could it be a comet, in such an obvious spot? Someone would have sighted it easily before now. It had to be a nebula, one she hadn't heard of. Yet . . . she studied the tiny blur again. It almost appeared to have a bright center, as would a comet or something with a comet's properties.

Hannah stared at the object until her eyes blurred, and then she gathered her skirts in her hand and leapt down the garret steps two at a time, slowing herself to a dignified pace before she stopped in front of her father's door. She counted to three, to calm herself, then knocked on the door as gently as she could.

'Hannah?' Her father opened the door in his dressing gown and nightcap. Hannah could see papers laid out upon the bed.

'I'm sorry to interrupt. I've seen something – I'm not sure what it is. I thought perhaps you could have a look.'

'What does thee think it is?' His gaze was indulgent, tender.

'I'm not sure. It's likely a nebula, but not one I've seen before.'

'Has thee consulted the catalogues?'

Hannah raised her eyebrows.

'Of course thee has. All right, give me a moment. If you think it's important, I'll come and look.'

Hannah whirled around and pounded back up to the walk. Five agonizing minutes passed before Nathaniel was beside her, peering through the Dollond. During that time, her mind danced among explanations, but landed each time upon the same conclusion. A current of excitement began to buzz in her chest and pound in her throat like a chemical reaction. But she would not let it spread until she knew for sure.

'You say there's nothing recorded for this region?' Her father squinted at the lens.

'Not by Admiral Smyth. But our copy of *Celestial Objects* is two years old.'

Hannah hopped from one foot to the other while he observed the object.

'It certainly could have some cometary properties,' he finally said.

'I thought so, too!' Hannah yelped. She was standing so

close behind him that when he rose, he almost knocked her over. 'I distinctly saw a bright nucleus.'

'Hannah,' her father said, his voice gentle, but firm. 'I'm sure you realize it's highly unlikely that if it is a comet, in such a location, that it's as yet undiscovered.'

'I know. I know that.' Panting a little, leaning into the eyepiece, she studied the tiny blur. 'It's most likely a nebula.'

'You can write to William in the morning if you like. Though you might want to wait and observe it again, to see if it changes position.'

'But when will I do that? If we're to leave tomorrow, I mean.'

Father and daughter stared at each other. When Hannah spoke, her words fell like wet snow, thick enough to stick.

'I should stay.'

'Hannah.'

'I know what you're going to say. But I have to know. The last time I found a comet –'

'The last time?' He looked at her as if she had said she'd sprouted wings once and flown to Trinidad.

'Yes. The comet Monsieur Rainault has earned priority for? You remember?'

'I read on the discovery.'

'I saw it earlier. I saw it and I didn't report it, because I thought I might be mistaken. I doubted myself.' She began to pace the walk.

'But why, Hannah? If thee thought thee'd seen a comet, why didn't thee give notice?'

She shook her head and wrapped her arms around her body.

'No one expected me to see anything. So I stopped expecting to. And then, when I did, I didn't trust myself.' Hannah raised her chin, though her hands were shaking. 'I won't do it again. I'll write to George right now and post it in the morning, and if what I've seen is nothing, I'll join thee in Philadelphia in a week's time. But I will not leave until I know for sure whether it's something or nothing. I cannot.'

Hannah stared into her father's familiar eyes. Her pulse was a drum corps in her ears, and her nose was running. She felt terrified but strong, as if she were swimming for her life.

He sighed, as if to fortify himself.

'As thee wishes,' he said. 'I only hope that thee is not disappointed. Again.'

20 mo 3, 1846. Nantucket.

Dear George,

Forgive the shortness of this letter and my poor handwriting, but I am writing this very late and with the last of my candle. I observed something this evening that has some cometary properties. See attached for exact RA and location, &c., and a sketch. I won't lie and say I shan't be severely disappointed if it turns out to be a nebula; but of course I will chart its actions again tomorrow, weather permitting.

Please advise at your earliest convenience whether you have knowledge of any object in the night sky at this location and what it looks like through your instruments.

Father removes for Philadelphia today but I have refused to join pending resolution of this matter (no pun intended!). Thus

*I await your reply anxiously and hope that you will not make me
wait among my boxes for too long.*

Your friend,
HGP

After Hannah had sealed the envelope, she remained at
her desk, as energized as if she'd just woken from the best
night's sleep of her life. Yet she wasn't satisfied by the letter to George, or her father's reluctant approval of her
plan to wait on Nantucket for her priority to be validated
or refuted.

I have done it is what she needed to say. *I believe it in my
heart, though I cannot yet prove it.*

There was only one person to whom she would utter
such a thought, and that was Isaac Martin. Hannah slid
her observing log along the desk until it was in front of
her, then pulled out the page from the back that still held
the two words she'd committed to it months earlier, and
smoothed it down on the table before her. Then she
picked up her quill.

20 mo 3, 1846
Nantucket via the Explorer

Dear Isaac:

*I am in hopes that this letter finds you well, and in fair winds, if it
finds you at all. And that if it does, you will read it through to the
end, and not tear it into pieces and toss it into the sea.*

*You may have heard about the fire here on Nantucket that
devastated our Town. It was exceedingly bad. The Atheneum*

burned to the ground, along with 1/3 of everything else. Much of it has been rebuilt but the wharves did burn, along with whatever portion of the fleet was docked, and while commerce continues everyone knows it will never be what it once was. Perhaps the Pearl will next sail from New Bedford, or Boston, and never again be floated into our Bay, which may not matter to you. But the idea of our Town reduced to a quaint haven for sea-goers saddens me.

Next: I believe I have found a Comet. I only just saw it tonight; it may have been seen by someone else in the United States or in Europe. For all I know, you may have seen it, too, as you gazed at the night sky where you are. If it does turn out that not a single observer at home or abroad did see 'my' comet before me, then I may be eligible for the King of Denmark's prize, which comes with enough currency to fund this and at least another year of modest living – and of course I know of no other kind.

While I await word, I have resolved that I shall not leave the Island, and if it takes longer than my Father will support, I shall subsist on pebbles and potatoes. I can teach, or tutor, or both; I'm thinking about starting a school of my own. Though I'm not sure many of Nantucket's families would entrust their children to me.

Finally, and there is no news in this, I wish to offer what I have not, until this point, been able to articulate in a letter, and barely to myself, which is my profound apologies for the way I behaved when we last met. I know that I wounded you. I did not write of it sooner because I was – and am – confounded by my feelings. I have no experience with these matters. Yet it is no excuse. I foundered when it was most important.

Now I must be direct. I have not stopped thinking of you; yet I cannot imagine anywhere that such thinking can lead. It is unproductive, at best, and distracting, at worst. Yet I cannot seem to stop, in spite of all my industry. I fear that you despise me. Or worse, that you pity me. I would understand either.

I write to ask your forgiveness, and in hopes that I may remain,

Your friend,
Hannah Gardner Price

24 March, 1846
Cambridge, MA

Dear Hannah,

You have done it! ('As far as we can ascertain at the present time,' my father says I must add.)

Please await our next — we've sent word to Professors Hanover and Munch at the Royal Observatory to give notice of your discovery and they will advise whether you are indeed the first to have seen what we can affirm is absolutely a comet — one which none among us, with all our instruments and accolades, did notice until you showed us where to look! If you are, you'll be eligible for the King of Denmark's prize.

In the meantime, write up an account of the sighting and we will submit on your behalf to the foreign journals. Well done! (I didn't doubt for a moment, of course.)

Your friend and great admirer,
GB

25. The Island

Word of Hannah's discovery completed its orbit from the Cambridge Observatory to its students and supporters to Miss Norris to the oldest and newest residents of Nantucket in less than two weeks. Hannah wandered into the kitchen that was no longer hers on the first day of May to find Elizabeth and William Hatter, the renters, waiting for her at the table. They'd agreed to let her keep her room while she waited for the Bonds to communicate the decision from Europe on whether she had – or had not – indeed been the first to see the comet.

Elizabeth gripped the edge of a plate of pancakes; both had the barely suppressed zeal of people bursting to share some exciting and unexpected news.

'Miss Price!' she bubbled the second Hannah entered the room. 'We've heard something extraordinary! Isn't that so, William?'

She glanced at her husband, who looked unusually alert, and pushed the plate and a fork in Hannah's direction. Living with the Hatters was like bouncing from season to season: she was constant, bubbling spring, and he was deep winter.

He nodded. 'Very impressive.'

Hannah slid onto the bench and took a bite of cold pancake.

'Have you found a property for your inn?' Hannah sank

in her seat. Were they leaving? She'd have to find new renters immediately. In spite of George's certainty that her comet was indeed hers, Nathaniel wasn't convinced that Hannah could – or should – remain on the Island and wait for formal confirmation. She'd talked him into a month of support; when that ran out, she'd have to find an income if she wished to stay, or follow her belongings to Philadelphia.

'No, my dear,' Elizabeth chirped. 'Though we're certainly scouring the seashore day and night. More syrup? No?'

Hannah shook her head..

'It's news of you, we mean. Of your great discovery!'

'Oh! The comet?'

'Well, of course!' Elizabeth picked up the bowl of syrup again, and Hannah again refused it.

'But how did you hear of it? It's not even confirmed I was the first to see it.'

'Well, the *Inquirer* made it seem as if your priority isn't a bit in doubt. See here.'

William snapped the newspaper into a crisp sheet and slid it over to Hannah, then leaned over to tap one long finger on a corner notice. She squinted at the tiny print:

Telescopic Comet Discovered by Miss Hannah Price;
  First Lady Contender for King of Denmark Prize Embroiled
  in Controversy Over Reporting Irregularities.
  Miss Hannah Price of Little India St, well known to Nan-
  tucketers as the former junior Librarian of our own Atheneum,
  has stunned the astronomy community of these United States by
  becoming the first to spot the luminous skyblazer at approximately

318

10pm on the night of 20 March. The mysterious object was lurking only a few degrees north of our own Pole Star, and through her diligent observations Miss Price did record its position and fire off a breathless note to Messrs. William and George Bond at the great observatory in Cambridge, asking those fine gentlemen to affirm her discovery.

They did at once confirm the lady's finding, but as it happens, the rules of the King's medal, which we have no doubt Miss Price deserves, require notice sent directly to the Royal Observatory in London.

All are in hopes that Justice will prevail in this matter, and that the King's medal will be awarded to our own Lady Skygazer, who is reported at present to be calculating the orbit of her fiery celestial jewel.

Hannah's face curled into disbelief as she read the brief article, and when she came to the end she flung the pages on the table as if they were covered in slime. The Hatters blinked in unison.

'Is it not an excellent notice, Miss Price?' Elizabeth asked, reaching over to smooth the pages. 'You're famous!'

'You don't understand,' Hannah said, feeling the need to move at once. She stood up and began to pace around the kitchen. 'My priority hasn't even been confirmed – not officially, in any case. Certainly not globally. And the King's medal – I had no idea I'd not complied with the rules.'

She slumped back onto the bench, her strength gone. The reality of her predicament was as glaring as the fresh black ink on the white page. If she wasn't eligible for the prize, there was no hope of her staying on-Island. Instead of being known as the recipient of the King of Denmark's prize, she'd be the astronomer who had failed to earn it. The *lady* astronomer who couldn't even follow the rules. Who would entrust her with their observations then? Her accomplishment would pale in comparison to her omission. She'd never be offered a contract that would provide an income.

The Hatters fell silent along with her. The kitchen felt like the Atheneum during quiet hours. Then William snapped to.

'Well, are the rules published? If they are, we can resolve that bit straightaway. I'm an attorney by training, you know. This whole inn-keeping business is Elizabeth's folly. I merely provide finance.'

'William is a brilliant interpreter of contracts, Miss Price. If the rules have any leeway, he's sure to find them,' his wife chirped.

'I have a copy upstairs,' Hannah said slowly, not allowing the glimmer of hope to blossom into anything brighter. The promise of disappointment was too great. 'I'll go and get them.'

A half an hour and three cold pancakes later, it was determined that Hannah had indeed slighted the rules by sending notice of her finding to Cambridge instead of London.

'Well,' William said, tapping the slip of paper outlining the contest rules and then smoothing it again, 'it does say that applicants must inform the Royal Observatory "at first opportunity." But we might argue that your remote location and lack of professional expertise made it seem impertinent for you to write directly to London without first confirming your finding locally. Just for the sake of argument, of course,' he added, seeing the look on Hannah's face.

'I suppose,' she muttered. 'I'll wait for word from the Bonds. I'm sure they've a better idea how these things work than any of us.'

'Well, in the meantime, fix your mind on the present. I'm certain you have all manner of exciting business to attend to,' Elizabeth said, and patted Hannah's arm. Then she folded the paper carefully and placed it on a high shelf of the kitchen, standing on her tiptoes to reach. Hannah remembered herself in just the same position as a little girl, striving to add something bright and beautiful to her shelf of specimens. Mrs Hatter could be no more than twenty years of age, Hannah realized, studying her profile. No wonder she was so excited about everything: her inn, the comet, the life stretching ahead of her. She'd probably be pregnant before the year was out.

'I thank both of you,' Hannah said, seized by a sudden rush of emotion. Where was *her* family at this crucial hour? Why must she rely on the assistance of strangers? She felt adrift, though she was sitting in her own kitchen, eating off the same dented pewter plate she'd washed and dried a thousand times. But her gratitude was real. The Hatters didn't have to help her. They weren't part of Meeting, though given her current standing it wouldn't much matter if they were. They'd mentioned being Unitarians, but they'd been at the house on First Day, so they clearly hadn't attended services.

Sunday, she reminded herself. The farther she got from Meeting and daily conversation with its members, the easier it became to shed its dozens of tiny restrictions, like a seam coming slowly undone. Her eyes drank in the bright pinks and dandelion yellows in the curtains Elizabeth had hung in the parlor, and she appreciated how the woven rugs that padded the floors softened the angles of the rooms. But her tongue still tripped over the days of the week and the months of the year, which seemed to beg to be numerically ordered rather than named like pets.

'You've been very kind to let me stay. I hope not to impose too much longer.'

'No imposition at all,' William said. 'We're honored to be temporarily installed in such a famous scientist's home.'

Elizabeth nodded her agreement and, going to stand behind her husband, rested her hands on his shoulders.

'Well, I'm truly grateful.' Hannah swallowed the lump in her throat and rose from the table. 'I'll see you at supper.' Once upstairs, she spent most of the day bent over her notebook, trying to compute the comet's orbit. At least the *Inquirer* had gotten that much right.

When she finally emerged, squinting in the late afternoon light, it seemed that every person on Nantucket had seen the notice in the paper. By the time she reached Main Street she'd been approached by a half dozen well-wishers, some hesitant, some hearty. Each time another acquaintance approached, Hannah was startled anew: she hadn't spoken with many of these people in months, or rather, they hadn't spoken with her. In the aftermath of her disownment from Meeting, she'd been unofficially shunned by nearly all its older members, few as they were.

But everyone she encountered this afternoon, regardless of religious affiliation, seemed to know more about the comet, her priority, and the King's prize than Hannah did. One woman told her she'd heard the prize was to be delivered by the King's consul in person by steamship; another congratulated her on discovering a new planet.

When she went to buy bread, Millicent Rotch – granddaughter of an elder and one of the few young people who remained at Meeting and addressed her neighbors as 'thee' regardless of their age or standing – leaned across the counter as she wrapped the loaf in paper.

'My mother disapproves of platform women,' she whispered when she handed it over. 'But I think thee is both smart and brave.'

'Platform women?' Hannah kept her voice low and tried not to laugh. 'Where would she get that idea about me?'

'Well, first there was that Negro man thee was going about with,' Millicent said. Her cheeks flushed even pinker, but her gaze was clear and steady. 'Lilian Archer said thee was helping the Antislavery Society convince the Atheneum trustees to allow their convention to meet there. And now the comet.'

'I never told her that,' Hannah snapped, though Millicent was only voicing what much of the Island had thought of her, at least until recently. She shook her head, a wave of indignation beginning to well up as she considered the fawning flocks of people she'd encountered that morning. Her neighbors were as base as the residents of any other part of the world. Any new scrap of fortune or calamity would eclipse the one that came before as easily as the sun sinking over the horizon. 'And I've never made a speech in my life.'

'Perhaps you should,' Millicent whispered. 'It's so exciting. I wish I had some occupation besides this. I'd love to study the Heavens. But I haven't the head for it.'

Hannah leaned over the counter.

'Well, every time I bake something, it either burns or turns to stone. And at least your work actually earns currency.'

Millicent sighed and looked around to see if anyone was near before she answered. 'It's my mother's currency, not mine.'

'Are you any good with maths?'

'I suppose. I keep our books.'

'Well, any time you want to learn the basics of astronomy, come and see me,' Hannah said.

Millicent's eyes went round as full moons.

'Really? But when would I?'

'Any time it's dark, Millicent.'

Her smile made Hannah happier than she'd felt since she'd ripped open George's letter. Let the Town mutter about her turning its women away from their fine, productive jobs. But her good mood didn't last.

As she walked past the Atheneum, Miss Norris came flying out, *Nantucket Inquirer* in hand.

'Miss Price, Miss Price!' she hooted.

'Miss Norris,' Hannah said, suppressing a smile. The older woman looked like a stuffed goose, her dark eyes beady bright and her plump arm waving, wing-like.

'I'm just thrilled. Thrilled!'

'It's not certain that I —'

'Nonsense! Thee did and thee has!'

'What I mean is, the matter isn't settled.'

'That old King should be deposed if he denies the award! That's what I think and so does everyone.' Miss Norris lowered her voice and tipped her wide neck toward Hannah like a conspirator. 'There's talk among the Trustees of reinstating thy position!'

Hannah felt her eyebrows rise into twin arches.

'Is there? No one's mentioned it to me.'

'Well, I don't think it's quite settled. But Dr Hall is strongly in favor.'

'I see.'

'I'm sure thee would do well to speak to him in person.'

Hannah nodded but didn't answer. The idea of speaking to Dr Hall about anything made her feel sick.

'I'll take it under advisement,' Hannah said, trying to be polite.

'Do. I'd love to have thee back.' Miss Norris lowered her voice and glanced around. 'I never agreed with the decision to keep thee out of the rebuilding. Even after what went on at Meeting. And as for that young man thee was teaching, well, I think all the outcry was for nothing. If one of his race was lucky enough to have thee as a teacher, I saw no harm in it. It's not as if thee were morally deranged. I say people behaved hysterically. Myself, I said Hannah Price is no more likely to enter into an improper relationship with a dog or pony!'

Hannah took a step back, feeling like she'd been slapped. The white wooden building behind the librarian was so bright, it practically glowed. Hannah shook her head, hoping to clear it; then she reached out and snatched the newspaper from Miss Norris' hand.

'You ought to check your facts,' she said, and turned her back on Miss Norris and the building.

'What? Miss Price? Hannah!'

As Hannah walked away, faint impressions of the columns danced in front of her eyes like wisps of smoke. She kept her head down as she went, trying to choke down the wad of fury that had sprung into her throat. A dog or pony. That's what Miss Norris equated Isaac with. Hannah couldn't have felt more disgusted and ashamed. Isaac was a man – he was a good man, a smart man. A man with ambition no different from her own. She ached to share her thoughts with him, to rest her head upon his shoulder.

It would never be. Once, when she was but sixteen, Hannah had caught the end of a speech by William Lloyd Garrison. He'd been speaking at the Boston Common, and Hannah had been in a carriage with her father and William Bond. They'd drawn the curtains and ordered the driver to take a different route, fearing a mob, but Hannah had heard the thunder from the platform as they clattered by: *I cannot but regard oppression in every form – and most of all, that which turns a man into a thing – with indignation and abhorrence!*

They'd all gone quiet, Hannah remembered, though William had nodded gravely.

That which turns a man into a thing . . . Or equates him with an animal, Hannah thought. Miss Norris would deny she held a shred of prejudice in her heart. She'd been vocally opposed to the segregation of the schoolchildren, and Hannah knew she opposed slavery. Yet the idea that Hannah could view Isaac Martin as anything other than a pupil in need of tutoring – that she could befriend him, respect him, love him – was unimaginable to her.

As she walked, Hannah turned this paradox over and over in her mind, searching for a way to reconcile these two truths, but found none. By the time she got upstairs to the garret, she was spent, though strangely calm. What would have been a revelation just two years earlier – that two competing Truths could in fact coexist in one mind – now seemed like a perplexing but obvious conclusion. She heard Isaac's voice as clearly as if he'd been standing beside her: *Black or white. This or that. How are you believing that all things proceed in this way?*

'I'm not,' she said out loud. 'They don't.' Her voice echoed off the walls. Flecks of dust swirled in the rays of light streaming through the window. She sat down at her desk and opened her notebook.

April 15, 1846. Nantucket.
via the Neptune

Dear Isaac,

Three weeks have elapsed since I wrote to you, so of course there is no possible way you could have received my letter and responded to it by now. Yet each day that passes it becomes more intolerable to me that I delayed so long in writing to begin with, and I imagine all manner of ideas you may have formed about me in the interim. Equally intolerable are the number of times in each day when I think of you but cannot communicate my ideas directly. The quill is a poor substitute for your company, especially without knowing if you are receiving these letters at all.

My thoughts wander. I am still awaiting formal confirmation of priority for my comet, and each day it does not come from Europe is another in which I doubt myself and must redouble my Faith. At these times I think of you the most. You have had to prove yourself in so many ways. It makes complaining about the limitations upon Women seem quaint by comparison. Yet I find it increasingly galling that the eyes of girls be trained on the measuring spoon and mixing bowl when the same attention to detail might be accorded the movement of stars across the prime vertical; that those who excel at attention to detail squander their capacities on the minutiae of domestic demands, and their energy on idle chatter.

I once abhorred platform women, feeling that railing at men would not change anything, but I begin to wonder if the firm and constant application of reason in combination with passion does not do some good; I think I come partly to this from the strong impression left upon me by Margaret Fuller, whose treatise on modern women I have finally read. Here I will copy out a passage for you:

'We would have every path laid open to women as freely as to men. If you ask me what offices they may fill, I reply – any. I do not care what case you put; let them be sea captains, if you will.'

It reminded me of games I once played with my brother, in which we explored the Earth from end to end from our 'ship' at Madaket. I suppose my new thinking on the matter of leaving v. remaining must be due in part to finding myself as free of all entanglements and obligations as you feel yourself to be, though I'm not sure I could ever move through the world with your ease.

Yet as time passes, all I held to be familiar and necessary as a buoy begins to resemble an anchor; perhaps I hold myself back in remaining, as Edward suggested, though where I might remove, even with means to choose my own place, is a mystery. You've seen more of the world than I; where might my place be?

Your True Friend,
HGP

26. Return to Cambridge

Cambridge in June crackled with students and visitors. Term had ended a few days earlier, and proud graduates strolled everywhere, trailed by parents and young ladies hoping a promise was imminent. Hannah studied them while she fanned herself with a pamphlet, trying to imagine herself as the former, then the latter. But she couldn't see herself in either role. Her feelings about the boys and their books were milky; she could no longer conjure the righteous indignation of earlier visits. As for the women, she had to remind herself not to judge, even though their flounces and rouged cheeks made her wince. For all she knew, they might be studying the stars at night as diligently as herself. Or writing sonnets. Or debating.

Watching them, though, she was reminded that her own position was no more certain than theirs. She'd been living in a strange suspended state in which her future was neither assured nor doomed. If Europe decided in her favor, the currency that came with the King's prize would secure her livelihood for a year at best; if it decided against her priority, she'd need to find paying work immediately, or she'd be right back where she started: choosing between a marriage of convenience or a move to Philadelphia.

She'd prepared herself for the latter, but that was before the comet had appeared before her lens. In the wake of her priority – if it was indeed to be accorded her – the idea of moving to Philadelphia and leaving her observations behind seemed a spectacular failure of imagination. To that end, the former had been playing in the background like distant music ever since she accepted George's latest invitation to visit.

She'd never formally answered his proposal, and as her remaining banknotes diminished with no word about the Prize and no letters from Isaac, the idea of aligning her fate with George's had become more difficult to dismiss. She still hadn't settled on a decision, but she meant to bring it up when the moment seemed right. Perhaps he had some new insight that would help crystallize the decision for both of them. She couldn't very well marry him unless he knew that she had no romantic feelings for him, and accepted that arrangement as mutually beneficial in some way; but she didn't want to hurt his feelings, or his chances to find a true match. Then again, weren't there some marriages that began as friendships but blossomed into love over time? Should she not be open to such a possibility in this case?

But the idea made her queasy, not because George was awful, but because he was not Isaac Martin, and feeling what she felt for Isaac for anyone else was impossible. Still, she spent a good portion of the trip trying to reason herself into or out of just such a decision.

The carriage ticked to a halt in front of the observatory before she could arrive at a conclusion, and the instant it stopped George himself flung open the door.

'My famous friend,' he said, making a little bow. Hannah laughed and took his arm as she stepped down and stretched her neck. The sight of his familiar tousled hair and pale face was comforting. She squeezed his elbow, hoping he wouldn't notice her blush and read anything into it.

'My loyal supporter,' she answered. 'Without your help I'm sure I'd still be hidden away in my garret, counting transits and teaching schoolchildren. Wait – I *am* still counting transits! And I'm sure I'll be teaching again sooner or later, since no other occupation has made itself apparent.'

'Bah,' he said, taking the valise her driver handed down. 'We'll have you set up in no time, I'm certain. Meanwhile, you're here and there's plenty to discuss.'

'Your sun is eternally shining,' Hannah said, hitching up her skirts and following him inside. 'It's amazing you're able to observe anything. Ah, but here's your secret.'

She stopped at the foot of the giant telescope, which loomed like an ogre, and laid her hand upon it. She wished she could put her cheek on the cool, polished tube.

'I might have some other tricks up my sleeve,' George said from the doorway.

'I thought you'd shown your hand,' Hannah called, meaning to tease him as always, then realizing that, in light of his proposal, her words had a double meaning. She drew a breath to broach the subject and tried to order her thoughts, but they were as sticky and tangled as wet clothes in a basket.

'Touché,' he said. He came and stood beside her, grinning like a schoolboy up to no good. 'But speaking of my hand . . . since you were honest enough to point me toward the possibility of – what was it you called it? A "true match"? – the almost unthinkable has occurred.'

'You've dedicated yourself to the pursuit of astronomical progress to the exclusion of all else?' Hannah said, wondering what he could be getting at.

'Well, not quite, though my father would certainly be forever indebted to you were it to be so. Rather, I've found myself ... that is ... well ...' He put her valise down, fumbling with the handle, and his bravado seemed to dissolve. Hannah wondered if he was having some kind of attack, or if he was about to repeat his proposal, or announce that he was moving to Nantucket to prove his affection. She took a small step back, trying to prepare a response.

'There's a lady,' he blurted.

Hannah blinked, too stunned to respond, and George found his voice again and leapt into the silence.

'She was visiting her brother, who was a student here these past years – quite a good student, actually, and not so full of hot air as his classmates, but I'd not taken notice of him much until he brought her along to observe an occultation – and, well, the family lives just south of here, and we've been corresponding. She's quite interesting, actually. Phenomenal at the piano, though that's incidental, of course; she's actually an accomplished botanist: knows more about flora and fauna than anyone I've met, and she's cultivated a greenhouse that's not to be believed.'

He's in love, Hannah thought, watching his eyes flash and his hands dance in the air as he went on about the lady's ability to divine one green thing from another. She smiled, though her chest tightened with a sharp sadness that felt like the snap of a twig. In an instant, the door that led to a life with George had closed, and though she hadn't wanted to pass through it, she was stung.

She put her hand on her friend's arm.

'She's truly lucky, George.'

He tilted his head and studied her face, and she didn't look away.

'Did I . . . I mean, were you . . . You never answered me so I assumed –'

She shook her head.

'You acted with perfect courtesy. Beyond courtesy. It was I who delayed in responding, even though I knew that in the interest of both our sanity and happiness, we'd do best to remain the closest of friends.'

George slumped with relief but didn't pull his arm away. His voice had a quiet sincerity she had rarely heard.

'I've always wanted only your happiness.'

'As I wish for yours,' she said, leaning in to put her free hand atop his. Hannah savored the sweetness of the moment, even as a final spark of doubt flared. Had she been mistaken in not accepting George? But she knew the answer.

'Well.' George straightened up and they extracted their hands at the same time, like children caught sneaking cookies. 'We had another visitor recently that will be of interest to you. He had to be off, but consented that we share a certain piece of news with you.'

He reached down and gripped her valise again, turning toward the hall that led to his father's office. At one time she would have snatched it from him, insisting it made no sense for him to struggle. Now she understood that he might want to carry it anyway. Not everything had to make perfect sense.

'Hannah Price, welcome, welcome. We couldn't be prouder if you were our own daughter,' the senior Bond gushed as George held the door open for Hannah. Embarrassed, she ducked into the small room. Its familiar jumble of tools and lenses, chronometers and sighting tubes, reminded Hannah of his old shop.

'Thank you, William. I hope I can live up to such praise.'

Warmed by his affection, Hannah sank into one of the chairs, shifting to avoid the springs. William spared no expense on instruments, but everything in his study was about to fall apart.

'How is your father faring in Philadelphia, then?' William asked, settling in the chair next to her while George perched on the desk.

'Well, I believe,' she said, pausing to consider. 'I haven't had much detail. We've rather been corresponding about my finding, and what it means, if it means anything at all. He mentioned that you'd asked the President of the College to post a note on my behalf to the Astronomer Royal in London.' She tilted her head at William. 'Can it be true?'

'Of course it's true!' William reached over to cuff her on the shoulder, then checked himself and gave her an awkward pat on the arm instead. 'You're far too humble for your own good, Hannah.'

'It's not humility at all! It's practicality. The likelihood of my having seen that comet, in that location, before anyone in the entire world, is – mathematically speaking – extraordinarily thin. Surely you agree.'

William and George exchanged a look, and then George said, 'May I?'

His father nodded, and the younger Bond shifted his body to face Hannah.

'What would you say the probability is? Of your priority, I mean.'

'I've not calculated it, George.'

'Guess.'

'I won't.'

'Humor me.'

Hannah refrained from rolling her eyes but sighed loudly.

'One in a million?'

'Well, then you're exceedingly lucky. We, of course, realize that your discovery was a result of your unflagging diligence and magnificent eyesight.'

'Get on with it, George,' William said.

'Right. Hannah, your priority has been confirmed by London. Comet Price is officially yours. Rome thought it was their prize, as one of their own saw it two days after you – but once we submitted your claim and explained the circumstances, etc., they decided in your favor.'

Hannah gripped the worn upholstery of the chair arms, feeling the fabric under her fingers, engulfed by the warm air of the room. It smelled like tobacco and ink; there was a metallic twinge of something ignited and then snuffed out. George's words dropped through her and disappeared into an invisible hollow.

'You're certain?' she asked.

Father and son laughed in unison; Hannah felt as if she were spinning gently, like a leaf in a current.

'Everyone is certain, Hannah,' George said. 'Except you, apparently.'

'I don't know what to say.' She glanced up at her old friend, as if he could tell her what she was supposed to do now that everything she'd worked and hoped for had come to fruition. But he only reached across the space between them and took her hand. Tears sprang to Hannah's eyes. She'd been carrying the weight of her ambition for so long that setting it down made her feel unmoored.

She let go of George's hand and stood up, then sat down again.

'What do I do now?' She looked from William to his son and back.

'Whatever you wish, my dear.'

'Well . . . I still need to earn a living.' Before she could contemplate how she might translate her priority into some kind of income, George burst out laughing.

'True!'

He seemed so delighted that Hannah wondered if he'd misunderstood her.

'That brings us back to the topic of our guest,' he said, hopping to his feet like a sparrow. 'Our other piece of news.'

'Did you mention Dr Bache's offer to Hannah?' William asked.

'Father! *I* wanted to tell her.'

William sighed and shook his head.

'It's not a parlor game, George.' The elder Bond turned toward Hannah. 'Dr Bache has taken on oversight of the Depot of Charts and Instruments. Including the *Nautical Almanac.*'

'And?' Hannah tried not to imagine anything. The chance was so slim. But hope gripped her ribs and squeezed.

'We were speaking of your superb mathematical skills, and of course of your recent discovery, and he expressed his desire to contract you as a computer. I think he said he needed someone to do the tables for Venus. Is that right, George?'

'Quite right.' George seemed to be resisting the urge to pout.

'Washington wants to hire me as a computer?' she repeated, knowing that she sounded doltish, but unable to overcome her disbelief and say anything smart.

'Starting immediately. He said, if you were amenable, to write a note straightaway and he'd send the terms, et cetera. It's not much money, I'm afraid, but I don't have to tell you that it's a prestigious appointment. To say the least.'

Hannah stared at George. Her priority confirmed; an income that would at least buoy her position if not keep her permanently afloat. She could stay on Nantucket, even without her father's support. And Comet Price would be recorded and reported for all time, blazing through the Heavens, bearing her name like a bright beacon. These were the facts. Yet she felt numb.

'Aren't you happy?'

George's eyes were full of concern.

'Yes,' she said. 'I'm very happy.'

'You don't look it.'

'I'm certain a sufficient display of emotion is imminent,' she muttered. He was right: she should be floating off her chair. But the victory felt shallow. The Bonds were *like* family, but they weren't family. Hannah ached for her father, for Edward. They should be here with her. In the next instant she thought of Isaac's wonderful eyes, the warmth of his body, the comfort of his faith. She wished, above all, that she could savor this moment with him.

She shook her head to rid it of longing. Had she not spent the last few years trying to unbind herself from the strictures placed upon her by men? Yet her shining moment paled without their validation. It was a weak showing at best. Surely she owed herself a bit more enthusiasm.

Energized, she hopped to her feet beside George.

'All right. What now?'

'That's better,' George said. 'We've arranged a viewing party. You're to become a part of history twice in one day.'

'We're to crack open the Heavens, dear,' William whispered, leaning toward her. 'Today we shall finally see if our Great Refractor was worth its trouble and expense!'

Five hours later, Hannah stood in a hushed semicircle of important men. Edward Everett, the President of Harvard College, was to her right; to her left stood Dr Asa Gray, the Secretary of the American Association of Arts and Sciences, and Professor Joseph Henry of the National Institute. Even Mr Whittle, the haughty observatory assistant George had introduced her to earlier that evening, looked suitably grave. Hannah suppressed a rare urge to giggle at the absurdity of her own presence at such a seminal event, and put her hands at her sides, then behind her back. Lamplight flickered on the somber faces of the men as they gazed up at the open dome and the sky beyond.

It was a liquid midnight, the moon bright as a silver fish in a dark sea. William had ascended the throne-like observing chair, and shouted directions to George, who was up on a pedestal at the foot of the mount.

Hannah heard William gasp as he leaned into the monolithic instrument. Two minutes later, he descended as if dazed and then swept his arms up toward the sky.

'Gentlemen! And lady! The Great Refractor is hereby in service.' Then he swiveled toward Hannah.

'Might I suggest that the lady astronomer be the first to ascend the throne of progress?' he said quietly.

All those present nodded in agreement.

Flushed and unnerved, she took William's hand and allowed him to guide her onto the first step. There she paused, but tugged her elbow free, and took the rest of the steps on her own, blood drumming in her ears and palms so slick she had to wipe them on her skirt for fear of harming the instrument. Below her, the pale crescent faces of the assembly peered skyward.

She leaned into the lens.

24 June, 1846.
Cambridge, Mass.

Tonight a slice of the Universe was offered to me, and I devoured that part of the Heavens that had been apportioned me with a rabid hunger. I was given the Moon; I have looked upon her with a clarity and closeness I never imagined possible. It was magnificent, seen through the great telescope at Cambridge, its luminosity pocked by shadow from the mountains and craters. I imagined that I could feel its power working upon my very blood, pulling me like a tide, great and fearful; and thoughts of tides led me to thoughts of Isaac. How he would be moved by its beauty, and how much better he would be able to describe it, in his language or mine.

I'm to be assigned a job computing the tables of Venus for our nautical almanac. I fear the contract speaks more to the influence of the Bonds than my own mathematical prowess – the ink is barely dry on the publication of 'my' comet's orbit. I cannot as yet write of it without that coy punctuation, in spite of the confirmation. It is Comet Price that shall be recorded.

Dr Henry from the forthcoming Smithsonian Institute came to supper with us on my final day at Cambridge and said he's certain I'll be awarded the King of Denmark's prize. All of which suggests that I might remain on Nantucket after all until the end of my days. Yet I still feel as if there are two Islands: the one Before – before the comet, before Isaac – and the one After. And they are not the same.

I imagine him upon the deck of the Pearl, lit by the same Moon with which I am now intimately familiar. This thought soothes me as I prepare to sleep.

27. Recognizable Objects

By the flickering light of a candle, Hannah examined her reflection: with her dark hair flowing loose around her face, the taut geometry of her cheekbones and jaw was softer, making her look less severe. More womanly, she thought. She squinted at the tiny lines etched into her forehead. They seemed to have expanded, like a root system. Maybe the candlelight made her look older. Or maybe twenty-seven *was* old. It was certainly close enough to thirty. In spite of a few grey hairs, though, and the lines in her face, she felt clearer than she had in years, and even she could see that her eyes seemed brighter than they once had, as if the intensity of her work now lit them from within.

She glanced over at her medal, which she'd hung on a peg right beside the mirror. It had only recently arrived, a full three months after she'd learned it would indeed be hers. The gold gleamed in the orange candlelight. The disc was the circumference of a crab apple; she stared at her name, which was inscribed on the front, then reached out and flipped it over.

Not in vain do we watch the setting and rising of the stars. Every time she looked at the sentence, her mind hovered and lingered on the same word: *we.* It had once seemed as impossible as a hailstorm of diamonds, yet here it was, inscribed in gold. And in ink: notices of her priority had made their way into newspapers up and down the eastern seaboard, resulting in a swell of sudden interest in her company.

You'll hardly believe that your famously unsocial twin has become something of a 'celebrity,' she'd written to Edward.

I've four invitations a week to dine here or there, speak at this or that function, or attend this or that lecture. I'm certain this will delight Mary, but I find it exhausting to even try and decide what to do, much less to do it. I've had to hire Millicent Rotch as an assistant, which might be the smartest thing I've done in years. Though her mother won't speak to me and now I have to go elsewhere to buy bread. It's a small price to pay for Millicent's help and company, though. Poor Mrs Riddell has had to assign me an entire cupboard for the mail! As you can imagine she was less than happy about it. A girl wrote to me from California, and another from England; mostly the letters are from ladies in New England, telling me about their own observations. I admit that I quite enjoy reading them, even if I haven't the time to answer every one. It seems I've unwittingly inspired hundreds of members of my Sex – from schoolgirls to wives to widows – to take up their telescopes with due diligence, in hopes of spotting a wanderer of their own. Taken all together, it's quite unbelievable – and wonderful – if time-consuming.

By the time she got downstairs, it was nearly six. She found Millicent at the table with a pile of correspondence at her elbow and a cup of tea in her hand. Her cheeks were as pink as they'd been when she was working at the bakery, if slightly less plump. Or maybe she just appeared taller, Hannah thought, watching her from the foot of the stairs, now that she had an occupation of her own choosing and stood up straight. Millicent had turned out to be less a fawning puppy than a tenacious shepherd. Their friendship had been a buoy through the long winter, and Hannah was grateful each day for her continued presence.

'Good morning!' she chirped when she saw Hannah. 'I've already read half of yesterday's mail, and I've only three questions for you!'

'Only three?' Hannah smiled at how quickly Millicent had dropped her plain speech once she'd left her mother's employ. Yet she still attended Meeting, though she never mentioned it; Hannah wondered if she'd been subjected to a visit by a committee concerned about her spiritual health when she took the job.

'What are they?'

'One: Do you want to address a convention of lady advocates for women's suffrage?'

Hannah paused.

'Do I? Where is it? And what do they want me to speak about?'

'It's in Seneca Falls, New York, and the invitation doesn't specify what you're to speak on. It just says you're one of a number of influential women whose presence would be welcome and whose voice should be heard. And, ah, what else . . .' She shuffled the pages in her hands. 'They will be drafting a Declaration of Sentiments on the matter of women's suffrage.'

Maybe she should attend; women ought to have the vote, of course. But the idea of speaking in public still made her feel like her bones had turned to soup.

'I'm not sure. What do you think?'

'I think they'd benefit enormously from the support of the first female fellow of the American Association of Astronomers.'

'Honorary Member. They crossed out *Fellow* on the certificate, remember?'

'Perhaps they were concerned you'd get the horrifying idea of actually voting at the next annual meeting,' Millicent said, raising her eyebrows and crossing her arms.

'Point taken. What if I sent along a statement of support? I do want to help the cause, but I don't feel prepared to make a speech on the matter.'

'I think it's a good first step. I'll add that you'll attend if your schedule permits. It's more than a year from now.'

Before Hannah could object, Millicent plowed ahead.

'Two: Might you consider making a donation to the Society for Betterment of Widows and Orphans?'

'I shall do so the moment I'm in a position to. Regrets.'

'I assumed as much. Three: There are two more young ladies who wish to join our lessons.'

'That's truly excellent,' Hannah said, making a swift calculation of the extra income. Mrs Hatter had already joined Millicent's astronomy sessions. As it turned out, teaching women was fun. They were diligent, and meticulous, and practically worshipped the material as Hannah herself had, though of course each lesson reminded her of Isaac. Thanks to him, her methodology had changed as well: rather than focus exclusively on mathematics, she now allowed time in each session for the students to study the skies without a specific task before them, simply to appreciate the majesty of the Heavens with their own eyes. To experience wonder. To imagine what they might behold someday.

'How did they learn of them, though? I've not advertised.'

Millicent cleared her throat and shuffled the papers as if she'd lost a page.

'The more the merrier!' Mrs Hatter had come into the kitchen without Hannah or Millicent noticing, and she dropped onto the bench opposite Millicent. 'Is there hot water?' Her husband had retreated to Boston weeks earlier, but she'd decided to stay on and 'get a feel for the place off-season,' as she put it.

Secretly, Hannah thought she wanted to be free of his dour face and mood. But it didn't matter: Mrs Hatter helped keep the house and, Hannah had to admit, lightened the atmosphere on Millicent's days off. When Hannah was alone on Little India Street, no matter how late she worked or how quickly she took her meals, it was impossible to escape her memories. So she was glad for the company, which eased the burden of her loneliness. Often the three women ate together. As Hannah breathed in the delicious warmth of the lamplit kitchen and the smell of the fresh bread Millicent had baked, she wondered if this was what it would have been like to have sisters, and an unfamiliar longing for the mysteries of girlhood rose in her chest. Had she grown up with the warmth of a mother or sisters, would she have learned to feel sooner, before it was too late?

She still had not heard a word from Isaac, and she wondered again and again what the reason was for his silence.

Had he not received her letters? Or had he decided that corresponding with her was not worth his time – meaning that she'd failed to communicate her feelings yet again?

There was no use in regretting what could not be, though. These women were here now; all she could do was cleave to what they offered and focus on her work.

'Here's a letter you'll want to read,' Millicent said, handing off a folded page to Hannah.

Hannah scanned the brief lines quickly:

1 September, 1846. Washington.

Dear Miss Price,

On behalf of the entire Coast Survey, I wish to express my pride in our association with the lady astronomer (and in myself for recognizing her talent). I offer my sincere congratulations to the tireless comet-seeker, and look forward to our ongoing connection. We are in hopes that she shall discover more Celestial objects, and again be the first American of her Sex to do so.

Warmest regards,
Alexander Dallas Bache
Superintendent, United States Coast Survey

'That's kind of him,' Hannah stammered, her hands shaking as if he were declaiming his pride to a roomful of peers instead of in a humble note meant for her eyes only. Dr Bache was the architect of a national project of immense scale and importance; she was amazed that he'd taken the time to write to her. She could barely contain her pride as she folded the note and put it in her pocket:

tonight she'd post it on the wall beside her medal, as a reminder of how far she had come.

'There's one other thing,' Millicent said, twirling a bit of string in her fingers. 'There's a note from Dr Hall here.'

She handed a brown folded note with a wax seal to Hannah.

'I didn't read it . . . but I recall his handwriting from school.' She shivered, and Hannah nodded in sympathy. She remembered those eviscerating notes that he had sent to students he'd deemed unprepared or lazy, though she'd never received one herself.

Hannah stared down at her name in his tight script. She never discussed – and tried not to think about – how much Dr Hall had wounded her. She hadn't spoken to him since the day she'd gone to him for help and discovered his betrayal. Her official disownment from Meeting had been certified with his signature, like an angry black scar. What could he have to say to her now?

When Hannah looked up, Millicent had busied herself with the correspondence again, as if she knew that Hannah would need a moment to compose her thoughts and her face. She had excellent instincts to go along with her mathematical skills. Hannah tucked the note into her pocket.

'Shall we go over the revisions for the article?'

Millicent nodded, and they bent their heads together over the document.

It was several hours before Hannah felt ready to read the note from Dr Hall. During a pause in their work, she slipped through the kitchen door to the garden and sat on the cold stone bench under the mulberry tree. The chill of the stone under her thighs reminded her of his duplicity, which was as she wanted it; she didn't want to be confused by her memories of the Dr Hall who'd lectured and tutored and challenged her. The Dr Hall who'd introduced her to the ideas of Le Verrier and Mary Somerville, who'd shown her how maths unlocked the mysteries of the Heavens in ways that observing could not. Without that Dr Hall, Hannah would have remained an assistant to her father; with his help, she had become . . . well, what was she, exactly?

She sat with the folded square in her hands as if it carried the weight of the Universe entire. *I'm an astronomer,* she thought. *I'm a computer for the* Nautical Almanac. *I'm a teacher.*

But she still felt herself a student, a striver. Dr Hall had proven to be selfish and weak, but a whisper of doubt crept in as she sat outside in the chilly late September afternoon. Hannah blew on her hands and then broke the seal and unfolded the note, the sticky weight of uncertainty making her clumsy.

Dear Hannah,

I hope that this note finds thee well, and not too preoccupied by thy successes to maintain thy studies. Even the greatest thinkers did make time for the expansion of knowledge, to add to their arsenal of wisdom!

I write now in my official capacity as Trustee of the Board of Directors of our beloved Atheneum. In recognition of thy many years of devoted service, I'm very happy to report that we have of late voted a unanimous resolution to offer thee the position of Head Curator. The unfortunate failure to offer thee a place in the

*rebuilding was an oversight that is much regretted now; I'm certain
that thee is familiar enough with the workings of Organizations
to understand how such an omission might have come to pass. In
any case, I remain thy devoted admirer, and hope that the position
is one that will suit. The salary of course will be commensurate
with thy vast experience.*

*If thee is amenable, I would like to come and explain more
about the position at thy earliest convenience.*

Respectfully &c.,
D. Hall

Hannah read the note through two times, then carefully folded it and put it back in her pocket. She wrapped
her arms around herself; the chill had become unpleasant.
But she stayed where she was, under the tree that had
stood in her garden as long as she could remember. It was
the tree Isaac had climbed when he came to see her his
last night on Nantucket; it was the tree she'd wept under
when she woke the next morning, with Isaac gone and the
Town in ruins around her. The small branches quivered
with a gust of wind, but no leaves dropped like portents
to tell her what to do.

With an Atheneum salary on top of what she'd earn
from the *Almanac*, she could afford a new telescope; maybe
she could even take up a subscription on Nantucket for a
proper observatory. But the offer rankled. The idea that
she was now acceptable, even desirable, as a member of
that institution where she'd been outcast just a year earlier
was awful. And it meant the worst of Dr Hall: that he had
been swayed purely by Hannah's newfound fame.

Anger swept through her, and she marched back into the house, casting the page into the kitchen fire as she went. But for the rest of the day, even as she compiled a new natural science curriculum for a girls' school in Ohio and read three journal articles that George had sent, she could not strike it from her thoughts:

I'm certain that thee is familiar enough with the workings of Organizations to understand how such an omission might have come to pass.

She wanted not to understand Dr Hall's meaning. Not to accord him a morsel of sympathy or understanding. But in truth she knew exactly how organizations worked, and that he was sending her a message. The ways that the minute and complicated forces of planets and nebulas, distant stars and dying suns, worked upon each other even at vast, invisible distances, creating an interlocking system in which one star, or planet, or sun, was inseparable from the system itself: this had been the subject of their most intense dialogues.

'The Solar System is exactly like an Organization, Hannah,' Dr Hall had explained. 'One unit may not operate outside the whole, for the forces that bear upon it are too powerful. It cannot avoid being acted upon by them any more than it can change its own Nature.'

Hannah had taken feverish notes as he spoke; she remembered drawing a star in the margin of her page and filling the space around it with planets and nebulas and other objects of her own imagining, all of them radiating toward the lone star in the center.

Was he suggesting that he was that lone star? That he'd tried to change the outcome of her disownment, and have her reinstated at the Atheneum, but been unable to sway the other Trustees? That he'd been on her side all along? But what about his veiled threat against her father? His failed proposal? His sinister note in her letterbox?

Sighing, Hannah rolled over and tried to find sleep, but when it came it was fitful and strange, filled with dark tides and empty rooms.

She awoke near dawn, and decided that she would listen to what Dr Hall had to say. From there, she'd have to trust herself to judge him wisely, if she could.

Dear Dr Hall, she wrote in the dim light. *I will come and see you on 2nd day. Please meet me at the Atheneum at half-noon.* – HGP.

She folded up the note and put it in the pocket of her dress, to deliver to his box later that morning; then, knowing that she would not sleep, she drifted downstairs to the kitchen to wait for first light.

28. An Offer

Hannah's hands shook as she tied on the bonnet Millicent had lent her for outings. She was due to meet Dr Hall at the Atheneum in fifteen minutes, but it was impossible to get anywhere on the Island in less than an hour unless she disguised herself. Putting it on was depressing. It felt like a betrayal of all that she had learned in the last year and a half: to walk with her head up, unhidden, for the first time in her life, guided by her own beliefs, her own principles.

And the bonnet didn't always do the trick. Some people paused only to say hello, but others stopped her in her tracks, going on about brothers with broken telescopes or articles they'd read about Herschel, and did she really think there were moon-men, and if so, would they be hostile, and had she truly been invited to the observatory in Rome, and if so, would she be expected to pray with Catholics?

Hannah had little to offer her admirers. She didn't see it as funny the way George Bond did. He claimed it was the price of fame, and didn't seem to sympathize when she explained that she'd wanted to *make* a contribution, not *be* the contribution. She was happy to talk about astronomy. But people wanted to know about her, not her comet. What she ate, what she read, with whom she corresponded. There had even been another short article in the *Inquirer* about her work with Millicent and the other women, sickeningly titled 'Lessons for Star-Gazing Ladies: Home-Grown Astronomer Price Trains Her Fair Students' Eyes Toward the Heavens.'

She'd been asked to contribute to at least a half dozen women's circulars, on topics that ranged from what could be gained from the study of the Heavens at an amateur level – which she'd promptly written and submitted – to proper etiquette for ladies at college. She'd declined to write that one, but penned the response herself. *Dear Madam*, she wrote.

I feel that I cannot do justice to the topic you have suggested to me, for not only have I never attended a college for women (nor any other kind), I see no reason there should be any difference in etiquette between male and female students at all.

Sincerely yours,
Hannah Gardner Price.

'Where are you off to?' Millicent asked, materializing beside Hannah at the door, watching her fumble with the bonnet strings.

'I need a book,' Hannah muttered, trying to undo the knot she'd made. Lying to Millicent made her itch, but she didn't want to reveal her errand to anyone before she knew what would come of it.

'Let me,' Millicent said, fingers flying before Hannah could wave her off. 'What book?'

'Did we get a reply from Washington?' Hannah asked, trying to change the subject. 'About the mural circle?'

'Not since you asked me twenty minutes ago.'

'I'm sorry. Have you got it?'

'Just. There.' Millicent retied the strings, a neat bow just under Hannah's chin, and tilted her face sideways. Hannah looked down at her, then over her head, trying to avoid making eye contact. 'I won't ask where you're really going, then. I can see when you want to keep a secret. But I hope it's a good one.'

Millicent ducked away and Hannah went out into the street. It was empty, the grey-shingled houses to either side quiet. The widow Miller across the street had passed on a month earlier, and her house was yet empty; several other houses had been let to renters Hannah didn't know. All the little gardens had gone brown and withered. She remembered the orange and yellow winter squashes that had once brightened the way to Main like little suns, even on the gloomiest autumn days. Cambridge must be magnificent in this season, Hannah thought. Bursting with new students and falling leaves.

The winter ahead was exciting in its own right, if daunting. There were articles waiting to be written, and two of George's for her to look over before he submitted them; he seemed to have acquired a new zeal for advancing his career, now that he was officially engaged to be married.

In addition, computing the tables for Venus required her daily attention, and there were her own students. Hannah smiled and focused her mind on the lessons she was planning for the women. Her bursting enthusiasm for their efforts still surprised her. It wasn't just that their hunger to learn relieved, at least for the few hours that they were present, the persistent gloom of Isaac's continued silence. It wasn't that they were particularly swift or excelled at observing, except for Millicent, who had a natural aptitude. But there was an ease to the arrangement, the freedom of forming her own lessons and experimenting with her teaching style. There was no one to frown if she praised her students too heartily; no one to judge her for accepting one who was a Catholic, and one newly arrived from England with her husband, a wealthy landowner building an enormous hotel in Madaket.

And, most important, there was the women's belief that with the knowledge of the Heavens that Hannah offered, they could – and would – contribute something, as she did. This belief was proof that times were changing. Colleges for women had begun to spring up, though Oberlin in Ohio was said to be on the verge of bankruptcy, and had only graduated a handful of women to date. The others were in such far-flung locations, they seemed mere abstractions. At least they offered more than teacher training – though, as Hannah had noted to Millicent, not one had a proper course in astronomy.

As she rounded the corner of Federal, she ducked her head to avoid eye contact with a clutch of pedestrians; then she was approaching the Atheneum, and she dragged her feet as she neared the steps. Hannah hesitated, wondering if she should turn around and go home. Instead, she sat down on the step, her back to a shining white column. She looked up. It soared to the height of the building, gleaming to the portico. ATHENEUM was leafed in gold, glinting in the morning light.

At the sight of it, Hannah felt as if she might cry, a great sorrow welling up for everything that had been lost with the old building. In each stately letter she saw a piece of her former self: her livelihood and her treasures, her favorite books and pamphlets, her inkwell and swiveling chair.

Images flickered across her mind like illustrations from that life: Here was the widow Ramsay, trailing through the stacks like a ghost, the hem of her skirt dredging dust from the floorboards. There were the Adams twins, fighting over the current issue of the *Youth's Companion*. Those boys were nineteen years of age now; they'd recently gone to California, toting new brides like toy trains. Hannah saw in her mind the hidden novels of upright Friends; the flowery notes of lovesick girls left behind in pattern books and poetry volumes; and finally – as if in answer to everything that could be learned from books – Isaac stretched out upon a bench, his beautiful eyes gazing up at the soaring ceiling. *It has a greatness of air.*

The world on and beyond the Island, in questions and answers, parchment and ink, history and philosophy. The ritual of minute interactions that lent a shape and meaning to her days she hadn't understood until it was taken from her.

She blinked at the gold lettering again, and a question flickered, then resolved.

Shall I die here?

It was a bizarre thing to think on; Hannah rarely, if ever, contemplated her own end. Death came for everyone, without explanation or warning. The sensation of her mother bending over her, holding something up for Hannah to see, washed over her, and she bowed her head, fighting back tears. Strange, how a memory could rise from the depths of one's past, like the mythical phoenix.

Edward had been there, too, she thought, though the image remained blurry. She imagined him and Mary now, surrounded by a hard bright expanse of desert. Heat rising in waves from the blazing white stones of Jerusalem, the city hoarding her ancient mysteries. Would he continue his journeys indefinitely? She imagined that his restlessness would settle. Time did surge ahead, but it was not a river emptying into a sea, to churn infinitely. There would be an end to her days – to all their days.

The door to the Atheneum opened, and Hannah jumped to her feet as Dr Hall stepped out and waved to someone leaving in the opposite direction. When he saw her, he froze, then straightened his back and lifted a hand in greeting.

'Hannah Price,' he said, nodding and waving her up the steps with a regal flourish. 'I'm pleased thee is here.'

When she got close enough, he held out his hand, and though she towered over him, she took it. His grip was claw-like. The lines on his face had deepened. He looked old.

Dr Hall ushered her into the huge main room of the bright building as if there had never been a break between them. He held his head up like a proud groom bearing home his bride.

But if this was home, she barely recognized it. The new space was as light as the old one had been dark. Windows that spanned from the floor to the ceiling brought the day into the room, and Hannah scanned the half-empty shelves that lined the walls for something familiar. Nothing was reminiscent of the old Atheneum except a few familiar journals scattered across the reading tables, and a wide wooden desk similar to Miss Norris' old one.

Even the head librarian seemed out of place in her long dark dress amid the bright new pillars and beams. Like a player on the wrong stage, Hannah thought as she followed Dr Hall into the center of the room.

Then familiar figures swooped in from every corner. Here came Miss Norris, and Mr Hillbright and Mr Coffey and Mr Starbuck; apparently, every trustee of the Atheneum had found some reason to be on hand that afternoon, and they hurried to offer explanations, which blurred together. Mr Hillbright said he'd read her account of the comet's passage and been shocked that no one in Europe had seen it first; Mr Starbuck wished to know if the King of Denmark's medal had arrived yet; Mr Coffey noted that he'd once had tea in London with the King's chargé d'affaires. Miss Norris fanned herself with a pamphlet.

'Miss Price and I have some business to attend to, as I'm sure everyone is aware,' Dr Hall intoned, and at once the trustees nodded and backed away in unison, as if at court. Hannah followed Dr Hall across the smooth planked floor in the direction of an alcove in the north corner. As they passed the children's section, Hannah remembered the Grimm brothers' tale about the brother and sister abandoned in the woods, trapped by a witch in her house of sweets. She'd always discouraged the children from reading fairy tales. There was no improvement in it. And they scared the young ones. But now she remembered that the little girl had freed them both, in the end.

Maybe she should have encouraged the children to read it after all.

Dr Hall opened a door into a dim room no bigger than a closet. One tiny window high above let a square of light in. An elaborate teak desk and two matching chairs took up most of the space. She wondered where he'd acquired them. There were hardly any books on the shelves. Had public funds purchased these luxuries?

'Do sit down,' Dr Hall said, stepping aside so that Hannah could get in, then squeezing past the edge of the desk to get into the ornate chair behind it. She wondered if his feet even touched the floor. The walls of the room were as bare as an interrogation chamber.

'Is this your office?' she asked, folding her hands together in her lap.

'Well, not exactly. It's a space I make use of when I need to conduct business. In my official capacity, that is.' He picked up a letter-opener from his desk and examined the edge, then placed it down again. It had a carved eagle at the top.

'Atheneum business must keep you quite busy,' she said, unsure of where to look. Her hand drifted toward her face, and she sat on it so she wouldn't bite her nails.

'I should say so.'

There was an awkward pause. Then they both tried to speak at once.

'I hope that –' Dr Hall said.

'I'm afraid I don't –' Hannah said at the same time.

He held up his hands as if quieting a classroom of unruly students.

'As thee has deduced, Hannah, I've asked thee here as a matter of Atheneum business.'

Hannah clasped and unclasped her free hand. *You're not a student,* she reminded herself. She pressed her face to her shoulder, inhaling her own particular scent. Wool and woodsmoke, apples from the cider she pressed last week. It was grounding.

'We're quite pleased with the new building,' Dr Hall said. 'It was completed in just over six months. Though the collections are severely lacking.' His eyebrows veed together in disapproval.

'I saw that you've acquired a few recent journals,' Hannah offered, trying to find something positive to say.

'True. But that's only because of personal connections.' He tilted his head at Hannah and raised a finger as he tried to recall something. 'Did thee happen to read upon the Bonds' most recent discovery?'

'Do you mean the eighth satellite of Saturn? I haven't read upon it yet. But I was able to look through the Great Refractor myself when I last visited.' She shivered at the memory.

'Did thee? That's stupendous. Stupendous, Hannah.' Dr Hall's eyes glowed with genuine awe, and Hannah felt embarrassed at what now seemed like a boast. Whatever his flaws, Dr Hall was her elder; he'd worked on higher mathematics his entire life, but the best he had to show for it was a school textbook used by a handful of primaries in Northern Massachusetts and a trusteeship at the Atheneum. He sat behind the desk, but she had surpassed him, and he knew it. It couldn't be easy for him. Perhaps it was his thwarted ambition, rather than lust, that had fueled his awful behavior in the first place. That would be easier for her to believe; it allowed at least a crumb of empathy.

'Perhaps thee could visit Cambridge one day,' Hannah offered. 'I'm certain the Bonds would be honored to have you.'

He stiffened.

'My work here keeps me extremely busy.'

'Of course,' Hannah said, wishing she could take back her words, the entire excursion. What had she hoped for? Some acknowledgment, an apology, something to right his betrayal? It was clear no such thing was forthcoming.

'That brings us to the business at hand,' Dr Hall said.

His face was clear and stern again, all traces of vulnerability and wonder gone as if through a trapdoor.

This is what it was like for Isaac, she thought. *Just trying to know my true feelings.*

'We – the Trustees – are in hopes that thee will consent to return to work here as the Head Curator and lead our campaign to rebuild our collections. We're certain that thy diligence and close knowledge of our former holdings suit thee for the position. Will thee accept?'

Time seemed to slow, so that each of his words hung in the air like clothes on a line. Specks of dust danced in the light coming through the small window. They went in every direction, with no apparent order. Yet there must be an order to them, as there was to all things in the Universe. According to Newton's laws, identical forces worked upon each speck of dust, each human being – upon her and upon Dr Hall, and upon Isaac, too. Her mind spun. Were they no different from each other than from a tree stump or a rock on their spinning orb in the darkness of infinity? Would their Creator have made them thus?

'To each action there is always an equal and opposite reaction,' Hannah said.

'Newton? I don't see the connection.' Dr Hall squinted at her across the desk.

She shook her head.

'I'm thinking about forces,' Hannah said. She folded her arms across her chest. Everything now seemed clear, sharply focused.

'What about them?'

'When I was my father's assistant, and thy student, my force upon our community – not to mention the rest of the world – was minuscule. I didn't shape events. I was simply moving in my orbit.'

'The past isn't relevant to our discussion, Hannah.' Dr Hall stroked the eagle on his letter-opener with his thumb. His voice suggested that the matter be closed. But his suggestions no longer mattered.

'But it is. I'll explain.' The idea, sparked, demanded fuel; Hannah let her mind expand to accommodate its light. The room was too small to pace, so she spread her knees apart so she could lean forward.

'As soon as another object – or person, in this case – came into orbit, it – he – acted upon me. My orbit shifted; I changed course.'

Hannah heard her own voice rising, her words falling faster and faster, but she didn't wish to slow down or stop herself.

'I was compelled to change course, you see. I had to.

And I did! Now I see it. I obeyed Mr Newton's second law. And then his third: Meeting rejected me, and I in turn rejected Meeting.'

She looked at Dr Hall, who was staring at her as if she'd just walked into the Atheneum in a red dress that showed her ankles. A moment later, his expression changed; he sat back in his seat and crossed his arms, looking at her with an almost paternal smile.

'Well then, my dear,' he asked, 'shall the Atheneum be part of this great Newtonian analogy? Will Miss Price be attracted by our offer of reinstatement?'

Now it was Hannah's turn to stare, struck dumb by his bemused smirk. Did he find her predicament laughable?

'Hannah,' he said, leaning toward her. 'Thee must understand the position of the Trustees: there would have been an outcry from the community if they allowed thee to keep thy position. There was talk – Well, your student was seen here. At night. Things were missing. Out of place.'

'You thought Isaac Martin was a thief? He'd no more steal from the Atheneum than you or I would.' Hannah shook her head. 'Is that why you sent that note? You believed I'd entrust a thief with the key to our most beloved institution?'

'It wasn't my belief. I defended thee.' Dr Hall's face lost its pleading look and hardened.

'Defended me from what?'

'From those who made allegations. Insulted thee. Accused thee of behavior unbecoming a representative of this institution. Of our Meeting. And worse.' He tapped his pointer finger upon the table to emphasize his words, as if drumming out a sentence.

Hannah shook her head. It was all clear to her now. She stood up and gripped the edges of the chair, energized, her thoughts unspooling into words.

'The truth is, the force that acted upon me has disappeared, replaced by others that are more attractive. My orbit appears stable once again. The dark menace is past. All traces of the aberration gone. So now I'm welcome. As if nothing ever happened. All will return to how it used to be. Is that what you thought when you asked me here?'

Dr Hall's mouth was a thin line, white around the edges. When he spoke, his voice was as smooth as cold marble.

'I thought thee would welcome the opportunity to lighten the stain thee brought upon thy name, and thy father's, by assisting in the rebuilding of our collections. I assumed thee would be grateful for the generosity and tolerance of those insulted by thy behavior. No amount of accolades or worldly pursuits will replace the loss of thy community. Without it, thee will drift through thy days, filled with regret. I thought thee was smarter than this, Hannah Price.'

An image of Isaac rose: he was commanding a ship, somewhere in the Pacific. Waves rose and fell; he charted a course that would steer his men safely across the open ocean, bring them to faraway continents, bring them riches, bring them home. He sighted all the stars and planets she had shown him: Aldebaran, Regulus, Pollux, Venus.

'Thee is correct,' she said, releasing her hold on the chair, releasing herself forever from whatever had bound her to this place. 'I am smarter.'

Then she stood and turned away, opening the little

door and floating back through the bright building, past Miss Norris and all the Trustees, past the rack of wide black hats that already looked as if they belonged in a museum, and out into what felt like the beginning of a new day in an unfamiliar place – something she'd once dreaded.

Yet she welcomed it, in her mind and her body, an idea taking root like a mangrove pod drifting, invisible, among the currents until it was bumped or blown upright.

15 September, 1846. Nantucket.
via the Franklin

Dear Isaac,

Since my last letter, I report that my medal has arrived from Europe after an exchange of letters among a dizzying array of men in an exhaustive display of detective work as to the nature of my failure to adhere to the specific rules of the prize. They managed to clear up the confusion amongst themselves. I did wonder that no one asked me about it directly, but being a mere Woman, I suppose they didn't think I had anything to contribute to the dialogue.

The Trustees of the Atheneum did offer me my old job back. I declined. The new building is nothing like the one in which we spent so many hours, though I suppose an objective observer would say it is a fine structure. But I no longer feel that my place is there. Certainly my heart aches each time I consider the time we shared in the old building. Which brings me to my next bit of news.

I've had an invitation to go to Europe for a nine-month journey, as chaperone to the young daughter of a writer (and patron of the Harvard Observatory), a Mr Hapwell, and his wife, Lucia. I've only met them once, at a dinner, but George and William Bond say they are desperate to have me for the journey — which makes me feel like an expensive valise — but they will pay a generous sum and in addition the Bonds will provide letters of introduction to everyone I care to meet in the astronomy world. They claim that news of my discovery is the talk of every star-gazers' salon on the Continent, though I cannot see how or why.

The plan is to travel to London, Paris, Rome, and Florence, which means I would be able to visit the observatories at Greenwich and at the Vatican, if I can get permission there; and I might even meet Mary Somerville as well. The idea of that is both terrifying and great; in case you don't remember, she's among the most revered mathematicians and astronomers, and currently living in Florence.

Florence! Once I would have shuddered at the idea of crossing the ocean, disembarking in a city in which I knew no one. So much has changed in me; today as I left the Atheneum I felt a sudden sharp desire to do exactly that. It was a longing I have not felt since childhood; I believe I've drawn some courage from the idea of your travels, which in length and distance dwarf my small journey. But I know they will contribute to my character and strength, as they have to yours. Edward was always the one in our family who thrilled to new places, new sights, new people. I trained my eyes on the Heavens and felt that was enough for me. I do yet spend the best part of each day in great wonder and awe at that expanse above us.

But where it once was my roof, my shelter and solace, now it seems to also be a door. To what I do not know. There is a kind of terror that sometimes rises in me when I think of what lies ahead, but I hope that in those moments, thinking of you will continue to bring me both perseverance and Faith.

367

I will depart in two weeks' time and am in hopes to hear from you before then. I long to hear your voice, even through the poor medium of parchment and ink. Without it I am less steady. But regardless I remain,

Your faithful friend,
Hannah Gardner Price

PART FOUR

May 1847 Florence

29. Coexistence

Hannah caught her reflection in the wavy glass of a café, and her hand fluttered to her new hat — a close-fitting silk the color of a fawn, with a narrow, deep-blue ribbon edging. It couldn't have been more different from her old bonnet, in shape or texture, and she couldn't hide her face behind it. This, according to Lucia Hapwell, was its best feature. The wife of the writer from Cambridge had taken one look at Hannah's outfit when she'd stepped off the steamer in London and assumed an expression somewhere between shock and pity before whisking her off to the milliner on Regent Street.

This particular hat had been a total indulgence, but Mrs Hapwell had insisted it was subtle and appropriate — not too showy, but 'suited for the salon.' Hannah didn't feel suited for any salon regardless of her headwear, but Mrs Hapwell promptly marched her from one shop to the next, insisting that she select from what seemed like an absurd number of choices in dress styles, colors, and fabrics, not to mention footwear and stockings. Stockings! Hannah had never before put a thing on her body she hadn't made herself, and the sensation of the silk against her bare skin felt almost dangerous in its luxury.

She could only imagine what Lydia Hussey would think. So she put Lydia out of her mind: the part of her life when Meeting elders determined what she could or could not wear was over.

That didn't make deciding such things for herself any easier. It took Hannah hours to decide among a set of dress patterns. She would never be comfortable enveloped in a concoction of ribbons and ruffles, but as she paged through store catalogues and the issues of *Godey's Lady's Book* that Mrs Hapwell had supplied, she slowly compiled a sense of what she might enjoy about contemporary fashions: a neckline that didn't choke her, for instance, or a choice of colors not restricted to the drabbest corners of the spectrum. The dress fitting itself had nearly mortified her, the seamstress's calloused hands looping round her waist, her thighs, but the first of the finished products – a deep-green day dress that reminded her of moss, in a soft, draping silk – felt wonderful and, even Hannah had to admit, flattered her complexion.

That had been the first of a series of lessons in city life, from commandeering a driver to making conversation at what felt to Hannah like harrowing speed. Mrs Hapwell had insisted that Hannah accompany her to a half dozen salons and suppers, theater outings and tea parties, before deeming her ready to deliver her own letters of introduction.

But standing in front of the enormous wooden door at her destination, clutching the envelope that George had entrusted to her, Hannah felt anything but ready to present herself. Before she could decide whether it would be worse to stay or flee, the door was hurled open as if by an angry elf, and there was Mary Somerville herself, a diminutive figure with a nimbus of white hair, bristling with energy at six and sixty.

'Come in, please. Come in!' she commanded. 'Albertina has the afternoon off, but thankfully she left something for us, so we shan't starve. Come! Close the door firmly, it sticks.'

Hannah obeyed, then trotted down the long hallway after her hostess, feeling the urge to tiptoe so she wouldn't scuff the floor-planks. They looked to be five hundred years old – like the door, like the Duomo, like everything in Italy Hannah had seen so far. It made her feel her own age acutely, and she wondered again why such an accomplished person had even made time to meet with her.

Mrs Somerville led Hannah into what could only be her study. The walls were papered in a deep scarlet, with worn rugs scattered about that looked as if they'd undergone an army of boots and slippers. A stack of books teetered on the small mahogany desk. On the small table between two overstuffed and uncomfortable chairs, a tea tray rested. A series of quills, inkpots, and nibs were lined up on the desk at precise angles to the books and the blotter, and Hannah was relieved by this humble evidence of a familiar impulse to order.

Mrs Somerville pointed Hannah into a chair and poured her a cup of tea before saying a single word more. A cascade of her accomplishments paraded across the bookshelves: *The Mechanism of the Heavens* . . . *On the Connexion of the Physical Sciences* . . . a half dozen prominent journal articles. The very notion of a planet beyond Uranus. All from the mind of this woman. It was awesome and terrifying, like being in the throne room of scientific progress.

'Tell me about your comet, then, Miss Price,' Mrs Somerville demanded the instant she'd settled on the other chair. 'It was the talk of the Continent last summer, you know.'

Hannah blinked and returned her cup to the saucer, her hand shaking.

'Well, I don't know about that,' she said. 'I can tell you that no one was more surprised than I to find my priority unchallenged.'

'But why should you be surprised?' Mrs Somerville stared at Hannah. Her gaze felt like a lighthouse beam, clear and cutting. 'From what I understand, your diligence – and the quality of your eye – is quite well-known.'

She paused, and clinked her own teacup down on the tray.

'No need for modesty here, my dear.'

'I don't mean to be modest!' Hannah said, wishing she could start over. 'Rather, my resources – our instruments – are nowhere near the caliber of those used by other sweepers, and they are no doubt as diligent as myself. We've only a Dollond – and not a new one, either.'

Mrs Somerville didn't respond, so Hannah leaned closer and raised her voice.

'I meant that the Dollond surprised everyone, especially me.'

Her hostess nodded vigorously.

'Sometimes an old workhorse can surpass a team of colts,' she said, and burst out laughing like a raucous schoolgirl. 'But what of the rest?'

'The rest?' Hannah wondered if she was being tested. She swallowed, and reminded herself that she'd been invited.

Mary Somerville waved a slender hand in the air above their heads as if to indicate the whole of the galaxy. 'Where does Miss Price turn her gaze these days? Toward the nebulae, I hope. Resolution should be the top priority for every astronomer in the world, I say.'

'Certainly, when I am able – that is, when I visit the Bonds.'

'Ah, William! And his boy.'

'George.'

'Yes. I saw them not a year ago at the international conference. Young Bond was quite interested in image-making. We've yet to make the attempt here on the Continent.'

'Indeed he is. In fact, he entrusted me with something to show you.'

Hannah drew a square envelope from the leather folder she'd carried in her trunk from place to place all the months of her journey, then unfolded the paper carefully and held out her treasure with two hands. They shook.

'What's this?' Mrs Somerville squinted, then used her hands as levers to rise from the chair. 'Can't see well. Nor hear. But everything else is in order. Come over to the window, dear, and show me.'

Hannah bore the photograph over like a jeweled crown on a satin cushion and laid it carefully on the window seat so Mrs Somerville could see it in the light.

'It is the very first of those images you speak of,' Hannah said, as slowly and clearly as she was able. 'It is a photograph of the stars Mizar and Alcor.'

'Yes,' Mrs Somerville whispered, leaning close over it. 'I see.'

'George took this a month ago. He's been able to get even clearer images since then. They're quite wonderful. He's devoting nearly all his time to spectroscopy – the lenses, of course, and how he might capture the colors of the stars as well as their luminosity.' Hannah heard the pride she felt in her voice. George had found his calling after all these years, and it dovetailed with William's relief that his son was contributing something he deemed scientifically worthy.

'Splendid!' Mrs Somerville tapped the photograph lightly with her finger. 'The future of knowledge, I predict. Here on the Continent we have the history, the practice, the instruments . . . but you Americans, you have the modern impulse. We must depend on your ingenuity!'

She reached over and squeezed Hannah's arm, her grip so firm, it sent a jolt through Hannah's body.

'Now let us go into the rose garden. I must walk each afternoon, lest these bones forget they yet have work ahead of them.'

Hannah trailed behind as Mrs Somerville listed the varieties she'd grown, their ages and qualities. In the last light of the day, the flowers blazed as if to defy their own transience.

'I had a letter from Dr Whewell recently,' Mrs Somerville said. 'I cannot abide the amount of time he spends on preposterous ideas. Why shouldn't another planet be inhabited by reasoned beings? I ask.' She paused, and Hannah realized she was expected to answer.

'I suppose it would be difficult to prove,' Hannah said carefully, not wanting to take sides.

'So what? A higher order of beings might people every

corner of the galaxy. The fact that we cannot yet prove their existence shouldn't encourage working to disprove the very possibility! It's anathema to truth.'

Hannah shook her head.

'I'm not sure I understand.'

'Reason is not the only path to enlightenment, my dear. One must have vision! And passion. One must not forsake feeling for fact.' She squinted at Hannah. 'Do you have much religious feeling?'

Hannah searched for a truthful answer.

'I did at one time. But my mind is unsettled. My father always quoted Edward Young.'

'"An undevout astronomer is mad."'

'Yes.' Hannah nodded, and her throat tightened, thinking of the tiny window through which she observed her first stars. The metronome ticked close to her ear; she counted seconds for her father. Mrs Somerville's clippers snapped dead branches.

'And yet, one must acknowledge the coexistence,' the older woman said.

'The coexistence?' Hannah felt strung between the past and the future, a timid girl beside an imposing elder. But she had contributed something; she was here.

'Of uncertainty and faith, my dear. No matter how fervent our passion for the works of our Creator, there will in minds such as our own always exist the potential for that which we cannot understand. For we are limited, are we not? We are simply prisoners in our current form, blown about by our emotions and so forth. It's a rare individual who can overcome her own Nature – and why should she? If this is our Nature, then I say we must embrace it until the next life.' Mrs Somerville stepped back to survey the shape she'd made. '"The Heavens declare the glory of God; and the firmament showeth forth his handiwork,"' she singsonged.

Snip, snip. Two final, slender branches fell to Earth, one at each woman's feet.

Mrs Somerville looked up and smiled like an indulgent grandmother, which made Hannah feel even more like a child. Hannah had devoted herself to everything she had been taught – all that she could apply reason to – at the expense of everything else. Forsaking feeling for fact was exactly what had cost her Isaac. What if she had chosen differently?

Mrs Somerville had children, and a husband, yet she'd made the greatest of contributions. She'd forsaken nothing. Or so it seemed. Of course, her situation was different. Such a union with Isaac would simply not have been possible.

'I expect to hear great things from you, Miss Price,' Mary Somerville called as Hannah went back through the enormous wooden doors. And then, as if she could read Hannah's thoughts, she added, 'Keep your mind open to possibility!'

As she left Mrs Somerville's, Hannah felt intimidated and enlivened, as if she had just woken from a powerful dream in which something important had been revealed. It glinted, just out of reach. But it was there.

As the months of travel wore on, though, the glimmer of promise and potential began to flicker. The longer Hannah spent wandering the streets of the clamorous cities, immersed in the jabber of foreign tongues and the treasures of the world's greatest museums, the farther away she felt from home.

Once you told me that you understood how time and distance are the same, at sea, Hannah wrote in one of a series of letters to Isaac, which she posted with less and less hope that he would receive or respond to. *How the longer you are away from home, the farther you feel from it. I understand this now, though it does not seem to apply to you; the longer I am away from you, the more I long to be near you.* Still, she kept writing, unsure if her missives were an act of penance or an act of faith. She only knew that she needed to share what she was experiencing with Isaac. She had to speak to him, even if he did not speak back.

Mrs Hapwell also instructed Hannah in the fine art of visiting, from what to put on her calling cards ('Just your name, dear: it speaks for itself') to which invitations to decline ('She only wants you there because she heard you were all the rage'). But the one place Hannah needed no help was in the observatories of Europe, where she found herself as at home among the instruments and charts as she had ever been, and welcomed as a peer, which shocked and amused her.

Even as she felt her mind expanding to accommodate both the modern innovations of the observatories and the antiquities and masterpieces of old in the museums, as the months wore on, and spring gave way to summer, Hannah missed home all the more. The hard sidewalks and soaring cathedrals of Europe were beginning to grind her down, the arches of one great structure blending into the pillars of another until she finally abandoned her *Handbook for Travellers on the Continent* in the Galleria dell'Accademia, unable to absorb another word, and circled back to the statue of David where she'd left her twelve-year-old charge, Desdemona.

The girl couldn't have been less like her mother: she was dreamy, lethargic, prone to losing anything not sewn to her person, and spectacularly unsociable. But she loved art, and as Hannah curled her hands around Desi's small shoulders, she found herself drawn into the lines of the male figure, the angles of his enormous fingers and feet. The curve of his knuckles, his jaw, his ear, made Hannah's mind leap to Isaac, and the familiar dull ache of longing thudded through her. Only when another visitor drew up beside her did she shake loose from the intoxicating memory and reluctantly steer Desi away.

The remaining weeks of her travels seemed to fly by, and as the day of her departure grew closer, Hannah found herself torn between conflicting sets of emotions. She was excited to see Edward and Mary, who'd returned to Nantucket in time for the birth of their son, Moses. She could hardly wait to meet her new nephew; to reunite with Millicent and Elizabeth; and to walk the familiar shores and breathe the sea air of home. But she was equally anxious about returning to a future that was almost as uncertain as it had been before she ever found the comet.

30. Homecoming

The carriage jolted over the cobblestones as they neared the port of New Bedford, and Hannah blinked herself awake and stretched her neck, mopping her brow with her damp handkerchief. She pulled back the curtain and looked out the window. Swarms of people were moving in the direction of the Nantucket packet. Men in pale suits and women in summer dresses lugged valises and baskets and small children in the direction of the ferry, while seamen of every hue cut through the crowds, chins up, chests out.

And as far as she could see, hundreds – maybe thousands – of barrels of oil were laid out in neat rows, covering nearly every foot of wharf. The heat shimmered the late June air above them as if they were holy. It reminded Hannah of the gilded halos around the portraits of saints she'd seen everywhere in Italy. The Madonnas and children, the Thomas Aquinases and Theresas.

She opened the window, letting in the hot, putrid air, then stuck her arm out and rapped on the roof.

'I'll walk from here,' she shouted to the driver, and leapt down when the team stilled. He passed her valise and tipped his cap, a gesture she was still uncomfortable with, even after nearly a year on the Continent, where the men bowed and dipped like toy boats every time a woman came within fifty paces. Hannah nodded, trying to be gracious, but when he offered to carry her valise to the ferry, she shook her head.

'No need,' she said, waving him off when he stood to leap down. 'It's quite light.'

One pair of new boots, five new dresses, her journal, and the hat upon her head: Hannah felt weightless as a dandelion, floating toward home. She still had no idea what would come next, but now that she was close enough to smell the salt in the air, the uncertainty had its own peculiar thrill; she felt sure-footed in spite of it.

She slowed down when she saw the line for the packet, which stretched nearly a quarter mile. It was only half-ten but she'd be lucky if she made it onto the noon boat. Sighing, she put down her valise and sat on it, fanning herself with a broadsheet as chatter whizzed through the air. When the line edged forward, Hannah rose and shuffled along. At this rate she'd never get home.

But the crowd was moving again, this time parting for a familiar ruddy face with hair and beard the color of a new penny atop a barrel-like body.

'Captain Smith,' Hannah called.

'Miss Price! Didn't recognize ye. Back from the travels, then? Magnificent. Excellent and good!' He beamed at her for a second before snatching up her valise as if it were a thimble, taking her elbow with his other hand and steering her though the throng toward the boat. His arm was as thick as a leg of lamb; she remembered him as a boy of fourteen or fifteen years, poring over diagrams of ships and riggings at the Atheneum. He looked much the same, only bigger.

'Coming through, let the lady astronomer through,

move it, you there! Out of her way, get!' His voice rang out as they moved toward the boat, and the sound of it made her smile even as she blushed. She'd heard it spoken, whispered, and announced in French, Italian, Spanish, and even German over the preceding months, but the sound of *lady astronomer* belted out in a New England port twang made her giddy with excitement.

To her surprise, the throng parted peacefully, edging their satchels and parasols and picnic baskets dutifully out of the way. Most of them stared as if she'd fallen from the moon. It couldn't be her attire, since none of these people knew just how different she looked from the woman who'd embarked from this same pier last year. But she felt a flutter of panic when she wondered what the people who *did* know her would think of her appearance. From hat to shoes, she resembled nothing so little as a member of the Society of Friends; and though she had no desire to rejoin Meeting or adhere to a Discipline she didn't accept, the idea that she had now crossed completely into the realm of outsider left her feeling sad and a bit hollow. The way she felt when she'd heard a haunting melody wafting from a Parisian café and learned that it was being played in what was known as the minor scale.

As the boat crossed Buzzards Bay and rounded the mainland past Falmouth, Hannah stood at the railing, facing east. The vessel dipped and rose, cold spray fizzing across her face. She squinted into the humid wind. The faint outline of Nantucket was just visible in the distance. Her heart ticked faster.

A minute later, she could see the new lighthouse on Sankaty Head.

The women gather on the headland and the harbor and stare at the light as if it will draw their men home faster, Mary had written.

By my reckoning, she who waits for love's return is shackled enough by her longing without a beacon with which to chart it, Hannah had responded.

The watery, distant light reminded her of Isaac's vision of his island, curled in the Atlantic Ocean like a green jewel in a velvet box. Staring into the opaque waters of the Bay, Hannah imagined him striding along the jungle paths amid his thousand shades of green.

Isaac could literally be anywhere on Earth, yet she felt that he was near, that he would return to this place. It was unreasonable. Every time she thought of him the same throb of sorrow passed through her like rain. The kind of disappointment she'd always imagined attended those bags of outgoing mail had its own vibration, she'd learned. An ache that reverberated in her bones each time she felt it. But she was used to it. She supposed it would be with her forever, like an extra heart thumping quietly in the background.

And here was the faint outline of rooftops, and the steeple of the Catholic church; here were the masts bobbing in the outer harbor, many fewer than she remembered, but familiar still; here was the crescent of Town and the sliver of beach below it; the storehouses and spindly outbuildings of the wharves; the browning green of summer sawgrass. Hannah was overtaken by a rush of love for her Island, and she gripped the railing as they drifted into the harbor, suddenly wide awake.

She was first in line as they tied in, and the moment they'd secured the ramp she strode down, pausing at the bottom. The wharves that were once as intimidating as canyons seemed much smaller than she remembered, the docks and oily waters and storehouses miniaturized. It was like standing in a diorama of a tiny grey town framed by cool sky.

Home. She turned the word around in her mouth like a marble. It was hers, to be sure. But as she stepped from the boat onto the creaking dock, and the footfalls of her fellow passengers fell away, she wondered at its newness.

As she approached Main Street, Hannah slowed down, then stopped altogether, turning in a circle at the corner of Federal. How could she be lost in her own backyard? She'd been away less than a year. Where was John Darling's Maps &c? Miller's outfitters? The rope and sail shop? Why were gaudy flags and bunting hanging from the veranda of the Hussey house?

Hannah took two steps back so she could read the street name. It was etched in stone, deep as ever: *Federal*. Then she noticed the new shingle, lettered shiny blue on yellow: NANTUCKET INN. Along the porch, young men and women sat on benches, with no apparent occupation besides conversation. Music tinkled inside, drifting out like smoke.

All around, women in pale, gauzy dresses, and men in summer suits passed arm in arm, strangers at leisure. Hannah resumed walking, staring at the row of new storefronts selling nautical trinkets, scrimshaw, and the like. One entire store seemed to hold only things shaped like whales. Bold advertisements pasted in every window touted new inns and hotels. Hannah felt as if she'd bought a ticket to the opera but landed at the circus.

'Miss. Miss! Come inside and have a look. A souvenir? Something for a special someone at home?' It took Hannah several seconds to realize that the shopkeeper, a stout young woman in a garish cotton summer dress the blinding color of pink hydrangeas, was addressing her.

She thinks I'm a tourist, Hannah realized. She shook her head, trying not to frown at the woman, who was only trolling for business. And Hannah *was* a tourist, in a sense. She was seeing the Island anew, just like the people on holiday around her; in comparison to the grand cities of Europe, the wide avenues and huge parks, the towering cathedrals and marble monuments, Nantucket Town looked as quaint as a dollhouse.

Just before she turned off Main, she caught a glimpse of a lone figure in a long, dark dress, moving slowly among the crowds. A bonnet in the style Hannah wore as a girl shielded her face. It was like looking at a living relic of a past that felt further distant than it should; Hannah had gone about wearing similar garments but a year earlier. People moved aside as if for a spirit as the woman glided through, turning to watch her pass with open curiosity, then closing rank again. Hannah watched until she lost sight of the woman in the crowd, then turned toward home.

At her gate, she stopped short, looking left and right to be sure she had the right house. Neat rows of summer squash, tomatoes, and wispy, fern-like carrot greens edged the east side of the house, along with squat cabbages and even a row of scraggly corn. Someone had coaxed the perennially droopy wisteria back to life, and it draped over a new arbor on the other side. It smelled like manure and sawdust, neither of which she associated with home. The porch had been swept clean of old rods and spars, the broken plank mended. It was tidy, but Hannah felt wistful for the lumpy detritus of the past. Even the door knocker's bird had a shiny, sharp new beak.

Just as she reached for it, the door swung open, and there was her family. Her father, his thinning swoop of grey hair, long earlobes poking out, a benevolent smile breaking the hard planes of his face; Edward's lean, angular jaw, so similar to Nathaniel's, but with a two-day beard newly peppered with silver, eyes permanently crinkled from laughing and squinting; Mary's bright golden braids, her sun- and wind-bronzed skin. She'd widened into a woman. In her arms was Hannah's nephew, Moses, three months old. He had a gummy grin and Mary's bright blue eyes under a fuzzy halo of shimmery hair.

Everyone's words tumbled out at once.

'Look at him,' Hannah cried, leaning in close to the baby, inhaling his sour-sweet essence.

'Look at you! Your hat . . . and the dress. You look beautiful,' Mary said.

'I'd hardly have recognized you. What have you done with my sister?' Edward held out the baby to Hannah, and when she took him in her arms, her brother stepped back to get a better look and Nathaniel stepped forward, putting a hand on each of Hannah's shoulders and squeezing gently.

'Thy absence was much felt,' he said, his voice gravelly with emotion.

Hannah reached one hand up to draw off her hat, and the baby promptly grabbed a long braid that she'd unhinged by accident, and yanked, giving her an excuse to swallow the lump in her throat.

'I wish you could have seen it with me, Father.' The familiar address had slipped out, and Hannah opened her mouth to rephrase in a more proper way, then closed it again. Her father knew as well as anyone that she had severed her ties with Meeting. Continuing to address him as she had before felt more fraudulent than respectful. Instead, she went on, too excited to share what she'd seen in her travels to ponder the issue. 'The instruments – Greenwich – and Liverpool! Did I not write to you about it?'

'No astronomy before dinner, please,' Edward said, reaching over to unlock the baby's chubby grip.

She smiled at Edward, nearly overcome by emotion.

'I can't believe you're a father,' Hannah whispered.

'I know. I should barely be allowed to guide another human being to the general store, much less through life itself.' Moses wiggled and kicked his legs with all his tiny might. 'Probably a good thing that he has your stubborn streak, Hannah.'

Hannah buried her nose in the soft flesh of the baby's neck, feeling herself expand everywhere – cheeks, heart, lungs. Giddy, she kissed his tiny nose, his ears. Edward and Mary stepped in and engulfed her, and everything dissolved in their embrace, the baby in the middle. She quickened to his warmth, which tugged at the core of her body. Moses screeched his delight and displeasure. Hannah stepped back and turned him so he faced his parents.

Mary sniffed loudly.

'Oh, don't cry. You'll only make me do the same,' Hannah said.

'Heartless Hannah about to cry?' Edward asked. 'Europe must be transformational indeed.'

'Let's not hover here like sheep,' Mary said, rustling them all into the hall. 'There's chicken, and a pie.'

As Hannah stepped through the door, her father put his arm around her shoulder and squeezed, and Hannah looked up at him. He looked more robust than when she'd last seen him. The planes of his face seemed fuller, less pinched. Marriage suited him, then.

'Where is Lucinda?' Hannah asked. 'I'd been hoping to meet her.'

'She was called to her sister's confinement, but is inestimably sorry she couldn't be here. She had all manner of plans for thy homecoming.'

Hannah smiled, and was rewarded with one in return. It was so rare that Nathaniel showed affection – and so long since she'd seen him at all – that Hannah felt as if she were physically basking in its glow, like sunlight after a long, dark winter.

The smell of food made her empty stomach roar. She hadn't eaten in nearly twelve hours, and as she followed her family into her house, pausing to drop her hat on her old peg, she passed the parlor without looking for the water globe or glancing at the lines of the upright chairs. The kitchen was still the kitchen she remembered, and she plunked down at the long, worn table and dug into the plate Mary slid before her, letting the conversation eddy around her.

When she'd mopped up the last bit of gravy from the

plate, Hannah looked up. Three faces stared at her, loving, expectant.

Hannah sat back in her chair and sighed with pleasure. She had longed for her family so often over the long winter she'd spent with the Hatters, and while she was abroad, that being seated among them – plus Moses – was as comforting as a warm bath.

'Your letters were wonderful,' Mary said, offering more pie, which Hannah declined. 'Though we got them out of order, so you were in Florence before you were in London. And I'm certain we missed a few.'

'Did you not get the ones I posted from Greenwich?'

Edward and Nathaniel shook their heads at the same time, and with the same staccato motion. Time had brought them closer in demeanor; Hannah wondered if they recognized it or would even acknowledge it.

'It was extraordinary,' she said, wondering how to even begin to share everything she'd seen. 'Charles II had enormous foresight, building such a place. The original octagonal room is used for storage now –'

'I'd heard as much,' Nathaniel offered, his eyes bright.

'– but the instruments themselves are impressive, and of course the Park is a beautiful setting for Professor Airy's work. Though he looks unfavorably upon the sprouting of new observatories of late. He thinks they contribute to inferior observations. Did you know that?'

Nathaniel nodded.

'William has told me that the Professor is quite outspoken on the matter. And yet, imagine if thee hadn't had access to thy telescope, daughter! The world would be less a true astronomer.'

Hannah felt a blush creep up her cheek at the unexpected praise from her father.

Edward smiled widely, as did Mary. Hannah reached across the table and grasped her father's hand.

'It was *your* telescope to begin with. Without your teaching and encouragement, no instrument on Earth could have brought me my comet.' Now tears really did spring to Hannah's eyes.

Her father squeezed her hand in answer, and Edward cleared his throat.

'On the subject of Greenwich, and Time, your friend George Bond is obsessed of late with the application of the telegraph.'

'Have you become enamored of scientific progress in my absence? That would truly be shocking. Though with all the changes I noted between the ferry dock and our front door, I shouldn't be surprised if you tell me you're to be appointed Astronomer Royal.'

'Things have changed greatly,' Mary chimed in, saving Edward from answering. 'After you left there was a rash of property sales: the Hussey house was the first, and there were some half-dozen more, all of which were operating as hotels by the time the first bulbs came up.'

Nathaniel nodded.

'It's been a financial boon for the Island, though perhaps not to the liking of all its residents.'

Edward shot Hannah a look she could read easily: *To say the least.*

Hannah sighed, allowing fatigue to settle in her body, the warmth of the room, the company of her loved ones to soothe her.

'I hope we can visit the Continent soon,' Mary was saying. 'We're looking into another expedition. Though of course it won't be as easy next time.' Her hand fluttered to the top of Moses' head.

Hannah felt her head nod. The voices of her family engulfed her like soft wings, and her eyes fluttered as Edward helped her from her seat.

'I can help clean up,' she muttered, but she was going up the stairs with Mary at her elbow, and here was her old room, and her bed, and before Mary had even unlaced her boots, Hannah was sound asleep.

31. Old News

When she woke up it was dark, and when she lit the candle she found that her trunk, which had arrived two days earlier, had already been unpacked in a freshly whitewashed room with a new-stuffed mattress and a soft quilt – a hundred squares of fabric in various shades of rose, from dusky sunset to blazing summer bloom. Hannah wondered if Mary, too, had reached the end of her tolerance for Discipline, or whether the quilt had been placed there strictly for Hannah's benefit. The floors were so clean, they shone. Sighing, Hannah changed into a pale blue dress, enjoying the sensation of the fabric on her legs and the round hooked rug under her bare feet. Then she laid out the carefully wrapped gifts she'd brought home: a pair of German binoculars for Edward, a delicate Florentine teacup for Mary, an iridium-tipped steel-nib pen and India ink for her father.

She picked her way along the hall with the ease she'd always had in the dark. At the foot of the stairs to the garret, she paused. A candle was lit above. Someone was working. Hannah padded up, soft as a cat. Two voices murmured within, and she pushed the door open a crack.

Her father and Edward sat side by side before her wide desk, their heads bent over a logbook. Hannah couldn't hear what they were saying. The light from the candle showed her the books and charts repopulating their corner of the room, as if they'd never been hidden away in crates, ready to ship; the glint of the Dollond on its stand caught her eye, and though it was as comforting as an old friend, it looked like a relic compared to the instruments she'd seen and used in Europe.

There were other changes: a leather armchair took up a whole corner of the room, and three new shelves held an array of objects she couldn't make out or recognize. Edward's old coat and woolen hat were back on the pegs near the stairs; a pile of Hannah's boxes were stacked in a far corner where the rocking horse used to be. Her gaze traveled to the stairway to the walk.

She imagined the depth of sky she could sweep with the telescopes she'd peered through in her travels. How the old star patterns of the sky over Nantucket – so familiar, she could draw them from memory – would reveal new aspects, things she couldn't even imagine. It would be like looking at a different sky altogether. *A different world,* Isaac had called it. She wished again that she might have shared it with him. That he could be part of her homecoming now.

Edward looked up.

'There you are,' he said, sliding his chair back. 'Come join us.'

Hannah hesitated.

'I don't want to intrude,' she whispered, hesitant to break the pleasant spell that seemed to bind them.

'Intrude? This is *your* room,' Edward said, and snapped his fingers as if to free her from an enchantment. 'We've only just managed to keep up without your help.'

Hannah smiled at his exaggeration, and pulled up the little stool between them. Her father scraped over a few inches to make room, and Hannah studied his form. He was wearing a suit of what seemed like very fine light-weight wool. It was a dark grey, and cut in a familiar style, but it had a light sheen. That's why he looked different, she realized: she'd never seen him in anything but the white shirt, dark pants, and buttoned coat that all the Friends wore. Hannah reached out two fingers and, taking the sleeve between them, marveled at its texture and weight, the array of tiny, perfect stitches.

'This is very nice,' she said, glancing up but not wanting to embarrass him with questions. It was the kind of tailored garment that cost a small fortune. Even though he was technically a Philadelphian now, she was shocked that he'd spent the money on it.

'Father's been contracted by the United States Mint,' Edward said, closing the logbook in front of him. 'In his position he's expected to appear – what's the word Lucinda used?' He glanced at Nathaniel.

'Like a member of modern society,' Nathaniel muttered.

'Are you and Lucinda not members of the Philadelphia Meeting?'

'Of course we are,' he said, patting her on the hand. 'And she looks forward to finally meeting thee.'

Hannah nodded, still focused on the combination of his suit's fine fabric and cut, his ruddy aspect and combed hair. Together, they lent him the look of – what? Hannah squinted and cocked her head, trying to figure out what he looked like, exactly, and could only come up with *banker* – which was exactly right.

'In any case, we've other business to discuss.' He pushed back his chair farther so that they sat in a semi-circle.

'We do? I've only just gotten off the boat. Have you lined up work for me already?'

He rewarded her with a smile, and a warm current of comfort swept through her.

'Now that I've secured the contract thy brother mentioned, I'm in a position to do something we dreamed of for many years. I've met with Dr Bache, in Washington, and of course spoken with William Bond and Dr Hall as well. All are in support of a new observatory. Small, but fully outfitted and able to contribute to all the local and national astronomical efforts.'

'Run by?'

'Run by thee. I'm certain you'll be able to find work enough to maintain thyself on the Island now, even if thee continues to choose . . .' He paused, fishing for a word. Hannah couldn't intuit what he was getting at. He cleared his throat. 'Even if thee doesn't marry. And of course I'll assist as the project gets under way. And thy brother will help, for whatever span of time he decides to grace us.'

Hannah was so shocked by the announcement that her thoughts puddled together all at once.

'You'll be the sole funder? That's terribly expensive,' was what she managed to say.

'Always practical Hannah,' Edward said, rolling his eyes and kicking her boot under the desk as if they were ten years old. She tried to kick him back but missed.

'I'm considering various funding options. Dr Hall has some interest in investing, and there's a good chance a subscription would be fruitful. There's a fair amount of labor involved, and Edward has been quite helpful. But Philadelphia is my primary residence now.'

He hesitated as if he wanted to say something else, and she remembered the garret as an empty shell, stripped of their presence down to its planks and beams. Nathaniel sighed and took off his spectacles, then bowed his head for a moment, rubbing his temples, and in that hunched position he looked elderly, and fragile. Hannah felt her throat tighten, a complex array of emotions vibrating at once.

The chance to have an observatory of their own, a place to discover and dream, had been their shared vision as long as she could remember. She imagined a small transit house atop the Bank, living in this house on her own, with the financial means to ignore marriage entirely. She could spend her days ciphering and her nights observing for as long as she wished; perhaps the offer to contribute to the Coast Survey would resurface. It would be the most orderly of lives. It made perfect sense.

But a speck of doubt floated by, light as a puff of pollen. *One must not forsake feeling for fact,* Mary Somerville had said. *Keep your mind open to possibility!* Now it sounded like a warning. Nathaniel and Edward were staring at her, expectant.

'That's an exceedingly generous offer,' Hannah said, choosing her words with care. 'It's a bit overwhelming. I hardly know what to say.'

Nathaniel blinked at her like a surprised owl.

'I rather thought thee would be more excited. I can understand thy brother's limited enthusiasm, but is this not what we hoped for?'

Edward looked as shocked as Nathaniel, but for once he remained mute, and she was grateful for the chance to gather her thoughts.

'It's true that Edward and I could not be more dissimilar in our inclinations and aptitudes,' she said, keeping her voice soft. 'These are our natures. I know thee has been disappointed by our choices in the past: Edward for shipping with the *Regiment,* rather than taking a profession, and myself for failing to marry some respectable individual, be it Dr Hall or George Bond.' She hoped her gentle tone would blunt the effect of what she was about to say.

'But in following the dictates of our own hearts and intellects, I believe we have chosen wisely. Had Edward gone on to University, he would have been miserable. And had I entered into a contract with a man I didn't love, I would be the same – and in all likelihood I would never have found my comet and gotten the opportunity to pursue my observations. At this exact moment, I'm not . . . I'm not certain of my course.'

Nathaniel didn't answer for several long seconds, but Hannah felt a swell of relief. Speaking her mind felt like laying down a tremendous burden. The salons of Europe, her audience with Mary Somerville, her visits to the great observatories – everywhere she had gone, people had asked for her thoughts and ideas; she'd witnessed passionate, emotional debates about everything from universal suffrage to the mathematical likelihood of a finite Universe.

'Thy travels have certainly impacted thee,' Nathaniel finally said. 'Perhaps after thee has rested, and given the notion more consideration, thee will conclude that this plan is indeed suited to thy nature and circumstances.'

Hannah bit her lip. She had wounded him; it was not what she'd meant to do. But before she could say anything else, Nathaniel sighed and pushed his chair back from the desk.

'In any case, we shan't resolve the future tonight. Nor the past.' He sat up straighter and clutched both arms of the chair in order to rise to his feet. Edward's hand snaked out to help, and Hannah's was still there, but Nathaniel swatted them both away.

'I shan't topple,' he said. 'But I will retire. I'm sure there's much catching up the two of thee have yet to do.'

Hannah rose to let him by, and as his footfalls echoed away, she slumped into the chair he'd just vacated, warm from his body, and propped her boot on the stool. Edward blew out a huge sigh.

'My goodness, Hannah. I should write to the *Mirror*: "Great Lady Astronomer Goes to Continent, Returns with Valise, Voice."' He shook his head but his voice was full of admiration. 'I've never heard you put your feelings into words. Especially in defense of yours truly. I'm touched. Really.'

Hannah shrugged, but her cheeks warmed.

'Heartless Hannah no more, I suppose,' she muttered, wanting to change the subject before she accidentally revealed the true source of her transformation.

Her twin stared at her, waiting, then crossed his arms.

'I'm as perplexed as Father at the moment, though I'll be delighted if you do decline the offer and decide to move away.'

'That's charitable.' Cross, Hannah pushed the stool away with her boot, then sat up and folded her arms to match his. 'I've only just arrived. Why must I decide today what I want to do?'

'You need not. But I'm sure that you of all people can see a hot iron when it's sitting in front of you.'

'I don't know what you're talking about.'

'Hannah!' Edward leaned forward as if she was missing a fundamental point. 'You're famous!'

'So what?' she shot back.

'Well, why would you want to stay here when you could go anywhere on Earth?'

She felt pinned in place by his intense stare, but it grounded her. This was the garret of her youth. Home. Her senses sharpened: old wood and new, the peculiar dust of this room, crumbling parchment and spiderweb and ink. Leather from the books; a hint of linseed oil. She glanced at the desk; someone had recently polished it. Its dull gleam beckoned. Hannah ran a loving finger across it.

'I honestly don't know if I want to stay or not.' Hannah examined the ragged edges of her fingernails. 'Though I'd hesitate to get involved with anything Dr Hall had a hand in. At least if I remain I'll be supported by my own industry, regardless of your comings and goings. Or that of any other man.'

'True enough. There's not a man on this Island right now who won't be away in a minute's time, bound for an eastern city or a western farm. But unless you wish to remain shackled to an empty bed for the rest of your days, consider whether you're willing to end up with a fellow with half your intellect, who'll expect you to follow him to some factory town or worse. You might have financial independence here, and every instrument at your disposal, but the rest of your life will be boxed in by the boundaries of this place, which you know better than anyone. And as you might have noticed, they now contain thousands of idlers in the summer and a ghost town in the winter.'

'Are we talking about my prospects again? Is that what this is about?' A vision popped into her head like a match struck in the dark: a warm spring day, the windows of the house thrown open to the breeze, green shoots rising in the garden. She would be working; a distant knock would bring her down the steps as it had two years earlier, and she would throw open the door to find Isaac Martin waiting. This time she would waste no time with formality; this time she would go toward him as if propelled by gravity itself. Lost in her imagining, Hannah heard Edward droning on as if through a veil.

'I'm only suggesting that the Island has changed – *is* changing. And you've changed, too. I can see it.' His voice dropped to a near whisper. 'I don't want you to stay here out of some misguided notion of loyalty, to this Island or to our father. Or because you're waiting for something. Or someone.'

Hannah's face must have revealed her sudden sense of panic that Edward had read her mind, because he held up his hands and shook his head.

'I didn't mean to – I'm not saying you have to marry. Just that I don't want you to spend your life in this tiny corner of the world.' He reached for her hand and she allowed him to take it, but she pressed her cheek to her shoulder to hide her face.

'I don't care about anything that happened here while I was aboard the *Regiment*. You know that. I trust your judgment to be as solid as the Heavens. But I do think there's a bigger role for you than even a Nantucket observatory could provide.'

There was a gentle tapping, and then Mary came into the room. She was clutching a bundle of papers, wrapped in a ribbon. Hannah sat up.

'Are those for me?' Hannah asked. Her skin tingled into gooseflesh.

'Oh. Yes. They're yours.' Mary handed them off and glanced at Edward. He rose, dropping Hannah's hand.

'We'll leave you to them,' he said gently. 'We can speak more later.'

Hannah nodded, staring at the sheaf of correspondence in her hand. She barely heard the door to the garret click shut. What she wanted to do was leaf through the whole bundle immediately, looking for a letter from Isaac. But she forced herself to begin at the top, stretching out her wait. Her hopes would be fulfilled, or dashed. He would have written – or not – and then she would have to face the clear truth of the situation. She had waited this long; she could wait a few minutes more.

The first letter was from Admiral Bache himself, inviting her to join an astronomical expedition to Northern Maine in a month's time; she quickened at the opportunity, until she got to the bottom and saw that her father had been invited, too. Was she in need of a chaperone? she wondered, and then winced at her own naïveté. It was political, of course. Not personal. She sighed and looked around for her calendar and journal before remembering that they were all downstairs.

The stack of letters nestled in her lap. She plucked the next one from the top: it was postmarked Cambridge and turned out to be a note from George about his latest experiment: photographing the rings of Neptune. *I could use your eye (not to mention your maths) here in Cambridge,* he wrote. *I can't offer you a paid position (though you know I would if I could), but if you're inclined to visit, I can guarantee you credit and authorship on anything we publish* ... Hannah folded it up after scanning the rest and put it with Dr Bache's letter to be answered. After that came three requests for articles or appearances and two dozen fan letters from individuals she had no acquaintance with, praising her accomplishments and wishing her, in one young girl's curling hand, 'more extraordinary luck in de-mystifying the Heavens.'

The stack was half-gone. Hannah seized the rest in her hands and was surprised to see, right at the top, her own name, in her own hand. She flipped the letter over: *Isaac Martin, via the Pearl, Pacific Grounds.*

Whereabouts unknown, someone had written across the top in red ink. It had been returned, then; Hannah squinted at it but couldn't remember when she'd penned it. She'd have to read it to find out. She put it aside and turned to the next one, finding the same inscription across her own handwriting, and then another, and another. Seven of her letters to Isaac in total, all posted from Nantucket before she'd gone overseas. All of them bearing the same angry red scrawl.

Whereabouts unknown.

She froze, clutching the sheaf of parchment, a record of her desire in black ink. Why hadn't her letters reached Isaac? Fear coursed through her like blood, and she had to order herself to calm down and think clearly.

It wasn't possible that the *Pearl* had gone down. When a Nantucket ship foundered, it was in the newspapers. People spoke of it; she would have known. At least a quarter of the crew was Nantucket-born. And none of the letters she'd written from overseas were in the pile. Her hand shaking, she placed the bundle down on the desk. No wonder he hadn't written: he'd not received her letters. They explained Edward's comments, too. Hannah felt her cheeks burning; he'd obviously seen these pile up in the mail slot, and knew that she'd been writing to someone who had simply disappeared.

There was only one letter left. Her heart hammering, Hannah reached for it, closing her eyes before flipping it over. *What do you wish for?* she heard herself wondering, long ago in the Atheneum. She answered without hesitation now, clutching the letter, seeing Isaac the way he had once convinced her to see her comet. As if she could conjure him. *Speak to me,* she thought.

She turned over the clean white square. Her heart thudded into her belly, heavy as an anchor.

Miss Hannah Gardner Price was neatly inscribed upon the front. It was not Isaac's handwriting. The return address was in St Lawrence Valley, New York. Hannah tried to recall if she knew anyone there – or where it was, exactly – but couldn't come up with anything. She broke the seal, hardly caring about the contents.

5 June, 1847.
Ithaca, New York.

Dear Miss Price,

*I write on the recommendation of our mutual acquaintances,
William and George Bond. As the Dean of Groton College, an
institution of higher learning for women, located in Tompkins
County in the great state of New York, it is my honor to offer you
the position of Instructor in the Department of Astronomy we
are in the process of establishing. Your duties would consist of
assisting us with the selection and installation of instruments in
our new Observatory; leading the Department in matters of
Curriculum; and of course teaching our women what they need to
know in order to take their place beside you in the new order of
our country's development, as scientists and astronomers . . .*

Hannah dropped the letter on the desk and gripped the
edge with both hands, feeling weak. She would have her
contribution, then. Her path could not be clearer if it
were blazed across a dark sky: shaping the minds and
sharpening the intellect of a whole generation of women –
that would be her path.

With that thought, the warmth of a private sun seemed
to be shining down on her, sensible, magnificent. She half
expected the luminous sensation to resolve into religious
feeling. She felt grateful; she felt humble; she felt excited
and nervous and incredulous. Was this the hand of God?
She wasn't sure. The hand she felt in the crafting of everything leading up to this moment was her own.

Slowly, she rose to her feet. The Dollond gleamed dully

in the wavering light of the candle, and Hannah went to it, laying a hand and then her forehead on the cool brass of the tube, as if it were a horse that had safely forded her across a river. *Thank you,* she thought. She rested there for another moment before she remembered that the letter from Groton had been the last. A cold current of sorrow cut through her relief like an icy wind. Isaac had not written. It was time to abandon hope of seeing him again; surely there was no mistaking the meaning of such a long, unbroken silence.

32. Independence Day

Are you coming?'

'I am.' Hannah wiped her brow with her elbow and snapped the last of the clean aprons in the humid July twilight before clipping it to the line, then ran upstairs to change into something cooler than the dark work dress she'd thrown on that morning. She had two choices: an old brown linen or a lightweight silk the color of new-churned butter that she'd bought in Italy but had never worn. She'd probably have little use for it in Groton; she might as well enjoy it now.

'They won't begin the fireworks till dark,' she said to Mary as she came downstairs. Her sister-in-law waited with Moses on her hip, jiggling him so that he bobbed like an apple in a tub. She looked Hannah up and down, her mouth a perfect rosebud O.

'I've never worn it before,' Hannah said, smoothing the skirt. 'Is it ridiculous?' It was silly to be nervous about what anyone thought of her attire, but she still felt her cheeks flush. It was impossible to discard one's old self entirely, Hannah thought, waiting for Mary's judgment.

'It's beautiful,' Mary said, reaching out and squeezing Hannah's hand. 'You look lit from inside.' The baby gummed at Mary's neck and she giggled, nuzzling into him. Hannah felt a now-familiar pang: a twinge of desire laced with a vaguely lurid curiosity. She wasn't sure whether it was her own intermittent longing that was by turns enticing and embarrassing, or whether it was motherhood itself that affected her, its viscous, redolent sensuality. Hannah had glimpsed Mary in the tub with the baby the evening before. He'd bobbed up and down on his back, resting on his mother's swollen breasts and soft belly. Mary's face had been beatific, like a Catholic painting of a saint. Hannah had withdrawn into the shadows behind the door but had watched for a moment before she forced herself to look away.

'I know, you want to see the parade. Right, Mo?' Mary planted a kiss on the baby's head.

'Let's go, then.' At the last moment, Hannah grabbed her threadbare grey shawl from the peg by the door, feeling like a child with a security blanket but immediately grateful for the soft fall of the weave around her shoulders.

The crowds on Main heading for the water swarmed thick and sweaty. There was no breeze, and Hannah's hair was heavy and damp at her neck. She linked her arm through Mary's to avoid losing her.

A bandstand had been set up at the corner of Main and Federal, in front of the Bank and across from the new hotel, and the air smelled like fresh paint and new wood. Sawdust carpeted the street, seeping into the cracks between the cobblestones. The strains of music reached their ears as they wove through the throngs, and though Hannah kept expecting to see people she knew, it was near dark before Lilian and John appeared, and then Nell, and finally Millicent, who flew into Hannah's arms as if she'd been released from a slingshot.

'I've been looking for you for days,' Hannah said, squeezing her friend's shoulders. 'I left two notes at your house. Where have you been?'

Millicent had been a consistent correspondent during Hannah's travels, keeping her updated on the social lives of Islanders Hannah was barely acquainted with, as well as entertaining her with stories of her daily trials as a teaching assistant at a penny school in New Guinea. But even Millicent's letters had been few and far between, with mysterious holes in the narratives left by earlier chapters that hadn't made it across the Atlantic.

'My mother said someone had been by but she didn't tell me who it was!' Millicent's eyes went wide. 'I heard you were on-Island but I didn't believe you'd show up and not come and find me. Or write to say so.' She narrowed her eyes at Hannah. 'Were you worried that I'd arrange a party of some sort?'

'I'm not so averse to festivities as to hide my plans from you,' Hannah said, squeezing Millicent's arm. 'I suppose your mother still blames me for diverting you from your destiny as a baker's assistant.'

Millicent sighed and linked her arm through Hannah's.

'Well, if I have any luck at all, I'll be out of her house soon enough.' She shot a shy sideways glance at Hannah, and a smile spread across her cheek.

'Millicent? What don't I know?'

'Not a *what*. A *whom*! And I hope to introduce you tonight, if I can find him.' She scanned the crowd. 'I'm going to go hunt him down. I'll find you!' And she sprang away, wading through the sea of people with a general's purpose.

A string of firecrackers exploded nearby, and Moses began to cry.

'The procession is starting,' Mary said, swinging the baby up onto her back and securing him with a swath of linen she produced from somewhere on her person. Hannah marveled at the efficiency of her gestures, her sure hands. People swirled around them, and they edged toward the margins where the crowd was thinner.

The engine companies paraded by like a ragtag militia, saluting the selectmen as they passed; then came the Cold Water Army, an intimidating pack of women with bright blue sashes whose collective belief in temperance had the effect of dousing the crowd with actual cold water: the festive hum died down, and only rose up again when the Masons marched by and the band struck up a rousing tune.

Hannah saw Dr Hall on the stage, gazing out over the crowd, and her eyes lingered on him for a moment. A swell of contempt twisted her gut. His betrayal still smarted; she had no desire to speak with him. When she turned back to Mary and the others, they'd disappeared. She was surrounded by strangers.

It was nearly dark. Boys roamed the crowd with baskets of candles for the procession. Hannah bought one and then waded into the river of Islanders lighting their wicks and holding their candles high. Hannah tried to spot Mary and the baby as the human tide began to snake through the streets, a buoyant stream of tiny flames, voices raised in song. She was lulled by the bobbing points of light, and drifted along as if in a dream, vaguely melancholy. She hadn't yet told her family about the offer from Groton

College. Today would be the day, she'd decided. When the parade was over, she would reveal her plans.

The procession turned the corner of Main, and Hannah paused to look again for her sister-in-law and nephew. The crowd parted and surged past like a river around a stone, but Mary and Moses were nowhere to be seen. Hannah edged carefully toward the storefronts, her candle wavering but still lit, and searched the faces in the crowd. Then she turned and tried to wade back in the direction she'd come from, elbowing and edging her way around the oncoming tide, head down, shoulders forward. She'd gotten only a few yards when someone gripped her elbow, holding her in place.

'If you please,' she said, wresting free before raising her chin and finding herself face-to-face with Isaac Martin.

Hannah felt her jaw drop, breath gusting in, her pulse fast and deep as thunder. It was impossible to form words. She raised her candle, a jerky motion lacking any grace, and squinted. It was him. He was staring back, equally surprised. The crowd jostled them closer to each other, then away, but he reached out and took her elbow again.

Questions sprinted through her head – Where had he come from? How long had he been on the Island? – and she felt a desperate rush of confusion. But she didn't pull her arm away, and he didn't let go. Like an awkward pair of dancers, then, they stumbled to the edge of the crowd, into the protective shadow of an overhanging roof.

The flickering light of a thousand candles wavered over his face. He looked frightened, and a little uncomfortable. *He doesn't know what to say,* Hannah realized, remembering the first moment she'd felt their sameness, under a similar overhang. She was seared by the memory, and her hand flew to his cheek as if to confirm that he was real. His cheek was rough, unshaven. He put his hand over hers, swallowed, leaned in, and spoke into her ear.

'I am looking everywhere for you,' he said.

At the sound of his voice – or maybe the scent of his skin, she wasn't sure – all the blood in her body rushed to her stomach, then to her feet. She hurled herself forward, and they engulfed each other without words. Seconds ticked by, which felt like hours, cocooned in each other's arms. Hannah felt as if she were suspended in a state of wonder, a beautiful darkness. When a sudden cry from the crowd pierced through, they broke apart. But the rush of bodies pushed on, insensible.

Still, she shook her head in warning, aware of the field of luminous faces just a few yards away. 'We should walk.'

He gave a brisk nod, glancing at the crowd, then reached for her hand, leading her directly back into the swell of bodies in the procession. It was too crowded for anyone to see her hand in his. Hannah allowed herself to be swept along, pressed close to Isaac's body by the crowd, clutching him tightly, nightfall now complete outside the nimbus of light from their candles. She pressed her face to his shoulder, inhaling his skin and his sea, everything about him that was familiar and yet foreign. The sheer relief of being close to him again felt like the tumblers of a lock falling open.

And on top of that, the smell of him made her feel what she imagined intoxication to be like: a hot, buzzing current running through her body, as undeniable as hunger. Like stubborn dreams, the sensation of his touch had returned to her body again and again over the years; the images that had flitted past before she could punch them away might as well have been disgraceful cartoons, flesh on flesh, a spectacle at best, an abomination to most, even to otherwise sane and decent people.

She moved forward, carried by the waves of people moving in the direction of the harbor, crushed too tight to speak. After a few minutes she heard the whiz and pop of the first fireworks. The procession surged forward. Isaac held on to her hand.

They went closer, the bright pop of cherry-red and white sparks high above them. Hundreds of faces tilted back and peered up like moon-lilies, drenched in wonder. Hannah looked, too, the bright display blazing over the waters of the harbor, lighting the ships and the masts, the rooftops and the shoreline, reflecting everything on the surface and above it in the mirror of the Bay, tipping the world upside down. Isaac moved behind her, circling her with both arms, leaning down as everyone looked up, burying his face in her neck. It was difficult to stand up straight. His hand was on her ribs, her belly, her thighs. So much heat, she felt branded. Her eyes fluttered, awash in light.

When the band struck up again and the crowd began to buzz, Isaac released her, tugging gently on her hand again before letting go. Feeling like a sleepwalker, she followed him through the crowd, weaving around the counting-house and along the edge of the wharves, continuing in silence down Pineapple Street.

They walked in silence until they reached Easton, enough room between them for a canoe, a flagpole, a coffin. The sounds and lights of the party faded. Isaac turned right and Hannah followed, heading back in the direction of the water on the other side of the harbor. When they reached the promontory at the very edge of the road, they went on by unspoken agreement, side by side now, until they stood at the very edge of the Island. In the distance, they could see the sparks still lighting over the water, the crowd a swaying skyscape of tiny candle flames.

They turned to face each other, closing the distance in an instant.

'When?'

His lips near the whorl of her ear.

'Today.'

She shivered.

'I wrote – I tried to tell you how sorry I am for how I – that I did not – that I could not tell you what was in my heart.' Hannah felt herself beginning to cry, great heaving sobs tearing through her chest as she tried to utter the words she had failed to say before.

But his hands were on her cheeks, then he was kneeling, and she was sinking with him. Pebbles and sand ground into her knees, their sting sharp and delicious as his lips took the words she might have spoken to explain her disappointment and her regret and everything else, but there were no words that she could conjure.

And she did not want words. Her body commanded her now. She did not try to speak again but gave all of her weight over to Isaac, her bones and the flesh around them, bridging the distance between them, releasing herself. She had never been so aware of her body; when he took the buttons of her dress one by one, investigating the triangle of skin between her neck and clavicle, the geometry of each rib, the softest and hardest places on her person, it was as if she had never seen or felt them herself.

Yet she'd been tethered to this body her whole life. It was the only thought she would remember later from the time that followed; how surprising it felt as each new part of her was revealed. Skin, flesh, freckle, bone. A dazzling Universe within and upon her.

Later – she wasn't sure how much – they rested, her head on his arm. They lay on her shawl, on a slight incline, facing the Harbor. A blanket of stars flickered overhead. Across the water, candles still wavered in the hands of invisible revelers.

'A miniature Heavens,' Hannah said. 'A thousand lights against the dark.' She sighed and shifted closer to him.

Here and there a tiny light bobbed in the dark and disappeared. The lighthouse beamed and diminished.

'There is so much I've wished to tell you,' Hannah whispered.

'Tell me.'

'I have seen so much. The observatories . . . in Europe. I've seen the colors of the stars. They're so beautiful.' The words caught in her throat.

Isaac leaned closer, rested his head in the cradle of her neck.

'Betelgeuse is red. Pure red, like an autumn rose. Red as blood. Rigel is blue. Others are lilac, some are yellow.' She sighed and turned her face toward the Heavens as if basking in their light. 'They are like a collection of precious stones, or . . . flowers. *Flores.*'

Isaac smiled, though his eyes were closed. He moved his cheek down to her chest, over her heart, and breathed against her as if buoyed by her vision of the jewel-colored stars.

'I found my comet,' Hannah whispered. 'I saw it first in my mind – as you showed me. And when I opened my eyes, it was there. As if it had been waiting for me.' She closed her eyes, imagining the wanderer as it had appeared to her, as clear and obvious as the sun.

A warm breeze came off the headland, and Hannah drew in a deep breath. It was the most familiar air: salt and seaweed and fish. Her own skin, her sweat, mixed with Isaac's, made it new.

'I am sorry I did not write,' Isaac said, propping himself up on an elbow so he could look down at her, his beautiful eyes solemn. 'I was wishing to protect you. And I did not hear from you, so –'

'I am sorry my letters didn't reach you. I don't know why they didn't.' Hannah shook her head. 'It doesn't matter, I suppose.'

'I wish I was receiving them. My journey was not . . . It was difficult.'

'The navigation, you mean?'

'This, too. But you should not be worrying: your teaching is excellent.' He grinned at her and Hannah leaned her cheek against his arms.

'What, then. Were you – were the men crude? Were there not enough provisions?' Her heart pummeled erratically at the thought of his suffering.

He sighed, cradling her head with his arm so that it nestled under his shoulder like a wing. For once she did not mind his pace, the time he took to gather his words like kindling.

'The men were as always. It is I who am changing.'

'How so?' The lights across the harbor had dwindled to a spark. Waiting for Isaac to answer, Hannah surveyed the sky. Altair, Deneb, Vega. Eagle, Swan, Lyre. Three constellations any child could pick out of the night sky. What would it be like to see the sky only in this way? A sparkling picture, pretty as a quilt. To lie each night beside a man and stare at the sky with no more care than for the next day's supper, for nicely tatted lace, ripe tomatoes, clean aprons?

Hannah thought of Moses, the tug she'd felt when his little body pressed against hers, and imagined herself mothering, laundering, adding and subtracting her husband's wage to add up to soup and silk and wool enough for the season. It was like imagining a duck in a desert. Then why was she thinking of it? Hannah squeezed her eyes shut and then popped them open again, grateful for the sight of her own sky and its endless, infinite geometry.

'When I am leaving my home I am yet a boy. I want only to avoid the army, to earn money, to have adventure. Also to help my family,' Isaac said. His voice wavered and Hannah glanced at him. He seemed to be struggling with a painful memory.

'I am everywhere in this world. I go north and west, Arctic and Pacific. After so much time I wish to advance my place – you are knowing all this.'

Hannah nodded but sensed there was more, and so did not move or speak. The soft lap of tiny breakers came into the quiet. Crickets rubbed their wings in the underbrush. Isaac swallowed – Hannah could hear the sound and put her hand to his throat to feel the throb of his muscles there. She felt him smile at her touch.

'And so,' she said, 'you secured your position upon the *Pearl*.'

He nodded.

'But before I can leave, I am stuck on this Island. Until I meet you. And this is changing me.'

Hannah concentrated on the meaning of his words. She felt gratified and confused in equal measure.

'Was it – is it a good change?' she ventured.

Isaac covered the top of her head with his broad palm, tilting her face to his.

'Not good or bad – only different.' He leaned in and kissed the top of her forehead, then turned back and rested again, his arms tucked under his head. 'I am doing only one thing for more than ten years. I am on the watch or in the fo'c'sle, I am taking orders, I am giving orders. I can say the same fifteen things in five languages, and I am hearing the same thing each day from dawn to dusk. The crew and the boats, the heave and the haul, topgallants, stuns'ls, lobscouse.' The music of his voice was unchanged.

He stopped short, as if he'd been caught unaware by his feelings on the matter, and Hannah was surprised, too. Isaac had always seemed to accept his role on a whaleship as obvious, necessary. He'd told her as much. But his voice betrayed him.

He grasped a fistful of sand and let it trickle out.

'I am spending more time on this Island than I have

spend on land since I leave home,' he said. 'If I am not meeting you, I would be spending all my time working and waiting. But you are showing me something different. Not only in the Heavens. Here. Upon the land.' Abruptly, he stood, and Hannah lowered her eyes, her cheeks warming at his nakedness.

He made no move to cover himself. Instead, he walked a few paces away, then continued on to the water. When she looked up, his back was to her, his body nearly invisible against the dark water, the crescent moon barely offering a silhouette.

'I no longer wish to crew a whaleship,' he said. 'I no longer wish for a life upon the sea.'

'I see,' Hannah whispered, pulling her shawl up and around herself. Then she raised her voice so he could hear. 'What do you wish for?'

She thought she could hear him smile, as if he, too, were remembering their long-ago conversation in the Atheneum. *I am not a child, imagining a life that cannot be. Dreaming without purpose,* he'd said. Did he now imagine a life that could include the impossible? Did he mean to include her?

'I once wished to go home,' he said, kneeling at the water's edge, dipping his hands in and splashing water over his head and neck. 'But I no longer have a home to go to.'

'What do you mean?'

'My parents – it was the end of their time. They are gone.'

Hannah rose and went to Isaac. She knelt beside him. His face contorted with grief, like a reflection in moving

419

water. She swept the shawl so that it enclosed him, too, and put her arms around him. Now it was he who gave his weight; it took all her strength to stay upright, and the balls of her feet dug into the cool sand. She shouldered him, he wept, the moon began its ascent.

'I am so sorry,' Hannah whispered. She wished she could look into his eyes, but they were closed. He rested his forehead on hers.

'It is as it must be,' he said, the calm returning to his voice as he separated from her. They stayed on the sand, kneeling, facing each other, as if in some religious ritual.

'And you have returned here from Flores? How?' Hannah asked, thinking that she should stop asking questions. He looked so tired. This close, she could see tiny lines around his eyes and lips that had not been there two years earlier.

'I leave the *Pearl* almost a year ago. We tied up with a ship that has just make the Atlantic crossing, and from a man from my island on that ship I learn that my parents are not well. I join an outbound crew, and when this ship puts in at Flores I leave to see my parents. It was May,' he said, settling back on the sand, cross-legged. 'They were very sick. He was dying. She could not see. Still he washed her feet. She prepared soup. Even on the edge of death. They must do these things.' His voice shook. Hannah settled beside him, then reached out and put a hand on his forearm.

'It took two months for them to pass to the next world. He went first, then she followed. I buried them, and then I had to decide what to do. The crop was bad. It was never good, but in the last years there was – how do you say it? When everything die.'

'Blight,' Hannah said.

'Yes. I cannot work this land. And after so many years I am a stranger to it. I could not know it again, without my family. No one is there anymore. It is not the same place I knew as a child. So I sell it. I leave, knowing I am never coming back. But I have gold, in a cloth the size of my hand.' He clenched his fist under Hannah's hand. 'I tie it to the inside of my shirt, like an extra heart. I took the bowl my mother used to grind spice, and the cane of my father that my grandfather carve. I have nothing else. This is everything. I leave with a merchant vessel, I crew with her to Boston. Then I take a train to Mattapoisett, then I walk to Fall River.'

'That's twenty miles,' Hannah interjected, horrified.

'A farmer drove me in his cart part of the way, looking back at me often to be sure I was not stealing his, what? His hay? There was nothing there.' He laughed, a short chuff of air. 'Then a fisherman took me to New Bedford, and I took the morning boat.'

'Why?' Hannah whispered. 'Why here?'

He reached for her face, his palm rough as tree bark on her cheek.

'This is the place I remembered what it is to love the land, to have a place to walk, to think, to learn. You made me think that I can . . .' He paused, and Hannah waited for him to find the word he needed. '. . . expand. So I choose to come here. To find land. And to see you, if you are here.'

'You didn't even know for certain if I was here?'

He shook his head. Hannah leaned back, resting her head on his thigh.

'What will you do?' he asked. 'Now that you have find what you seek?'

Hannah paused, remembering the clean white envelope from Groton engraved with her name. It had lifted her like a balloon when she saw it earlier in the week; now its hard edges seemed like small knives piercing her heart.

'I'm not sure the comet was really what I sought,' Hannah said slowly. 'It was a path to what I wanted. A doorway. But now I know that there are other such passages.'

'What did you want?' Isaac asked, stroking her hair.

'To contribute something. Some knowledge. To matter, in a worldly sense. But more than that I wanted to advance myself – but I had such a limited idea of what my self comprised. Do you understand?'

She tilted her head back to see his face, but it was impassive.

'Before I met you, I saw only with my eyes. Judged only with my mind. Myself and everyone. I had no reason to consult my feelings, much less put my faith in them. You showed me how to do that. Even if I could not act upon it until now.'

She fell silent, gathering strength.

'I've been asked to move to northern New York State. To teach astronomy at a college. A college for women.'

The breeze had stilled again. Hannah reached down and gathered a handful of sand, then let it sift out through her fist. She was home, and not home. Isaac had returned. How could she part from him again?

422

'So you will go,' he said.

His words were like a cold wave breaking over her. Hannah sat up and wrapped her arms around her knees.

'You sound certain.' A knot of panic rose to her throat. Did he not want her to stay?

He sat up and moved close in beside her, mirroring her posture, and looked at her.

'How would I hold you here? Your world has also . . . expanded.' He swept his arm out before them, indicating the sea before them and all that lay beyond it. Then he brought his hand to rest on her knee. She covered it with her own, marveling by moonlight at the contrast.

'What if I chose to stay?' Hannah asked. Her voice felt small.

Isaac tipped his head down so that it rested on hers.

'You said I was teaching you to find the truth of what you feel.'

'Taught. Yes.'

'Then look there and tell me that we can live here, on this Island, together. Without hiding. Without caring what happens after?'

Though Hannah couldn't see his face, she knew its sorrow.

'It would be my choice,' she said. 'And things may change. The country is changing. Attitudes are changing.' She tried to cling to the reason therein, but she knew that her words had the heft of dragonfly wing.

He didn't say anything else. In the distance, the lighthouse bell tolled.

'You must go,' he whispered. 'You will know where to find me.'

He turned her face to him and kissed her. The salt from her tears burned her lips.

Later, sometime before dawn, they walked along the shore. Hannah shivered, pulling her shawl tight around her shoulders.

'I met Mary Somerville,' Hannah said. 'During my travels. She's a famous scientist.'

'I remember,' Isaac said.

'She told me that faith and uncertainty must coexist.'

'Yes.'

'She believes in what cannot be proven. She said I must not forsake passion for reason.'

'And what do you believe?'

Hannah stopped, pulling Isaac to a halt so that they stood facing each other. She shivered. He put his hands on her shoulders and she lifted her chin, meeting his gaze, feeling herself grow taller until she was towering as a lamppost, a tree, a lighthouse.

'I believe this is the first time in my life I have understood myself completely.'

She let the shawl slip to the ground. The sea was warm, and nearly still, as they waded out, ankle, knee, thigh, chest. Hannah struck out, away from the shoreline, her legs kicking cleanly so there was nearly no wake, her rhythm smooth and steady. She did not look for Isaac or look back at the shore. With each stroke, she felt some part of herself disappear. First sweat and sand, then skin and nail, then flesh itself, leaving only a shell. As she swam, she wished for nothing, desired nothing, as if past and future could be annulled by the sea, leaving only the present.

When she was far out, the water cool and dark and deep,

she turned on her back and floated, the night sky a dark curtain overhead, sprinkled with stars she knew but declined to name. She let her eyes drift closer to closing, so that the objects above blurred together, indistinct and cloudy, a beautiful mystery she could not decipher. Without intention, without thought, Hannah floated, needing nothing but the water on which she was carried, light as a feather.

August 10, 1847.
Nantucket.

Dear Isaac:

I write by the very last of my candle; my trunk is packed and ready, and in a few hours, before dawn, I shall be bound for New York. When you left upon the Pearl, I felt as if a light were being extinguished. So did my life darken in your absence. Now, though, when I regard the events that followed, unfolding all the way until you found me again right up until this moment, it seems that without that darkness we could not have emerged into the light of these last golden weeks. I would have remained submerged in what I thought I knew. My 'black-and-white' as you once called it. I would have denied my heart any flight it attempted without the endorsement of my mind and the approval of my elders; my orbit would have been confined, static. I would not have risked an aberration that could take me off my charted course.

Even when I consider all the suffering we did weather, I would not choose to deny myself the light you did bring. How could I? You have always understood what Mary Somerville told me about Faith and uncertainty. I did once think them incompatible; yet they are inseparable. I shall bring this knowledge with me on my journey, and keep it close as the malachite you did give me so long ago. One of many treasures you bestowed upon me.

I know there will be days when I am unable to penetrate the veils of mystery that yet shroud the Heavens, when I feel as if all the work of my life has barely yielded a single insight, when I feel as if my contributions are so very limited. Yet I shall not despair, but think of you, wherever in the world you might be, living under the same stars.

Your devoted friend,
HGP

August 11, 1847. Nantucket.

Dear Hannah,

After I read your letter, I went to the headland at dawn, and watched the sun rise, and the boat that would carry you away come in, and then go out, like a tide. I was too far to see you but I knew you were there.

You say that your contributions are small, but you are more like your Comet than you know. All over this Earth people know of you, and observe you with wonder. It is you who creates the light you speak of, through Knowledge. I choose to stay in this place because it is where I am learning to See. I am learning this from you.

I am the fixed star now, and you are the Wanderer. Know that I will watch for you in every night sky, and find you in each Sun rise. When and if you return to this place, I shall be here, like the Pole Star, anchored in place, rooted at last.

Your faithful friend,
Isaac Martin

Epilogue
June 1889 Nantucket

'Tell me again why this is necessary.'

'I don't need to tell you. You'll just have to trust your old mother.'

'I trust you. But I don't like watching you struggle to trudge through mud on some unexplained mission related to Aunt Hannah.'

'Well, there are many things I don't like, Moses. Yet they must be done.'

Mary sighs, and steps carefully over a stone in the road. The way to and from the old Newtown Gate is crowded with beachgoers, the thousands who descend at the start of each summer and inhabit the streets of Town and the hotels that line the shore from there to 'Sconset until the last days of August.

'It's busy for seventh day,' Mary comments.

'Saturday is always like this.'

'Saturday.' She rolls the word around. 'Turn here.'

Off the main road, there are fewer people, and nearly all are dark-skinned. Moses and Mary wave their greetings to the familiar faces of New Guinea. They walk for another half mile, Mary feeling it in her hip, though she does not pause until they reach the old farmhouse set back from the road, surrounded by a neat, low fence recently whitewashed and mended.

'Mr Martin's place?'

'He was a friend of your aunt. For longer than you've been alive. I believe they've written to each other every week since she moved off-Island.'

'I didn't know.'

Isaac sees the old woman and the middle-aged man coming up the path to the house and rises to his feet from where he is sitting on the porch. He shades his eyes. Mary still favors the old style of dress, high-necked and dark-hued. Nothing about her eyes has aged.

'Mrs Price. It's good to see you.'

'And you.'

Moses and Isaac shake hands.

'I'm going to sit with Mr Martin a bit,' Mary says to her eldest son.

'Shall I wait?'

'You go on. He'll see me back home.'

Isaac nods and helps Mary into the chair on the porch. It overlooks the small yard, which blooms so improbably, it seems an oasis amid the yellow-green and dust brown of the surrounding fields. Mary breathes in the deep, twilight smell, fighting tears. A trellis, heavy with Nantucket roses, climbs the wall beside her, and the flowers comfort her.

'Isaac,' Mary says into the buzzing air. 'Hannah has passed.'

Isaac had settled at her feet, on the step facing the garden, so she cannot see his face, and wonders if he has heard. She is about to repeat it when he speaks.

'I knew it before you came,' he says slowly. 'I had a dream.'

'A dream?'

He nods. In the dream he saw Hannah as she was at twenty-five, her dark hair loose. It had been night; she was asleep. Something woke her, a heavy acrid smell, a dim, distant thunder. Rising, ghost-like in white linen, she moved to the window. Isaac observed, unseen, as she drifted through the house – he realizes now it was the house on Little India, the old house – and up into her garret observatory, which both is and is not the one he remembers. Rather, this room holds all the things he remembers, the specimens and logbooks, the telescope and rocking horse, but all of it is bathed in an orange light streaming from the open arc of a giant dome atop the house. He had not expected such a grand structure on the small house, but it was so.

Hannah ascended the stair in full stride, wanting to see, needing to know. It was not the comet she sought, but something else. At the top of the stair she turned the crank on a small wheel and the whole of the roof began to revolve and then dissolve, diminishing with each turn until there was only sky, a blazing sky so bright that in the dream Hannah shielded her eyes, then released herself and rose, or the stair itself dropped away, and, blinded, Isaac closed his own eyes.

'Yes,' he says to Mary. 'The stars were all burning at once.'

They sit, quiet, in the stillness.

'I'd like to see the lighting ceremony,' Mary says. 'Would you take me?'

Isaac nods and offers her his arm. Then he brings out his horse and cart and helps her up. They drive together through the deepening twilight as far as the old ironworks;

Isaac has owned it for two decades, and as they draw up, the workers changing shifts wave.

Mary steps carefully. Already, the crowds have gathered along Main, the ladies in fashionable dresses, poufing and puffing in every direction, clinging to men in straw hats. They make way for the old woman in her plain dress and the dignified black man who accompanies her. Mary ignores them. She knows that when they look at her they see a ghost, a relic of the old Island, and she does not care any more than a tree cares what a raindrop thinks of its roots.

'Let's go up to the top of Step Lane. The Veranda House is to be lit first, but we'll see it all from there,' she says to Isaac.

He nods, and they turn on Center, skirting the crowds along Water Street, and make their way up to the very top of the steep and narrow path. They can hear the voices booming from the bandstand, the Mayor no doubt touting his own role in the bringing of electric current, as if history itself had not borne this like a tide to their tiny Island. Slowly, by some signal, all the lamps are blown out at once, and an eerie quiet seeps over the path along with the dark. Quiet descends all the way down into the Town, thousands of voices stilled, waiting, reverent, invisible.

When they turn on the current, the vast hotel on the hillside bursts into view, a hundred electric lamps popping at once, like so many stars. After the Veranda, the Springfield is lit, then the Nantucket, and after the hotels come the lamps along Main Street. The Island blooms with light. All those around them on the high lane look down at Town. Isaac looks up.

Mizor and Alcor, Arcturus and Spica, Denebola and Regulus are disappearing, as if bowing their heads against the sudden blaze. Isaac lowers his head, too, then, and closes his eyes.

Forty miles away, on the mainland, for the first time, those who turn their gaze east, toward the horizon, observe a bright haze, a nimbus of light piercing the night sky where before there was only darkness.

Author's Note

I had never heard of Maria Mitchell before taking a day trip to Nantucket in 1996. On the ferry, I picked up a flyer aimed at tourists, directing newcomers to Nantucket's attractions. In one corner, a squib caught my eye: *Come and see the home of the famous girl astronomer from Nantucket!* The text explained that Maria Mitchell, born in 1818 to a large Quaker family, had shown interest and aptitude for observing the stars from a very young age. In spite of her isolated location and having only a high school education, she'd discovered a comet in 1847 and earned a medal from the King of Denmark for doing so. She went on to become the first professional female astronomer in America, and the founding professor of astronomy at Vassar College.

Girl astronomer. I couldn't get the phrase out of my head. What, I wondered, would compel a teenage girl to spend her nights alone on the roof of her house, staring at the stars for hours on end, sweeping the skies in hopes of spotting something so few people had the opportunity to see? The commitment required was beyond my understanding. I walked along the still-cobblestoned Main Street of Nantucket Town until I reached the side lane where the Mitchells had lived and observed. The little house and its garden of wildflowers bewitched me; my imagining of young Maria and her telescope took flight.

That half-day trip inspired a fifteen-year journey. I researched Maria Mitchell's life and work, thinking that I wanted to write *about* her; what I ended up with, all these years and almost as many drafts later, is a novel that uses her work and accomplishments – not to mention the time period and many details from her life – as a leaping-off place for the journey of a character of my own creation: Hannah Gardner Price.

Hannah and Maria share a number of attributes: diligence and intellectual rigor; impatience with the constraints upon women's freedom and education; a job at the Nantucket Atheneum; and a father and mentor without whose guidance they might not have progressed. Maria Mitchell and her father, William, worked for the U. S. Coast Survey, and enjoyed a cordial relationship with their friends, William Cranch Bond and George Phillips Bond of Cambridge, overseers of the Harvard Observatory (though my characterizations of the Bonds, including George's romantic interest in Hannah, are entirely invented). The Mitchells were members of the Society of Friends at a particularly rigid moment in that body's history: though fond of the Edward Young quote that appears in this novel (*'An undevout astronomer is mad'*), Maria Mitchell was indeed disowned from Meeting at age twenty-five (albeit in a much less dramatic fashion than Hannah) after professing that her mind was 'unsettled on religious matters.'

Many of the details of Hannah's home and professional life were drawn from my visits to the Mitchell house and archives on Nantucket, from Maria Mitchell's journals, and from her sister Phebe's recollections of the family's early years. Among those scenes inspired by the above sources are: the laying of the meridian stones outside the Pacific National Bank (which was done by Maria Mitchell's father); and the meeting with Mary Somerville, which took place in 1858, eleven years later than Hannah's scene with her occurs in the novel. Hannah's astronomy journals are modeled after those kept by Maria Mitchell. In addition, the circumstances of the award from the King of Denmark; her work for the *Nautical Almanac* (which wasn't actually published in the United States until 1852); and her membership in various astronomical and scientific societies were drawn from real activities.

I placed Hannah at certain real events that Maria Mitchell was not present for, such as the first use of the Great Refractor at Harvard (which happened in 1847, not 1846). Miss Mitchell was living on Nantucket in 1846 when a massive fire destroyed a third of the town, but there's no record of what she did during the conflagration other than (allegedly) burning her own journals rather than risk her privacy should the fire reach their home and blow the pages into the street. To the best of my knowledge, the astronomy that appears in the book is accurate for the time period in which it is portrayed, with the exception of the meteor shower Eta Aquarids, which was not discovered until the 1860s; the discovery of the eighth satellite of Saturn, which actually occurred in 1848; and the photograph of the stars Mizor and Alcor that Hannah Price carries to Europe in 1847. That photograph was actually taken in 1857.

In every other way, Hannah Gardner Price's story is a product of my imagination. Her twin brother and the rest of her family life, her actions, and her personal relationships, including the one with Isaac Martin, are entirely fictional. In inventing Hannah's journey, I tried to remain faithful to the spirit of Maria Mitchell: independent, industrious, and above all truthful.

As a novelist, I'm grateful I came across Miss Mitchell's story as a source of inspiration; as a woman, I'm thankful for her lifelong advocacy on behalf of women's education and women's suffrage. Without women like her who paved the way for their peers in every profession, the life I have crafted for myself – not to mention this book – would not have been possible.

Sources

The initial inspiration for this book came from the writings of Maria Mitchell, as provided to me by the Maria Mitchell Association archive on Nantucket, and as collected in the volumes noted below (though none from her young adulthood have survived to the present day).

In constructing daily life among Nantucket's Quaker community in the mid-nineteenth century, the practice of astronomy and celestial navigation at that time, as well as life on a whaleship, I drew on a number of additional sources, the most salient of which I've listed here:

Albers, Henry. *Maria Mitchell: A Life in Journals and Letters.* Clinton Corners, N. Y.: College Avenue Press, 2001.

Bacon, Margaret Hope. *The Quiet Rebels: The Story of the Quakers in America.* Wallingford, Pa.: Pendle Hill Publications, 1999.

Birns, Susan M. 'Nineteenth-Century Black Life on Nantucket.' Research paper UMass 15, University of Massachusetts Humanities Program on Nantucket, 1975.

Bolster, W. Jeffrey. '"To Feel Like a Man": Black Seamen in the Northern States, 1800–1860.' *The Journal of American History* 76, no. 4 (March 1990).

Bowditch, Nathaniel. *The New American Practical Navigator: Being an Epitome of Navigation.* New York: E. & G. W. Blunt, 1841.

Dell, Burnham N. 'Quakerism on Nantucket.' *Historic Nantucket* 2, no. 3 (January 1955).

Ferris, Timothy. *Coming of Age in the Milky Way*. New York: William Morrow, 1988.

Gormley, Beatrice. *Maria Mitchell: The Soul of an Astronomer*. Grand Rapids, Mich.: William B. Eerdmans, 1995.

Johnson, Robert, Jr. *Nantucket's People of Color: Essays on History, Politics, and Community*. University Press of America, 2006. Errata and commentary by the Nantucket Historical Association.

Karttunen, Frances Ruley. *The Other Islanders: People Who Pulled Nantucket's Oars*. New Bedford, Mass.: Spinner Publications, 2005.

Kelly, Catherine E. *In the New England Fashion: Reshaping Women's Lives in the Nineteenth Century*. Ithaca, N. Y.: Cornell University, 1999.

Leach, Robert J., and Peter Gow. *Quaker Nantucket: The Religious Community Behind the Whaling Empire*. Nantucket, Mass.: Mill Hill Press, 1996.

Linebaugh, Barbara. *The African School and the Integration of Nantucket Public Schools, 1825–1847*. Brookline, Mass.: Boston University, 1978.

Loomis, Elias. *The Recent Progress of Astronomy; Especially in the United States*. New York: Harper & Brothers, 1850.

Mitchell, Maria. *Maria Mitchell: Life, Letters, and Journals*. Compiled by Phebe Mitchell Kendall. Boston: Lee and Shepard, 1896.

Norling, Lisa. *Captain Ahab Had a Wife: New England Women and the Whalefishery, 1720–1870*. Chapel Hill: University of North Carolina, 2000.

Panek, Richard. *Seeing and Believing: How the Telescope Opened Our Eyes and Minds to the Heavens*. New York: Penguin, 1998.

Philbrick, Nathaniel. *In the Heart of the Sea: The Tragedy of the Whaleship*. Essex, New York: Viking, 2000.

Rey, H. A. *The Stars: A New Way to See Them*. New York: Houghton Mifflin, 2008.

Sobel, Dava: *Longitude: The True Story of a Lone Genius Who Solved the Greatest Scientific Problem of His Time*. New York: Walker, 2007.

In addition, relevant issues of the *Nantucket Inquirer* and the *Nantucket Mirror* were extremely helpful to my research, as were additional articles from *Proceedings of the Nantucket Historical Association* and *Historic Nantucket*.

I also drew on the following American Antiquarian Society holdings: Chase family papers, Abigail Gardner Drew diaries, Abigail Foster Kelley papers, and especially the Gardner Family Papers, from which came the text of the fluttering note in chapter 21 of the book ('Absence must be longer than life . . .'). The 'vast Leviathan' note in the same chapter is from William Hazlitt's *Notes of a Journey Through France and Italy*.

The Meriwether Lewis quote in chapter 9 ('I had as yet done but little . . .') is from *The Journals of the Lewis and Clark Expedition,* edited by Gary E. Moulton (Lincoln: University of Nebraska Press, 1983–2001). The citations in chapter 24 are from Margaret Fuller's *Woman in the Nineteenth Century* ('We would have every path laid open to women . . .') and an 1854 address by William Lloyd Garrison delivered at the Broadway Tabernacle in New York ('I cannot but regard oppression in every form . . .'). The image of the celestial sphere as the underside of a giant umbrella is drawn from H. A. Rey's *The Stars: A New Way to See Them*.

Acknowledgments

While researching and writing this book, I was assisted by dozens of individuals, organizations, and texts. My deepest thanks:

For the gift of time, space, freedom from chores, and the inspiration of my fellow residents: The Millay Colony, *Fundación Valparaíso*, the Constance Saltonstall Foundation, the Edward Albee Foundation, and Jentel. Special thanks to Drake Patten, Judy Barringer, Neltje and Mary Jane Edwards.

For the gift of research assistance and the guidance of my fellow scholars: The Maria Mitchell Association, the American Antiquarian Society, the Nantucket Historical Association, the Kendall Library of the New Bedford Whaling Museum, and MTV Labs' Seed Money Grant. Special thanks to Joanne Chaiken, David D. Hall, Cindy Lobel, James Moran, Elizabeth Oldham, Jim Secord, Manisha Sinha, and especially to Dr Joann Eisberg, Chaffey College, for her invaluable consultation on the astronomy and historical instruments that appear in the book.

For providing a house, a room, and/or a desk to call my own: Graham Johnson, Ry and Japhet Koteen, the Monchik family, the Writers' Room, Paragraph, and the Brooklyn Writers Space.

For believing: Julie Barer and Sarah McGrath, agent

and editor extraordinaire. I can't believe my great good luck.

For bringing this book to fruition: Katie Freeman, Leah Heifferon, Jynne Dilling Martin, Kate Stark, Sarah Stein, and Anna Weiner.

For reading, commenting, editing, cheerleading, gainful employment, encouragement, instruction, and friendship: Allison Amend, Tom Bailey, David Bosnick, Tina Chang, Nicki Bush Duffy, Catherine Dunne, Jennifer Cody Epstein, Betsy Forhan, the Guerrero family, Judy Isikow, Elspeth McCusker, Jennifer Milich, Lauren Monchik, Leigh Newman, Liz Rosenberg, and Peter Rubens. Very special thanks to Hannah Tinti.

For lifelong moral support: My parents, Ona and Maurice Brill.

For the ultimate gift: My daughters, Isabel and Alma.

And finally, for faith: Ivan Guerrero, silent sage, peaceful warrior, husband of my dreams. You have made the life I imagined possible.